Also by Julia Brannan

HISTORICAL FICTION

The Jacobite Chronicles
Book One: Mask of Duplicity
Book Two: The Mask Revealed
Book Three: The Gathering Storm
Book Four: The Storm Breaks
Book Five: Pursuit of Princes
Book Six: Tides of Fortune

Jacobite Chronicles Stories
The Whore's Tale: Sarah

CONTEMPORARY FICTION

A Seventy-Five Percent Solution

The Eccentric's Tale: Harriet

A Jacobite Chronicles Story

Julia Brannan

Copyright© 2019 by Julia Brannan

Julia Brannan has asserted her right to be identified as the author of this work under the Copyright, Designs and Patents Act 1988

All rights reserved. No part of this publication may be reproduced, distributed, or transmitted in any form or by any means, including photocopying, recording, or other electronic or mechanical methods, without the prior written permission of the publisher, except in the case of brief quotations embodied in critical reviews and certain other non-commercial uses permitted by copyright law.

DISCLAIMER

This novel is a work of fiction, and except in the case of historical fact, any resemblance to actual persons, living or dead, is purely coincidental

Formatting by Polgarus Studio

Cover design by najlaqamberdesigns.com

Cover model: Elizabeth Ann Cairns

Dedicated to the memory of Ann and John Cairns

vi

ACKNOWLEDGEMENTS

First of all, as ever, I'd like to thank Jason Gardiner and Alyson Cairns, my soulmates and best friends, who put up with me on a day-to-day basis, who are now sharing my wonderful new life in Scotland, and who understand my need for solitude, but are always there for me. They've both supported me through every stage of my writing, and, indeed, in all my other endeavours, both sensible and madcap!

Thanks to the long-suffering Mary Brady, friend and first critic, who reads the chapters as I write them, critiques them for me and reassures me that I can actually write stuff people will want to read, and to my beta readers Angela, Claire, Roma and Susan (as well as Jason and Alyson) for their valued and honest opinions. I can't stress how important you are!

Thanks also go to Mandy Condon, who sends me useful articles, has already determined the cast list for the film of my books, and who has been a wonderful and supportive friend for over twenty years. Long may that continue!

My gratitude also to fellow author Kym Grosso, who has been extremely supportive and has generously given me the benefit of her experience in the minefield of indie publishing. She's saved me a lot of time, money and tears, and I value her friendship and support enormously. Her books have now been optioned for TV, and I'm so proud of her!

Also a thank you goes to the National Trust for Scotland, who are stocking my books at the gift shop in Culloden Visitor Centre and to the Clan Cameron Museum, which also stocks the Jacobite Chronicles. Both sites are well worth a visit, should you be in the area.

And thanks as always go to Jason at Polgarus Studio for doing an excellent job of formatting my books, to the talented and very patient Najla Qamber, who does all my covers, puts up with my lack of artistic ability, and still manages to somehow understand exactly what I want my covers to look like! Also to Maria Elena, who makes my newsletters look professional, and revamped my website for me. It looks lovely now!

To all my wonderful readers, who not only buy my books, but take the time and effort to give me feedback, to review them on Amazon and Goodreads, and to recommend me to others, by word of mouth and on social media – thank you so much. You keep me going on those dark days when I'd rather do anything than stare at a blank screen for hours while my brain turns to mush…you are amazing! Without all of you I would be nothing, and I appreciate you more than you know.

A special thanks to Melanie and Claire! You know why.

And finally, to Bob and Dee. You are wonderful people and I love you.

ABOUT THE AUTHOR

Julia has been a voracious reader since childhood, using books to escape the miseries of a turbulent adolescence. After leaving university with a degree in English Language and Literature, she spent her twenties trying to be a sensible and responsible person, even going so far as to work for the Civil Service for six years.

Then she gave up trying to conform, resigned her well-paid but boring job and resolved to spend the rest of her life living as she wanted to, not as others would like her to. She has since had a variety of jobs, including telesales, Post Office clerk, primary school teacher, and painter and gilder.

In her spare time she is still a voracious reader, and enjoys keeping fit, exploring the beautiful countryside around her home, and travelling the world. Life hasn't always been good, but it has rarely been boring. Until recently she lived in the beautiful Brecon Beacons in Wales, but in June she moved to Scotland, and now lives in a log cabin in rural Aberdeenshire, so has new countryside to explore!

A few years ago she decided that rather than just escape into other people's books, she would quite like to create some of her own and so combined her passion for history and literature to write the Jacobite Chronicles. She's now writing the side stories of some of the minor characters, and is researching for her next series, The Road to Rebellion, which will go back to the start of the whole Jacobite movement.

People seem to enjoy reading her books as much as she enjoys writing them, so now, apart from a tiny amount of editing work, she is a full-time writer. She has plunged into the contemporary genre too, but her first love will always be historical fiction.

PROLOGUE

November 1678

Stephen, Duke of Darlington, had dreaded the great honour the king was now bestowing upon him, knowing it to be a very mixed blessing indeed. Anyone with any sense who had enjoyed (or endured) being visited by a monarch knew that.

But regardless of whether King Charles II was visiting to demonstrate his approval of and partiality for him, or was merely trying to ascertain whether the duke's family was truly loyal to the Stuart monarchy, Stephen knew that this was his chance to reverse the results of his father's disastrous decision thirty years previously to actively support Parliament in its war against the current king's father rather than just keep his head down, a decision which had initially ensured the family's survival, but had not stood it in such good stead since the restoration.

King Charles had never actually demonstrated any disapproval of the Ashleigh family, but then that was not his way. On his restoration he had promised not to persecute anyone who had fought for Cromwell, excepting only those who responsible for his father's execution, and he had kept that promise. But he had not shown many of those who had actively fought against him any favour either. For eighteen years the Ashleighs had managed to survive, mainly because Stephen's father, as well as being a master of reckless decisions, had also been a master of parsimony. He would have had an apoplexy had he known how much this week's monarchical visit was costing his son.

But the old duke was dead and the young duke needed to repair the damage, if his family was to come in from the cold and rise as he wished them to. His wife would be delighted to be received at Court, and had already privately agreed that even were she asked to be a lady-in-waiting to one of the king's mistresses rather than Queen Catherine herself, she would agree. Anything to be back in favour.

Stephen glanced across at the king and his brother James, who were currently sitting on cushioned and gilded chairs of state at the front of the great chamber, among their courtiers, chatting and laughing together. It was a shame that their wives had not been able to join them, but at least that had saved *some* expense. They seemed to have enjoyed the earlier concert, and now Stephen's eldest daughter and his youngest brother would perform a small scene from Shakespeare's *Tempest,* then the music would continue until supper, after which there would be a firework display over the lake as a grand finale to their visit.

Both Charles and James were known to love children, so even if Harriet and Percy messed up their lines it should be a pleasing interlude, and would show the duke and duchess as fond parents, something Charles would approve of. Their two younger daughters, aged three and one, were already asleep in the nursery, but at six Harriet was old enough to at least play a small part in social occasions.

So far, all had gone well. Very well. Already the king had suggested that the duke and duchess might wish to attend the Christmas festivities, although no formal invitation had been issued as yet. Just this evening to get through. In the morning the royal guests would depart, and then Stephen and Amelia would wait and pray for the invitation that would tell them they had been accepted back into the royal fold.

As the curtain was pulled back from the small stage, Stephen reached across and captured his wife Amelia's hand, squeezing it reassuringly and lovingly. The couple sat back and awaited the entrance of the children, who had been practising this scene for weeks.

Some amount of urgent whispering came from the side of the stage, after which a small, somewhat portly boy dressed in artificially distressed courtly clothes appeared rather abruptly, as though having been propelled onstage rather than using his own means. In his arms he clutched a small log in a death grip. He surprising sweetness. One eye was clear grey, the other bright red and rapidly swelling.

The king bit his lip to stop himself laughing and upsetting the children, James coughed into his handkerchief, his eyes bright, and Stephen buried his face in his hands.

Harriet turned and stalked across to Percy so abruptly that the alarmed boy clearly thought she was going to attack him, and raised the log he was holding, evidently intending to use it as a weapon if necessary. Amelia started to stand.

"Alas, now, pray you,

Work not so hard: I would the lightning had

Burnt up…" Here the child hesitated, and shot Percy a look of unadulterated hatred, "…those logs that you are enjoin'd to pile!" she continued.

Charles glanced back to the girl's worried mother.

"Sit, my lady," he whispered. "Your daughter has most excellent comic timing."

She did. A titter ran through the audience, which was acutely aware that if lightning had missed the logs and obliterated the unfortunate Percy instead, Harriet would have been overjoyed. Which would have indeed been excellent if Shakespeare had intended the scene to be comic, rather than one of budding love between two innocent young people.

The scene continued, with the two children standing belligerently opposite each other as though about to engage in mortal combat, whilst delivering lines of utter adoration with beautiful and well-rehearsed expression. The audience was almost prostrate with repressed laughter.

"Hear my soul speak," Percy managed, before screwing up his face and sneezing. The second pad shot out of his nostril, along with a spray of blood, which pattered on the floor and on Harriet's dress. He looked at it and grinned. "The very instant that I saw you, did my heart fly to your service; there resides, to make me slave to it; and for your sake am I this patient log-man." He raised the log, and Harriet stepped smartly back out of the way.

"Do you love me?" she asked, clearly as utterly disgusted by this thought as by the blood on her dress.

"Oh God," Stephen heard the king murmur, his shoulders shaking with mirth. He glanced at his wife, whose face wore an stared at the audience for a moment in utter panic, his wide eyes growing even wider when he heard his older brother's suppressed groan.

The king, smiling broadly, applauded encouragingly, and the rest of the audience joined in. On the stage Percy relaxed a little, stepped forward and bowed. One of the plugs which had been hastily pushed up the nostrils of his red and swelling nose fell out, and when the boy straightened a thin trickle of blood ran down his face, eventually joining the considerable amount of gore that already decorated the front of his costume.

"A scene from *The Tempest,* Act III, scene I, if it please Your Majesty," Percy said in a voice rendered somewhat muffled by his injured nose.

"It pleases me greatly," called the king. "Let us hear it, young master!"

"There be some sports are painful, and their labour
Delight in them sets off: some kinds of baseness
Are nobly undergone, and most poor matters
Point to rich ends," the child recited thickly. He moved across the stage to the corner, putting the log down, still speaking his lines and, in fairness, making an admirable job of them, excepting the indistinctness of some of the consonants. He moved back to the side of the stage and accepted another log from an unseen hand, then sniffed loudly and licked the blood off his top lip.

"I must remove
Some thousands of these logs, and pile them up,
Upon a sore injunction: my sweet mistress
Weeps when she sees me work, and says, such baseness
Had never like executor. I forget:
But these sweet thoughts do even refresh my labours,
Most busy lest, when I do it," he continued.

At this point, the boy's 'sweet mistress' marched belligerently onstage, her costume a confection of shimmering silk, her blonde hair elaborately ringleted, falling to her waist. A small chorus of 'ahhs' from the female members of the audience at the cuteness of the six-year-old Harriet was extinguished abruptly as the little girl scowled ferociously at the unfortunate log-bearer before turning to the audience, on whom she bestowed an equal glare before curtseying perfectly to the king and smiling at him with

THE ECCENTRIC'S TALE: HARRIET

expression that mirrored his thoughts – as disastrous as this scene was, it appeared to be amusing the monarch hugely, which could be no bad thing. He relaxed a little, and then more as the scene ended and the two children exited the stage, before returning to glare at each other and bow and curtsey to the royal guests, to rapturous applause.

King Charles beckoned the little performers to come down from the stage and join him. Stephen and Amelia relaxed. The children had been taught how to conduct themselves if the king should address them personally.

Harriet curtseyed deeply to the king.

"I'm honoured, Your Most Gracious Majesty," she said.

"I am delighted that you enjoyed our performance, Your Majesty," Percy added.

"Well, it was quite unique," said the king sincerely. "I have seen *The Tempest* several times, but will admit that I have never seen a performance which affected me as yours did. I will remember it for a long time. I'm sure you will too, brother."

"Oh, most assuredly," agreed Prince James, smiling.

Harriet turned to the prince and curtseyed again.

"Thank you, your Royal Papist Arse-cloth to Louis," she said, her childish voice clear and piping.

The silence that fell upon the room was instant and profound. Harriet straightened, saw James' shocked expression. Behind him her father started to rise from his seat, his face white. And then the king spoke and her father froze, half-standing.

"Come, child," King Charles said, reaching across and lifting her onto his knee. "Do you like marchpane?"

She nodded, although her eyes filled with tears, aware that she had done something wrong. The king popped a small piece of marzipan in her mouth, and she looked up at him. His brown eyes were not full of laughter now as they had been a moment before, but they were still warm as he observed her. He had a lovely face. It was not handsome, but it was lived in, and friendly. She smiled up at him uncertainly.

"Now," he said, "that was a most interesting title you just bestowed upon my brother. Normally people address him as 'Your Royal Highness,' you know."

"Yes," Harriet said, after she'd swallowed her mouthful of

almonds and sugar. "Mama taught me to say that, but then I heard Papa tell her that we would now have to call him a new title, so I thought I would remember that, and use it to please you." She looked apprehensively at James, who was clearly anything but pleased.

"It is not your fault, child," James said gently, "but I think it better if you forget that title and use Your Royal Highness in future."

"I will, and I'm sorry if I upset you," she said sincerely. This was the first time she had met the royal brothers, but she had seen them from the nursery window during the course of their stay, and once had seen them from across the lawns, Charles walking very quickly around the gardens as was his way, James matching his pace, both of them chatting and laughing together, clearly very close. She had instinctively warmed to them, loving their relaxed and affectionate relationship, and had wanted to run across the garden then to say hello. But she had been forbidden to introduce herself, had been told to wait until she was addressed personally by one of the royal brothers.

And now she had been, and had offended him. She bit her lip, and Charles reached out his arm and embraced her.

"Think no more of it, sweeting," he said. "I would that all my courtiers were as innocent and honest as you are. Even those who would seem our friends can be preparing a knife in the dark. But I do not think you would do that, eh?"

"No, never, Your Majesty!" she replied.

"Well, that is good to hear," he said. "Now, what happened here between you? It's clear that you have argued. I hope you did not strike your niece, young sir?"

Percy coloured.

"I…I did, Your Majesty," he said in a very small voice.

"Well, it is not very chivalrous to hit a lady, you know," Charles stated.

"I know, Your Majesty," Percy whispered.

"I hit him first, though," Harriet interceded.

"You hit him first?" Charles said.

"Well, it is not very ladylike to hit someone, you know," James said, parodying his brother. He did not look as shocked now, but his lips were still held in a tight thin line.

THE ECCENTRIC'S TALE: HARRIET

"No, I know. Mama and Papa tell me that all the time," Harriet admitted. "But it's hard not to hit Percy, because he's so…because he annoys me so much," she amended, realising that Percy was already dying of embarrassment and that, as much as she hated him, to denounce him as a pompous idiot would be a bit unfair. After all, the king had not offered *him* a piece of marchpane, nor was *he* sitting on the king's knee. That was victory enough.

"I think we must forgive you your lack of chivalry on this occasion then, sir, as it seems clear you were provoked," Charles said. "And your performance was quite entrancing. I congratulate you both. Now, I hear the musicians tuning their instruments. Are you staying for the music, or must you go?"

"Their nurse will take them to bed now, if it please Your Majesty," Amelia said, standing and moving forward, her face a picture of distress. Charles glanced from her to her husband, who could not bring himself to meet his monarch's gaze, staring instead at his feet. Harriet started to dismount from the king's knee, but his hand came to her waist, halting her.

"No, it does not please me," he said, his tone light, his expression cold. "I would like very much to retain the company of these delightful, *honest* children for a little longer. Would you like to stay and hear the concert?" he asked them. Both children nodded, their eyes shining. "It is settled, then," he said, and making a little room on his seat, he patted the space beside him. "I think that, being almost a young man now, you will not want to sit on my knee," Charles said to the eight-year-old boy, "but you cannot object to sharing my seat."

Chairs were set out on the stage, and the musicians appeared and began to prepare for their concert. Soft but halting conversation started among the audience. Stephen and Amelia sat rigid, silent. Percy sat between the king and Prince James, feeling very important.

Harriet relaxed on the king's knee, turning so that she could see the stage and leaning back against his chest. He kept his arm round her, one large hand resting on her knee. What a lovely, lovely man he was, to allow her the rare treat of staying for the concert! She looked at James and smiled, and he smiled back at her, his eyes warm. She was sure he was not too offended that she had messed up his title a little. And if he was not offended, then her parents would not be very angry with her. Certainly the king liked her, thought her delightful and honest. Papa and Mama would be happy about that.

Although she had hit Percy, even though she had promised that she would try to be friends with him just for this evening. But it was impossible to be friendly with him, because he was horrible, lording it over her just because he was a boy and her uncle, even though he was only two years older than her. Even so she shouldn't have hit him, not because of him, but because it had upset Jemima, her nurse, who she loved, and would have disappointed Mama and Papa, who she also loved.

Ah, but even so, what a wonderful evening it was! On impulse she reached across and wrapped her little hand around the king's large thumb. He raised his hand to his lips and gently kissed her fingers.

Then the concert started, and monarch and child, who both loved music, forgot everything, and allowed themselves to become lost in the exquisite performance.

CHAPTER ONE

The duke and duchess stood by the window of their private apartments on the first floor of Ash Hall, gazing down at their beautifully designed formal gardens, which even at this bleak time of year were a delight to walk in if the weather was clement, as it was today. In truth the couple were paying no attention whatsoever to the decorative results from the painstaking toil of the team of gardeners, but were instead observing the tall, long-legged figure of the monarch engaged in his habitual morning exercise, today being taken at an uncharacteristically slow pace. At the pace of a six-year-old, in fact, who was currently holding the king's hand whilst stretching the other arm out to show him something of interest which lay out of sight of her watching parents above.

"Really, I could strangle her," Stephen commented, "if I could get her away from Charles for five minutes, that is."

"It was hardly her fault, you know. You only have yourself to blame. I've told you more than once about indiscreet comments. He has really taken to her," Amelia mused. "I suppose that's something, at least. He *does* love children. Look at how he dotes on his bastards. It's such a tragedy that the queen is barren."

"What do you mean, I only have myself to blame?" Stephen said. "It's come to something when a man can't speak freely in his own house without it being reported directly back to the king, and by his own child!"

Amelia looked at her husband with an expression of frustration mingled with sympathy. "We both know that you wouldn't harm a hair of Harriet's head. You adore her. And we also both know that any comments as extreme as the one she unwittingly repeated to him should, if spoken at all, only be done in whispers when alone in our rooms, and not with a great flourish in the library for all to hear!"

Stephen sighed, and looked down. Charles and Harriet were now standing by the lake, still hand in hand.

"She wasn't even in the room," Stephen said defensively.

"No, she told me that she was walking past outside, and saw you bowing elaborately and saying it. She genuinely thought it was his new title. But even if she hadn't, servants are everywhere, Stephen. I know we're so accustomed to them that we hardly notice they're there, but letting them hear potentially treasonous statements is not advisable at any time, and right now, when the king must feel insecure on so many fronts, it's positively dangerous. He needs people who he *knows* will stand by him through the storm."

"And he no longer thinks we will. Even though I would have done, you know. Whatever my doubts about James, I believe Charles to be an excellent monarch."

"I know you do. But he loves his brother, and he needs people who will support him in his endeavour to stop the Exclusion Act from being passed, which would prevent James from succeeding him. You cannot support Charles and not James. They are a close family, as are we. If you are against one, you are against all."

"Yes, you're right. I said it impetuously, and for your ears only. But it's too late now. At least if a servant had told Charles I could have denied it as a malicious lie," Stephen said. That was true. But he could hardly claim his own daughter was a liar, when she had so clearly said it in pure innocence, understanding neither its meaning nor how catastrophic the consequences would be for her family. "It's only what many other nobles are thinking right now, you know," he added.

"I do know that. But the sensible ones are not telling Charles that to his face. They're waiting to see what happens. And in truth, I think it's all a fuss about nothing."

"Many other nobles would not agree with you there, my sweet. And I am one of them."

"No, but you're all allowing your ridiculous horror of Catholics to cloud your judgement. And before you remind me of Bloody Mary's reign," she said, holding up a hand, "that was a

THE ECCENTRIC'S TALE: HARRIET

hundred and fifty years ago, when a large number of the population were still secretly Catholics. It's a very different situation now. There are only a handful of them in the entire country, and I don't believe they have any wish to massacre Protestants or forcibly convert us. Most of them would be happy if they could just practice their faith openly."

"Even so, having a Catholic king could change everything," Stephen argued.

"Maybe, although in honesty I doubt it. But James is not the king."

"He will be though! The queen is clearly barren, but Charles refuses to divorce her and marry a more fertile woman."

"He does. I admire him for that, truth be told. He might have a goodly number of mistresses, but he is at least willing to stand by his wife in that. That's one reason why it's so obvious that this so-called Popish Plot that's stirred up such panic is a tissue of lies, and Titus Oates a madman. Why, the queen would no more attempt to poison her husband than I would. She loves him and would lose much if he died. It's ridiculous. And in any case, look at him, Stephen," she said, pointing out of the window at the king, who, presumably tired of the dilatory walking speed had now lifted his diminutive tour guide into his arms and was walking round the lake at his normal brisk pace, "he's not yet fifty, and in the peak of health. Any number of things could happen. The queen could die and Charles remarry and have legitimate children. James could predecease him, or give up his faith. I can understand all this fuss about the Test Act to exclude Catholics to a point, but I think it's exaggerated. James is no more the arse-cloth of Louis, as you so delicately put it, than Charles is."

"I hope you're right, my love. But whatever he is, our chances of returning to favour are gone."

"Maybe. But Charles is still here. That has to count for something."

This morning, while his brother's luggage was being loaded into carts, King Charles had cheerfully announced his intention to stay a little longer with the duke and duchess, if that was not an inconvenience. He was having such an *interesting* time.

The duke and duchess had given the only possible answer to that, with the result that although James had left with the briefest of icy farewells, Charles was now staying for another week at least.

"Maybe he's giving us another chance to prove ourselves loyal," Amelia added.

Stephen snorted. "If you believe that, you're as innocent as Harriet," he said. "He's doing what Queen Elizabeth used to do."

"What was that?"

"If she thought a subject might rise against her, but had nothing that she could arrest them for, she would sometimes favour them greatly with a prolonged visit, ensuring she ruined them financially by doing so, and so rendering them powerless to rise against her."

"Do you really think that's what he's doing?" Amelia asked.

"I'm certain of it. At the very least he's giving us a severe warning. This morning he told me that he had an excellent idea, and thinks that Percy and Harriet would be delighted to see a professional performance of *The Tempest*. He has sent for all his players to join us for a few days. Which means that as well as accommodating him and all his household, I will also have to accommodate all his players, and have the great chamber altered to provide a suitable stage for a professional play. We are already in debt, Amelia, due to my father's idiocy. If Charles stays for a week, we will survive, just. If he stays for longer, we will struggle. Especially as it is highly unlikely that we will be returned to his favour afterwards. And he knows that. He is very astute."

Down below in the gardens their eldest and much-loved if somewhat exasperating daughter, completely unaware of her parents' distress, was happily telling her new friend the king how overjoyed she would be to see *The Tempest* performed by proper actors.

"Because Percy and I are not proper actors, you know," she informed him, in case he was unaware of that fact. "We did practice for hours and hours though. It was very boring sometimes, and Percy was very annoying. But he always is."

They had walked halfway round the lake and were now sitting on a stone bench on the far side, looking back at the house.

"Why do you dislike your uncle so? He seemed a fine little man to me," Charles commented.

"That's because he'd been told to behave himself. We both had," Harriet said. "I shouldn't have hit him. I'm sorry for that."

"I'm glad to hear it. I'm sure he was in a lot of pain."

THE ECCENTRIC'S TALE: HARRIET

"Oh, I'm not sorry about that. I hope he *was* in a lot of pain. I'm sick of him telling me I'm stupid and ugly and trying to order me about all the time, just because he's my uncle and a boy. I didn't mean to make his nose bleed though, because he had to perform for you, and you probably couldn't hear all his lines, which was a shame because he said them very well. And I'm sorry because I know Mama and Papa were disappointed in me, even though they haven't told me they were, and I hate that, because I love them. And Jemima too. She's my nurse, and she's very kind."

Charles glanced down at the little blonde head with its mop of now unruly ringlets and grinned. This was one reason why he loved children, as he loved dogs. They were honest, and uncomplicated. If they liked you, they let you know. If they didn't like you, they let you know. They had no ulterior motives. It was so refreshing to enjoy their simple company, when one was surrounded by treachery and duplicity constantly. This child, though, was particularly candid. Even at such a tender age most aristocratic children had learnt *some* artifice. But this one was as refreshing as a cool breeze on a sultry day.

"You should try to get along with your family, you know," he said. "Sometimes they are all that stand between you and your enemies."

"You mean your brother?" Harriet asked.

Charles was shocked. He had been referring to James, yes, but he had not expected her to comprehend that. At the moment he was all that was stopping the country from tearing his brother apart. He loved James very much, appreciated his unswerving loyalty, rare in royal brothers, but wished he would see sense, appreciate how terrified people were of Catholicism, understand how tenuous was his grip on the throne, and how easily it could all be swept away again, as it had been in their father's day. The days of absolute monarchy were over, in Britain at least, and Charles had only kept his throne by a mixture of charisma, intelligence and an ability to play the game, whereas James seemed to have learnt nothing from their father's mistakes.

He glanced down at the child, who was sitting quietly, patiently waiting for him to answer. She was really quite exceptional.

"My brother?" he repeated, employing a tactic he usually used with adults to get more information before committing himself to a reply.

"Yes. I watched you walking in the gardens. You love each other very much, don't you?" she said.

Charles smiled.

"Yes, we do. As I'm sure you do your sisters," he said. "We have been through a lot together, James and I."

"I do love my sisters. Sophia, at least, now she's starting to talk. Melanie is boring, because she's too little to do anything yet except make messes. But I hope we love each other like you and your brother do when we're old like you are. I'm sorry I said a bad thing to him."

"Don't worry about it, child."

"I'm sure Papa is sorry too. He was very happy that you were coming to see us. Papa is wonderful. I love him, and Mama. I'm sure he would not have said a bad thing if he'd known that it would upset Prince James. I know I wouldn't."

Charles reached down and ruffled her hair.

"I am sure you wouldn't. But you would always tell me what you really think, I believe."

Harriet's brow furrowed.

"Yes, of course. Why would I tell you something I didn't really think? That would be stupid," she said.

Charles laughed out loud at that, loud enough that Stephen and Amelia, still standing at the open window, heard him.

"Oh God, what has she said now?" Stephen groaned.

Amelia reached across and squeezed his hand.

"I don't know, but right now, I think she may be the key to his favour. Or at the very least, to his not rejecting us completely. He is very taken with her, that's clear. She *is* an unusual girl."

Stephen rolled his eyes to heaven, but his wife had a point. Whatever the king thought of the parents, it was obvious that he enjoyed Harriet's company very much. And if he did, maybe, just maybe, he would refrain from bankrupting the family she belonged to.

* * *

"What did he say?" Amelia asked the second her husband crossed the threshold of her dressing room. Locking the stable door after the horse had bolted, Stephen looked down the corridor to ensure it was devoid of eavesdroppers before coming in and closing the

THE ECCENTRIC'S TALE: HARRIET

door. Amelia had been on tenterhooks since the king had drawn Stephen away into the gardens for a few private words as he was departing. She had directed the servants to help load the mass of belongings into the baggage train, and then had waved farewell to the assorted actors, courtiers and staff as they left, leaving only the king's coach and guard waiting on the driveway. Then, having already bid the king farewell, and aware of how desperate and impatient she must look hovering at the entrance, she had repaired to her private rooms, where she had massacred a piece of needlework until her husband appeared.

Stephen poured them both a glass of wine and sat down, observing the messy stitches, which told him a lot about his wife's state of mind. He would get right to the point then.

"He was gracious and charming," he began. "And—"

"Of course he was," Amelia interrupted. "He'd be gracious and charming to his executioner, if it came to it. That means nothing, with Charles. What did he *say?*"

Stephen forgave his wife her uncustomary lapse of manners, in view of the circumstances.

"Well, first of all, as this was the first time I've been alone with him since that night, I apologised most profusely. And he told me that he appreciates apologies and usually accepts them, if they are sincere."

"Oh. Do you think he thought yours was?"

"It's impossible to tell with him, but I doubt it. He also told me that our daughter is utterly delightful and on no account must she be punished for her innocence and honesty. He hopes she will ever remain so. I replied that the fault was mine, not Harriet's, that I would not punish her for my own error. And *that* he smiled at. He then said she told him that we spend a lot of time with her and her sisters and that she loves us and Jemima very much, which he found encouraging."

Amelia smiled. It was true, but she was glad the king, who was devoted to his children, had been told that by someone he could believe.

"Charles told me that he was sure I would take a poor view of anyone who insulted any member of my family, for it is clear that I love you all. And that he feels exactly the same way about his family. And that was the closest he came to telling me I was still out of favour."

Amelia thought for a moment. For Charles, who was rarely aggressive or even impolite to anyone, that was both a criticism and a warning.

"So we have spent a great deal of money and are no closer to returning to Court," she said sadly.

"We aren't, no. But he did say that he will see how everything goes, that Harriet has permission to write to him if she wishes to, once she learns to write, and that if she does, she should write freely about whatever she wants. When she is older, fourteen or fifteen maybe, he may be pleased to offer her a place at Court."

"Oh!" Amelia exclaimed. "But that is wonderful!"

"It is," Stephen said. "But it means we have to survive for another eight years in the shadows, and that all our hopes of a return to royal favour lie with *Harriet*, of all people. Because he was very insistent that she be allowed free rein in her letters."

"She's not *that* bad," Amelia said doubtfully. Stephen shot her an incredulous look. "She takes after her father," she added tactlessly.

"And her grandfather," Stephen added. For all his faults, indiscretion clearly being one of them, Stephen always admitted when he was wrong, and would apologise and take responsibility for his faults with good grace. It was one of his most endearing qualities, and one his eldest daughter shared with him. For all her childish enmity towards Percy, Harriet would never let him take the blame for something she had done or had instigated.

"Well, all we can do is tighten our belts then, as surreptitiously as possible, not say *anything* indiscreet except when alone, in whispers, and pray that Harriet keeps the king's favour," Amelia said.

"Yes, and I think that instead of waiting until she is nine before she learns to write, as her tutor recommends, we must start her instruction immediately. I don't want there to be three years of silence before the king hears from her. We must keep the affection he has for her fresh in his mind."

* * *

June 1679

"Good God," said Stephen in despair. "We can't send *that!*"

Amelia looked at the liberally ink-blotted sheet of illegible

THE ECCENTRIC'S TALE: HARRIET

scrawl on the desk in front of them. In one corner was a distinct fingerprint, a tiny one. She smiled fondly.

"He did say she must be allowed to write what she wanted," she pointed out.

"What she's actually written isn't the issue. I can't make out any of it after 'Dere Your Majistie,' he said. "And neither will he. He'll think we're raising an idiot. Or that her teacher is a local farmer's son rather than a highly respected tutor. What the hell am I paying the man for?"

"In fairness, Stephen, poor Mr Hale is an excellent tutor. There is a reason children don't normally learn to write until they are older. Her hands are too small to hold a quill properly. I think this is an admirable attempt. She's only just turning seven, after all."

Stephen reviewed the blotchy mess with this in mind.

"I suppose you're right," he admitted. "But we still can't send this to the king, because he won't be able to read it at all."

"No he won't. But I do think we should send it. He has children of his own. He will appreciate her hard work and dedication, at least."

"Hmmm," Stephen commented doubtfully.

"What he won't appreciate, and what I need to speak to you about, as the topic has been raised, is that Harriet is not the most docile pupil. Her tutor's hands are tied because you refuse to allow him to discipline her, and she finds anything that involves sitting in one place for more than five minutes intolerable, and says so. I haven't been able to get her to even think about embroidery yet. It has nearly killed the poor man to get her this far in her writing. I'm not sure how long he will remain here, if he cannot control her."

"You want me to give permission for him to beat our daughter?!" Stephen cried.

"Not exactly beat her, no. But she needs to start learning that she cannot just do what she wants, to curb her energy. She's rapidly becoming uncontrollable. It cannot continue."

Stephen ran his hand lightly over the tiny inky fingerprint and smiled. Amelia, catching the look and empathising with the emotion behind it, leaned across and took his hand in hers.

"I know she is the apple of your eye, my love. She is of mine, too. She is our firstborn, and she has many lovely qualities. She's friendly and caring. She's intelligent and interested in everything too, and is very open and honest which is wonderful, and which is what, I believe, attracted the king to her. And it is lovely to watch her delight in everything. I don't want her to be sad for even a moment, but that's not possible."

"That's true," Stephen admitted. He picked the letter up, and sighed. "I think we have to take her in hand and quickly, not only because she holds the family's future in her hands, but because her sisters will follow her example if we don't. She's wild, but delightful as she is she's not a baby any more, and we are going to have to start to mould her, or she will never fit in at Court, or anywhere else for that matter. If we have no sons, she will inherit too. If there's anything left by that time. She must learn to discipline herself, and to do what she doesn't like, when necessary."

* * *

September 1679

Dere Your Majistie,

I am sorrie it has took so long for me to Rite this Letter to You, but I had to lurn to Write as I cud only Rede before. It wos verry horibul as I had to sit for days in the Summer and lurn to form mie Leters insted of runing outside, but now Papa sed mie hand is gud enuf for me to Right too You.

"Dear God," said Stephen, perusing his daughter's painful first letter to the king. "Her hand is good enough, but her spelling is appalling. She's spelt 'write' three different ways already."

"Charles won't mind that. At least you can read it now," Amelia pointed out.

"'Evry time I walk in the Gardens I think of you and I hope you can cum back soon and stay again, as you were verry nice to talk too and I miss you. I am lurning too grow flours now, wich is fun. I hope you rember me.' Oh, well, that will please him, I think!" Stephen said, smiling. He bent his head again. "'Percy is still stoopid and nastie to me but I hav only hitt him some few times as You sed it was nott laydelike. I dont wont to bee a layde. I want to bee a man wen I am big so I can doo intrestin things. Your Majisties obeedeent servant, Harriet.'"

There was silence for a few moments.

"Well, it took a downturn at the end," Stephen commented drily.

"Is it good enough to send?" Amelia asked. "She has sweated hard over this, and there's nothing the king can take offense at. I think he'll find it amusing. And it will bring us to his mind again, in a good way."

"Yes. And he certainly won't think for one minute that we've told her what she must write. Yes, let's send it. She does know he may not reply?"

"I've told her the king is very busy, yes. I haven't told her that he likes writing letters about as much as she does."

"Doesn't he? How do you know that?" Stephen asked.

"I know we are not in favour, but several of my acquaintances are, and so are their husbands. It's well known that the king's counsellors have the devil's own job getting him to deal with any paperwork. That's where he gets the reputation for being lazy from, Lady Parrish told me, although he works extremely hard at everything else to do with kingship."

"Ah. Well, let us prepare to console Harriet then, if he fails to respond."

In the event, the king replied within a month, rendering Harriet mad with joy. She had been waiting impatiently at the door every time the footman went to the post, although being from the monarch, the reply was in the end delivered to the door by a courier. Mother, father and daughter looked at the letter excitedly.

"My very first letter!" Harriet said ecstatically. "Can I open it?"

"Of course you can!" Amelia replied. "It's for you. And a great honour, for the king himself to write to you. Break the seal carefully."

She did, and read it slowly, frowning over the curls of some of the letters that were unfamiliar to her.

"'My Dear Lady Harriet,'" she read. "Oh! I spelt 'dear' wrongly in my letter! I must remember that. 'I was very happy to receive your letter, and I certainly remember you fondly. I am honoured you have learned to write just so that you can write to me.'" She looked up. "I haven't learned it *just* to write to him, have I? I can write to anyone now, I suppose. I don't know if I want to, though. It's hard work and it makes my hand ache. I'm glad I don't know anyone else who lives a long way away."

"What else does he say?" Stephen asked, resisting with difficulty the urge to tear the letter from his daughter's hand and read it quickly.

"'I am happy to hear that you have only hit Percy sometimes, although I hope that soon you will be able to write to me that you no longer hit him at all.' I don't know if I can do that, because it would be a lie," Harriet commented. "'I enjoyed walking in the gardens with you too, and maybe one day we will do it again, certainly when you come to live at Court. You must learn how to be a fine lady so that you can do that. It is not always interesting to be a man, my dear.'" She looked up from the letter to her parents. "It seems interesting to me. The boys get to do archery and learn sword fighting, while I have to learn letters and to play the harpsichord, which is boring," she said.

"But the boys have to learn letters too. And you love music," Amelia said.

"I love *listening* to music. But I don't like having to learn to play it. You can't enjoy listening to it if you're playing it, or you make a mistake."

"What else does he say?" Stephen asked again, before the conversation got derailed.

"Just that he hopes I will write again," Harriet said. "Which I will, because it's very nice to get letters. It means someone cares about you, if they take all that time to do something so difficult and boring, just to make you happy."

After she'd left, Stephen and Amelia read the letter again.

"He said 'when' not 'if' you come to live at Court," Stephen commented, grasping at straws somewhat.

"He did. But I think the most important thing is that he

THE ECCENTRIC'S TALE: HARRIET

actually wrote to her, *and* that he wrote the letter himself," Amelia said. "He didn't dictate it. This is incredible!"

"How do you know that?" Stephen asked.

"I've seen his handwriting before. It's smooth and flowing. He used to write most of his letters himself, especially before he was king. He dictates a lot more of them now, of course, because he's so busy and hates writing, as I said before. I can't believe it!"

She looked at her husband, and the pair exchanged an excited smile.

"Harriet really has no idea how much of an honour it is for the King of Great Britain to write to her, does she?" Stephen said.

"No, and I'm not sure that I want her to. It's delightful that she judges people by their personalities rather than their status, and I think Charles saw that. She liked him for himself alone. She will need to learn appropriate conduct with different classes of people, though. But not yet. She has so much else to learn. We can leave that till a little later."

* * *

The correspondence between the king and Harriet continued, and once she had really mastered the use of the quill pen and no longer found the mechanics of writing so difficult, she enjoyed writing to him, partly because she was allowed to write whatever she wanted, within reason, and partly because she really liked Charles. He was one of the few adults who had taken her seriously, had listened to her opinions as though they were important, and had replied accordingly to her.

Most adults (except for her parents) treated you as an irritating nonentity when you were a child, something to be endured or ordered about until you were old enough to be of use. Of course her parents ordered her about, more and more as she grew older and had to learn to do lots of things that she hated – in the main things that involved sitting down for hours at a time – but they loved her, as they loved Sophia and Melanie, and had loved little Stephen, named for his father, even though he had only lived for a few weeks.

After he died they had all worn black for a long time, and Charles had actually sent a personal message of sympathy to her parents when she'd written to tell him of the death of her tiny brother. She was glad he'd done that, because it cheered them more than any of the other messages they'd received.

They were not wearing black any more, which was nice, because black was very dull, and warm in the spring, which it now was. Harriet loved the spring, although she had loved it a lot more when she was younger and had been able to just run around outside in it.

The flowers that she'd been allowed to plant in the garden, helped by one of the under-gardeners, were also growing now. The wallflowers were beautiful, and smelled wonderful, attracting bees, which Jeremiah said would help them to make honey. He had told her that at one time the petals of wallflowers were made into a conserve to help with gout pains, but she was glad they weren't now, because it was lovely watching the bees come to them, and smelling the wonderful scent. The daffodils were also blooming, and she'd been given sunflower seeds to plant, which she had done a couple of weeks ago. The gardener Jeremiah had told her that they grew very quickly and very tall, much taller than the tallest man she'd ever met.

The tallest man she'd ever met was King Charles, so she had written to him to tell him about the seeds and what Jeremiah had said, and had asked him if he could visit her when the flower was grown, to see if it really *was* taller than him. He had written back to say that he did not think he could this year, but that she should measure it, and he would tell her if it was taller than he was.

She enjoyed writing to the king, even though it meant she had to sit down for a time. But it was a lot harder to sit indoors for hours and do lessons, sew stupid pictures on cloth or learn to play music she didn't even like on the harpsichord, when the sun was shining outside. It was easier to do that in the winter, when it was cold, dull and rainy, although even getting cold and wet would have been more fun than embroidering a rose, as she was now doing. She would much rather be outside, learning how to grow them. She loved the rich smell of soil, the physical labour of digging and planting seeds, and the pure joy when tiny green shoots started to appear, which made her feel like she thought God must have done when he'd created the Earth.

Harriet looked at the grubby piece of needlework she'd been working on for weeks, and then at her mother, and her sister

THE ECCENTRIC'S TALE: HARRIET

Sophia, now seven, who was sitting opposite her near the window and apparently enjoying learning to sew a stem.

She sighed loudly and theatrically, causing her mother to glance across at her.

"It will not finish itself, you know," Amelia commented.

"I know. I just don't see why I can't paint a rose on the cloth," Harriet said. "It would be a lot quicker."

"You hate painting," Sophia commented. "You don't like anything that you have to sit down to do."

Harriet shot her sister a venomous look.

"That's true," she admitted. "But at least I wouldn't have to sit down for as long to paint a rose, and it would look much nicer than this, too." She looked at her mother hopefully.

"I'm sure it would," Amelia said. "But when the garment it was painted on was cleaned, it would be ruined. Whereas this will survive for years, longer than you, even. You don't want to be remembered in the future as someone who couldn't embroider roses, do you?"

"I don't really mind," said Harriet. "I'd rather be remembered for *growing* roses, real ones. There's a lot to do in the gardens right now. I could be out helping Jeremiah."

"No you couldn't. Jeremiah is paid to do his job, along with all the other gardeners," Amelia said. Fewer gardeners than there had been, because economies had to be made, but she didn't mention that. "You need to learn to be a lady, and one of the things ladies should be able to do is embroidery."

"I don't see why ladies need to do embroidery. It's boring. When I'm grown up, if I want a rose on my dress I'll pay someone to embroider it for me, so I can do things that interest me instead. I want to be remembered as someone who did wonderful things. Worthwhile things."

"Like what?" Sophia asked.

"Like learning how to fight with swords, and then winning a great battle for the king," Harriet said, prompted by the sound of sword practice on the lawn.

"You can't win battles if you're a lady," Sophia said. "That's what men do."

"I wish I was a man," Harriet said with such intense feeling that her mother, who had been about to give her a lecture on womanly duties, gave in.

23

"You can't learn swordplay because swords are too heavy for a girl, but if you finish that petal you're working on – and neatly, I'll ask James to give you an archery lesson, if you want," Amelia said.

Never, in Harriet's eight years of life, had Amelia seen her daughter sit so still and so concentrated for so long as she did for the next two hours. Except of course when she was writing to her great friend King Charles. But then she enjoyed doing that, whereas she despised embroidery. At the end of that time, she handed a remarkably neat rose to her mother and then shot out of the room with extremely unladylike speed to have her lesson.

Amelia looked at the embroidery and smiled. She too had learnt a lesson today. She had just learnt how to make her daughter do tasks she hated, well.

It was a lesson she would employ repeatedly over the next few months, with the result that Harriet learned basic bookkeeping, how to hem handkerchiefs, three more pieces on the harpsichord, and two new dances.

She also learnt how to hit the bullseye on a target almost every time she shot, even on windy days, and how to load a pistol, although she was not allowed to attempt to fire it until her mother or father gave their permission for her to do so.

* * *

October 1681

"So how do you make a hotbed?" Harriet asked.

Jeremiah, who was at the top of a ladder plucking the last of the apples from the branches, having refused to allow Harriet to climb up, looked down at where she stood below him, deftly catching the fruit as he dropped it and placing it carefully in the baskets, so it wouldn't bruise.

"Look at the state of you, my lady. Your dress is all mud. You'll be in trouble if your mother sees you."

Harriet glanced down at the numerous grass and mud stains on her dress, unconcerned.

"It's not one of my good dresses," she said.

"Even so…Jem could do this, and you go in and clean up," Jeremiah said doubtfully. He had seen the disapproving looks that

THE ECCENTRIC'S TALE: HARRIET

the nurse Jemima had cast when she'd seen Lady Harriet and the gardener together engaged in some muddy duty, and he did not want to get into trouble with the duke or duchess.

"Don't worry. It's not your fault I'm dirty," Harriet reassured him. "Who's Jem?"

"Bless you, Jem's my son – about the same age as you, he is, my lady. You'll have seen him working in the gardens, I expect."

"I didn't know you had a son!" Harriet exclaimed. "So what does your wife do? Have I seen her?"

"No, my wife died, not long after Jem was born. You won't remember that, you being just a babe in arms yourself. When I got married, His Grace let us move into the little cottage together, which was very kind of him, because a lot of people dismiss servants if they marry."

"Do they? Why?" Harriet asked.

"I don't rightly know. You'd have to ask your parents. Anyway, when my wife died Jem was only a few months old, and I thought I'd lose my job for certain then, because a servant with a small baby to look after is a liability. But your mother and father were wonderful – they let me stay, and gave me work to do in the part of the gardens where I could hear if Jem cried, and go and tend to him. And then when he was four he started to work with me."

"He started work when he was only four? But he was still too small, surely?"

"Bless you, my lady, no. Lots of children start work at that age, especially if their parents are poor. They need to earn their keep as early as they can."

Harriet fell silent then, deep in thought, and Jeremiah carried on picking apples and passing them to her to put in the basket.

"I need to learn about the servants," Harriet announced to her parents that evening at dinner.

"You need to learn about a lot of things," her mother said. "But yes, the servants are part of that. One day when you're an adult you'll have servants of your own, and you need to know how to control them and look after them. You're old enough now to start learning about that, and other things."

"It's high time you did," her father added. "You can start to spend more time with your mother, learn what she does. Because it's the wife's job usually to look after household affairs and the domestic servants, and the husband's to deal with estate business and the outdoor servants."

"Will I do that instead of my lessons?" Harriet asked eagerly.

"Certainly not," her father said. "You need to work hard at your French, which is poor, from what Mr Hale tells me. Perhaps you should start writing to the king in French instead of English."

Harriet instantly became a picture of distress.

"But I spent *years* learning to spell and write English properly so that I could write to him!" she cried.

"You did. And you spell and write very well now. In English," her father commented. "So if you now have to write in French, I'm sure that will improve too."

"But…but the king won't understand my letters then. He's English!" Harriet said desperately.

"His French is fluent, Harriet," her mother told her. "After all, he lived there for a long time, before he became king, and his sister was married to King Louis' brother."

"Yes, but if we both understand English perfectly, why do I have to start writing to him in a language that I can't express myself properly in?"

"Because if you do, you will learn to express yourself properly in it," her father said logically.

"And if you do, the king will be *very* impressed with you, and it might influence his decision to allow you to go to Court, which would help all of us," her mother said, upset at the distress of her daughter, and aware that she was becoming exasperated, which Stephen would not take kindly to. He had been much more stern with his daughter of late, with mixed results.

"Oh." Harriet digested this for a minute, along with her venison stew. "Maybe at first I could write just a part of my letter in French, rather than all of it?" she suggested pleadingly.

Stephen, opening his mouth to refuse this, caught the expression on his wife's face, and amended what he'd been about to say.

"Very well, then. From now on you must write one page in French, and the rest can be in English. And from next week you and your mother can arrange a time when you can learn about what she does, which will stand you in good stead for when you marry and have a house of your own to look after."

"I'm never going to marry," Harriet said with great certainty. "But I do want to have a house to look after. Why don't people like to have married servants?"

* * *

From then on, Harriet spent two afternoons a week learning how to run a household by supervising Mrs Armitage the housekeeper, who was responsible for managing most of the female staff, except the lady's maid, nurse, and cook, who were Amelia's direct responsibility. She learnt about discussing menus, receiving and paying visits, and checking the household accounts (much of which was normally the man's job, but Amelia, having an excellent head for figures, performed this task).

"It is always useful, if you can, to keep an eye on the accounts, to ensure that money is being well spent, and that your steward is trustworthy. Of course I have no worries in that regard about Mr Noakes, but it's important for all households that we know how much we're spending, especially ones in which economies have to be made," Amelia said.

"Do we have to make economies, Mama?" Harriet asked. She had never thought about where everything she enjoyed came from. It was just there.

"Yes, my darling, we do now. Your grandfather made the wrong choice in who to support in the past, which resulted in our family losing royal favour. Over time this has left your father in debt, and although he fought not to, recently he has had to sell part of the estate, which brought in much-needed money for us. This means that we have now lost the income from those lands forever. So we have to make some economies. It is one reason why we do not travel to London for the season."

"And the other one is because I called Prince James a papist arse-cloth of Louis," Harriet added sadly.

Amelia, surprised her daughter still remembered that, looked up from the menu she was perusing, and caught the glitter in Harriet's grey eyes. She reached across and took her daughter's hand.

"You appreciate honesty, so I will not lie to you. That certainly did not help our fortunes, no. But don't blame yourself. You were six and had no idea what the words meant, and your father should not have said them for you to overhear. So if our current predicament is anyone's fault, it is your father's, and your grandfather's. But we are not poor, and your future is looking bright. The king thinks very highly of you – if he did not, he would not have maintained a correspondence with you for three years. And one day you will go to Court, and maybe then we will come to London and be welcomed there again."

"But I will have to learn how to behave properly at Court," Harriet said. "Does it mean I will have to sit down a lot?"

Amelia laughed.

"You will. But you will also ride out to hunt, which you enjoy. And dance, which you also enjoy now you know the steps."

"I'd rather ride than dance," Harriet said. "And I'd rather plant things than do either of those. Do you manage the gardens too?"

"No. Your father manages the gardens and the staff there. But that's not so in every household. When you marry, maybe your husband will allow you to design and manage the gardens." Although she would not be encouraged to actually do the heavy garden work, but Amelia did not tell Harriet that. Better to disappoint her a little at a time.

* * *

Late October 1782

"So," said Harriet to Jem, the under-gardener's son, who she'd made a point of getting to know once she'd found out they were the same age, and with whom she was now standing next to a long trench, which she'd helped him to dig. "I don't want to get married, but I keep being told I will have to one day, because that's what all ladies have to do."

Jem leaned on his spade and looked across the grounds rather than at her, as he always did when thinking hard.

"That's what men and women does," he said. "They gets married, and then they has babies, and that's how the world keeps going. It's no different for us than it is for you rich folks, except you has a lot more things. So we needs children who can grow up and work so we can all eat, and so they can look after us so's we

THE ECCENTRIC'S TALE: HARRIET

won't starve when we's old, and people like you needs children to leave all the money and lands and things you've got to, so they can keep looking after it and the people who works on it."

"Yes, but if I get married, I'm supposed to do what my husband tells me, because he's a man and I'm a woman, and I'm sick of doing what other people tell me to do instead of what I want to do."

"You's doing what you wants to do now though, en't you?" Jem said, pushing a lock of fair hair that had come loose from his ponytail behind his ear.

"Well, yes, but later I've got to sit in the drawing room during visiting and sew a stupid flower while I listen to conversation, so I can start learning what ladies talk about. But I'd rather be here with you."

"What time have you got to do that?" Jem asked.

"At ten."

Jem glanced up at the weak wintry sun, screwing up his bright blue eyes as he did, calculating the time.

"We'd best get on then, if you wants to learn how to make a hotbed," he said.

"I do. Go on, then. So the trench is about two feet deep, and you've got brick and wood round it. What do we do next?"

"We puts horse shit in it," Jem said, pointing at the pile of manure outside the stable block, "a thick layer along the bottom. And then straw on top of that. But we won't have time to do all that before you has to go in to visit."

"We might. I'll help you do it," Harriet said.

The children worked happily together, Jem spading the manure into the wheelbarrow, Harriet wheeling it across to the trench and tipping it in, both of them getting hot and dirty in the process. Then he jumped into the trench and started spreading the manure across it.

"So you spreads it smooth, and then puts straw on top, and then the frame with the glass panes goes on top of that, with hinges so's you can lift it to work and to let the air in if it gets too hot," Jem said. Harriet jumped down beside him and helped him spread the manure. "Your shoes is awful dirty," he commented doubtfully.

"But what makes it so hot? Is it just the sun shining on the glass? If it is, what happens when it's not sunny? Do the melons and cucumbers die? Because there's no room for braziers in here."

"No. There's little worms in the shit and the straw that works to turn it into soil. You're hot now, even though it's cold out here, en't you?"

She nodded. She was, she was even sweating, her hair lank, damp patches under her arms.

"Well, it's the same for the little worms. They works hard and they gives off a lot of heat, and that makes it really warm in there, because there's a lot of them, and because the heat can't get out. The straw round the sides of the bed outside helps to keep the heat in. And once they've done all the work, and the shit and straw turns to soil, they stops working, and then we has to replace it, or the hot bed gets cold and the plants die. But then we puts the soil they've made on the garden, because it's nice and rich and helps the plants to grow."

"That's really clever!" Harriet said. "I like that. So what other things can you grow in here?"

Instead of answering, Jem cocked his head like an alerted wild animal, listening. Harriet really liked Jem. He was clever, not about writing and French and stupid things like embroidery and music, but about interesting things, like plants. He could grow anything, his father Jeremiah said. And there was something wild, natural about him. She got the feeling that he would be able to go and live in the forest like a fox or a hare, and be perfectly at home there. He behaved as if he was free, somehow. She knew he wasn't, not really. He had to do what his father told him to do, and he was a servant too. But he *seemed* free, and that really called to her.

"Your nurse is calling you," he said. "You'd best go now."

And he had hearing like a wild animal too. She hadn't heard a thing.

"What time is it?" she asked.

He glanced up at the sky.

"About ten, I'd say."

"Oh God!" she cried, and leaping out of the trench, she picked up her skirts and ran in the most unladylike way possible back to the house.

CHAPTER TWO

"It was impossible. I couldn't even invent a reason why she would be late joining us, not after she'd just treated all of us to the sight of her dashing across the lawn with her skirts hitched up round her knees, covered in dirt with her hair flying all over the place. I'm just glad that I went out to see what was wrong and managed to catch her in the hallway. Otherwise she'd have burst in on us as she was. And she smelt dreadful! She'd been shovelling manure with one of the gardeners' sons, it seems."

"Jeremiah Wilson's boy?" Stephen asked.

"Yes. Apparently she wanted to know how a hotbed was made, and decided to help him rather than just watch. She was soaked with sweat, too, even though it's October. She looked more like a beggar than a duke's daughter."

"Where is she now?"

"In her room. Her shoes were completely ruined and she had to have a bath, immediately. She was so disgraceful that I was hoping the ladies wouldn't recognise her, but unfortunately Lady Renton did and joyfully announced it to the room."

Really, this just cannot go on," Stephen said. "She's not a baby any more and should know better. She has to learn to think about the consequences of her actions."

"Hopefully that's what she's doing in her room right now," Amelia said.

"She's spending far too much time with the gardener's boy. Last week she told me that Jem's her best friend, apart from the king," Stephen commented.

"Well, at least we can say her acquaintance is diverse," Amelia said, amused in spite of her irritation by Harriet's blithe disregard for social status, although she agreed that her daughter's conduct had to be amended, and quickly.

"How on earth will she ever be able to attend Court, when the time comes that King Charles summons her? I know he appreciates her honesty, but he won't want a wild savage running around the palace. He said that when she was fourteen or fifteen he would send for her. That gives us enough time to make a lady of her, but we have to start right now," Stephen said. "I blame myself. I should have been more severe with her much earlier, instead of letting her have her own way all the time."

Amelia sighed.

"We're both at fault, partly because we love her so, and partly because she's such a sweet child. She's not wicked at all, just thoughtless and carefree. She asked me if Jem could join her in her lessons, because he's trying to teach himself to read and wants to be a head gardener one day," she said.

"What did you tell her?" Stephen asked.

"I said no, although I did wonder if she might enjoy classroom work more if she had someone of her own age learning with her. Sophia's a completely different sort of child, very placid, and Melanie's too young. I think Harriet likes Jem because he's intelligent, as she is."

"Yes, but he's a gardener's son!" Stephen said. "And she's far ahead of him in learning in any case. This friendship has to be stopped. It's one thing caring for the servants' welfare, but quite another becoming bosom friends with them. She needs to learn to make friends with girls of her own kind, otherwise she'll never fit in."

"She was really sorry that she was late and had upset me," Amelia commented. "And she promised that next time the ladies call she will stay clean, and be on her very best behaviour with them."

"That's very gracious of her," Stephen said sarcastically. Amelia looked at him, shocked. "I'm sorry, my darling. I know how genuinely sorry she is when she disappoints us, and it's charming, but it's not enough if she doesn't learn from it and change. You know how I adore her, but I've been thinking that we are really doing her no favours allowing her to run wild as she does. Not just because so much depends on her being accepted

THE ECCENTRIC'S TALE: HARRIET

at Court, but because she will never find a husband, or be happy, if she doesn't learn how to behave in polite society. Things have to change. We both must be much firmer with her, starting immediately."

* * *

For the next few days Harriet, knowing how upset her parents were with her, made an enormous effort to behave herself as it seemed a young lady should. She worked hard at her lessons, learnt a new melody on the harpsichord, and endured endless hours of mastering a new embroidery stitch that her sister Sophia was already proficient at even though she was two years younger than Harriet. She didn't ask if she could engage in archery practice, or do anything in the garden, she sat erect in her chair, spoke quite fluently with her parents in French at dinner, and wrote a complete letter to King Charles in French which took her a whole day, in which she told him that she had displeased her parents by making a hotbed, but was now attempting to be a proper lady because she was so sorry for shocking her mother's friends by allowing them to see her covered in horse shit. And she had not hit Percy, even when he had told her she was no better than a Scotchwoman, although she had admitted to the king that she didn't know any Scotchwomen, so had no idea why being no better than one was a bad thing. Did he know any, and if so, what were they like?

At the end of the week it stopped raining, and Harriet, still on her best behaviour, politely asked her mother if she could go for a walk in the gardens. Amelia, having observed her daughter closely over the last few days, and appreciating the huge effort she was making to behave as Sophia did naturally, said she could, of course. It was clear the child desperately needed to burn off some of her incessant energy.

"And you may join the archery lesson later if you wish, as you have behaved so well," Amelia told her daughter, and was rewarded with a radiant smile.

Harriet walked round the gravel paths of the gardens briskly, enjoying the crisp November air which lifted her hair and blew her cloak around her shoulders. It was wonderful to be outdoors again, after a week inside. If it hadn't stopped raining, she didn't know what she would have done. The lack of exercise had almost killed her this week, but after the shameful spectacle she'd made of herself in front of her mother's friends, it didn't seem right to ask if she could go for a walk in the rain, because she knew that most ladies wouldn't, although it was perfectly acceptable to go for a walk in dry weather, even when it was cold. It was acceptable to be interested in gardening too, but not to climb trees, do any digging, or anything which involved getting very dirty or sweaty.

She really did want to please her parents. She hated it when they were disappointed with her. But there was so much that she was interested in that it seemingly wasn't appropriate for ladies to do, and it didn't make any sense to her why ladies shouldn't do anything that they were able to do, if they wanted to. Men did. But she loved her parents and wanted to please them, and so she would try harder to do it. It was worth doing something quiet and boring, if it made her mother or father smile and praise her.

She walked round the lake and down the path on the other side of it as far as the walled garden, and contemplated going to the dairy, but then decided against that, because her mother had said she would show her a duchess's dairy duties later this week. She did have time to look at the hotbed that had caused all the trouble last week though, before the archery began. She would only look at it, not actually *do* anything in it, so as not to get dirty.

When she arrived there, one of the gardeners, a man she only knew by name, was busily packing straw round the sides of the hotbed. Jem had told her that straw was packed round it because it kept the heat in, and that was why some poorer people had straw mattresses on the ground, because they couldn't afford beds and the straw stopped the cold from the floor getting through to them when they were sleeping.

"Hello, Matthew," she said. The man looked up and dipped his head to her.

"Good morning, my lady. A nice day for a walk," he replied.

"It is. How are you today?" Her mother had told her always to ask how the servants were, to show you cared. This was one instruction Harriet found easy to remember, because she *did* care.

"I'm very well indeed, thank you for asking," he replied.

"I helped Jem to put the horse shit in there last week," she

THE ECCENTRIC'S TALE: HARRIET

explained. "Is it hot yet?"

"It is, my lady. After four days it was very hot in there, and so now I've just put the soil on top. You can see, the glass is misty – that's because it's so hot the water is misting the window!"

She came a bit closer to look. It was!

"That's amazing!" she said. "Jem told me it got very hot, but I didn't realise it was hot enough to make the water steam!"

"It's too hot to plant anything now, because it'd shrivel, but the soil will cool it down enough so we can put seeds in soon," he said.

"Why didn't Jem put the soil in?" she asked. "He told me he was going to. I was going to help him, but I've had to stay inside because I was naughty."

"Jem isn't here any more, my lady. He left last week, his father too."

"What? Why?" Harriet asked. "He didn't tell me he was leaving!"

Matthew reddened.

"I'm sure I don't know. It was all very sudden. Begging your pardon, my lady, but I'd best get on," he said.

Harriet stood in shock for a minute, staring at the hotbed, until she realised that Matthew was becoming distinctly uncomfortable by her silent presence. Then she walked away, and set off back to the house, her archery lesson forgotten. Her mother would know why they'd left. No, her father. He was responsible for the outdoor servants, she had learned that.

* * *

"I have dismissed them both," her father said when she managed to track him down in the stables, where he was checking on one of the horses which had developed a limp.

"Why?" she asked.

"That's not your concern, Harriet," he replied, stroking the mare's leg before standing up. "The outdoor servants are the man's responsibility. It's the indoor servants that you will be responsible for when you marry."

"But Jeremiah was kind to me, and Jem is my friend, so they *are* my concern!" Harriet argued.

"Harriet, I know we told you that you must take care of the servants, and have an interest in them, but that does not mean

35

you should make them your best friends! They are not of the same class as you are. There must always be a slight distance between a master or mistress and servants, to ensure that respect and obedience are maintained." Stephen realised how pompous he sounded, but even so, the principle was right. It was difficult to discipline an employee if you treated them as your equal.

"You dismissed them because Jem is my friend, didn't you? Because I helped him shovel shit into the hotbed," Harriet said.

"Harriet, shit is not a very ladylike word," Stephen reproved her. "Dung or manure are more appropriate."

"Why? Shit is just a word, just some letters put together to make a name. Why is shit unladylike, but dung isn't?"

There was a silence while Stephen realised that his daughter had a point. He had no idea why shit was bad but dung wasn't. It just was. Some things just were. Like servants not being your best friends.

"You haven't answered my question," Harriet injected into the silence. "Did you dismiss them because you don't like me having Jem as my friend? Or because I asked Mama if he could learn to read with me?"

Stephen reddened slightly, giving the astute Harriet her answer.

"That's not fair, Papa," she said. "Jem didn't *ask* if he could learn to read with me. That was my idea, and I didn't even tell him I was going to ask if he could. And if you wanted me to stop being friends with Jem you could have told me."

"And if I had, you would have argued with me, as you are doing now," Stephen said, "which is not something a child should do with her father."

"But you've always told me to question things!" Harriet said.

"Yes, but not my decisions. I have made this one, it is done and it is your place to accept it, not to question it!" Stephen shouted.

Harriet stared at him, shocked. Her father rarely shouted at her, and then only when she'd done something terrible. But it was not terrible to ask a question. He had always encouraged her to ask questions, both her parents had. She felt the tears prickle on her eyelids and swallowed hard, then turned and walked away.

Stephen leaned on the stable door feeling suddenly exhausted, realising he had not handled that very well. He was not a natural disciplinarian, but he could not allow his daughter to carry on as she was, for her own sake as much as theirs. Soon she would have to mix with other titled ladies, and she would be ridiculed and scorned, which would hurt her far more than he had just done, he told himself.

It did not make him feel any better.

* * *

"I'm a little worried about Lady Harriet, Your Grace," Jemima said that evening to Amelia. "I think she might be sickening for something."

"What? Harriet?" Amelia said, shocked. Harriet was *never* ill! It was Sophia who had every childhood ailment, passing them on to Melanie, while her eldest daughter never contracted anything worse than an occasional cold.

"Yes, Your Grace. She came back from the gardens earlier, said she'd had a quarrel with His Grace, and that she was going to lie down. I just thought she was upset – she looked as though she'd been crying. But she's still in bed, and she said she doesn't want anything to eat this evening."

Amelia's brow furrowed. That was not like Harriet at all. She was not one to let anything upset her for long, and she had a very healthy appetite.

"Does she have a temperature?" Amelia asked as she put her sewing down and set off to the nursery, Jemima following behind.

"No, she feels quite cool, but she's not behaving as she normally does at all."

"Jemima tells me you don't want to eat tonight," Amelia said to her daughter, sitting on the edge of the bed and holding up the candle to examine her face. Her colour looked good, at least, not flushed, or pale.

"I can't eat," Harriet said. "I'm too sad."

"Why are you sad? Is it because you had an argument with Papa?"

"No. Well, yes, but I'm sad because he dismissed Jem and his papa, and it's my fault. And I can't eat, knowing that."

"Your father dismissed Jeremiah?" Amelia said. Why would he do that? The man had been with them for years, and his work was excellent. She must ask him about it.

"Yes, and when I asked him why, he shouted at me, even though he's always told me to question things. And he said I shouldn't use the word shit, but I've already sent a letter to King Charles with it in."

Amelia blinked.

"Well, I think the king has probably heard the word before, sweeting. I wouldn't be upset about that. I'm sure he won't be offended. And I'm sure Papa didn't mean to shout at you."

"He did," Harriet said. "He told me I have to accept his decisions."

"Well, you do, really, just as I have to. Because he's the duke, and the master here," Amelia said, seeing an opportunity to educate her daughter.

"Even when he's wrong?" Harriet asked.

Amelia sighed. It was lovely to have a clever daughter. But sometimes it would be a relief if she didn't ask such awkward questions and instead accepted things, as Sophia did.

"I'll go and have a chat with him," Amelia said. "If Jemima brings up another tray for you, will you try to eat something? It would make me happy if you do."

"I can't," Harriet said firmly. "I'm too unhappy."

"No," Stephen said, when Amelia asked him if he'd go and talk to their daughter, who was very upset about the gardener being dismissed. "I've said all she needs to know. I'm not going to start explaining myself to her. She has to learn to accept my decisions. One day she'll be married and will have to accept her husband's decisions too. This is a good start."

"Explain yourself to me then, even if I am only your wife," Amelia said a little tartly. "Why did you dismiss Jeremiah? I thought he was an excellent worker."

"He is," Stephen replied. "But his son and Harriet are far too close, and it's not appropriate. He's a boy, and a servant too!"

"They're ten years old, Stephen!" Amelia said. "Are you afraid he's going to try to seduce her in the shrubbery?"

"No, of course not!" Stephen replied hotly, reddening. "But he's her best friend! She needs to start becoming acquainted with young girls of her own age and class, and she won't do that if she's

THE ECCENTRIC'S TALE: HARRIET

shovelling shit with the gardener's son!"

"She told me she's written 'shit' to the king, but you told her it's a bad word, too," Amelia said.

"If she's upset about that, then I'll tell her the king won't be angry," Stephen said, "but I'm not arguing with a child about my decisions regarding the servants."

"Stephen," Amelia said, "she's not upset about that. She's been writing to the king for four years. She knows he won't be angry about her using the word shit. He was after all close friends with Rochester, who had a mouth like a sewer!"

"Dear God, don't compare our daughter with that rakehell!" Stephen said. "He died of the pox!"

"I'm not comparing Harriet to Rochester. I'm only saying that the king is not easily shocked. But that's not why she's upset. She's upset because you've dismissed the gardener and she thinks it's her fault. She's too upset to eat. Why didn't you just tell her not to see Jem any more, instead of getting rid of him?"

"I couldn't be sure that she wouldn't keep seeing Jem. I can't watch her all the time," Stephen replied. "She goes her own way, we both know that. And now she has to learn that she must change. If we remove the temptation, it'll be easier for her. It's done now, and there's an end to it. Just leave her. She'll eat when she's hungry," he finished.

She did not eat when she was hungry. Four days passed with father and daughter in deadlock, Harriet refusing to eat because she was 'upset', and Stephen refusing to go and discuss the matter with her.

On the fifth day Amelia sent for the doctor, partly to make sure that Harriet wasn't actually ill and partly hoping the doctor would be able to persuade her to eat.

After examining her daughter, Mr Stokes came to Amelia's dressing room, as she'd requested.

"I can't find anything wrong with her," he admitted. "She has no fever and her urine is a good colour and taste. I questioned her closely, but she has no symptoms at all, apart from feeling weak and dizzy if she stands up and not passing stools any more. But as you said she's not eaten for four days, that's not surprising. She told me she's too unhappy to eat. Has there been a tragedy of some sort, the death of a beloved pet, perhaps?"

Only if you consider having two members of your family as stubborn as mules a tragedy, Amelia thought.

"No. But there has been a disagreement between Harriet and her father, which has upset her," she said.

"Ah," replied the doctor. "I have seen this sort of thing before, children holding their breath until they swoon, that kind of thing, to try to get their own way. You must be firm with her, not let her rule you. She will eat once she realises she cannot win. As long as she is drinking, which she is, she will be in no danger for some days yet. Call me again if you are concerned."

After he'd gone, Amelia sat for a while staring at her reflection in her dressing-room mirror and trying to think of what to do. The doctor was wrong; Harriet had always accepted being admonished when she'd done wrong. She was not a child who threw tantrums, and had never behaved in this way before. Although in honesty, neither had Stephen.

Amelia sighed. She would leave them both to it for another two days, see if one of them bent.

Neither of them bent.

* * *

"I don't actually *feel* hungry any more," Harriet admitted to her mother. "So it doesn't bother me not to eat now."

"It bothers me, though," Amelia said. "It bothers Papa and Jemima too. If you don't eat you will die. You are already weaker, you told me that, and you feel sick. You *must* eat. You cannot carry on like this. And your father will not change his mind, as is his right. You must accept that Jeremiah and Jem are gone and are not coming back. We don't know where they are now."

"But I can't accept that!" Harriet wailed. "It's all my fault! Jeremiah told me how wonderful you both were, because you'd let him stay when he got married, and had given him work near the house when his wife died so he could look after Jem. He was really happy here, and so was Jem – he wanted to be head gardener one day. And now they could be begging in the street, because father just dismissed them! They must be so unhappy. How can I eat when they might be starving because of me?"

"Really, darling, you are being a little dramatic," Amelia said.

THE ECCENTRIC'S TALE: HARRIET

"They were both excellent workers. I'm sure they've found another position by now."

"But you don't know if they have," Harriet said. "You just said you don't know where they are. It's not fair that they're being punished because I did something wrong! Why didn't Papa explain to me that he didn't want me to be Jem's friend?"

"You would have argued with him about it if he had."

"I might have done," Harriet agreed, "but I would rather have ended the friendship with Jem, even if it made me lonely, than know they might be starving to death. It's so cruel of Papa. I don't understand him," Harriet said. "I don't ever want to get married if men are kind and loving like he is, and then suddenly become cruel for no reason."

Amelia resisted the urge to knock her head on the doorpost with frustration, and went back to her room to think out her next move. Really, she should knock *their* heads on the doorpost instead! Stephen's harder than Harriet's, being honest.

She waited until they were in bed, alone, until he couldn't use urgent business as an excuse to avoid discussing this subject that he clearly felt very uncomfortable about. Uncomfortable because he knew he was in the wrong, Amelia thought.

"I don't want to talk about it," Stephen interrupted firmly when Amelia broached the subject that night.

"Well, we're going to have to," she replied. "We've been married for many years, and I know you very well, so don't play the tyrant with me. It doesn't suit you, and I don't want it to. I talked to Harriet today and I don't believe she's not eating to wage a battle of wills with you."

He cast her an incredulous look.

"She's upset, really upset. We told her she needs to take care for the servants, that they are our family, and we are responsible for their wellbeing. And that is what she's doing. In an extreme way, as Harriet is wont to do, but I can understand her. She is afraid Jeremiah and Jem might be unemployed and starving, and she is dismayed that they've been treated unjustly, which they have. And she cannot believe her father can be so cruel, because she loves you."

Stephen bit his lip, and looked away.

"I cannot just give way to her on this, or we will never be able to control her. She must learn to accept our authority," he said.

"She does need to learn that. But she's intelligent, and has a keen understanding of justice and injustice. It's the injustice of this that she is fighting against, and I admire her for it, in truth. We cannot tell her she must be caring and responsible, and then tell her she must accept it if we are not! We must set the example for her to follow. I know she's stubborn and headstrong. So are you. So am I. And we are at fault for not reining her in earlier. But this is not the way to do it, Stephen, you must see that. If you were in her position now, knowing what I've just told you, would you give in?" He opened his mouth and she gently put her finger on it. "No, think before you answer. Because if you are comfortable with your decision to dismiss Jeremiah, then you are not the man I have been happily married to for twelve years. Speak honestly to me, as you always have."

He thought for a minute, and then he sighed.

"No, I am not comfortable with my decision," he said. "I am not naturally a hard man, Amelia, we both know that. But we also both know that we have been too soft with Harriet. I think I may have made the wrong decision, been too hard, yes. But there is a danger that if I just ask them to come back, Harriet will think she can get her own way every time, and that would not be good."

"No, it would not. I've given a lot of thought to this topic over the last days. It's tearing me apart to see you both estranged, who love each other so much. Harriet is intelligent, and she loves us both. She accepts things much better if she understands them. I know it is the way of many parents to just lay down the law to their children and expect to be obeyed, but that will not work with her. It would not have worked with me, nor with you."

"No, it wouldn't," he admitted. "It didn't, did it, when your parents tried to stop us from marrying because they did not approve of my father's support of Cromwell?"

"No. We met secretly anyway. But if my parents had explained the possible long-term consequences of your father's decision to me, instead of just ordering me to stop seeing you, I might have listened to them," Amelia said.

Stephen's eyes widened.

"Might you?" he asked. "Are you sorry—"

"I have never been sorry for one minute that I married you," she interrupted. "You have made me happier than I could have imagined, with or without the king's favour. But I am giving you an example of how my parents' heavy-handedness actually pushed us together, the opposite of what they intended. That's what's happening now. I truly believe that if you go to see Harriet and admit you made a mistake, but that you were concerned about the friendship and why, not only will she accept that, but she will love you and respect you more for it. And then we have to find out where Jeremiah and his son are, and make sure they are looked after. She will not see it as winning a victory. She will see it as her father doing the right thing, and she will be more inclined to listen to you in the future and follow your advice, when you *explain* things to her."

Sensibly, she did not labour the point any more, but left her husband to think about it, trusting to him to come to the right conclusion.

In the morning he went to see his daughter. They were together for over an hour, after which he came out, told Jemima to send for some soup, but not to let Harriet eat too much at once, and then he set about finding out where Jeremiah was.

It took him two days to find they were living in a stable. Jeremiah had not managed to obtain work yet, but Jem was mucking out the stables at the coach house in town, which he hated, but which earned them a place to sleep and some food.

Two days after that they were back in the cottage, and Harriet had agreed not to see as much of Jem, and to start learning how to be a lady in earnest, because if she was to be a lady at the Court of King Charles, she would *have* to learn how to behave appropriately, and how to make friends with the other ladies at Court. Otherwise she would be miserable, and so would Charles.

And so would her parents, who were desperate, socially and financially, to be accepted back in royal circles, for which Harriet was the key. Although that they did not tell her.

* * *

December 1682

So far, all was going well. Although Amelia had been on tenterhooks for the first few minutes of the afternoon social gathering of ladies,

Harriet had so far behaved faultlessly.

She was sitting opposite her mother in the formal circle of chairs which was the standard arrangement for these affairs. Personally Amelia thought it would be more cosy and sensible to arrange the chairs around small tables and let the ladies form their own more intimate groups, not least because she could then allow the spiteful ones to sit together and tear the county to shreds whilst she engaged with those ladies whose company she actually liked. But that was not how these things were done. She had suggested it once, but the other ladies had been horrified, reacting as though she had suggested placing a turd in the middle of the room for them to comment on. It seemed that sort of arrangement would be far too outrageous.

So she sat and politely listened while Lady Renton destroyed the reputation of a young man she'd never heard of and then went on to comment on the lack of feeling of a daughter of a lady of their acquaintance (absent today, of course) who had had the temerity to wear a scarlet dress in public!

Harriet's head had popped up at this, but then she had caught her mother's faint shake of the head and the question on her lips was swallowed back. She had been schooled prior to the social in how to behave, Amelia trying to think of every possible eventuality.

"When the ladies come in, John will announce them, and we will stand and greet them. I will tell them how happy I am that they could come today and escort them to a chair, while you will curtsey. If they greet you, you will wish them a good day and say you're delighted to make their acquaintance. Then for today I want you just to listen and observe what happens. Only speak if someone asks you a question. Then next time, when you understand the routine, maybe you can contribute a little more," Amelia had told her.

Twenty minutes into the afternoon gathering, Amelia started to relax a little. Really, Harriet was being so good. She was not swinging her legs or fidgeting as she usually did when sitting down, and she was immaculately dressed, not a hair out of place. She didn't even have a bored expression on her face. Amelia determined that when this meeting was over, she would take her daughter out riding, rain or not, as a reward for the ordeal she had endured.

THE ECCENTRIC'S TALE: HARRIET

"Ladies, I really wanted to ask your opinion of my fontange!" Lady Elman leapt in when Lady Renton took a breath in between ending the character assassination of one person and starting the next. Everyone looked at the two-foot-high confection of lace, wire and ribbons on top of that lady's head.

"It is rather higher than I have seen before," Amelia said politely. Most ladies wore a small lace and ribbon cap on top of their curled hair since it had become popular in France, but this was an enormous and cumbersome version. Lady Elman had had to duck when she'd entered the room to avoid hitting it on the doorframe.

"I know," Lady Elman said. "This is the first time I've worn it. But my new ladies' maid is from Paris, and she tells me that the ladies at the French Court are wearing theirs higher and higher now. Everyone in England will be wearing them like this soon!"

"Then you are at the forefront of fashion!" another lady cried.

"But how does it look?" Lady Elman asked. Her eyes met those of the quiet little girl, who was observing the fontange with great interest.

"It looks very uncomfortable," Harriet said.

"Oh, it is, Lady Harriet," Lady Elman replied proudly. She turned her head so that Harriet could see the enormous pile of curls which climbed up the back of the three tiers of stiff, wired lace. "You have to put egg white on your hair for days beforehand to stiffen it, and it took simply *hours* for Madeleine to create the style last night, and then I had to sleep sitting in a chair, because if I'd laid down it would have been quite ruined!"

"Well, I'm flattered that you took so much trouble to attend my little gathering," Amelia said. "You really didn't need to, you know. We are always quite informal."

"Oh, I know that, Your Grace, but next week I am going down to London to attend a soiree at Whitehall, and I wanted your opinions on whether it would be acceptable or not before I go."

"The king lives at Whitehall," Harriet volunteered, before looking at her mother, wide-eyed, realising that she was not answering an actual question. Amelia smiled reassuringly.

"He does indeed, Lady Harriet," Lady Elman said. "I will be meeting him there, and the queen, and I so want to look my very best. What do you think?"

"I think it's horrible," Harriet said confidently, having been asked a direct question now. "It makes your head look very long, and you have lines on your face as though you're in pain."

A moment's silence greeted this opinion, but Lady Elman replied before Amelia could leap in.

"I am a little," she confided. "My neck is stiff from sitting up all night, and I have to hold my head straight so that the fontange doesn't slide to the left or right. But I'm sure I will become accustomed to it before I go to the palace."

"It seems an awful lot of effort for something that looks so silly and gives you lines," Harriet commented. "Old people don't like lines on their faces, do they? I'm sure the king would far prefer you to look happy and young. He likes happy people. And it smells, too. I can smell it even from here. The king won't like that either."

"Who are you to presume what King Charles will or won't like?" Lady Renton broke in somewhat hostilely, angry that Lady Elman, who was her cousin, was being embarrassed by a child. And a child that, last time she'd seen her, had looked like a filthy street urchin!

"He's my best friend," Harriet announced. "We write to each other all the time."

"Oh, if you wrote to him I'm sure he told his secretary to send a polite reply to you, that's all," Lady Renton said condescendingly. "The king rarely writes to anybody and in any case has far more important things to do than correspond with a child."

"No, he does write to her quite regularly, in his own hand. I'm familiar with his handwriting," Amelia replied defensively. How dare the woman be so nasty to her daughter! She glanced at Harriet, expecting her to be distressed, but if the child was, she showed no signs of it. She had turned her face to Lady Renton, and was eyeing her speculatively.

"Yes, he does," she said now, then turned to Lady Elman. "He told me that both the gentlemen and ladies wear some quite ridiculous fashions at Court, so I am sure you would please him and be far more comfortable if you wore something a little smaller, my lady. Then you'll be able to concentrate on being happy, which will certainly please him."

"Well, His Majesty clearly tells you a lot. Who would have

THE ECCENTRIC'S TALE: HARRIET

thought he would confide in *such* a child as you?" Lady Renton said nastily. "What other wisdom has he imparted to you then?"

Before the outraged Amelia could intervene, Harriet turned her clear grey eyes to the older woman's brown ones, and smiled.

"Oh, I'm sure I cannot divulge anything the king confides in me to *such* a woman as you," she said in an innocent and friendly tone. "He has however written, not in confidence, so this I *can* tell you, that he abhors people who spread vicious tales about others behind their backs, when they have no chance to defend themselves. He said it is *craven* of them. I hadn't heard the word before so had to ask its meaning."

Amelia would never forget the expression on the Countess of Renton's face. She closed her eyes momentarily, torn between her impulse to hug Harriet for comprehensively annihilating the unbearably vicious and snobbish woman, and her need to rescue the afternoon, and Lady Elman, who she *did* actually like, even if the woman was a bit silly.

"Harriet, my dear, would you go and tell the footman that we're ready for refreshments now?" she said, although she could have rung the bell on the table next to her, as the footman was waiting directly outside the drawing room door in case he was needed.

Harriet, being intelligent, knew that, and therefore also knew that she had failed, in spite of all her efforts to follow her instructions, and that her mother was giving her a reason to leave before she committed any more indiscretions, rather than just dismissing her. She climbed down from her chair, curtseyed exquisitely to the ladies, then left the room.

She then went up to the nursery, where Jemima, somewhat surprised to see her so early, asked her what was wrong, at which Harriet burst into tears and cried inconsolably on her nurse's lap for a full fifteen minutes.

As soon as the visitors left Amelia bounded up to the nursery with a lack of feminine grace that Lady Renton would have gleefully informed the county of, had she seen it.

"Why didn't you come back after speaking to the footman?" Amelia asked her daughter gently on seeing her red eyes and blotchy face.

47

"I thought you wanted me to leave because I'd done something terrible," Harriet said, her eyes filling with tears again.

"No, sweeting, I wanted to give you a chance to move about a bit. You'd been sitting so still and so beautifully, and I know how hard that is for you."

"Oh! So I didn't do anything terrible? Only that fat old woman was so cross with me, and when I looked at you, you had your eyes squeezed tight shut, so I thought…" She sniffed loudly, and blew her nose.

Amelia thought for a minute. Aware of how anxious Harriet was to please her parents, and the titanic effort she'd made, Amelia didn't want to sound too critical.

"I'm not angry with you," she began. "I'm so used to these social gatherings, I forgot how…complicated they can be. You really shouldn't have told Lady Elman that her headdress was horrible."

"But she asked me what I thought, Mama, she was looking directly at me when she asked it! And you told me to answer direct questions!" Harriet said.

"You're right, I did. I really should have told you not to answer any questions unless they were *about* you, so it's my fault, not yours," Amelia said.

"Why shouldn't I have told her her headdress was horrible, Mama? It was! Didn't you think so, too?"

"Yes, I did. But at these conversations with ladies, you must always be polite and complimentary before you are truthful," Amelia replied. "I should have told you that."

Harriet's face screwed up in puzzlement.

"But I liked her," she said after a moment. "And she was so excited about going to see the king and queen. I didn't want him to think she looked stupid or dull, which he would if she wore that silly thing. And she smelt terrible. I didn't realise it was her until she explained about the egg whites. Isn't it better to tell her the truth? And then she can wear something nicer that smells better, and the king will like her too and she'll have a lovely visit with him! If it had been that horrible woman who hates everyone I might have told *her* she looked nice though," Harriet mused.

It was really, really difficult to argue with someone when you actually agreed with them. Amelia exchanged a glance with

THE ECCENTRIC'S TALE: HARRIET

Jemima, who was trying very hard to keep her expression serious, although her eyes were sparkling with suppressed laughter.

"Harriet, did King Charles *really* write what you told Lady Renton? About his likes and dislikes?" Amelia asked.

"Yes. I wouldn't lie and say he wrote something he didn't," Harriet said, but then she bit her lip and looked a little ashamed. "But I *did* know that it would annoy her if I told her, because she's just the sort of person the king doesn't like, a nasty old gossip. She already didn't like me because I'm a friend of the king's and she isn't, which is very silly of her. I'm sorry, Mama. I really shouldn't have said what I did, but I couldn't help myself."

At that Amelia grinned, and Jemima, who had had the misfortune of being on the wrong end of Lady Renton's tongue in the past, laughed out loud, before clapping her hand over her mouth.

"Let's go to my dressing room, out of Jemima, Sophia and Melanie's way," Amelia said, trying to keep the hilarity out of her voice. "We'll sit there, just the two of us, and I'll send for some of the refreshments you missed, and we'll have a little chat about the day. A nice little chat," she added, seeing Harriet's alarmed expression. "I'm not angry with you, I already told you that. Quite the opposite, but we do need to talk about the visit while it's fresh in our minds."

* * *

"How I kept from laughing out loud when Harriet crushed that vicious old bitch I'll really never know," Amelia told her husband later that evening in the bedroom when he got back from estate business and the children were all in bed asleep. "The expression on her face…I don't think she's ever been spoken to like that. She visits absolutely *everyone* and people are so afraid of having their reputations destroyed by her that they won't do anything to cross her at all. It was wonderful."

"Did you explain to Harriet that the old bitch will now tell everyone in the nobility what a rude and uncivilised child she is?" Stephen asked, but smiling.

"Not in those words, no, but I did explain that to her, yes. And she told me that she really didn't care what Lady Renton thought of her at all, and that anyone who decided they didn't like her without meeting her, based on that woman's malicious tongue wasn't worth caring about either. So I told her that Lady Renton is a countess and has a lot of influence with a good number of important people. And Harriet said, 'well, she can't have *that* much influence, because she was so very envious of my friendship with the king, envious enough to be nasty to my face rather than behind my back, which means she would *like* to be his friend, but isn't. Maybe she's met him and he told her he didn't like her. I hope so. It would serve her right if he did'."

Stephen snorted with laughter at that.

"I think maybe we're worrying too much about Harriet being upset if she doesn't fit in, you know. She really doesn't seem to care a fig what people think about her," he said.

"No, she doesn't. I must admit she made me feel quite the coward, because I've wanted to tell that horrible woman what I think of her for years, but was too worried that she'd malign me to others. But now Harriet's done it for me, I feel absolutely light-hearted that I won't have to endure her company again, and I realised that I don't really care either about people who believe her malicious lies. But at the same time, I feel like that because I have you and other genuine friends too, who I know love me. It gives me security."

"And Harriet has us and her sisters, who she knows love her," Stephen pointed out. "We will always be there for her."

"But we won't, darling. One day she will have to make her own way in the world, and for that she will need friends of her own age. She is a very loving, caring child, and without friends she will be lonely. I don't want that for her."

"Neither do I. But please tell me you didn't chide her for standing up to that harridan."

"No. How could I? She was wonderful – not directly rude to the woman, but made her views so clear that even her silly cousin understood. She will need to stand up for herself in time. I knew she would be able to do that, but until today I didn't realise she would do it so well – Lady Renton couldn't reply without acknowledging that she knew she was a nasty gossip, which she'd never do. But what I *did* discuss with her was the forthrightness of her opinion about the fontange on Lady Elman's head."

"Hmmm. I really don't understand why you women put

yourself through all that agony to wear such ridiculous-looking things," Stephen said.

"Men do it too. Wigs are just as ridiculous, really, especially when you have to shave your own perfectly good hair off just to wear a hot, itchy, vermin-ridden thing on your head!" Amelia retorted.

"That's true, although mine is not vermin-ridden. But I don't have to sit up all night so that it won't look a mess," Stephen pointed out.

"We're becoming distracted," Amelia said, fumbling with the catch of her necklace. She had dismissed her ladies' maid so that they could speak in private. Stephen, noticing, came over to the dressing table and undid the clasp, handed her the necklace to put in its case, then started to unlace her corset for her. "Thank you," she said. "We had a little chat about how to word criticism more delicately, because I realise that Harriet will never be able to tell an outright lie to someone if they ask her opinion, and it's not really fair of me to ask her to. I've decided to do a little play-acting with her, asking her to give me opinions on various matters in the most tactful way possible, and then I'll have another social afternoon."

"Without Lady Renton, I would imagine," Stephen replied, unbuttoning his waistcoat.

"I think it will be a long time before we see her again, thank God," Amelia replied. Dressed now only in her chemise she stood and stretched luxuriously, before moving across to help her husband disrobe.

Then they became decidedly distracted for some considerable time. After making love, as it was cosy in the room and neither of them had to disturb the other by rising at some ungodly hour in the morning, Stephen did not return to his own bedchamber and instead they lay together, enjoying the warmth and feel of each other's naked bodies, drinking wine and talking intimately about the small affairs of the day, as long-standing partners who still care deeply for each other do.

"I would have Harriet enjoy a love such as ours," Amelia said, sipping wine, her head on her husband's shoulder, his arm wrapped round her, his hand gently fondling her breast. "I would like that very much for her."

"That is a tall order for anyone, my love," he replied. "We have been very fortunate. Few people of our standing marry for love, and in truth I think that often such unions fail when the romance fades, as it must. In general I think it better to marry someone with whom you have common interests for practical reasons, and then learn to love each other in time. It's a far more solid basis for a marriage."

"That's true. But however it happens, I dearly wish that for her. We must look for a husband worthy of her, and not only in title or wealth."

"We will, when the time comes. But first let us teach her how to conduct herself with others of her class. But now it is late, and we should sleep."

He reached across and put his empty glass on the table at the side of the bed, and was about to snuff out the candle when Amelia spoke again.

"Oh! I almost forgot! When I was talking to Harriet today, she told me that the king wrote to her some time ago telling her to stop using 'Your Majesty' all the time when writing to him, as friends such as they were had no need to stand on such ceremony with each other in private, although he trusted that when they met in public she would conduct herself with appropriate formality."

Stephen stopped and turned back to her, his eyes wide.

"What? My God, are you sure? This is not one of Harriet's presumptions, because she has no regard for status?"

"No. I thought as you, and when I questioned her she ran to her room and found his letter – she keeps them all in a box, in the order he sent them. And she showed it to me."

"Do you have it with you?"

"No, I gave it back to her. They are her greatest treasures, and rightly so. But I memorised the sentence, which read, 'I beg of you, do not treat me with so much ceremony in addressing me with so many Majesties, for we are friends, and friends require no such formality in private correspondence, although you must remember to do so in public'."

"But this is wonderful! To hell with the Renton woman and that stupid hat. Why didn't you tell me this immediately?" Stephen cried.

"I'm sorry, you're right. I should have. I can't believe it slipped

THE ECCENTRIC'S TALE: HARRIET

my mind. It's a fontange, by the way, not a hat."

"To hell with the fontange, then. He must think very highly of Harriet to tell her to dispense with formality," he mused.

"We know that already. He would not write to her regularly if he did not find her letters interesting, after all."

"No. But to tell her to dispense with all formality indicates that he thinks very highly of her indeed. And it also indicates that he intends to bring her to Court, and trusts her to behave appropriately in public, and not to forget herself."

"Which we do not," Amelia said.

Stephen lay back in bed and looked at the bedhangings for a minute, thinking.

"I don't think it's that we don't trust her, it's that she doesn't *know* how to behave in some situations, and so she behaves with others as she'd want them to behave with her. I'm sure if she was wearing some ridiculous ha…fontange that made her look a fool, she would appreciate someone telling her outright rather than beating about the bush. But if she understands why the king needs to be treated with formality in public, then she can be trusted to behave appropriately. And clearly he believes that she appreciates that. Why did she suddenly tell you this?" he asked.

"Once she knew I truly wasn't angry with the way she'd spoken to Lady Renton, she said that she would love to have told her that Charles had ordered her to stop calling him Your Majesty all the time, because it would probably have given her an apoplexy. But that she couldn't say that, because it was a secret between them. She only told me because she believed he would not mind that, as I am her mother and she is still a child. So yes, she can be trusted in that way."

Stephen still lay looking at the bedhangings, a beatific smile on his face.

"This is wonderful," he breathed. "I really believe now that we need not worry. We just need to wait until Harriet is a little older, teach her how to word her comments appropriately by explaining the reasons to her, and the king will invite us to Whitehall in due course. I have hoped for that, but now it is, I believe, a certainty."

Amelia turned her head and kissed his shoulder.

"We must just be patient," she said.

"Yes. But we are accomplished at that, you and I, even if our daughter is not," he replied.

At that she laughed, and licking his index finger and thumb he reached across and snuffed out the candle without disturbing their embrace, which really was delightful.

Life really was delightful.

CHAPTER THREE

December 1684

For the last few days the house had been in uproar. Every inch of the enormous building had been painstakingly cleaned and aired, huge fires had burned in every room for four days to thoroughly warm them, a tennis court had been constructed in one of the smaller chambers on the ground floor, tapestries had been unrolled, cleaned and hung, and an enormous amount of food and extra candles ordered in. The duke, duchess and their three daughters all had brand new luxurious costumes, which had cost a fortune, even more so as they'd had to be made in a great hurry.

And now Stephen stood at his bedchamber window, dressed in his new knee-length royal blue justaucorps coat, the heavy lace of his cravat tied with a matching blue bow, his wife next to him in an equally rich heavy silk manteaux gown in emerald green, with a lavishly embroidered stomacher, her wrists and throat encircled by emeralds. Indeed the colour of the dress had been chosen to match the finest jewels Amelia still possessed, the rubies and sapphires having been sold to relieve debt some time ago.

"I don't know why we went to all this effort, when he's hardly noticed us in the two days he's been here," Stephen said somewhat huffily. "Instead of spending a fortune on our own clothes, we could have just bought a new gown for Harriet, and met him in our dressing-gowns."

"Oh, he's noticed us, you can be sure of that," Amelia replied, gazing down at the couple sitting on the opposite side of the lake. "And, in fairness, when he sent the messenger to announce his visit, he did stress that he did not want us to arrange any entertainments, or go to any trouble."

"He did. But he would know full well that *everyone* who is called upon to entertain a member of the royal family is not going to just throw another log on the fire and wait until he turns up!"

"No, but I'm glad you didn't arrange a great ball or concert for him. It seems he really meant it when he said he wanted a peaceful visit. At least we didn't have *that* expense. And if all goes as well as it appears to be doing, we'll be able to wear our new costumes at Court," Amelia consoled him.

"It does *seem* to be going well, doesn't it?" Stephen commented, watching his daughter speaking with animation to her 'best friend' the king, who was laughing at whatever she was saying. She raised her hands as high as she could and circled her head.

"Yes. She's telling him about Lady Elman's fontange," Amelia said. "I can tell by her hand gestures."

Harriet was indeed telling King Charles about the fontange, and that afterwards her mother had told her that if someone asked your opinion on something and you liked it, it was perfectly acceptable to speak your opinion directly, whereas if you didn't like it, you then had to say so in a very careful way, so as not to offend the person.

"So since then I've spent a lot of time learning how to use an awful lot of silly words to tell someone their hat is horrible without *really* telling them," she said, "when it would be so much simpler to just say that, and then spend the rest of the time talking about something more interesting. But Mama said it's extremely important that I do as she says in this, otherwise I will never have any friends."

"Well, then," said the king, "let's see how much you have learned. Tell me, what do you think of my coat?"

Harriet looked at it for a moment.

"Oh, that's easy," she replied. "It's beautiful. The gold embroidery sparkles in the sun, which is lovely, and the deep red suits your dark complexion and hair."

"Hmm. Am I wearing anything you don't like, then?"

"Your shoes," she replied instantly, "but I'm only telling you because you asked me to. I wouldn't otherwise, not any more. I wouldn't mention them at all, and then if you asked me directly what I thought of them, I would say a great many evasive things."

"You told me also because we are friends. And good friends can be honest with each other. In fact for my part, I treasure genuine and honest friends above most other things," the king replied. Harriet smiled at him, relieved.

"Tell me then – forget we are friends for the moment - what do you think of my shoes, Lady Harriet? They are quite new, you know!" he simpered, making her laugh. This time she took longer to reply.

"They are exquisitely made, Your Majesty," she said finally, "and the leather looks as soft as butter. I'm sure they are very comfortable to wear, and the red of the heels matches that of your coat perfectly. I do think that a lower heel might suit you better though. You are naturally so magnificently tall, that with the added height they give you you could appear somewhat overpowering, which you may not wish to do."

"Oh well done!" the king said, applauding. "Your mother has taught you well. So, is it really just the heels you don't like? You can be honest now."

"I don't like the heels, no. I don't really like the buckles either. I'm sure they're real diamonds, because you *are* the king after all, but they look a little showy to me. I prefer plainer things. But Mama said that if I don't like anything about the item I've been asked to comment on, I should just comment on *one* thing I don't like, and only elaborate if they ask me to. And before I mention the bad thing, I must always say something good about it, even if I have to invent it."

"That's excellent advice, Harriet. Because you must always remember, if someone asks your opinion about something, it's usually because they have chosen it themselves, and therefore like it, and hope you will too. So if you don't like it, you must take that into consideration so as not to hurt them. If you're too brutal they see it as an attack on them."

"Yes, Mama explained that. But it's really very silly. If people don't want to know what I think, they really shouldn't ask me. And if you tell me you hate my shoes, you're hardly attacking *me,* are you? If anything you're being kind, giving me your honest opinion so that I won't look like a fool. It's just so difficult to have to think about the implications of everything I say all the time. It's tiring. And usually the social visits are tiring anyway, because I have to sit still for a long time and listen to a lot of talk about things I'm not interested in, like who's cuckolding who, and how many ribbons you should be wearing this season. But I have to do it, so that I can make friends and be accepted by society."

"You do," Charles agreed.

"But the society I've met so far I don't like at all. I don't really want friends that are boring. I'd rather just do what I like, and be on my own."

"And what do you like?"

"I like gardening. It's wonderful planting seeds and then watching them grow. I like riding, and walking, and having watched you and Papa play tennis this morning, I'd like to try that, too. And archery. I'm very good at that. I wanted to learn swordplay when I was younger, but Papa said ladies can't do that. It must be wonderful for you, being the king, because you can do whatever you like."

"Good Lord, whatever gave you that idea?" the king said.

"Well, there isn't anyone higher than you in the land, so no one can tell you what to do, can they?"

"God is higher than me. I must answer to Him one day."

"Yes, but *everyone* must answer to Him. But He won't tell you not to go riding, or not to walk in the mud."

"No. But the higher your position, the more responsibility you have. It's not those higher than myself I have to consider, but those lower than I am. As the king, I'm responsible for the wellbeing of all my subjects, and that's a very heavy responsibility indeed. If I just went riding or walking in the mud all day, then the country would be in a bad way, or if I declared war on another country just because I like swordplay, then thousands of men might die, and that would be my doing."

"I hadn't thought of it like that," Harriet said. "I just thought you had the very best of everything and lived in a great palace, and could spend your days doing whatever you wanted."

"I do have the best and live in a palace, but I spend hours dealing with business, talking to people I don't always like, and having to think about what I say to them and how I must say it, to get the result I want. It's the same for you. One day you will marry and have a household to manage, as your mother and father

THE ECCENTRIC'S TALE: HARRIET

do now, and you will have to take care of all your servants, and do the best you can for them, as I do for my subjects. So you have to spend time dealing with estate business, whether you like to or not, because it's your duty to do so. And if you don't, not only you, but all those who depend on you, servants and tenants, will suffer."

"But you don't have to listen to stupid conversation to try to make friends with people you don't even like. You must have lots of friends anyway, because *everyone* wants to be friends with the king, don't they?"

"You are thirteen now?" he asked.

"Nearly," she replied. "I will be, in February. Why do you ask?"

"Harriet," he said, turning suddenly towards her, and taking her small hand in his large one, "you are almost a woman now. I have written to tell you that when you are a woman, I will consider asking you and your parents to come to Court, and that is one of the reasons I am here now. I wanted to see you, see how you have matured. But if you come to Court, you must not assume that everyone is my friend. Nor must you assume that people who speak kindly to you are *your* friends either."

"Why would you have people at Court who are not your friends?" she asked.

"I am the king, and you are a duke's daughter, and as you have no brothers, an heiress. And this we have in common; people will take great pains to become our friends, not because they care for us, not at all – they might even hate us – but because they want what they think we can give them. In my case, that is position, power and wealth. In your case it will be perhaps your hand in marriage, not because they love or even like you, but for the lands or title they hope to gain. For others it will be for the prestige of knowing a duke's daughter, for apart from royalty, dukes are the highest aristocrats in the country. It's vital that you do not take people at their face value, for if you do, you will be destroyed."

"Is that how it is for you?" she asked, staring at him with shock.

"Yes, that's how it is for me, and always has been. Even my enemies will play my friends, in the hope of discovering my weaknesses so they can pull me down. I have to play their game, and play it better than them to make sure I win. Many people hate me merely because I *am* the king, and they will feel the same for you, because you are an aristocrat, and in my favour."

Impulsively she leaned forward and embraced him.

"That is so sad," she mumbled into his coat. Touched by her concern he wrapped his arm round her and drew her to him, then stroked her hair. "I'm not your friend because you're the king, you know," she said, lifting her head to look up into his face. "You must never think that. I'm your friend because you're wonderful and I love you. I don't care a fig about you being the king."

He laughed then and leaned down, kissing the top of her head.

"I know it, child, and it means the world to me," he said.

In the bedroom Stephen started.

"My God," he said, suddenly alarmed. "You don't think…"

"No, I don't," Amelia replied in spite of the fact that he had let his sentence trail off rather than finishing it. "I know he has a reputation for debauchery, and a good number of mistresses, but he is not a man to ruin a child, I'm sure of that. It's an affectionate embrace, not a seductive one."

"Are you sure?" Stephen said.

"Yes. Watch. In any case, he is a man who has been on public display his whole life. He knows that he is being observed by everyone in the house. Do you really think he'd try to seduce our twelve-year-old daughter in front of fifty witnesses?"

She had a point. And even as she finished her sentence, the couple they were watching broke the embrace, but continued to hold hands, the king speaking to his small companion earnestly.

"I wonder what he's saying to her?" Stephen remarked.

"We can ask Harriet later. If it's not a confidence she'll tell us, you know that."

The king had completely enveloped her hand in his, which was lovely, because his hand was very warm and hers was cold, and also because she felt protected by him, and it was much nicer to talk to him face-to-face than write to him and then wait weeks for his reply.

"I have a lot of people around me who claim to be my friends, as you will have, but it takes me time to discover who is genuine and who is not," the king was saying earnestly to her. "Once I am

THE ECCENTRIC'S TALE: HARRIET

sure of someone, then I will give them my friendship. Until then I am friendly, but wary of what I tell them, wary of how much I reveal. I'm telling you this because you will have to be the same, and up to now you have been sheltered, but that is about to end and you must be careful of who you confide in. Friends are true diamonds, but they're extremely rare and you have to sort through a lot of paste to find one."

"You are my friend," Harriet said. "And Jem, he is too, although I don't see him as much as I did."

"Jem is the gardener's boy?" Charles asked, showing that he took note of what she wrote to him.

"Yes. I think that's all the friends I have, except for my family and Jemima. Well, not Percy, because we hate each other, but Mama and Papa, and my sisters."

"Family are very important, and we must always consider them," King Charles said. "They are a part of us, for they share our blood. My brother and I don't always agree, but he is loyal to me, as I am to him. I hope it will be so with you and your sisters."

"Sophia and I are very different, but I love her. Melanie is more interesting, and now she's seven we're starting to talk more together. But I can't like Percy, even if he is family. He's only an uncle, though. Do they count?"

"Not as much maybe as siblings or parents, but it would make me happy if you could reconcile with your uncle," Charles said, smiling.

If you want me to, then I'll try," Harriet said. "But it won't be easy. So once you know that someone is paste, do you throw them away?" she asked.

"No. This is the other important lesson you will have to learn when you come out into society," he said. "And it's one that is hard for an honest and straightforward person like yourself to learn. Often it is necessary to be friendly to people who you don't like at all, or who don't like you. In fact, if you want to do as you like, it's vital."

"Why? That doesn't make any sense to me," she said.

"Because you might need those people to help you achieve what you want. So, for instance, if I need more money to do something I want to do, I have to call Parliament to ask for it. Not everyone in Parliament is my true friend, but I need them to vote for what I want. Do you think they would vote for me if I'd been rude to them because they bored me or I knew they didn't really like me?"

"No, I suppose they wouldn't, if they didn't have to," Harriet said. "Can't you just tell them how to vote, though, because you're the king?"

"No, child, I can't. The days of absolute monarchy are gone. Now if I've been nice to them, even if they don't really like me, they will look at my request more favourably and may vote for me, hoping I'll show them favour when they want something. If I've been cruel to them they will vote against it, even if they think it's a good idea, just because they want to hit back at me for hurting them. You should keep your enemies as close to you as possible, and in your debt, if you can."

She sat for a moment, thinking about this, letting it sink in, sensing that it might be important to her life.

"I don't really want to have to be nice to people who don't like me, though," she said. "I don't know if I could be."

"No, I'm not telling you to be nice to avowed enemies. But as well as helping you to get what you want, being nice to people and avoiding hurtful speech is kind, and we should all be kind to each other. The world needs more kindness, God knows. You are a caring child, and should find it easier to do that," Charles said.

"Yes, that is easier. I could never be nice to Percy, because we're enemies. But I will try to reconcile with him, for your sake. And although I thought Lady Elman was silly and not someone I want to be friends with, I was sorry that I hurt her with my comments about her horrible fontange. So that makes good sense to me. Thank you," she said. "I'll try to do that."

"I'm very glad to hear it. I am your king and can command you in all things," he said, but his eyes were gentle, "although I think you're a child who does not take well to commands, so it is as your friend I ask you – take note of your parents, for they love you. Some parents are cruel or pay no attention to their children. You must do as they advise, for they have your interests at heart, not just their own. I ask you to promise me you will do that. I would have you keep your honesty, but you must remember when it's appropriate to speak that aloud and when not to. But with myself you should always speak as you think, and I ask you to promise me that too."

THE ECCENTRIC'S TALE: HARRIET

"I promise both of those," Harriet replied immediately. "They're easy promises to make."

"Good. And I promise to watch out for you when you come to Whitehall. Now I am growing cold, but I think another game of tennis will warm me. Let's go back to the house."

She stood with him, but was disappointed that their talk was over. He was going home this evening after an early dinner and she wouldn't have him to herself again. Keeping hold of her hand, he started to walk briskly back to the house.

"You have grown tall," he said. "Last time we walked I had to carry you, because you could not match my pace."

"I was only six then, though, and wasn't even as tall as your waist," she said. "Now I am level with your chest, although I'm small for my age, my Mama says."

"You have time to grow. And I am very tall," he said. "You will soon be as tall as the queen."

They reached the house, the door opening as they arrived, and Harriet curtseyed perfectly to him, ready to say farewell until dinner.

"Now, as your king, I command you to change into a gown that is not as heavy and cumbersome as that delightful formal costume you're wearing," he said with mock severity. "For you will never be able to learn tennis in such an outfit. I will meet you in the tennis room in half an hour."

The joyous smile on her face was well worth the fact that he knew he would have to play very gently and slowly with her. She would be even more excited when she found out that it was a game few women played, as when played at full speed it was extremely physical and tiring.

Once changed into lighter clothing, King Charles went back downstairs. The duke and duchess were in the hallway, and he greeted them warmly.

"Ah! Just the man I wish to see!" he cried. "Do you have a tennis racquet suitable for Harriet? Perhaps you still have the one you used as a boy?"

"For Harriet, Your Majesty?" Stephen replied, clearly stunned.

"Yes. She is a most active person, as of course you know, and I think a game of tennis will burn her energy, and render her less excitable for the dinner you've arranged later. I'm assuming she will be eating with us, as she's now almost a woman, and you have clearly worked hard at teaching her appropriate behaviour?"

"Indeed she will be, and her sister Sophia as well, as she is now ten, if it please you," Amelia replied.

"Excellent! I will be gentle in teaching her, I promise you. She is changing into appropriate clothing now. It will pass the time most agreeably, and perhaps we will get a chance to further her instruction at Whitehall? You could teach her a little more during the winter, and then when the roads are passable, in February, maybe March, I will summon you to Court, if you wish."

There was a profound silence as the couple absorbed that this was the moment they had been hoping for since the old duke had died, so many years ago. Then they both sank to their knees and kissed the king's proffered hand.

"We would be delighted to attend you at Court, Your Majesty," Stephen said, his face radiant. "You do us great honour."

"I do," the king replied. "I think it is time to forget the past, although I warn you my brother is not so ready to, so you must be patient with him and prove yourself loyal, to him and to me."

"That will not be difficult, for we are indeed both your loyal and devoted subjects," Stephen affirmed.

"I am very happy to hear that. You have a most exceptional daughter, and she will of course accompany you when you come. I have a great interest in her, and would see her happy. I think that when she reaches womanhood, we must between us ensure that she marries someone worthy not only of her birth, but of her personality. I would see her happy and fulfilled, as I'm sure you would."

"Indeed we would, Your Majesty," Amelia said.

"She is delightful and a credit to you. I would not see her free spirit subdued. I like fire in a woman, and would see her achieve her potential. Ah, and here she is! Come, child. Your father will fetch his racquet, which may be a little heavy for you, but which will do to teach you the basic rules. Then if you like the game I'm sure he will purchase suitable equipment for you, and maybe have some appropriate clothing made for you to play in." He bent his head to her parents, then turned to lead their daughter to the tennis room.

THE ECCENTRIC'S TALE: HARRIET

"Do you know," he said to her as they walked away, "my wife, when I first married her, would sometimes wear men's clothing, which was a trend at Court at the time, and which she very much enjoyed the freedom of doing, although I think it would perhaps not be wise for you to do that, as you will wish to make a favourable impression with my courtiers and not start with a scandal." At the door of the room, he looked back over his shoulder at the duke and duchess, who were watching their monarch and daughter, their faces radiant.

He winked at them, then bestowed an equally radiant smile on them, before disappearing into the room.

Stephen and Amelia stood frozen, unable to believe this wonderful change of fortune.

"The racquet," Amelia hinted after a moment. Stephen jumped as though shot and ran across the hall and up a few stairs, before running back down again and taking his wife in a brief but painful embrace.

"We have done it!" he said, and then letting her go, he ran upstairs to fetch his tennis racquet, leaving Amelia blushing and somewhat crushed in the hallway.

* * *

After dinner, which was a great success, and after which Stephen in his flush of joy gave the cook a pay rise, Harriet was allowed to stay downstairs to say farewell to the king, because it was after all due to her that the whole family was about to be accepted at Court.

"The tennis lesson was wonderful, Papa," Harriet said as the family waited in the hall for the king to descend from his apartments, "will you play with me, so I can improve?"

"Of course I will," Stephen said happily. "Tomorrow we will order a racquet and some suitable clothes for you. We will make an expert of you before you go to Court!"

"Before *we* go to Court," Harriet said. "The king told me he had invited you and that you were pleased, and we must look for a messenger from him. But he will write to me before that, he said."

"You have done very well, Harriet," her father said.

The king came down, farewells were said, and he went to his

coach and climbed in, before re-opening the coach door and calling to Harriet, who ran across. The coachman had already taken the steps away, but the king leaned down and lifted her easily into the coach, sitting her opposite him.

"I have thought of a way to help you remember how to behave at Court," he said, "and I would tell you now. Your parents have taught you much, and I will watch over you when I can, but I am a busy man, so I will give you this advice; imagine that at the palace there are many spiders' webs, and at the centre of each web is a courtier. When you are there you must acknowledge the spiders according to their rank, as your parents will show you, and you must be friendly and polite at all times to them. But you must always remember they are in the centre of a web even if you cannot see it. You must ensure that you avoid the webs, but with tact and diplomacy, for if you are caught, you will be eaten, like a fly. Can you remember that?"

"Yes," she said. "It's easy, because I can see it as a picture in my head. But it doesn't make the palace sound a very nice place."

"It's a very nice place," he said, laughing, "as long as you avoid the webs. And I think you will, because you are a clever child. Now go, and we will meet again soon."

He lifted her down from the carriage, and waved to her parents. They stood and watched until his coach had disappeared from sight, then they went in.

Once inside Harriet told them what he had said to her in the coach.

"I didn't want to tell you on the steps with servants all around, as I think the king lifted me into the coach so that no one else would hear what he said," she commented. "I don't think the courtiers would like to know he thinks of them as spiders."

"You're learning quickly," her father said, smiling. "No, he would not want everyone to know that. He trusts you, and it's a great honour for anyone to do that, but a king most of all."

"He is wonderful, isn't he?" Harriet cried. "I couldn't wish for a better friend."

Indeed she couldn't, her parents agreed as they chatted together in the library later.

"Please don't tell me you still think he might want to make her his mistress," Amelia commented after they'd discussed the new clothes they'd need to order, and what they'd need to sell to buy them.

"No, I don't. It was just that his embrace was so sudden. I wasn't expecting it. And his Court is renowned for its depravity, you know."

"Yes, all the more so if you're the son of a Commonwealth Puritanical soldier," Amelia teased.

"Well, yes. To Father, Charles was the Devil incarnate. I just wish he hadn't expressed his opinion quite so loudly. But putting that aside, it is a pleasure-loving place and a young lady's virtue is not safe there," Stephen pointed out.

"No, although the king is no longer a young man, and so his Court may be more sedate now. And we will be there to help her. And being truthful, I would be far more worried if Harriet were a beauty, but she is quite plain, which may put off the more frivolous rakes."

"True. But she is still a duke's daughter, an heiress and on extraordinarily good terms with the king. I think that may outweigh the lack of beauty. And she is not ugly!"

"I didn't say she was. She reminds me of the king in that way," Amelia said.

"What? She looks nothing like him! She is fair with grey eyes, and he is dark. And a man," Stephen added, earning himself a withering look from his wife.

"No, I mean that the king is by no means a handsome man, as Harriet is not a pretty girl. But he has some quality even so that draws people to him, and makes him appear more handsome than he actually is."

"It's called kingship," Stephen said acidly.

"No, he would have it even if he were a pauper, although it's magnified by his status. Even though he can be ruthless, I think at heart he is a good, kind man who cares for others, and that makes his eyes sparkle, his smile genuine, and so his face attractive. And Harriet has the same thing. When she smiles at you her whole face lights up, because her smiles are honest. And when you speak she really listens to you, which is very attractive. The king is the same. It's very endearing. On first sight you might think both of them plain, but when you get to know them, their personalities make them beautiful."

"Unless you're on the wrong side of their cutting tongue, or try to thwart their desires," Stephen said.

"True. Charles has learned to blunt his cutting tongue when appropriate. Now we must spend the next months blunting hers and refining it," Amelia replied.

"We must, but not *too* much," Stephen said. "I have been wondering why the king, who you say hates writing so much, has maintained a correspondence with Harriet for so long. I know some of it is because he's amused by her honesty and unconscious humour, and her complete lack of pretentiousness. It must be refreshing to have a friend who really wants nothing more from him than friendship. But I think it's more than that with him."

"What do you think it is, then?" Amelia asked.

"I think he has recognised that we are a close family, and by keeping us out in the cold for so long and then showing great favour to Harriet, he is hoping to acquire the loyalty and support of a ducal family without having to spend anything to get it."

"That's very cunning, if you're right," Amelia said. "And he will have to spend *something* if we are to go to Court, or we will be bankrupt and no use to anyone."

"That's true. But he won't mind laying out some money on a certainty. And of course he's cunning, and very duplicitous. Those are the qualities his father lacked. It was that and his inflexibility which lost him the throne and his life. The current Charles will bend rather than break. And that along with his cunning are the qualities that have kept him on the throne for so long."

* * *

The next two months passed in a blur for Harriet. She had been ecstatic when told that from now on she would only spend the mornings in the schoolroom with her tutor, but she was soon disabused of the thought that she could spend the rest of the day doing as she wished.

Instead she spent it learning how to converse properly, which topics were appropriate and which were not, how to address various members of the nobility on meeting them, and how to walk and sit perfectly. First of all she practised these arts only with her mother, but after a couple of weeks, time now being of the

THE ECCENTRIC'S TALE: HARRIET

essence, Harriet started to accompany her mother on her social visits, to the theatre, to some evening soirees and balls, and shopping.

Her two younger sisters Sophia and Melanie were green with envy, and when Harriet arrived home from her excursions, throwing herself down in a chair in the nursery, they would pester her endlessly with questions. If Sophia and Melanie wanted to hear about how magical and fairytale-like her excursions were, they were disappointed, mainly because Harriet found little about her new life exciting. The beautiful elaborate gowns she now had to wear were restrictive and uncomfortable rather than glamorous, the time spent beautifying herself she considered wasted, "because, you know," she explained to them, "no amount of powder and curling will ever make *me* beautiful," and most of the events she went to were tedious in the extreme.

"I'm sure that if I'd been to a ball at the Earl's house I'd have remembered more about it than the fact that the pins were pulling at my hair and the Count of Shrewsbury had bad breath and trampled my feet when he danced with me!" Melanie grumbled after having heard her sister's dull account of the dance she'd been to the previous evening.

"Well you asked me what it was like, and that's what it was like. After the dance I had to sit down because my feet hurt so much, and then Lady Elman sat next to me and spent hours talking to me about the latest fashions and how beautiful the flower arrangements were. I think I'd rather have had my feet trampled some more than endure that. But at least it was good practice in being kind to someone who was boring me to death," Harriet mused.

"So what did the flower arrangements look like?" Melanie asked.

"I didn't really look at them. I was too busy remembering to sit up straight and behave correctly. They were pink and purple, I remember that," Harriet replied.

"You're impossible, Harriet, you really are," Sophia said, disgruntled.

Later in bed she thought about it, and realised that she was being a bit unfair to her sisters. She knew how tedious nursery life was – hadn't she lived it herself for years? She owed it to them to think of some nicer things to say about her excursions. And looking for the pleasant aspects would maybe help her to feel happier about them.

So the next time she went with her mother to afternoon visiting, she made an effort to forget how much her back hurt from having to sit still and erect on an uncomfortable chair, and instead paid attention to the dresses the ladies were wearing, the way the room was decorated, the taste of the exquisite little cakes, and some of the less boring conversation. When she got home she recounted all those things to her sisters, and, watching the joy on their faces as they imagined the beautiful surroundings she'd spent her afternoon in, Harriet realised that the visits weren't *that* bad after all, and it was lovely to make her sisters happy. It was kind, as the king had told her she should ever be.

Even so, it was much easier to enthuse about her tennis lessons. Once her racquet arrived her father taught her how to play, and having overheard the king's comments about Queen Catherine wearing male clothing when she'd first come to England, he got one of the ladies' maids to cut down an old outfit of his for her to wear, after he'd made her promise *only* to wear it for tennis games and never, under any circumstances outside the house.

Wearing men's clothing was wonderful and Harriet was determined to broach the subject somehow with the queen, if they met. Maybe Queen Catherine could start a new fashion, and if she did then everyone would copy it, and she would be able to wear these fabulous clothes that allowed her to move so much more freely than gowns did.

She was a natural at tennis, loving the speed and ferocity of it, and came on in leaps and bounds. The king would be in for a surprise if he chose to have a game with her at Whitehall, Stephen thought happily.

She was less of a natural at playing cards, however, as she really seemed to have no ability to either remember the rules or to keep a neutral expression on her face if her hand was good or bad. In the end Amelia told her that when they went to Court, or indeed to anyone's house where cards were played, she would do better to either offer to play the harpsichord instead (but not sing, because she could not carry a tune) whilst the people played, or to stand behind her mother to learn by watching, although if she did she should keep her fan over the lower half of her face so her facial expression would not be seen.

"And when we are at Court, never, under any circumstances, even if you master the games, play Unlimited Loo," Amelia said.

"Why not?"

"Because that is how fortunes are lost, and God knows we can't afford to lose *anything* right now!" Amelia said. "In fact, don't play any games where money is involved. There are courtiers who will try to take advantage of your inexperience, and if you lose we would have to pay or lose respect. No account would be taken of your youth."

"Yes, the king told me that. I haven't forgotten the spiders in the web," Harriet said.

* * *

In January the materials for costumes were ordered, and Harriet found herself having to stand still for fittings, which could take hours. By now she was getting used to disciplining herself and looking interested or happy, even when she was intensely bored. Amelia was now relaxing more with her too, knowing that while Harriet was naturally honest, she was also naturally trustworthy, and would never repeat anything that had been told to her in confidence. So, on the return journey from various excursions, mother and daughter would exchange sometimes vicious and cutting opinions on the personalities of the people they had just spent several hours smiling at and talking pleasantly to. It relieved a lot of tension, and Amelia found herself enjoying these times with her daughter much more than she'd expected to, and much more than she did when visiting alone.

The boredom of standing for fittings was relieved by the utter joy of Sophia and Melanie, who had been permitted to watch, if they didn't get underfoot. Sophia, who loved sewing, was particularly attentive, asking the seamstress all sorts of pertinent questions about how the garments were measured, cut and sewn.

The king had written to her in January, saying that he had not forgotten his promise and was sure that she and her parents would enjoy their visit to Whitehall, and that he would send for them soon. Maybe it would not be so bad going to Court after all,

Harriet thought as February dawned and excitement in the household built. After all the king, her best friend, would be there, and so would her parents, who she had grown even closer to during the recent hectic preparations for their return to favour. She would meet lots of new people, and surely *some* of them would become her friends.

She was still nervous, knowing how important this Court visit would be for her parents. Their whole future depended on it. Aware that she was the person who, if innocently, had delayed them being received at Court, she felt the burden of responsibility for making it right. But she knew that, with care, she could do it. She already had the king's favour, which was a good start.

And she would no doubt have an enormous fund of stories to entertain her sisters with on her return. She had grown closer to them, too, in the last months.

* * *

Mid-February 1685

The duke and duchess were enjoying breakfast alone, Harriet, who now often joined them, having decided to breakfast in the nursery with her sisters so she could tell them the details of last night's concert that she'd attended.

"She's really doing extraordinarily well," Amelia said as she sipped her chocolate. "I am making sure to compliment her regularly, because I know how much effort it takes for her to sit still for hours."

"As much effort as it would take Sophia to get covered in mud from head to toe in five minutes, I expect," Stephen replied. "Harriet managed that very well, though, last week."

Amelia laughed. Sophia was an extremely clean child, always had been, while Harriet seemed to attract dirt like a magnet.

"She didn't *intend* to fall in the pond," she said, remembering the previous week when Harriet, having been rewarded after a particularly tedious visit by being told to go outside and have a brisk walk in the gardens, had instead showed Melanie what great fun it was to roll down the grass slope to the edge of the lake. Except that she hadn't stopped at the edge of the lake, instead rolling straight into the muddy shallows in spite of frantic efforts

THE ECCENTRIC'S TALE: HARRIET

to stop herself. The two children had returned to the house, both of them giggling nervously, both of them drenched and covered, as Stephen had just remarked, in mud, Harriet from falling in and Melanie from helping to drag her out. "I was worried they'd catch pneumonia," Amelia added.

"Melanie maybe, but Harriet? She's strong as an ox, that one. She really *should* have been a boy," Stephen said.

"It would have made our lives easier if she had been," Amelia said sadly.

He looked across at her.

"Don't feel bad about not giving me a boy," he said. "You've given me three beautiful healthy children, and above all that, you've given me yourself. That alone has made me happier than I deserve to be. And we still have time to try for more children in any case!"

She smiled warmly across the table at him.

"Even so, we will need to think about the title, if we do have no sons. Harriet cannot inherit the dukedom, even if—"

She was interrupted by a polite knock on the breakfast room door, followed by the appearance of Mr Noakes with the morning mail on a tray. As he approached the table, Stephen glanced up from the paper he was perusing, and then his expression changed to one of such alarm that Amelia turned to see what was wrong. The steward was as white as a sheet, and tears stood in his eyes.

"My God, man, what's wrong?" Stephen asked. "Has something happened to Andrew?" Andrew was the footman who normally collected the mail and brought it to the breakfast room.

"No, Your Grace," Mr Noakes said falteringly. "He brought the mail as usual. But there was a proclamation too, and when I saw it, I thought…" he stopped for a moment to pull himself together, "I thought I'd bring it myself."

Stephen looked at the folded sheet of paper on the tray, puzzled.

"Well then, give it to me," he said.

Noakes handed it over, his face a mask of distress. Stephen unfolded and read it, while Amelia looked on anxiously, her chocolate forgotten. She saw his eyes close, his face blanch as white as the steward's.

"Dear God, no," Stephen said softly.

JULIA BRANNAN

"What is it?" she asked, alarmed. He lifted his eyes from the paper, looking ten years older than he had a moment ago.

"There is no gentle way to tell you this," he said. "The king is dead."

For one long moment she could not take it in, and the words, though spoken clearly, seemed foreign to her, incomprehensible. And then reality broke through, and her first thought was not for the king, nor for their shattered hopes, but for Harriet.

"Do the other servants know?" she asked Noakes, who was still standing there, distraught. As one of the senior servants, the one who took care of the finances, he knew better than anyone how desperately the duke needed to return to royal favour, how much money they had borrowed recently to prepare for their return to Court, and what this news would mean to them, practically speaking at least.

"I don't think so, Your Grace," he said. "I asked Andrew if he'd read the proclamation, but he said he's a slow reader and hadn't had the time, as it was raining and he wanted to get back before he got too wet. But news like this will spread very quickly anyway, which is why I wanted you to hear it in private, so you have time to compose yourselves. I know what a blow this must be, and I am so very sorry," he finished.

"That was very considerate of you," Amelia said, somewhat shakily. "Thank you. Could you please go up to the nursery and ask Lady Harriet to come down immediately? Don't tell her why, even if she asks. And then after she is here, please arrange for all the staff, indoor and out, to assemble in the hall in an hour, so that we can tell them all together."

Noakes bowed and left the room immediately.

"James is the king now. We are finished," Stephen said as soon as they were alone again. He took out his handkerchief, blew his nose and wiped the tears from his cheeks.

Later Amelia would register that her husband had not cried like this even when his father died. As soft-hearted as he was, he was a man, and men did not openly cry, particularly ones whose fathers had beaten them every time they'd shown the slightest human emotion. The last time she'd seen him cry was when little Stephen had died, which had told her how desperately he wanted a son, although he was too kind to admit that to her, knowing it would hurt her. The

THE ECCENTRIC'S TALE: HARRIET

king's death would have terrible consequences for them.

But right now she could not think about the death of their dreams, or their financial plight, because firstly she had to think of how to tell her eldest daughter that her best, really the only true friend she had outside her family, was dead.

There came another knock on the door, and the subject of Amelia's frantic thoughts entered the room, her expression wary and concerned.

"You sent for me?" she asked hesitantly, clearly wondering what she'd done wrong.

"You have not done anything wrong," Amelia said immediately, her heart clenching as she saw the momentary relief on her daughter's face, knowing she was about to receive the worst blow of her young life.

"Come and sit down, sweeting," Stephen said gently, attempting and failing to smile at her.

"What's happened?" she asked, moving to the table but remaining standing, her hands on the back of a chair.

"We have some very bad news that we have to tell you," Amelia said. "You must be very brave now. Sit down."

She pulled out the chair and sat down, her face puzzled.

"Is it Jem?" she asked. "Has something happened to him?"

Amelia had forgotten how much Harriet thought of the gardener's son, even though she'd hardly seen him in the last two years, having kept her promise to stop spending time with him. Clearly the amount of time she spent with a person did not change how she felt for them. This was going to be horrible.

To her surprise, instead of telling Harriet himself, Stephen passed the proclamation across for her to read.

"Whereas it hath pleased Almighty God to call to his mercy our late sovereign lord King Charles the Second, of blessed memory, by whose decease the imperial crowns of England, Scotland, France and Ireland, are solely and rightfully come to the high and mighty Prince James…" she read out loud. Then she stopped and looked up, her brow creased. "What does it mean?" she asked, although she was certainly intelligent enough to understand the words.

Amelia reached across the table and captured her daughter's hand, which was trembling slightly. She did know at some level, then.

"The king is dead, sweetheart," she said.

Harriet looked at her mother uncomprehendingly.

"He can't be," she said. "He wrote to me just two weeks ago! He wasn't ill. He would have told me if he was. He's never ill."

Now was not the time to tell her that the king had in fact almost died some six years previously; presumably he had not told her. She had only been seven at the time. It was irrelevant anyway.

"People die all the time, Harriet. I am so, so sorry," Amelia said. Harriet's hand squeezed her mother's convulsively, and she closed her eyes tightly for a moment, then shook her head in denial.

"He can't be," she repeated softly. "I couldn't bear it if he was. He can't be."

She opened her eyes and looked at her mother, her mouth twisting in grief and shock. And then, for the first and last time in her life, she fainted, sliding gracefully off the chair onto the breakfast-room floor.

CHAPTER FOUR

Harriet stood at her bedroom window, as she often had over the last two weeks since she had learnt about the king's death, looking across the grounds to the lake, to the bench where they had sat together the last time she had seen him.

If she closed her eyes she could still feel the warm pressure of his large strong hand enfolding hers, and the gentle touch of his lips on her hair as he'd kissed her when she embraced him. She would never feel that again, would never hear his voice, see his smile, receive a letter from him. It was all gone, forever.

It was unbearable even to think that, let alone live it, but she had to bear it, she knew that. Everyone lost people they loved, and they had to deal with it and carry on. Her mother and father had lost little Stephen, who they had loved. She hadn't really loved him, because in her mind he had not become a person yet, had not done anything to make her love and miss him, was just a bundle really. But her parents had grieved for him and had carried on, and she must do the same.

Her heart twisted painfully in her chest and she opened her eyes again, staring blindly out of the window, her tears blurring the rain-drenched landscape outside. How could someone so strong, so big, so full of life as the king was, just die? How could that happen?

Even as she asked herself the question for the thousandth time, she knew it was a silly one. She was old enough now to know that it was not just the old and frail or the very young and vulnerable who died suddenly; it could happen to anyone, no matter how strong and vital, and did. The king had not died suddenly, she now knew. He had had an apoplexy, and had lived for several days, the doctors doing everything they could to save him, but failing.

That did not make it any more bearable for her, though. She hated to think of him suffering for days, but was sure he'd done it bravely. And now his brother, James, was King James II. The papist arse-cloth of Louis.

Oh God.

She turned away from the window, went to the bed and sat down. She had spent the best part of the last two weeks either walking ferociously around the gardens or in the bedroom she had recently been moved to from the nursery, because at thirteen she was almost a woman. Her parents had allowed her the time to grieve in her own way, one of them visiting her each day just to make sure that she was eating properly and to see if she wanted to talk, or be consoled.

It was very kind of them to give her that time, because it was exactly what she needed, and they knew that because they loved her, as she loved them. And because of that she had to start to think of them now, of their grief, and of what she could do to console them.

They would not be grieving in the same way that she was, because Charles had not been their personal friend. But the promise of his favour had been their future, and they must be terribly upset that that had now gone. Charles had told her to be kind, and her parents needed her to pull herself together, because it was not fair that they should worry about the future *and* about her, as she knew they were. She could at least take one worry away from them.

She dried her eyes, blew her nose, and then went to her dressing table to tidy her hair and make herself look as recovered as possible so she could go down and tell them, convincingly, that she was going to be fine.

Once she was presentable she went downstairs to the library, where she knew her father at least was likely to be at this time of day, unless he had an estate matter to deal with. If not, her mother might well be there writing letters.

The door was slightly open, and she had just raised her hand to knock on it when her father spoke, and the distress in his voice froze her.

THE ECCENTRIC'S TALE: HARRIET

"God, Amelia, I don't know what we're going to do," he was saying. "I've spent the last days examining every aspect of our finances. Unless we cut back to the bone on everything, including servants, which I don't want to do for their sakes as well as ours, we're not going to raise enough money to even keep up with our debt payments, let alone pay them off."

"How much did you spend on clothes and entertainments for Charles?" Amelia asked.

"A goodly sum, but we could survive that if it was all the debt we had. But you know my father raised a lot of money for Cromwell's parliament by taking out loans, thinking that in time he would recuperate that with a good Parliamentary income. He didn't of course, because Cromwell died not long afterward, and it was a miracle he wasn't attainted and the estate forfeited after the restoration. It was only King Charles' Act of Indemnity and Oblivion that stopped that happening. Until now I have managed to just about keep my head above water. But that cannot continue, not now we know that we have no chance of returning to Court in the foreseeable future. My debtors must know that my prospects are bleak too, and if they call in the loans rather than continuing to accept minimal payments, we are lost. So I have two choices; either I sell more land to pay some of the debts, which of course will reduce our future income from the tenants and resources, or I cut back dramatically on our standard of living, and try to keep our lands until something happens."

"What sort of something?" Amelia asked.

"I don't know. Maybe James will forgive me, or die. If he dies his daughter Mary will inherit, and she is a Protestant, so maybe we will be able to get back into favour. Or if one of our daughters marries very well, maybe."

"They won't do that without dowries though," Amelia pointed out. "Which it seems we don't have."

"They might. Or at least Harriet might," Stephen said.

Harriet, who was starting to feel guilty about eavesdropping, had been about to announce her presence, but on mention of her name, waited.

"How?" Amelia asked.

"At the moment we have no male heirs, so if Harriet marries and has a son, then that son would inherit the dukedom," Stephen said.

"What? That can't be right. I thought that your brother John would inherit first, and then Percy if John died before you without a son?"

"Yes, normally that would be the case, but it's different with us, because my great-grandfather had no sons or brothers, and so he took out letters patent with a special remainder to keep the dukedom in his bloodline. It stated that if no sons were born to him, then his eldest living daughter and her male heir would inherit instead."

"Why haven't you told me this before?" Amelia asked.

"Because I didn't know. Father never told me, if he even knew himself. He had three sons, so it didn't matter. But the special remainder still applies. I found it while I was going through all the ancient documents, trying to find anything that could stop me having to sell land or drastically reduce our standard of living."

"So Harriet will inherit everything when you die?"

"Yes. She will be the Duchess of Darlington. And if she has a son, he will be the next duke."

Harriet stepped away from the door and very quietly went back upstairs. She knew that she could not have walked in at that point without revealing by her facial expression that she'd overheard her parents talking, and they would not think well of her eavesdropping.

Back in her bedroom, she sat on the bed and thought.

From what she had just overheard, the future of not just the title, but the whole family depended on her making a great marriage. Sophia and Melanie would not be able to do that without monetary dowries, but she did not need money to marry well, because, effectively, she had the dowry of a dukedom, which was the highest title in the land apart from royalty. If she gave her husband a son, he would one day become the duke, a glittering prize for any suitor wishing to rise in nobility. Well worth marrying a plain woman with no dowry for.

She laughed quietly and mirthlessly to herself, thinking that of the three daughters, she was the one who had the least interest in marriage or titles, and could not even *imagine* having to give birth to a squalling brat. But she had to do it, for two reasons; because her family were the most important thing in her life – Charles had

THE ECCENTRIC'S TALE: HARRIET

been right about that - and she held their future in her hands; and because it was her fault they were in this position in the first place.

She did not go back downstairs that evening, needing time to come to terms with the new responsibility she was about to take on. Last time she had seen the king, he had told her that she was almost a woman.

Now she was thirteen, and if that did not quite make her a woman physically, certainly listening to her parents' conversation had made her a woman mentally. It was time to put away childish things, to accept that as much as she desired freedom, she could not have it, not without paying a price that would be far too high – the misery and destitution of her parents and sisters, and of herself too. And in honesty, even if she remained unmarried she would not be free – she would be beholden to her male relatives, as she had no income of her own. Not so bad while Papa was solvent, but she would not want to be dependent on Uncle John, and she would starve before she asked Percy for anything. She closed her eyes and sighed, and when she opened them again she had decided on her future, and would put her mind completely to attaining it.

She took some comfort in knowing that if the king was looking down on her now, he would be pleased with the decision she had just made.

She smiled, and then undressed herself, which took some time, but she didn't call her maid because she wanted to be alone. And then she knelt by her bed and prayed for the soul of King Charles, that he would be received into Heaven, and for the strength to go through with the decision she had just made.

Tomorrow she would go downstairs to breakfast and announce that she wanted to start learning the rest of the duties she would need to know to be a good wife when she was a little older. She would tell them that the king had wanted her to look to her future, and that she intended to do just that. They would accept that then, she hoped, would put it down to her grief and reverence for her friend, and would not question her sudden determination to pursue a marital future that she had, until now, made utterly clear she had no interest in.

* * *

April 1688

Harriet stood loosely, breathing deeply until she felt her heart slow and her mind clear. Then she nocked the arrow, gripped the string, and lifted the bow. She drew the string back to her anchor point at the back of her jawbone, and then looked down the lawn to her target. Fifty yards away was a circular archery butt. However she was not focussing on that, but on a two-inch-wide wand stuck into the ground a few yards in front of the butt, which was what she was aiming to hit.

She knew that her archery master was watching her, and eleven-year-old Melanie too, who had also now started learning the sport. And more importantly, from the edge of her vision she'd seen Percy approaching, striding across the lawn from the house as she started to draw the string.

She let everything go; her rivalry with her uncle over archery, over everything, his voice as he called hello, not to be friendly but to distract her, and the rising of her intention from a hope to a necessity that she hit this wand, which he had not yet hit in three weeks of trying.

Everything vanished from her sight and her mind except the tiny stick of wood in the ground, and then she relaxed the fingers of her right hand, letting the string slip past them and watched as her arrow flew, straight and true, splitting the wand of wood about four feet from the ground. She felt the ecstasy of triumph rise in her, and then she lowered the bow, picked up another arrow and nocked it.

"Oh, well done, my lady," her archery master said, his voice laced with joy and pride, for it was a testament to his teaching as well as her natural ability that she had achieved such a feat.

Percy was standing to the right of her, just out of sight, but she could feel the waves of malevolence and envy radiating from him. She lifted the bow, intending to shoot again immediately, this time aiming lower down the wand, knowing that if she hit it again he could not claim it was a fluke, as he surely would otherwise. She knew she shouldn't try to make him jealous, but in spite of reining in her tongue as much as she could, her relationship with her uncle had not warmed noticeably in the last years. She couldn't remember what had caused them to become sworn enemies,

THE ECCENTRIC'S TALE: HARRIET

didn't know if there had ever been any event or whether it was an instinctive thing, but it no longer mattered. The truth was, they just hated each other and always had.

"So, your father has finally found someone stupid or blind enough to marry you, it seems," Percy's pompous voice came from behind her. She ignored him, knowing he was just trying to distract her. She knew her parents were looking for a suitable marriage partner now she was sixteen, but they would not tell him before her if they had found a possible suitor. She pulled the string back, and focussed on the wand.

"At least the fool will get a virgin, I suppose, which is something," he continued. "No one would be stupid enough to try to fuck something as ugly as you for fun. Although it's probably just as well Charles died before you got to Court, because he couldn't wait to get up your skirts, could he? God knows why. He'd fuck anything though, everyone knew that."

Harriet swivelled smoothly on the balls of her feet, so that the arrow now pointed directly at her uncle's chest.

"My lady—" began the archery master, no doubt intending to tell her she should never turn from the target with a nocked arrow in case it was accidentally loosed.

"Stay still," she commanded Percy as he instinctively made to move. "And apologise. Now."

"What for? For telling the truth? Everyone who looks at you can see you're ugly," he said, smiling, clearly glad that he'd hurt her.

"Apologise for your insult to the king," she said.

"I didn't insult the king. Charles isn't the king any more. He's just a rotting corpse," Percy persisted.

"Either you apologise, or I'll shoot you," she said icily, her hand steady as a rock. "Your choice."

Now, for the first time, his face registered alarm. Good. He knew she was serious.

"You can't shoot me," he said, his voice shaking slightly. "You'd hang!"

"Right now I think it would be worth it," she said. "But I doubt King James would let me hang when he found out I'd been defending his brother's honour. Now apologise before my arm grows tired and I shoot you accidentally."

He licked his lips, which had turned as white as the rest of his face.

"I'm not apologising," he said. "You wouldn't dare—"

"Oh yes she would," Melanie interrupted. "She hates you. In truth I don't like you either. Apologise, you idiot. You know you're in the wrong, and it's not worth dying for."

Behind Percy Harriet saw her father emerge from the house and start running across the lawn towards them at full speed. She returned her focus to her uncle and smiled.

"You're just about to make me so very, very happy," she said, and drew the string a fraction of an inch further back preparatory to releasing the arrow.

"I'm sorry!" Percy shouted suddenly, then registered the momentary disappointment on her face and realised that she really had not been calling his bluff, but had intended to shoot him, and in another second would have done.

He stared at her wide-eyed for a few seconds, then, to his everlasting shame, his eyes rolled back in his head and he crumpled to the ground.

Harriet turned the bow back toward the target, aimed and released the arrow, watching as it sailed past the wand into the butt behind it.

"Damn it," she said softly, then turning, stepped round Percy and set off across the lawn to meet her father, who had slowed now he had seen that she had not in fact murdered his brother.

"What the hell was that all about?" he said angrily as she reached him.

"Percy said you've found me a suitor," she replied calmly. "Is it true?"

"You threatened to kill him because he told you that?" Stephen said, deeply shocked.

"No. I wouldn't do that, although if it's true I'd rather you'd told me before him. He insulted me, but I wouldn't have threatened him for that either. He insults me all the time, after all. But he told me that the king wanted to fuck me when I got to Court, because he'd fuck anything, and no one insults King Charles to me."

Stephen's face reddened.

"He actually said those words?"

THE ECCENTRIC'S TALE: HARRIET

"Not exactly those words, no. And he said more than that. But if you mean the word 'fuck', yes. Ask Melanie, and Nat. They both heard him. And please don't reprimand Nat, Papa. He tried to make me stop, and I ignored him. He's taught me the rules of archery, but I broke them deliberately."

"Go to the library," Stephen said. "Your mother's already there. I'll meet you in a few minutes."

Then he walked past her to his unconscious brother, his archery master who was gently attempting to revive him, and Melanie, who was still sitting on the grass, looking somewhat amused.

Fifteen minutes later Percy had been revived by Stephen slapping him awake once he had ascertained the exact nature of the insult, and then had received a tongue-lashing, not just for insulting the dead king and Harriet, but for using foul language in front of his daughters and for eavesdropping on a private conversation in the library.

When he protested that Harriet had threatened to kill him, was insane and should be committed to Bethlehem Hospital, Stephen had informed him coldly that if he didn't leave the premises immediately he would kill him himself. Then, once his brother had left, Stephen walked slowly back to the house, trying to quell both his anger at Percy and his approval of his daughter's loyalty to her friend, her icy composure, and her honesty, all of which he found utterly admirable.

Ever since that day three years ago, when she had come to the library and informed her parents out of the blue that she wanted to learn how to be a good wife because she was no longer a child, she had put every ounce of her considerable energy into learning all the skills she would need to run an aristocratic household.

Initially her parents had thought it was a passing phase, that perhaps King Charles had asked her to learn feminine skills and that in her grief she was trying to please him. But as time went on and she devoted all her efforts to learning everything she would need to know, including things she found utterly abhorrent, like embroidery, fashion and other subjects she had no interest in, so that she could converse with women she also had no interest in, both Amelia and Stephen had come to believe that she had finally softened, and had accepted her duty as a female.

And in fairness, he thought now as he neared the house, she *had* accepted her duty as a female. But today's incident had shown that she had not softened, not at all.

She really should have been a boy, he thought, his heart full of a pride he could not display when he arrived in the library, because he really could not show his approval of her threatening to kill his brother, even if she would not have carried out the threat. Really, Stephen thought, Percy was an obnoxious little shit, always had been, and showed no sign of mellowing as he turned eighteen. Mama had thrown all her affection onto her last-born after Papa died, and it had utterly ruined him.

He could not show that, either. Reaching the library, he moulded his features into what he hoped was an appropriate expression, and walked in.

Amelia and Harriet were already sitting on a sofa near the shelves of books, talking earnestly. They both looked up as he came in.

"Percy's gone home with a flea in his ear," Stephen said. "He should not have spoken in such an uncouth manner, nor should he have been listening at the door. You really shouldn't have threatened him like that though. What would you have done if your finger had slipped?"

"Killed him, I suppose," Harriet replied indifferently. "But my finger wouldn't have slipped, Papa. I really am an expert. If I'd shot him, it would have been intentional."

"Would you really have shot him, if he hadn't apologised?" Stephen asked.

"Yes, of course I would," Harriet replied. "There's no point in making a threat unless you're willing to carry it out, is there?" Seeing the look of shock on their faces, she elaborated. "I wouldn't have killed him, if that's what you're concerned about. I threatened to shoot him, not kill him. It's not my fault if he didn't listen properly. If he hadn't apologised for what he said about the king I would have changed my aim from his heart to a painful but non-fatal place."

"Harriet," Amelia said after a moment, "you really can't shoot people for insulting those you care for."

"Why not? Men do it, don't they? Maybe I should have challenged him to a duel instead. I suppose that would have been fairer."

THE ECCENTRIC'S TALE: HARRIET

"Ladies don't duel. That's something gentlemen do," Stephen pointed out. "You really must prom—"

"Please don't say what you're going to, Papa," Harriet interrupted. "You can't ask me to listen to someone insult a person I care deeply for and just accept it. I won't do it. I've subdued myself for the last three years, learning everything I need to learn to make a very good marriage and hopefully by doing so raise this family again. Now I can talk to idiots, and listen to tedious conversation for hours without screaming. I can host dinner parties, play numerous tunes on the harpsichord, dance and speak French. I can even embroider pointless pictures on cloth that look like what they're supposed to be. I know how to do accounts, and to write letters to people I don't give a damn about. All these are things I hate doing, but I'm doing them for us, to restore the family.

"But please, Papa, don't ask me to make a promise I cannot keep. I cannot and will not stand back and flutter helplessly while someone slanders a person I love, whether it's King Charles or one of you. I will always defend those I love. I have learned to let go of so much of myself in the last years, but I will not let go of this. If I do, I will lose all respect for myself."

There was a long silence as both parents absorbed a number of things about their eldest daughter, including what a huge effort she was making for them, and the fact that whatever she had to face in her future, being thought feeble would not be one of them. Or at least anyone stupid enough to think that would soon discover their error.

"So then, Mama was telling me that you have found a suitor for me, someone who you think might be ideal?" Harriet said after a while, breaking the silence.

"Yes," Stephen said after a moment. "We have found a possible suitor. He's a Marquess, so only one step down from me, as it were. He's Marquess of Hereford."

"Hereford?" Harriet replied.

"Yes, but he doesn't live there. He lives in Hertfordshire, which is a lot closer to London than we are, and which means it will be easy for you to attend Court, but still spend a lot of time on his country estate. It's only about three hours' drive from Whitehall."

"It's very large, and really beautiful, we've been told. We know how much you love the countryside, so we thought you might like that you won't have to be in London most of the time," Amelia commented. "If you're interested in him, then we will of course visit his home so you can see that as well as him. He has invited us already."

Harriet nodded thoughtfully.

"I don't know London of course, or if I'd enjoy the city, but yes, I do love green places. So he's accepted at Court then, I assume," she said. "I also assume he's extremely rich as well as being in favour with King James?"

"He is. He's also only a few years older than you – in his late twenties, and quite handsome. He seems to be very personable too. We have heard nothing objectionable about him at all, although if you meet him and don't like him, then you must tell us. We really will not make you marry someone you dislike. We would never do that."

Harriet smiled. They really wouldn't, because they cared so much for her. Charles had been right, they were exceptional parents, deserving of her sacrifice for them.

"If he's already a marquess though, will he want to marry someone like me without a dowry?" she asked.

"Someone like you? You say that as though you are not an excellent prospect!" Amelia remarked.

"Well, I'm not, am I? I have no dowry – in fact he will need to agree to settle your debts, Papa, or I won't consider him. I'm very plain, and not exactly witty or gracious. All I have in my favour is the special remainder in the dukedom, isn't it?"

Stephen and Amelia gasped in unison, and Harriet closed her eyes for a second, angry with herself for letting the secret she'd kept for three years slip in an unguarded moment.

"I'm sorry," she said. "I should have waited for you to tell me that."

"Who told you about the special remainder?" Stephen asked. "Was it Percy listening at doors again?"

"No. I heard you talking about it in here, not long after the king died. I came down to tell you I was going to be alright, because I knew you were worried about me, and I heard you talking about it, so I went back upstairs, because I didn't know what to say. I didn't want you to think I was nosey."

"And you've kept that to yourself for three years?" Stephen said.

"Yes. I didn't know how to broach the subject, so just thought I'd get on with making myself as eligible as possible, in the hopes of saving the family. Is he a Catholic?"

"What?" Stephen said, still astounded that his straightforward honest daughter had kept a secret from him for three years. He was learning a lot about her today.

"The marquess. Is he Catholic? Is that why James likes him?"

"No," Amelia replied. "He's Anglican, but has no objections to serving with Catholics and supports the king's attempts at toleration. It's said that he has expressed an interest in learning more about the Catholic faith, which is one reason why James favours him so. He's willing to pay all our debts when you have a son, and to make a will leaving you a third of his estate if he dies before you, which is very generous."

"But if I don't have a son and he dies, what then?" Harriet asked.

"It's the custom for the widow to receive a third of her husband's estate anyway, in that case," Stephen told her.

"Custom," Harriet repeated. "Hmmm. How desperate is he for his son to be a duke?"

"I don't know, but he's unlikely to get a dukedom any other way," Stephen replied. "The marquess would have to do something extraordinary to be elevated by James. If he hasn't done it by now, he's unlikely to. And then, I am the *sixth* Duke of Darlington, which also carries some status – his son would be the seventh, therefore it would appear as though his title was established, rather than newly created by an unpopular monarch."

"Stephen!" Amelia exclaimed.

"No one is listening, I trust Harriet, and James *is* unpopular, partly because he's a Catholic, and partly because he hasn't got the charisma or ability to play the political game that his brother had," Stephen countered. "A lot of people are waiting for him to die, as his eldest daughter is a Protestant."

"Unless Queen Mary has a boy this time," Amelia said.

"The queen is with child?" Harriet asked, thereby demonstrating how little attention she paid to social events, as it had been the talk of the last few weeks. Neither parent commented on this.

"Yes. If the child lives and is a boy the Catholic succession will be assured, as the heir is certain to be raised in the Roman faith."

"And the Marquess of Hereford will be secure in his place and we will not, unless we all suddenly become Catholics, or I marry him," Harriet commented.

"Yes, but we still don't want you to feel you have to—"

"Let me meet him, then," Harriet interrupted. "And his house, which I assume I'll be managing, to an extent. When can we go?"

"Harriet, you are looking at this very coolly," Amelia said.

"Of course I am," Harriet replied, surprised. "I'm sure you'd look at any business transaction in the same way, weighing up the advantages and disadvantages of undertaking it."

Amelia moved forward, taking Harriet's hands in hers.

"Harriet, we are hoping very much that it will be more than that, that you will find happiness with him, if you marry him. And you absolutely must promise us that if you really dislike him, you will tell us. We would not force you to marry against your will. We are both resolved on that."

Harriet squeezed her mother's hands, and smiled.

"I know you are. I know how much you love me, and I love you very much too. You and my sisters are everything to me. It means a lot that you will allow me to make my own decision. So let us make arrangements to meet my prospective husband."

It did not occur to either parent until very much later, that Harriet had not promised them anything at all.

* * *

May 1688

In the end the whole family travelled to Hertfordshire to Broadfields Hall, on Harriet's insistence.

"After all," she said, "I want you to tell me honestly what you think of him. If I do marry him, he will become part of our family, especially as he has no siblings and both his parents are dead too. He will no doubt be glad to acquire such a lovely family." She said this with great certainty, as though being part of the Ashleigh family was the highest honour in the world. Which to her it was. Stephen and Amelia exchanged a private smile over it as they all

THE ECCENTRIC'S TALE: HARRIET

clattered along in the coach, which had been hired as the expensive private carriage had been forsaken two years previously as one of the economies.

"It's an awfully long way away from our house, isn't it?" Sophia commented anxiously.

"It's not as far as it seems," Stephen said. "After all, we set off quite late on Monday, and had a leisurely drive yesterday too. And don't forget we could have arrived last night, except that it was too late to pay a social call."

"Yes, and we're in a coach, which is always slower. If I rode the whole way instead, I could probably do it in one long day, if I set off very early," Harriet commented, then intercepted the glance between her parents. "If I needed to," she added. "I know it's not considered acceptable for a marchioness or whatever I'd be to gallop headlong across the country."

"No, and it's not safe, either," Amelia pointed out. "You would need to be in a coach, with a guard."

"I really need to learn to shoot properly," Harriet mused, which did not overly reassure her parents, but they had no chance to comment further, as they now arrived at the open gates of Broadfields Hall, at which were standing two liveried servants who bowed deeply to them as they passed. They carried on for some time along a tree-lined drive, past a maze and formal gardens, until they arrived at the house itself.

"My God, it's enormous!" Melanie breathed.

It was indeed enormous. Their own house was very grand too. But this one showed the extreme wealth of the owner, as it had from the moment they had driven through the gates. The formal gardens by their nature would take a veritable army of gardeners to maintain, and the outside of the three-storied cream-coloured house was immaculate, the windows glittering in the late spring sunshine.

"Everything looks as though it's just been cleaned," Sophia said, who was such a lover of military precision and symmetry that her father had nicknamed her 'Soldier Sophie'.

As they drew up a host of liveried footmen appeared to greet them and help them down from the coach, while their trunks were spirited away to the various rooms they would stay in tonight, and a young man came down the steps of the house to meet them.

Harriet, who had not commented on either the house or gardens yet, observed him from inside the coach, noting that the servants all lowered their heads and bowed deeply to him as he passed them, whether he looked their way or not. He was tall, slim, and, as her parents had told her, quite handsome, in that his features were very regular. *Sophia will approve of the symmetry of the man,* she thought, driving away a momentary worry about what he would think of her when he saw her. *I can't change what I look like,* she told herself fiercely, *and in any case, it's the prospective title I bring that he wants. It doesn't matter whether I'm beautiful or not.*

Annoyed by her flutter of uncustomary concern for her appearance, she stepped down from the coach, remembering to accept the hand of the footman as though incapable of walking down three small steps unaided. She was used now to the ridiculous ways of society ladies, although that did not make them any more acceptable to her.

The marquess was greeting her parents, and as she appeared on the drive, now turned to her. If he was disappointed by what he saw, he didn't show it at all.

"Lady Harriet," he said, his voice rich and deep, "welcome to my home. I hope you like it."

"I do so far," she replied bluntly. "You have a very fine garden, Lord Hereford."

"Later I hope you will do me the honour of allowing me to show you my estate. After you have rested a little, and eaten dinner, of course. It will be ready in an hour, but if you all need longer to rest, please tell me, and I can easily delay it to suit."

Knowing how horrified the kitchen staff would be were their no doubt immaculately planned and crafted meal to be delayed, and the amount of panic and work that would involve, both Amelia and Harriet stated together that they would be very happy to eat in an hour, after which they were shown to their rooms where basins of warm scented water, soap and towels had been thoughtfully provided.

Harriet, now alone, sat on the richly carved and gilded four-poster bed, looked around the room and whistled softly to herself in an unladylike manner, before going to the window and looking out across the enormous expanse of gardens. In the distance could be seen a tower, which she would no doubt be shown later

THE ECCENTRIC'S TALE: HARRIET

when she toured the estate with her suitor. She was not overawed by what she had seen so far; after all, Ash Hall was magnificent. But it was also starting to show the lack of attention of penury; they now had only enough servants to care for the family and maintain the rooms they lived in. Other rooms had been closed off, and even the inhabited rooms sported cobwebs in the corners and dust on high, difficult to reach surfaces. It was true that their maids worked very hard, but there were only enough of them to keep the house superficially clean.

On impulse she picked up a chair and standing on it, ran her hand across the top of the frame of a painting, then looked at her unsoiled fingers. Not a mote of dust, anywhere. If the whole house was like that, and the gardens too, then he must have an enormous number of staff. His clothes were exquisitely tailored as well, something she had learned from listening to endless conversations about fashion.

There came a light tap on the door, and before Harriet could jump down from the chair it opened and Melanie came in.

"What are you doing?" she asked.

"I'm seeing if there's any dust on the picture frame," Harriet explained. Melanie's expression turned to one of complete disbelief. "I wanted to see if all these servants are just to impress me, or if they're real," she elaborated.

"Why wouldn't they be real?" Melanie asked, coming and sitting on the couch at the end of the bed.

"Well, if he's just pretending to be enormously wealthy to get me to marry him, then he could have hired all those footmen we saw, and spruced up a few rooms. But he wouldn't have got someone to dust the top of the picture frames, because we wouldn't see that."

"You are clever," Melanie said. "I would never think of that."

"You would if you were about to make the most important decision of your life," Harriet said.

Melanie stroked the heavy silk of the gold-fringed bedhangings.

"I suppose I would," she agreed. "What do you think of him, then?"

"I don't know yet, I only saw him for a moment," Harriet replied.

"He's quite handsome, in a boring kind of way," Melanie said. "Sophia thinks he's perfect to look at."

Harriet laughed.

"Haven't you got to change for dinner?" she said.

"Yes. So have you. I just wanted to see what your first impression of him was, that's all."

"He seems like chocolate," Harriet answered after a moment. With Sophia she would have had to elaborate on that, but Melanie understood immediately. Dark brown eyes, rich dark hair, a deep rich voice, smooth and luxurious.

"Yes," she said. "He does." She stood and moved to the door, then stopped, her hand on the knob. "You don't like chocolate," she added.

"No. So let's hope he isn't what he seems," Harriet replied.

After an enormous luncheon, which included roasted lobsters, cheesecakes, marrow puddings, salad, fruit and a variety of wines, the marquess repeated his invitation to drive Harriet around the estate, which she accepted.

"Could we walk a little, maybe round the formal gardens first?" she asked. "It will help me to digest the food. Which was delightful," she added.

"Of course," the marquess replied immediately. "What an excellent idea. There's nothing like a gentle stroll after a healthy meal."

They strolled around the beautifully clipped knot gardens at the front of the house at a pace somewhat slower than Harriet would have liked, although it did allow her to see this part of her future gardens in more detail. Stephen and Amelia followed, far enough behind to preserve propriety without being able to hear what the couple were saying.

At the moment the marquess was saying that his father had redesigned the gardens in the latest style, which was all the fashion in Holland, France and Italy, it seemed, and was slowly making its way to England.

"Although he died before he could finish, sadly. But I have continued with his plan, and it is now almost complete. Does it please you?" he asked.

"It is new to me," she replied, unwilling to admit that she found it too artificial-looking for her tastes. There wasn't a leaf or blade of grass out of place. She was very aware that she was unusual in enjoying more natural gardens, with swathes of flowers and winding paths, and didn't want to reveal any more of herself than she needed to at this juncture. She did, however, want him to reveal himself. "Do I please you?" she asked, and felt the muscle of his forearm tense under his hand, the first natural reaction of any kind he had shown so far today.

"Of course," he replied smoothly a moment later. "Who would not be pleased by such a refined young lady?"

Oh, well put, she thought.

"Come, my lord, let us be frank for a moment," she ventured. "I am not beautiful. My mirror tells me that. Does that disturb you?"

"I find you most attractive," he said. "Your eyes are particularly fine. Now you must answer the same question, I think. Do I please you?"

"You have made my family very welcome here, and your home is wonderful," she replied evasively.

"Thank you. But you have not answered my question. I did not ask you if my house pleased you, but if I did," he said.

Damn.

"You are very well-proportioned, and your looks are perfect. As I observed to my sister earlier, you remind me of chocolate," she elaborated.

He smiled.

"Thank you," he said. "That is very kind of you."

"Not at all. It was the truth. I try to speak the truth whenever possible," she said, feeling slightly guilty, although in fairness she *had* spoken the truth. Almost everyone loved chocolate, so he was not to know she hated it, found it extremely bitter unless mixed with a lot of sugar, after which it was too sweet for her taste. In any case he would think she was making the comparison because of his hair and eye colour, and maybe his outfit, which was also brown, rather than his overly sweet, smooth and possibly false demeanour, concealing something bitter that he wanted to keep from her.

Now, I really would like to show you the tower, which you may have seen from your bedroom window. It's the oldest building on the estate, built by my ancestor in the fourteenth century," he continued. "But it is a little far. May I drive you there?"

"Yes, you may," she agreed. She wanted them to be alone, completely alone, for what she wished to say.

She waited, allowing him to tell her about the lands, that they grew most of their own food, and had an extensive farm and brewery as well, which he would show her another day, if she would do him the honour of paying another visit before their wedding. And then he took her to the tower, where they got out of the carriage and walked up the crumbling spiral staircase, emerging onto the crenelated walkway at the top.

"My ancestor built it to stake his claim to the land," the marquess explained, "and so that he could see any potential invaders. He may have built a keep here too, but this tower is all that remains."

"It's certainly a wonderful view," Harriet said. It was. The hall glowed a rich cream in the afternoon, the river behind it sparkling in the sunshine. She could be happy here, if the circumstances were right. It was a wonderful estate, and very well kept. He had not done all this just to impress her, she knew that now. Years of painstaking work had been put into it, and his pride in it was clearly genuine. That much she was sure of. "You have put a great deal of love and attention into your estate," she said. "It is truly beautiful. You are right to be proud of it."

"I *am* proud of it, that's true," he said, gazing out across his land. "I would not see the title become extinct, as it may do."

"Which is where I come in," she commented.

He seemed to come back from a long way away, and she realised that he had probably not meant to speak his thoughts aloud. Honesty at last, then. He looked shocked, as though horrified to have uttered a sincere sentence.

"It was most uncouth of me to speak in such a way," he said. "My deepest apologies. I do of course hope for us to be happy together." He had recovered himself now, and the brief but refreshing honesty was gone, the last sentence ringing disturbingly false. She suddenly disliked him, but knew that she had no reason to do so other than instinct, so she looked towards the house for a moment as though absorbed, and subdued the unfair feelings. Even so, she needed to broach a subject he would not want to talk about, and she needed to do it now. It was not fair to give

THE ECCENTRIC'S TALE: HARRIET

him false hope if she could not go through with this liaison.

"May I ask you a question, my lord?" she said after a moment.

"My name is Raphael," he said, "and of course, you may ask me anything you wish about the estate. I will do my best to answer."

"Raphael," she said, realising that she had not known his real name until this minute, and had not cared, because it did not affect her family's welfare or hers. What she was about to ask did though, so she took a moment to formulate the question.

"I am very pleased with your house, and of what I have seen of the estate," she said. "And you have made myself and my family most welcome. I know you have no living family, and I would like it very much if you come to consider my parents and sisters as your own. But I would like to be frank with you, and I hope it does not offend you. We both know that we are standing here because we are considering marriage to each other, and that marriage is proposed for practical rather than emotional reasons."

"That is true," he agreed, his voice guarded now. "But I do hold you in the highest esteem."

"I'm very happy to hear that," she said. "I too hold you in high esteem and I'm sure you will understand what I say now. If I marry you, then I will in effect give over everything of myself to you, as you will not to me." When he opened his mouth to object she continued quickly. "I mean legally. When a man and woman marry, they become one person in the eyes of the law, with the woman subject to the man. I know that is not your doing but the law of the land, but because of that, there are certain things I would like to safeguard before I agree to marry you."

"And they are?" he asked.

"You have told my father that you will pay off his debts when I give you a son, and that you will make a will after we are married leaving a third of your estate to me if you die. Is this correct?"

"It is," he said, "although I hope not to die for many years."

"I must tell you, Raphael, that without intending to insult you, I am not willing to commit myself utterly to you unless I have all the documentation in place before we marry, as it is normal to do."

"I assure you that my word is my bond, as a gentleman!" he protested, clearly outraged.

"I'm sure it is," she replied calmly. "And you have done nothing today to prove otherwise. I really have no wish to offend you. But I implore you to see my side of the situation - once we are married, you will have complete legal authority over me. I would therefore prefer if you were to make some undertakings prior to the marriage. After all, it will not make a lot of difference to you to keep your sincere promises earlier than you had anticipated, but it will make me happy, which you have said you wish me to be."

"What undertakings do you wish me to make?"

"As we both know, my father has the rank you desire, and you have the money he desires. You cannot achieve a dukedom for your son without me, and my family cannot achieve an appropriate lifestyle for their status without you. I wish you to pay off all of my father's debts as you marry me, not when I have had a son. And I would wish you to make a will to take effect on our wedding day, leaving everything to me if you die, unless I have a son before that happens, in which case I would ask for the customary third of your estate as you have already promised, the rest going to our son, who would receive the final third when I die."

It was good to see, just for a second, a natural, outraged expression on his face.

"You ask a lot, my lady," he said after a moment. "If I may be brutal, you do not bring a substantial dowry with you as is customary, but you expect me to pay out a good deal of money, with no guarantee of a return, as it were."

"I do. Our marriage is a gamble, as we both know. But you are wrong. I *do* bring a dowry, and one that is far more important to you than money, which you have demonstrated so well today you possess an enormous amount of. I bring you the prospect of not only giving you a son to continue the marquessate in your direct line, but also of making that son a seventh duke. I am sixteen, and could reasonably give you over twenty children in the next years, at least one of which is sure to be a boy. When my father dies I will inherit his estate, which in reality means that you will inherit it, and our son will inherit both our estates in his turn, which will make your name the most powerful in the country, next to the king's. I believe that possibility to be worth the gamble of a few thousand pounds now and a will that will not be proved for many years yet. There's a good chance I will die before you anyway, in childbirth. And I will not watch my family struggle after I marry, while we live in luxury. What do you say?"

He was clearly flabbergasted by her brutal honesty, although he did not say that. But it was only right that he had some concept of what he was taking on if he married her, she thought. She watched with interest as he thought about what she'd said, of which he clearly disapproved, in spite of his attempt to hide it.

"We bring equal, if different cards to the table," she added. "My family is in need of money, which you have. You are in need of heirs, which I can give you."

"I hope. You are asking a great deal," he said. "I will have to give this some thought."

She was not asking *such* a great deal, in fact, and he must know that. In aristocratic marriages, it was customary for a considerable amount of negotiation to take place before the wedding, and a large part of that negotiation was to get the financial agreements in place. It was *not* normal for the bride-to-be to become directly involved though, which was probably why he was annoyed. She was supposed to be concerning herself with flowers and gowns, and seating arrangements.

But all she was asking was for the agreements to be legally binding, not merely promised. And if he truly intended to fulfil the agreements after the wedding and birth, why was he so reluctant to commit himself a few weeks or months early? Was he in fact hoping to cheat her father, who was a good man, the sort of man who would accept that a gentleman's word was his bond? If so, she wanted no more to do with him.

She nodded to herself, and he clearly assumed that she was acquiescing to his desire.

"Shall we continue?" he said. "There is a great deal more that I would like to show you."

"No," she answered. "There really is no need. If I am not going to marry you, then I have seen enough. Thank you for a most interesting tour, though. Let us return to the house, and I can tell my parents that they need to find another suitor for me. They will be disappointed, but I am sure it won't be difficult to find another nobleman who wishes to rise to a dukedom, and is only too willing to fulfil my wishes in order to make my wedding day a happy one."

She turned, and lifting her skirts descended the stairs, not quite as gracefully as she had ascended them, because she no longer needed to impress him in any way. She had dismissed him completely from her mind, and it seemed he was astute enough to recognise that from her manner, and to realise that the dismissal was not a feminine ploy, but genuine.

"You drive a hard bargain, Lady Harriet," he said as she climbed into the carriage without accepting his outstretched hand to assist her.

"I have offended you, and I had no wish to, but this issue is too important to me and to my family for me not to address it, my lord," she replied. "I have only the one asset to sell, and it is precious. I will not give it away for a promise alone. I will keep it until I see hard cash. For yourself, perhaps you *do* have a chance of receiving a dukedom from the king, but I suspect the attempt will cost you a lot more than it would to agree to my request – and no amount of money paid to the king will make your son a seventh duke, will it?"

"Very well," he said unhappily. "I will send my lawyer to your father in the next days."

"Thank you," she replied. "And when the documents are signed, I will accept your proposal, gladly. Now I hope we can put this behind us, and enjoy the rest of this delightful day together."

Judging by the frosty atmosphere that prevailed for the first part of the return journey it seemed as though he at least could not put it behind him, which she understood. Men were not good at conceding anything, especially to women, and he was not happy that he had to or would lose her. And while part of her couldn't care less as long as she won the battle for her family's future, she had learnt the importance of sweetening bitter pills in the last years.

So, as they drew closer to the house Harriet made some comments on his exquisite taste in garden design, and on the beauty of the tulips, and mentioned that although they had some in their gardens, she had never seen so many varieties before. Upon which he explained that they did indeed have over a hundred different kinds of tulip, and that they had been a great

THE ECCENTRIC'S TALE: HARRIET

favourite of his grandmother's, who had even travelled to Holland herself after the *tulpenwoede* to buy a *Semper Augustus*, which in the *tulpenwoede* had cost as much as a beautiful house.

"Although she did not pay that much for it, you understand, because the prices crashed when the tulip bubble burst, but they were still very expensive. It was white, with crimson flames running through its petals, quite extraordinary. Are you interested in flowers?" he asked.

"Yes, very much," Harriet replied. "Do you still have the tulip?"

"We do, but that particular one is indoors, as it is extremely rare and valuable, even now. It has finished blooming for this year, but there is a painting of it in one of the state rooms, if you would like to see it," he said.

She replied that she would, and was so genuinely excited by this that he was mollified somewhat, and by the time they descended at the house no one would have known that they had had an unpleasant conversation earlier.

In the evening the entertainments were varied, and designed to show off his wealth and breeding. There was no dancing, as they were but a small party, but they played cards, there were fireworks after dark, and he had his own troupe of musicians who played delightfully that evening and again in a nearby room whilst they breakfasted the next morning. The food was delicious, the wines exquisite, the floral displays around the house beautiful, and servants were on hand to do absolutely everything. In the time she was there, Harriet did not have to open one door, pack or unpack any items, refill her glass or plate, or in fact do anything apart from enjoy herself.

None of which she cared a damn about. She had just secured her family's future. Or she hoped she had, and would be sure in the next few days.

She did not make idle threats. Her uncle knew that now, and hopefully, so did the marquess. If he did not comply with her demands, she would not marry him.

CHAPTER FIVE

June 1688

The young couple sat, or rather lay together in the gardens on a little grassy slope at the edge of a copse of trees. It was a glorious summer day. Jem, barefoot and stockingless, lay on his side, head propped up on one elbow, while Harriet lay on her back, knees bent, hands cupped in front of her face, blowing furiously between her thumbs.

"I can't do this," she said finally, red-faced and frustrated.

"Yes you can. It's just practice is all," Jem replied. "And you have to stretch the blade of grass really tight between the top and bottom of your thumbs. Try a thicker piece of grass, it's easier to make a sound." He sat up and examined the area around him, before locating a likely specimen. "Here," he said, handing her a straight, thick blade. "Now, you traps it between your—"

"You trap it," Harriet corrected automatically. They had an agreement; she corrected his speech so that in time he would sound more refined, and he taught her interesting things. Today's lesson was how to make a whistle out of a piece of grass.

"You trap it between the base of your thumbs and the top, but make sure you stretch it tight. Cup your hands, and then you blows through...you blow through the little space, and if you do it right, it makes a noise, and you can change the kind of noise by making your mouth bigger or opening your hands out. Keep practising, and you'll do it."

Birds sang in the trees, bees buzzed by, the sun shone, and assorted blowing noises and frustrated sounds came from Harriet's cupped hands, followed after a few minutes by a loud

THE ECCENTRIC'S TALE: HARRIET

and piercing whistle, which set the more nervous birds to flight. Harriet's face emerged from behind her hands, scarlet with effort, but with an ear-to-ear grin.

"I did it!" she announced.

"You did! I knew you would."

"That was really loud! Much louder than I expected."

"It's because you was…were blowing so hard. Now you've done it once, you can play with it and make different sounds."

A little more time passed, punctuated by various whistling noises.

"So it seems you're really going to go, then," Jem commented. The whistling stopped, replaced by a sigh.

"Yes, I am," Harriet replied. "He's done what I asked him to do, so it's just a matter of setting the date and sorting out the documents really. Papa is doing that. The wedding will be here though, mainly because I have a lot of relatives, whereas he's an only child and his parents are dead. He hasn't mentioned if he has uncles and cousins who want to come, but if he does I don't think they live near him, whereas most of the Ashleighs live within a day's ride of here, so it's more practical, I suppose."

"You don't sound very excited. I always thought girls got very excited about getting married and then having babies. Isn't it what they all want to do?"

Harriet discarded the grass and put her arms behind her head, staring up at the cloudless sky. "I don't know," she said after a minute. "I don't really care what other girls want to do. It's not what I want to do, that's all I know. But I have to, really, for the family."

He didn't ask her why she had to. Even if she never mentioned it, probably never even thought about it, he knew he was a servant and she was nobility, and there were lines you didn't cross. Asking about the private affairs of the family was one of them.

"What's he like?" he asked instead.

"He's like the opposite to you," she said, and when he didn't respond she glanced across at him, to see a puzzled look on his face. "You're like a summer day in the countryside, all sunshine and blue skies, wild and free," she elaborated. He was; his hair was a dark golden blond, eyes the blue of the sky above, the corners creased by laughter lines even though he was only sixteen, because he was outdoors all the time and always smiling, always merry, as much a part of the landscape as the trees and the wildlife, or so he seemed to her. "And he's like a winter night in the town, dark hair, dark eyes, pale skin, and very cool, controlled, restrained and unnatural somehow, like the town."

Jem's expression was concerned now, rather than puzzled.

"He don't sound like a good match for you, then," he said.

"Doesn't, not don't. But that's just my first impression of him, and I'm probably imagining things. I told Melanie he was like chocolate, partly because of his hair and eyes, and his voice is deep and smooth, but then when I look at you, it seems that he's the opposite of you. But I'm probably wrong on both counts. I don't really know him. He's very polite and courteous, and he's done what I asked, which is fair." She sat up and rested her chin on her knees. "He's like his house and garden. There's absolutely nothing out of place, not a weed anywhere, not a speck of dust. It's all immaculate."

"Hmmm. Do you think he'll make you happy?"

She turned her head to meet his troubled look.

"As happy as I'm going to be, I suppose," she said. "I'm never going to get what I really want, am I? So I might as well help the family, and live in a beautiful place."

"Can't you have what you want?" he asked.

"No. It was all a childish dream when we talked about being free, doing whatever we liked and sailing off all over the world, wasn't it? You already knew that. I knew some of it – I knew I couldn't be a man, of course. I just didn't know that I couldn't do manly things then. I thought that if I was able to do them *physically*, then there was no reason why I shouldn't do them. But the world isn't like that. So if I can carry on with archery and riding, go for long walks and do things in the gardens, I'll be contented enough, I think. Your dream of being a head gardener was always more achievable."

"Maybe, but I still need to learn to read and write properly if I'm going to be one. I haven't got time, with the gardeners being cut back. I should be working now, really."

"That's going to change," Harriet said. "Papa will employ more servants again soon, and you should have some free time then."

THE ECCENTRIC'S TALE: HARRIET

"It's still hard though, because I don't know anyone who can read well to teach me. I know the sound of each letter, but when they're put together in words, they don't make sense to me."

"I wanted to talk to you about that," Harriet said. "But I got distracted with the whistle. I want you to come with me when I go to Hertfordshire. When I was there, Raphael told me about these really rare tulips he's got, and there was a painting of one of them in the house. It was beautiful, and one bulb used to cost as much as a big house!"

Jem whistled through his teeth.

"You're not serious!" he said. "A big house? One flower? Was he teasing you?"

"No, I don't think he's the sort to tease. And we'd just had a disagreement, so neither of us was in a teasing mood. But I thought I'd like to experiment, maybe build some hotbeds, or a big hothouse, and try growing some unusual flowers and other plants. You could help me. And I could teach you to read properly, and then one day you could be my head gardener!"

If she'd expected him to jump at the offer, she was disappointed.

"You could bring your father with you, of course," she said after a minute of non-reaction from him. "I'd have to ask Raphael, but he's already given me something much more important, so I don't think he'd object to you coming with me."

"He might," Jem said then. "He might not be happy that you're so friendly with me."

"Like Papa wasn't, you mean. Maybe. But we'd just have to be more careful for a while, keep all the stupid proprieties, have you take off your hat and bow and so on to me, call me my lady or whatever marchionesses are called until we settled in. And then we could relax more, like we do now. As long as I do all the other things that ladies are supposed to do, the boring things, I'm sure he'll be satisfied."

"I'm not so sure about that," Jem said. She looked at him, and caught the expression he tried to hide.

"What is it?" she asked. "You know something you're not telling me."

"It's nothing," he said. "Just gossip. And I know you don't like gossip."

"No, I don't. But neither do you, so if whatever you've heard is making you turn down my offer, then you think it's true. And I respect your opinion, so I want to know what it is. I won't tell him, or anyone what you say, if it might get you in trouble."

He thought for a minute.

"The marquess doesn't have a good reputation where servants are concerned," he said.

"How do you know that?" she asked. "You don't know anyone who knows him, do you?"

"No, but you know things about other nobles that you've never met, don't you? Because people who *do* know them come and tell you about what they do, and what they're like. And sometimes it's just nasty gossip, but sometimes it's useful, because it tells you whether to be wary when you do meet them. It's the same with servants. We're like a club, servants to the nobility, and while you're in the drawing room talking to Countess Whatsername, her coachman or ladies' maid is in the kitchen or forecourt talking to us. I don't pay heed to the normal gossip, but I do to whether someone's very good or very bad to work for, so that one day if I need a job, I'll know who to avoid."

That all made sense.

"So what do they say about Raphael, then?"

"They say that he's very severe with his staff, will beat or dismiss them if he thinks they're not showing respect – I don't mean being rude or disobeying orders, but if they look him in the face, or don't bow deep enough to him, that sort of thing. And their sleeping places, food and other things are horrible too."

"Why don't they leave, then? Surely they can get work elsewhere?" Harriet commented.

"Not without a character, or not with nobles, anyway. So they'd have to take a lower status position at best, I think. I don't really know. I didn't ask why they don't leave. I just thought I won't ever work for him."

"But you'd be working for me, not him," Harriet pointed out.

Jem looked at her sceptically, one eyebrow raised, and after a minute she sighed.

"No, you're right. Damn it to hell," she said. "But if I get there, and find that he's not like that at all, would you come then?"

"His Grace is wonderful to work for," Jem said. "I'm very

THE ECCENTRIC'S TALE: HARRIET

happy here, and so is Da. But yes, I would consider it, if you asked. Because I'll miss you when you go."

She smiled then, but sadly.

"I'll miss you terribly," she admitted. "You're my only real friend, outside of my family. I was hoping you'd say yes and come with me, so I'd at least have one person around who liked me for who I really am."

"If you really want me to come, I'll do it anyway," he said. Impulsively she scooted across to him and grabbed his hand, squeezing it.

"You're a true friend, Jem," she told him. "But I won't ask you to come and work for a tyrant, because you couldn't do it, and if you were unhappy I would be too. If it's just a nasty rumour, I'll send a message to you, or tell you when I come back to visit."

"You'll make new friends," Jem said. "Friends of your own kind, and then you'll be happy."

"You *are* my own kind," she said. "We like a lot of the same things, and each other, and that's what matters, not stupid titles and clothes."

She leaned in again then, hugging him, and he wrapped his arms around her, wanting to comfort her, knowing how unhappy she was about this marriage and how much it was costing her not to show it to her family.

He did not tell her that the rest of the world did not see it like that, because she already knew that. Nor did he mention that if her husband found her behaving so familiarly with a gardener, never mind embracing him, he'd likely kill him. He might object to *any* other man she was so familiar with, nobles included, if he was a jealous sort. But a friendship with a mere servant would not be tolerated by any titled husband, jealous or not. Harriet had never seen, and hopefully never would see just how cruel a man could be to his wife without breaking any laws, or arousing any criticism even.

Jem would not be a party to making her life unbearable. He thought too much of her to do that. Better that she be lonely at first. In time she would adapt, and make the best she could of her life.

So he sat and allowed her to embrace him for as long as she needed to, because it was a platonic embrace, and because there was no one watching who might misinterpret it. And in his mind he said a silent farewell to her. He would cry later, alone in the woodland, when the night and trees concealed his emotions, which he knew were inappropriate and must be hidden.

While he was sitting in the branches of a tree that evening, tears in his eyes, watching the moon rise, Harriet sat in her room at the window, looking across the moonlit gardens and remembering walking down the open colonnades to the inner courtyard at Broadfields Hall with Raphael. She remembered him telling her that he was contemplating enclosing the colonnades to create a more convenient corridor, sheltered from the weather. And she remembered a maid coming towards them, so preoccupied with carrying a host of cleaning implements that she had not seen them until she was mere yards from them, after which a look of utter terror had crossed her face and she had turned immediately to the wall, stepping so that she was pressed against it, her back to them until they had passed. Harriet had commented on this very strange behaviour, and realised now that Raphael had evaded the question, and had continued to talk about the prospective alterations as though nothing out of the ordinary had happened.

Perhaps for him nothing out of the ordinary *had* happened. Perhaps all the servants were expected to squash themselves into walls or bow to the ground whenever their lord and master appeared. And perhaps they did that not from respect but from fear of the consequences if they did not.

She could not change her mind now. And certainly not because of servants' gossip and an uneasy feeling. Harriet had not realised how heavy a burden the debt had been to her parents until it was paid, as it had been a few days ago. She had seen them in the hallway as she came downstairs, Papa lifting Mama from the floor and swinging her round as though she was a child, both of them laughing, both of them looking younger than they had in a long time.

She could not take that away from them, *would* not take that away from them.

She had also discovered this evening that the queen had gone into labour two days ago and had been delivered of a baby boy. In London it seemed there had been bonfires and bells had been

THE ECCENTRIC'S TALE: HARRIET

rung to celebrate the birth, although not as many as would be expected following the birth of the child who would be the next king. And that was because all the people who were reluctantly enduring the reign of the Catholic King James knowing that when he died his Protestant daughter would take the throne, now knew that if this baby lived the Catholic succession would be assured.

She was not that interested in politics, but from a personal point of view it meant that her devoutly Anglican family would be unlikely ever to be accepted back at Court, unless she married this marquess who was a right-hand man of the king, and made a better impression the next time she met James than she had the last.

And of course her father wanted the dukedom to continue through his line, even if it *was* the female line, which she would also hopefully manage. Her mother's womb had not quickened in ten years, and was unlikely to now she was in her forties.

She would go through with this.

At least when she was married she *would* have control of some of the servants, the indoor servants at least. That would be expected of her, as the mistress of the house. And when she did, she could make changes. Not instantly and massively, as she would have done when an impulsive child, but subtly and carefully. One really important thing her mother had taught her was that a lady was much more likely to get what she wanted from a man by being passive and persuasive rather than confrontational. She had not had the time to be passive and persuasive with Raphael about her marriage settlement, but would try not to be so direct in future, as he clearly didn't appreciate it. However this marriage turned out for her, she had made her parents happy and could at least make her servants happier, if the rumours Jem had heard were true.

And that would be some consolation.

* * *

The wedding was a very long party to be endured, from Harriet's point of view. She had attended a few in the past, and this one was pretty much the same as them, in that there were a lot of people there, some of whom she didn't know and many of whom she didn't like, all of whom pretended to be ecstatic that she was marrying such a wonderful man, and told her she was beautiful even though she knew she wasn't.

The main difference between this wedding and the others that she had attended, apart from the fact that she was the bride, was that there was much more of everything; more people, flowers, jewels, courses at the meal, and music. This was because, in royal favour or not, the marriage of a duke's daughter to a marquess was of great societal importance, something Harriet hadn't considered at all. She realised that she should have done, because it was true that their son, who half the guests had already decided would certainly appear in nine months, would one day inherit an enormous amount of land and wealth and would therefore be one of the most powerful nobles in the land.

She was therefore a little surprised that the king himself was not in attendance, but it seemed he was somewhat preoccupied, not with the birth of his son as she'd expected, but with the trial of some bishops who had done something he didn't like, and who he'd expected to be convicted because he was the king and wanted them to be. But instead the bishops had been acquitted yesterday and the resultant celebrations in London had far outdone those of the prince's birth, so it had been thought unwise for the king to go out in public.

The day seemed to go on for ever. Raphael, who had hardly spoken to her since uttering his vows during the ceremony, and had so far only touched her hand to lead her to dinner and to dance with her afterwards, was, as she'd expected, immaculate in his rich silk brocade outfit, and perfect in his behaviour, if very cool and unromantic. Harriet considered that a blessing, because if she'd had to listen to him making effusive insincere declarations of love as well as enduring all the tears and joyful comments of the guests, she thought she would have gone mad. Although she wished he had shown *some* sign that he was happy to have married her. As much as she hated to admit it, she was nervous, and a little friendliness from her spouse would have helped to calm her.

As well as being nervous she was very uncomfortable, because her silver embroidered and jewel-encrusted dress was heavy and cumbersome and the weather was hot, so by the end of the ceremony she was already sweating profusely, whereas Raphael's skin of course was not even moist, his hand cool and dry as he led her into dinner, and equally cool and dry as he led her in the dancing later.

She would have given a lot to be able to escape the celebrations for a while, to kick off her shoes and run barefoot across the grass to the cottage where Jem lived, to sit in the copse of trees with him and speak honestly, of things she cared about. But of course she could not do that, partly because as the bride she was the centre of attention, and partly because if she did and was discovered, it would be Jem who'd be punished, not her.

So she smiled, and ate, and danced, and accepted the many compliments and good wishes that were showered on her, and put all her energy into showing her parents how much she appreciated the enormous effort they'd put into organising this, and waited for the moment it would all end and she could go to her room and have a little peace.

Except of course she couldn't go to her room and have a little peace, but instead had to go to the room that would normally be reserved for a royal visit, which had last been slept in by King Charles, who she missed enormously this evening. She tried not to think of what was to happen in the bedroom. Her mother had given her some idea of what was expected of her, and over the years she had witnessed various farm animals copulating, but neither that nor her husband's glacial demeanour allayed her fears about the imminent loss of her virginity. Part of her wanted the eating and dancing to go on forever, while another part of her just wanted to get the whole thing over with. Anticipation of a bad event was usually worse than the realisation, she knew that. But the knowledge did nothing to allay her fears, and by the time she was led off to bed by the other ladies she was terrified, though she did her utmost not to show it.

After being ceremoniously undressed, she and Raphael had to sit up in the enormous bed while the guests paraded through the chamber wishing them a fruitful union. After a full hour of this Harriet's terror had been dulled somewhat by boredom, with the result that she uttered a sigh of relief when the door finally closed and they were alone.

"God, I thought they'd never bugger off and leave us to it," she said, kicking off the bedclothes and jumping down from the bed before walking across the room to open the window and shutters, letting some cool air into the room. She stood there for a minute, inhaling the fresh sweet air deeply. If she could only go for a walk in the cool summer night, she'd probably be ready for what was to come. But she could hardly do that. She was married now, had to consider her husband, could not just do what she wanted any more.

"I'm sorry," she said, turning back to see the perfect marquess still sitting up as he'd been a moment ago, looking at her. "I should have asked if you minded me opening the window. Do you mind?"

"No," he replied. "I don't mind that, but I do mind your use of coarse language. That is not what I expect from my wife."

She thought for a minute, casting her mind back over what she'd said, then smiled at him. "Ah, you mean 'bugger'. I won't use it or any other curses in front of others, of course. But it's been a long day, and as we're alone now, I didn't think it would matter."

"I would prefer it if you did not use such language at all, whether alone or not," he replied coldly. "Now, come to bed. I am tired, but we need to consummate this marriage, so let's get on with it, then we can sleep. Who knows, if we're lucky you'll fulfil your part of the bargain straight away."

It was not the most romantic invitation to make love, but as Harriet had neither had one before nor wanted one now, she merely took another deep breath, braced herself and returned to bed to endure whatever was to come, hoping it would be over quickly at least so she could get some sleep.

Tomorrow she would have to say goodbye to her parents and sisters, and if she could get away for a while, to Jem. She was not looking forward to that, but would deal with it better if she'd had a good night's sleep, she knew.

* * *

She said a tearful farewell to her parents and sisters the following morning, and made them promise to come and visit her in her new home as soon as they possibly could, hoping that her parents didn't notice the distinct lack of enthusiasm in the voice of her new husband as he agreed to this. If anything, now the celebrations were over he seemed anxious to be away as quickly as possible, but she carefully ignored all his hints and gestures, and

THE ECCENTRIC'S TALE: HARRIET

took a very leisurely farewell of everyone.

In truth she didn't want to leave them at all, partly because she loved them desperately and knew she would miss them terribly, and partly because Raphael was already showing signs of not being the perfect husband he had taken such pains to pretend he would be before the wedding. She was not a fool – she had known that the face he had shown to her and her family had been at least partly a mask, as in fact was hers, but she had not expected him to discard the mask quite so quickly as he had – in fact the moment they had been alone in bed together, when he had, as he had suggested, 'got on with it', with no concern for the fact that she was a virgin, and no attempt to make her first sexual experience pleasant. Instead he had dispensed with any kissing or tenderness, simply climbing on top of her, spreading her legs, and clinically depriving her of her maidenhead before climbing off again and going to sleep.

It was as well that she was not the sort of girl whose head was full of romantic notions, but even so, she had hoped for a little more consideration than that. She'd seen horses copulate with more tenderness than he'd shown. But at least it had been over pretty quickly, and had not been as terrifying as she'd thought, although it had been painful.

This morning, sore, and tired from not sleeping properly, she had firmly reminded herself that she preferred honesty to false kindness and that at least it seemed she would not have to pretend to be in love with him. She could occupy herself fully with looking after the house and gardens when she got to Broadfields Hall, and hopefully when she'd given him a son he'd leave her alone.

In spite of Raphael's seeming indifference to her last night, he had watched her like a hawk this morning, with the result that she had been unable to escape for even a minute, let alone for long enough to say a personal goodbye to Jem. Her father, considerate as ever, assembled all the servants in the driveway to wave the happy couple off on their new life, and, already sick of Raphael's sighs of impatience and clear desire to be gone, Harriet took the time to address each servant by name, thanking them for their service and telling them she would see them when she came home for visits, which she intended to do as often as possible.

When she got to Jem she took his hand and squeezed it hard,

a pressure he returned, after which he glanced at her husband, who was standing by the coach, arms folded. Then he looked back at her, his blue eyes full of merriment and nodded slightly, telling her that he knew exactly what she was doing, and approved. In that moment she would have given almost anything to be able to stay here, to wake up now and find that it had all been a nightmare.

But it had not all been a nightmare. Her father was out of debt, her marriage had been consummated, and she now had to make the best of her future as the Marchioness of Hereford.

So she drove off with her husband amidst a sea of 'good lucks' and waving handkerchiefs, and with a huge effort managed not to cry, feeling perhaps unfairly that if she did he would enjoy her grief at leaving her home of sixteen years.

When they arrived at her new home the following day she was greeted by more celebrations, organised by the steward and housekeeper and attended by all the staff and tenants of the estate, which Harriet found touching. It was nice to be welcomed to her new home by someone, because her husband had been somewhat sullen for a good part of the journey home, occupying himself by reading a book for much of the previous day's journey, and by scratching himself today, following a night in a particularly infested bed, which had not improved his mood. Harriet had made no attempt to cajole him out of his sullenness, considering that she had far more reason to be unhappy than he did, and while she was happy to meet him halfway, she was not about to start her married life by begging him to cheer up and thus encouraging his sulky behaviour. To hell with him. If he wanted to be miserable, let him get on with it.

So she had amused herself by looking out of the window and dozing until they arrived home, where she complimented the steward sincerely on his welcome speech which was very prettily delivered, and then threw herself with enthusiasm into the dinner which was attended by the local dignitaries, with music provided by the servants, some of whom were really quite accomplished. It ended with a torchlit parade to the tower she had last seen when she had given Raphael his ultimatum, where fireworks were set off and were followed by another speech, this time by the housekeeper.

THE ECCENTRIC'S TALE: HARRIET

By the time they got to bed she was exhausted, and really hoped he would leave her alone tonight, as she was still a bit sore from her wedding night. Her hopes were not fulfilled, but at least he complimented her for the way she had behaved that evening, stating that she had made a very good impression on the local gentry, and that he was pleased with her for doing so. Then, after claiming his conjugal rights, to her surprise he got out of bed and left the room, wishing her a goodnight at the door and not returning.

So it was that she discovered two things; firstly that it was quite normal for aristocratic couples to sleep in adjoining bedrooms, sharing a bed only when having sexual intercourse; and secondly, just how in love with each other her parents were, and seemingly had always been, because on many occasions as a child, on waking from a bad dream, if her nurse was asleep Harriet would make her sleepy way to her parents' room in the middle of the night to find them both in the same bed, and always ready to offer comfort to her or her sisters. She had taken it for granted, had thought that all married couples slept together.

She was not sorry in this case though, to find she had been mistaken. If she had to endure his clearly dutiful, emotionless invasion of her, at least she didn't have to endure his snoring and indifferent presence for the rest of the night.

It was not a good start to what could well be a very long union, she knew. But it was what it was, and, now that the nuptial celebrations were presumably over, she would accept that, and strive to structure as happy and meaningful a life for herself as she could within the new framework of her marriage.

* * *

September 1688

Harriet stood on the top of the tower, rested her elbows on the crenelated battlements and looked across at the house, the house she was supposed to call home, but instead thought of as hell. She was not supposed to be here on the tower, but right now she couldn't care less. Increasingly it seemed that she was not supposed to be anywhere except in her rooms, unless there was some sort of social event, a dinner or concert, when she was supposed to be wherever her husband wanted her to be, showing how happy she was in her marriage with this perfect cultured man and how fascinated she was by the conversation of his friends' wives.

And against every ounce of her personality she had done it, and had not questioned him. For nearly three months she had tried her absolute utmost to be a pleasing wife to him, which she felt would have taxed most women, let alone someone of her nature.

She had done it for her parents, because she knew they wanted her to be happy and had spent years teaching her how to conform so she could be, and she knew she had to give their teachings a chance. She had done it for him, knowing that he resented her forcing him into paying out for goods he had not yet received. A lot of men would resent being bested by a woman, so in recompense she had decided to play the passive obedient wife until she had birthed the longed-for heir, fulfilling her part of the bargain. And she had done it for herself, thinking that if she did what he wanted, behaved as he wished, then he would soften and allow her some freedoms which would make her life bearable.

And absolutely nothing she had done had excited the slightest approval from him. In fact things had gone from bad to worse as the time passed.

The fucking (because that's what it was – in no way could what they did be called making love) continued, night after night, and presumably would until she got with child. She now saw it as a necessary nightly chore to be endured, and accepted it. Her courses also continued and had come again today, which was one reason why she was standing here now, where she could be alone to think. About what he would deny her next.

In her first month she had been able to walk all over the gardens, or take the little cart and drive around them, but when she had asked the groom to saddle a horse for her to go out into the estate with the purpose of becoming acquainted with the tenants, the Master of Horse had told her that her husband had given orders that she was not allowed to leave the gardens without him. She had bitten her tongue and accepted it, and had not even raised the topic with Raphael at dinner, partly because she'd vowed not to question his decisions at first, and partly because she suspected he might get pleasure from pointing out that he did not have to give her reasons for any of his decisions.

So she had walked around the gardens, had engaged in a little archery practice, had raided Raphael's library, and started to plan alterations to the garden, or at least to build a hothouse, which he surely could not object to, as if successful it would provide exotic fruits and flowers for the interminable dinners he gave. However, when she'd brought up the topic he *had* objected, telling her that if he wanted a hothouse he would already have built one, that they were prodigiously expensive to both build and maintain, and he had spent enough money on her already.

The next time she had gone to his library, a red-faced footman had been standing at the door, saying that Lord Hereford had ordered him not to allow her access to the room, as much of the reading matter was unsuitable for ladies. Presumably being denied the use of the library was punishment for daring to request a hothouse.

In late July her courses had come, and of a sudden the archery butts and bows were in a locked room to which no one had the key; the archery master was nowhere to be found, and it seemed that archery was too dangerous a sport for ladies to practice unsupervised. It was also unsuitable for ladies to go hunting it seemed, so while her husband and his friends charged all over the countryside in pursuit of game, thoroughly enjoying themselves, Harriet, who was an expert rider and as good a shot as any of them, sat in the drawing room sipping tea and listening to insipid and tedious conversation, in which she feigned great interest, something she had thankfully learned to do from her mother.

No longer allowed to read, she wrote long letters to her parents, although she was finding it increasingly difficult to think of things to write about, because she didn't do anything interesting. She didn't want to tell them how miserable and bored she was because it would make them unhappy, and they could do nothing to help her, so there was no point. She found herself waiting for the replies as avidly as she had awaited those of King Charles when she was a child.

If only he was still alive. He would not let her be restricted so, she was sure. She had expected to be taken to King James' Court soon after her wedding, as Raphael was one of the king's right-hand men and James would surely want to meet his trusted courtier's bride. But Raphael had told her the king had weighty matters on his mind at the moment and could not take time for such trivialities. When she had asked what the weighty matters were, he had told her they were nothing she would understand or needed to concern herself with.

She had spent an awful lot of August biting her tongue and punching her pillow in a most unladylike way, followed by stomping round the gardens, scowling. The gardens were boring. Everything was clipped to within an inch of its life, a mass of gardeners swarming over the area like ants every day, and every one dropped to his knees the moment she approached, head bowed until she passed.

She had an urge to mockingly pronounce some great Latin benediction over them as the pope might do, because all this bowing and scraping made her feel ridiculous, as though she was some sort of false deity. But if word got back to Raphael he'd be incensed at her mocking the king's religion, and she knew that servants gossiped. The last thing she wanted to do was repeat her blunder of ten years previously and alienate James again.

At the end of August her courses came again, and a few days later Raphael announced that over the next weeks he expected to have to spend a lot more time at the palace. While she was concentrating on not looking as gleeful as she felt about this, he told her that he had engaged a companion for her, so that she would not be lonely while he was away.

As he never spoke more than a few words to her each day and clearly didn't give a damn whether she was lonely or not, this was ridiculous and led Harriet to suspect immediately that the woman had been engaged to spy on her. As someone who treasured her time alone, the thought of having someone shadowing her at all times was unbearable, but she had not voiced these thoughts, instead saying that there was really no need for him to go to such expense, as she knew she had as yet not justified the money he had already spent on her. If he would allow her access to his library while he was away, and to the archery equipment, she would be quite happy to occupy herself.

To which he had replied that he wouldn't hear of it, and that it was no trouble at all. And so, two days later a thin po-faced

THE ECCENTRIC'S TALE: HARRIET

woman, introduced as Mrs Grave, a surname that profoundly suited her, took her place at Harriet's side. Within hours Harriet was sure that her suspicions were founded. Mrs Grave was the least suitable woman Harriet could imagine to be a companion, not only for her, but for any lady.

For a start, she had no conversation. At all. Any attempts Harriet made to start one were met with monosyllabic answers. She was not interested in music, gardening, embroidery, politics, riding, dancing - she seemed to have no interest in anything except attaching herself to Harriet's side at all times, even sleeping on a pallet at the foot of the bed at night.

Any joy Harriet had at not having to face her sullen husband over the breakfast table, or endure his equally sullen sexual assaults on her at night was obliterated by the perpetual gloomy presence of her 'companion'.

And *still* she had endured it, doing her best to pretend the woman wasn't in the room with her, ignoring her completely as much as possible, but doing nothing that could be interpreted as hostile. She told herself that it was not Mrs Grave's fault, that the woman was probably desperate for the money Raphael paid her to be a spy, but although that helped to curb her irritation at the constant presence, it did not lift her resentment and misery.

And then today at the end of September, her courses had come again, and she wondered what petty spiteful act Raphael would think of now. Because he could do anything he wanted, short of commit violence against her, and in fact he could even do that within reason.

She had been married for three months, and they were both young. This increasingly unbearable existence could go on for countless years if she didn't give him a damn boy child, and maybe even if she did. Already she was growing to hate him. But she was growing to hate herself more for just lying down and letting him walk all over her, in the hopes that he would come round in time.

She needed to think. And in order to do that, she needed to be alone. So whilst having breakfast she informed the serving footman that she would like some wine with her food, and ordered him to fetch the key to the wine cellar from the steward. When he had and asked what wine she would like, she told him that she would accompany him to the cellar, as she really could not decide without seeing for herself.

It was most irregular, but she was the marchioness and he was a servant, and as his lordship was away, no one could object to it. No order had been issued banning her from entering the wine cellar. So they went down, Mrs Grave following, as it was now clear that she had been ordered to accompany Harriet absolutely everywhere. *It's a miracle she doesn't stand over me while I have a shit,* Harriet thought.

Once in the cellar Harriet told the footman to wait at the door while she made her choice, then dawdled around, moving into the depths of the extensive rooms with a candle until she was at the farthest point of the cellars she could get to.

And then, suddenly, having memorised her route, she blew out the candle and made a run for it, charging up the steps to the startled footman, pushing him through the door and then closing and locking it.

"Thank you," she said calmly. "I find that the walk has in fact driven away my desire for wine after all. And for food, in fact. I shall take a turn around the gardens instead, as it's such a lovely day."

The footman looked at the door, and at the extinguished candle in his mistress's hand. Following his gaze, she smiled and handed the candlestick to him.

"I see no reason for you to remain here, or anywhere in the immediate vicinity. If you would return that to the breakfast room, I would be grateful," she said. "And I will return the key to the steward. Later. When I have finished my walk. You may tell anyone who asks that I was most insistent upon that."

Then she turned and walked away, but not before she had heard the quickly smothered laugh, had seen the footman's grin of amusement and understanding of what she had just done, and had realised that, even if it was unfair to call on them for support, she perhaps had *some* allies among the staff.

She walked around the gardens slowly, enjoying the bliss of being alone, not giving a damn that the miserable spying bitch was in the cellar, in the dark. She had had enough. She climbed up the spiral stairs to the top of the tower, the tower that Raphael had told her last week, just before he'd left for London, she must not climb again, because it was too dangerous for ladies to ascend alone. To hell with him. He knew she enjoyed standing at the top, looking at the view, feeling the wind blowing through her hair, remembering when she had made him capitulate to her wishes so that she would accept his marriage proposal.

He hated her for doing that and was going to make her pay, in increments, forever. She knew that now. Nothing she could do would make him forgive her.

She stood there and cast her mind back to when he had raised a topic with her in the dining room when there had been just the two of them dining with half a dozen footmen waiting on them. When had that been? Only a few weeks after their wedding, anyway.

"I wished to speak to you about Mr Harrison," Raphael had begun, wiping his mouth with a napkin and laying his knife and fork down on the plate, a signal at which the servants had to remove both the marquess and marchioness's plates, regardless of whether she'd finished her meal or not. Harriet had forked a huge pile of salmon into her mouth before it was whisked away, ignoring Raphael's look of disapproval at her bulging cheeks. Unable to speak, she'd chewed and waited for him to continue.

"He said that you came to visit him today, and asked some most intrusive questions about his work. He was concerned that he was no longer trusted."

Harriet had swallowed, taken a mouthful of wine, and now swallowed again.

"I went to see the steward to introduce myself properly, as I intend to do with the housekeeper tomorrow," she'd said. "I gave him no hint that I didn't trust him. I merely said that I would like to learn what he does. I'm not sure why he is so sensitive."

Raphael had eyed her with obvious disdain.

"He is not sensitive," he stated. "Mr Harrison has been with me for many years, and I trust him implicitly. He expected, as did I, that as a duke's daughter you would know the steward is responsible to the head of the household, not his wife. Therefore he quite reasonably thought his standard of work was being examined. You need not concern yourself with either him or the housekeeper. They are both experienced and capable, and have been running the house perfectly for years."

"My mother, the *duchess*," Harriet had responded, "taught me that it is the duty of a wife as the female head of the house to know all the affairs of the household, and to keep an eye on the senior servants."

"It is hardly my fault nor my steward's that your family were too impecunious to employ sufficient staff to run the house adequately," Raphael had said. "But my house is not run in such a slipshod manner, and you will respect that. You are not, nor will you ever be the head of the household, so you need not trouble yourself with anything regarding that. Your proper duties should be enough for you. I would have thought your mother would have taught you that."

She had picked up her fork and played with it, managing with an effort not to stab him in the eye and wipe the self-righteous sneer off his face forever.

"Clearly the proper duties of a duchess differ from those of the lower nobility," she had responded instead, watching with satisfaction as his sneer vanished. "Pray tell me the duties of a marchioness, then."

"Your primary duty, madam, is to give me a son. And while I'm waiting for you to do that, to entertain my friends' wives, behave meekly and with decorum and not get involved in things beyond your female understanding," he'd replied.

She had known then that this was going to be really hard. But she had also known that any protests she made would go unheeded. So until she proved her fecundity, she'd thought, she had only two choices; try to please him, or go to war with him. And as much as the latter option had appealed to her, she had known that ultimately she would lose if she did that, because he had all the weapons and would enjoy wielding them against her.

She had thought then that it was better not to give him the satisfaction of knowing how much he was getting to her. It would be good practice in subduing her volatile emotions, and when she went to court and met the king, she would do her utmost to make a friend of him or the queen, because what she needed was a powerful friend, as she had had in King Charles.

But Raphael had not taken her to Court, and probably had no intention of doing so, unless commanded to. He would not come

THE ECCENTRIC'S TALE: HARRIET

round in time, she knew that now. Beneath his groomed, cultured exterior and immaculate clothes lay a mean-minded petty tyrant, who would never forgive her for making him pay more than he had wanted to, to have her.

And she had let this spiteful creature insult her parents, who were worth a hundred of him, had let him lord it over her, thinking he would mellow eventually.

He would not mellow eventually. She might have to lie back and suffer him to sweat and pant over her every night as he tried pathetically to impregnate her, but she did *not* have to just meekly accept his petty tyranny. She did not want his kindness, his admiration, his affection. She did not want his forgiveness either, and never had, she realised now.

When she had met him before the wedding she had thought that the cool, controlled perfectly mannered face he had presented to her was a front, had hoped that beneath that was a real, living breathing human being with emotions, someone she could get to know, learn to like at least, if not to love.

When she was a small child her father had taken her to see an automaton, a model of a soldier that played a drum. She had been fascinated by it, but had found it a little unsettling too. In one way it seemed very lifelike – the eyes had opened and closed, the head had turned on its neck and it had really played the drum. But she had found it disturbing because although it *appeared* alive, it wasn't. It was rigid, and had no personality, no emotions, no sense of right and wrong. She had had nightmares about it for weeks afterwards, dreaming that it was walking across her bed, about to kill her.

And standing here, alone for the first time in weeks, with time and space to think, she realised that she felt the same way about her husband. He was like an automaton; cold, controlled, not quite human. She had never heard him laugh, raise his voice, be shocked or amused – he seemed to be emotionless, apart from this petty spite that was driving him to make her life miserable. She did not want him to love her, or to like her. She did not want his forgiveness. She did not want anything from him, except for him to leave her alone.

She despised him, as he clearly despised her.

But worse than that, she despised herself, for meekly lying

down and letting this emotionless puppet walk all over her. What was wrong with her? This was not what her mother had intended her to do when she had taught her to tame her wildness and behave acceptably in society. It would not make her parents happy to know that their daughter had become a doormat.

She had never let anyone do that to her before. And, she vowed now, she would never let anyone do that to her again, whatever the consequences.

If he was going to make her life miserable, then she could at least make his life miserable too. She could not use the methods he was using; she would have to be devious. But she was done with meek capitulation. Just knowing that raised her spirits, made her smile as the wind lifted her hair playfully and blew it across her face. She looked across the gardens to the house, wondering if the footman had told anyone about what she had done to her companion, wondering if word would get back to Raphael. And not caring one iota whether it did or not.

Right, you bastard, she thought, *if you want war, I'll give you war.*

Harriet Ashleigh, daughter of the sixth Duke of Darlington, descendant of royalty, albeit on the wrong side of the blanket, was back, and was about to put her mother's teachings to much better use than she had in the last months.

CHAPTER SIX

October 1688

Harriet stood five steps up on the staircase, looking at the mass of servants assembled in the enormous marble-floored hall. Every face was looking up at her, and every face had a worried expression, except for one, which had an expression of disapproval and contempt.

Ignoring the rest, Harriet decided to deal with the disapproving one first. She had already given Mrs Grave the day off and had insisted she go into town, going so far as to call the carriage for her and see her off the premises herself. Her companion had done her utmost to refuse, but Harriet was not a duke's daughter for nothing. She knew how to be imperious. She was done with being submissive to her husband, so didn't really care what he would think about her actions.

Now she turned to the steward.

"Thank you for instructing the servants to assemble here, Mr Harrison," she said. "What I am about to say does not apply to you, and as you tell me continuously, you are a very busy man. I would not keep you from your business affairs. You may go."

"No, I will stay and listen. Although I am busy, it's true," he replied.

"Indeed. Even more so now you have to write to Lord Hereford and inform him of my unconventional action today," Harriet replied. Some of the worried expressions in the hall now became amused instead. "But you mistake me, sir. I am not *asking* but *commanding* you to go. Now," she added coldly, when he still hesitated.

"This is most irregular," he began. "I think you should—"

"Mr Harrison," Harriet interrupted, "it may have escaped your notice that I did not in fact marry you, but the marquess, and that I am neither required nor do I desire to pay any attention at all to what you think. If my husband has something to say about my actions, he can tell me himself. When he comes home. In the meantime you will obey me, sir, or you will be ejected."

A wave of titters ran across the hall, and the steward, red-faced, departed. He would certainly write to Raphael immediately, Harriet thought, but although her husband was taking great pains to keep her ignorant of what was going on at Whitehall, that something *was* going on she was certain. And something momentous too. Hopefully momentous enough to keep him away from home for a long time, although he could not stop this meeting in any case.

"That's better," she said to herself, although seventy pairs of ears, now listening intently, heard her. She brought her mind back to the present moment, and smiled across the sea of faces. My God, did they really have this many servants, just to look after two of them?

"Please don't be worried," she began, "I haven't called you here to give you bad news, not at all. I merely wanted to introduce myself to you." The expressions now became puzzled. "Yes, I know I've been here for some time, and you all know I am the marchioness, but that is not what I mean by 'introduce'," she explained. "When I lived with my parents, we considered our servants to be part of the family. I knew all their names, and if they had any concerns they knew that they could come to one of us for advice or assistance. I've been here for four months now, and not only do I not know your names, but I don't even know your faces, because every time I come within ten feet of you, you either drop to your knees and lower your heads or you squash yourselves into the wall until I've passed.

"I have to admit I've never seen such extraordinary behaviour before. I'm a marchioness, not a goddess. None of the servants at my father's house behave in such a way, and he's a duke, so I'm not sure why a marquess's servants should have to. I know my husband has commanded it, and I know he is your employer. But I also wanted you to know that I neither like it, nor do I wish you to behave this way to me, at least when Lord Hereford is not at home. However, if you feel you must continue to kneel or turn away from me, I will understand completely. I would also like you to know that if you have any worries or concerns that you wish to discuss with me, I will be very happy to listen to you, in confidence, and if I can help you in any way, I will. In short, I would very much like to get to know you all a little better than I do at the moment. Thank you for your hard work in the house and gardens. It's very much appreciated. That's all I wanted to say."

She stopped, and watched as the expressions changed, some of them becoming wary, but many regarding her with the beginnings of warmth, of friendliness. She was glad now that she hadn't decided to address them from the first-floor balcony as Raphael would have done; there was already too much distance between her and the staff. Here on the stairs she was almost amongst them, and they appreciated the gesture.

Suddenly to her surprise someone started to clap their hands, and then another person joined them, and another, until almost everyone was clapping. Harriet smiled, then curtseyed to them exactly as an actress would on the stage, and they understood and laughed. Then as the meeting was over, they started to disperse, but over half of them came to her before they left and told her their names, and what their job was in the household, and she chatted with them as though she was their equal. Which, in a way she was, as she was just as dependent on Raphael as they were, but sadly could not just walk out of her job as his wife, as they could leave theirs if they wished.

That being said, she had just fired her first shot in the war with her husband, and it felt very, very good.

* * *

Harriet waited for two days, knowing that Harrison would have probably dispatched a letter to Raphael as soon as whoever was on his side had informed him of the contents of the meeting. But Raphael did not come haring home. So he either didn't think her action was important, or the situation at Court was serious enough to stop him returning to discipline her. It would be useful to find out which was the case, and to see if her talk to the staff had had the desired result.

So she sent Mrs Grave off to find a particular shade of green silk thread for the leaf she was embroidering on a waistcoat that Raphael would never wear, because neither her love of pointless sewing nor her love for her husband had increased in the last few months, and both of those factors were reflected in the quality of the embroidery.

Then she ran down to the servants' hall, appearing abruptly in the middle of their lunch. There was a panic and clatter as everyone stood. Harriet raised her hand.

"Please sit down and carry on with your meal," she said. "I have no wish to disturb you. I only wanted to ask if any of you has a newspaper that I could look at. The library is locked, so I cannot access Lord Hereford's periodicals."

No one sat down, but at least they didn't all crash to their knees or leap for the wall, which was something. There was a moment's silence, and then one of the footmen spoke.

"I take the London Gazette, my lady," he said. "We…some of us take turns to read it. It's in my room, but I can fetch it if you'd like."

She bestowed one of her warmest smiles on him.

"That would be absolutely delightful, Brian," she said. She'd made a huge effort to memorise the names of all the servants who'd introduced themselves to her two days ago, and was now rewarded with a look of gratitude. He shot off to get the paper, and Harriet smiled at the others.

"For God's sake, sit down," she said. "Don't let your food go cold. If you don't I'll have to leave, and if I do, that Grave woman will find me and tell me off for consorting with you all."

One of the maids burst out laughing then stifled it, but the atmosphere relaxed and everyone sat down. After a minute Brian returned with the newspaper, which he handed to her with a bow. A normal bow.

"Could I keep this for a short time?" Harriet asked. "I'll return it once I've read it of course."

"I'd be honoured, my lady," he said, blushing.

Mrs Grave was nowhere in sight when Harriet got back to her room, but better safe than sorry, so grabbing a candle she retired to the privy, and sitting down, began to read. The paper was only

THE ECCENTRIC'S TALE: HARRIET

two pages long; she could read that in the time it took someone to empty their bowels.

In the end it was the sound of Mrs Grave knocking tentatively on the door that roused her from her perusal.

"Are you ill, my lady?" the woman asked. "You have been there for a long time."

Had she? How long had she been there? She had read the paper once, and then, not believing her own eyes, had read it again. And again. And then she'd sat, staring at the candle flame until the tapping on the door roused her. She shook her head to clear it, then the tapping came again.

"I am well," Harriet replied. "Just a little costive, that is all. I will be out in a minute."

"Shall I ask a maid to prepare a tincture of valerian or liquorice for you?" Mrs Grave asked when Harriet emerged a few minutes later.

"Yes, thank you, that would be very kind. I won't take any now, as I did manage to relieve myself a little, but if I have a tincture to hand, I can use it later if needed."

I have to get into the library, she thought. Raphael would have past periodicals there. She had to know how long this had been going on, and could not demonstrate her utter ignorance of nationwide affairs by asking the servants to enlighten her. That would undermine her position and authority with them, as Raphael knew. That would have been part of his reason for denying her access to his reading materials, knowing that if the master did not respect his wife, his servants would have no great need to either. Of course that was only effective if the wife in question chose to accept being disrespected. Which this wife no longer did.

The following morning, some time after drinking a cup of the strong sweet chocolate she hated with her companion, which disguised the taste of the laxative in one of the cups beautifully, Harriet made her way downstairs. As usual, there was a footman sitting outside the library door, partly to be on hand to answer the door, and partly to show that the room was out of bounds. He stood as she appeared, and made a normal bow to her. A good sign.

"Good morning, Paul," Harriet said cheerfully. "How are you today?"

"I'm very well, thank you for asking, my lady," he replied, then followed the line of her gaze, which had moved to the library door. He had been at lunch yesterday when she'd invaded the servants' hall.

"Is Mrs Grave not in attendance on you, my lady?" he asked.

"No," Harriet replied. "She is, sadly, most horribly indisposed. A flux, which came upon her quite suddenly this morning. I believe she will be indisposed for some hours."

"Ah. In that case, I can tell you that the key to the library has most unfortunately been misplaced," Paul said, smiling broadly. "I have been told to sit here because the door is unlocked, to make sure no one goes in. Mr Harrison is conducting a search for the key at the moment."

"Is he?" Harriet said.

"Indeed. I'm sure he'll find it – eventually. But in the meantime I cannot always watch the library door, you will understand, as I need to also answer the front door to anyone who calls."

Harriet grinned.

"I believe I just heard someone knock," she said.

"I believe you did," Paul replied, moving toward the front door.

Once inside, the door firmly closed, she lost no time in finding what she was after, and sat in a chair to read the newspapers and catch up on political events from her wedding day until now. Once again she was aroused by a light tap on the door, and hurriedly gathering the papers together she replaced them on the shelf, then exited the room.

"It seems Mr Harrison has found the key," Paul said softly. "I think he will come to lock the door in a few minutes."

"I am very grateful, Paul," she said. "I always believe loyalty should be rewarded, and when I am in a position to do so, I will."

"My lady?" he said, as she turned away.

She turned back, expecting he was going to ask her for something immediately, and hoping she could grant it.

"I just wanted to thank you for what you said to us all," he told her. "It meant a lot to us – to most of us."

"Thank you," she replied. "I meant every word I said."

"We know that, my lady," he said. "That's why we'll help you, when we can."

THE ECCENTRIC'S TALE: HARRIET

She had hoped that the talk to the servants would soften them towards her a little, make them more well disposed towards her. But already they had facilitated her spending a few hours in the library and reading all the news Raphael was keeping from her. She knew the key had not been lost, but hidden, just to allow her to do as she wished.

She had forgotten how powerful servants really were, and how important it could be to have them as discreet allies. She smiled and went upstairs to see whether Mrs Grave was any better.

* * *

The following day Raphael returned home mid-morning, and summoned her to his rooms half an hour later. Harriet entered to find him pacing up and down the room like a caged lion. When he heard the door open he turned and frowned at her, his face slightly flushed, but whether that was from the exertion of the ride home to discipline her or from temper, she had no idea.

"Good morning, Raphael," she said calmly. "I have asked cook to provide a meal for you. Shall I have the fire lit in your bedroom?"

"I cannot stay," he replied. "I must return to Whitehall this afternoon. I came because Mr—"

"Yes, of course you must," she interrupted sweetly. "How goes the war? Have the Dutch sailed yet? Will you be fighting for the king, or is your role a more administrative one?"

The look of utter shock on his face warmed her heart.

"I cannot believe you thought that I would not find out at some point that the whole country is on the brink of war. After all, everyone else knows, from the ploughman to the scullery maid. Indeed I am at a loss to know why you tried to conceal it from me," she said sarcastically.

"It is none of your concern," he replied petulantly.

"Of course it's my concern!" she cried. "James is *my* king as well as yours. I could be raising men from the servants and tenants to fight for him, as every noblewoman whose husband is away will be doing. I could be making preparations in case we do end up fighting the Dutch, as seems very likely. Did you think I would just sit embroidering flowers and enduring that tedious woman's monosyllabic conversation while the country burned around me, and not notice?"

131

"You are being hysterical," he said. "This is why—"

"I am *not* being hysterical, I am being angry," she replied. "By keeping me in the dark you are undermining my authority with everyone, including the servants. That is beneath even you, Raphael, and does you no credit."

Now he flushed crimson and strode toward her, no doubt expecting her to back away, become submissive, as she had been for far too long. She stood her ground.

"I am here because it seems you have been trying to *exert* your authority with the servants," he shouted.

"That is Harrison's supposition, not the truth. He was not there. I called them together to introduce myself properly to them, as it is my place, indeed my wifely duty to do. It was the first opportunity I have had to do so, and I took it. That is all. I am hardly to blame if Harrison has brought you galloping here because of his erroneous assumptions.

"But I am glad he did, because we need to discuss this likely war," she continued, moving past him to the couch and sitting down. She might as well make the most of his shock at her uncustomary assertiveness. "I assume then, as one of the king's most trusted courtiers, you will be taking up arms for him?"

"Why, are you trying to tell me you would care if I were injured or killed?" Raphael asked mockingly.

"No. You have not done anything to make me care if you died," Harriet replied with a brutal honesty that shocked him, judging by the expression on his face. "But even so, I need to know if my husband is to go and fight. And we must raise men for the king. Every loyal landowner will be expected to do that."

"It has not come to that yet," he said.

"Oh. Are the newspapers lying then? *The Gazette* says that some twenty thousand men will sail for England next week, and that Newcastle, Derby, Jermyn and others are raising men to fight them. Is that not so?"

"I cannot stand here bandying words with you, madam, about things you do not comprehend," he replied. "I must return. You will summon no more meetings, nor do anything out of the ordinary without first asking my permission. Do you understand?"

She stared at him, understanding far better than he wished her to.

THE ECCENTRIC'S TALE: HARRIET

"My God," she murmured. "You are his right-hand man, yet you are thinking to abandon him."

He flushed scarlet and would not meet her eye when he answered, which told her far more than any words could.

"You will go to your rooms, and you will stay there until I write and tell you otherwise," he shouted, and then, turning away from her, he left the room abruptly.

She sat and listened to the door slam, then the front door, then the clatter of the horse's hooves as it galloped down the drive. She didn't care about his ridiculous order to stay in her rooms, which she had no intention of obeying. She cared about only one thing.

He was thinking to abandon his king, the man to whom he had pledged allegiance, who he had served, who was no doubt counting on him in his time of need.

She was married to a coward.

She was married to a traitor.

How the hell had it come to an invasion? Everyone had known James was a Catholic for years – there had been plenty of attempts to pass a law excluding him from inheriting the throne when Charles was king, but no one had tried to stop him being crowned once Charles was dead. It was true that since becoming king he had made some stupid decisions, including having a lot of Catholics around him and attempting to impose universal toleration of all faiths on a nation that was not only intolerant of Catholics, but hostile to them. But every king made stupid decisions.

So why, four years into his reign, would James' own daughter and her husband agree to try to usurp him, agree to plunge the whole country into another civil war, just forty years after the last one? Was history about to repeat itself, as it had with James' father? And would her husband, who had sworn allegiance, now betray him and sign his execution warrant?

No. He would rise. Surely he would rise and fight for his king.

* * *

He did not rise and fight for his king.

But in fairness, neither did many others. Instead King James' son-in-law, Prince William of Orange, landed in south-west England in November and almost immediately men rallied to him, leaving King James and his army thoroughly demoralised. Even James' second daughter Anne deserted him, and soon the trickle became a flood, with officers and noblemen either actively joining William or doing nothing at all. Raphael was one of those who did nothing at all.

Depressed, ill, and utterly despairing of victory, in December King James fled the country, managing on his second attempt to join his wife and son, who had already made their way to France.

With the throne now empty, on 13th February 1689, James' eldest daughter Mary and her husband, William of Orange, became King and Queen of Great Britain.

Although Raphael was only one of many of the king's trusted men who had refused to help him, this cut no ice with his wife, who from that day on regarded him with utter contempt. Having made the best use of the library and the servants' cooperation while Raphael was away, she understood better now why James had lost his throne. It was not only James' religious beliefs which had put terror into his Protestant subjects, but the fact that he had also tried to regain absolute power, a very dangerous thing to attempt in today's political climate. But he had already been fifty-two when he became king, and his heir, Mary, was a Protestant. Many of his subjects remembered the civil war that had resulted from the last ejection of a king from his throne, and had thought to passively resist his attempts at absolutism and religious toleration and wait patiently for James to die and Mary to take over.

But then in 1688 the queen had given birth to a prince. A Catholic prince. And in spite of the malicious rumours that the pregnancy had been fake and the boy baby smuggled in in a warming pan, in truth there had been witnesses to the birth. Unless something was done, this would be the start of a long-lasting Catholic dynasty.

And the fear of a Catholic absolutist dynasty had been greater than the fear of another civil war. It was, finally, as simple as that, but had galvanised the people in power to take action and invite William and Mary to depose James, although a good many of his subjects were outraged or at the least deeply uneasy at this casual removal of a monarch ordained by God to reign. After all, it was not for man to contest God's will. But in the main, in England at least, whatever their opinion, those disturbed by events did not take action to restore James, which was all that mattered.

It was true that Harriet's parents had gone to Court to welcome the new King William and Queen Mary and to pledge allegiance to them, but they had never been James' close confidantes – he had ignored them completely, and now he had fallen their star was finally rising.

But in Harriet's view, for whom trust and loyalty was *everything*, deserting your king when you had been his trusted counsellor for over four years was despicable. And the fact that Raphael had acted pragmatically to save himself and his estate did not make his action honourable. Charles had been her king and her friend, and she would have died or killed for him without hesitation if it had come to it. She had thought that was what all friends did for each other. Perhaps true friends *did* do that. In which case determining who was genuine, out of all the people who professed friendship, was instead the issue.

Although she had never been to Court, she had not forgotten King Charles' warning about the spiders and the webs, although it was only now that it occurred to her that she was actually living with one of the duplicitous, traitorous spiders, and that the courtiers' webs were not confined to Whitehall. She had been caught in Raphael's web for some time, but was now cutting the threads, one by one. Or at least disturbing them, rather than lying passively waiting to be devoured as she had been previously.

* * *

September 1690

Abandoning James might have allowed Raphael to continue living in luxury in England rather than having to join his king in exile, but it had not assured him of a place at the new Court, so he was now at home most of the time, with the result that his relationship with Harriet had deteriorated rapidly, and by mutual agreement they spent the minimum amount of time possible together.

Due to his presence the library was once more out of bounds for her, but Harriet was able to keep up with current affairs due to a benevolent fairy, who left the *London Gazette* under her pillow on a regular basis, and removed it again a few days later. So it was that she discovered that King James, far from accepting his exile, and prompted by King Louis of France, had set sail for Ireland, hoping to gain enough support there to launch an attempt on England to regain his throne. It had been taken seriously enough for King William himself to sail to Ireland and fight at the head of what was now his British army, which had ultimately resulted in the defeat of James' army and his return to exile in France.

Of course Harriet knew that the *London Gazette* was the Court newspaper, so she was effectively only obtaining a one-sided view of events, but whether William and Mary were truly as popular as the *Gazette* made out or not, they had not been dislodged from the throne, and any risings for the exiled king, whether reported or not, had not been successful. Neither William nor Mary had called on Raphael to attend them at Court, but whether that was because they suspected his loyalty due to his service to James or whether they thought as little of cowards and turncoats as she did, Harriet did not know, and could not ask.

The house was large enough for them to hardly meet at all, but they still endured each other's company for the now infrequent social events, and for the regular copulations which had, after two years, still not resulted in a pregnancy. Raphael took great pains to make sure she was aware of his authority over her constantly, by denying her access to any room or activity he knew she enjoyed, whilst he, of course, went out hunting and visiting friends regularly. In two years she had neither ridden a horse nor passed beyond the garden gates.

In private with him she was acerbic, not giving a damn what he thought of her any more. If he was determined to hate her, she would damn well give him reason to. After all, what could he do to her? There were only two ways to get rid of unwanted wives; one was to attempt to divorce them, which would cause an unholy scandal, and which she would welcome in any case; and the other was to have them declared insane and committed to a madhouse, which she could imagine him relishing, but for two things. Firstly, if he did that she would never give him the heir he so badly wanted, nor her father's dukedom. And secondly her parents, now hopefully rising in power and influence, would never allow him to do that to her.

In public, however, up to now she had continued to behave as a marchioness would be expected to, and in fact made a great effort to be the epitome of respectability and sociability with the stultifyingly boring guests she was obliged to entertain. When her husband was present at such events they were polite but cool with each other, but as most noble marriages were made for practical rather than emotional reasons, no one thought this coolness out of the ordinary.

This was thanks to another of King Charles' pieces of advice to her; "Often it is necessary to be friendly to people who you don't like at all, or who don't like you," he had said. "In fact, if you want to do as you like, it's vital." One day she hoped somehow to get away from Raphael, and to do as she liked, and to do so she might need the assistance of some of these titled, influential people.

She had hoped that going to war with Raphael would give her satisfaction, would make the long days more meaningful. It had restored her self-respect, but that was the only positive. It had also made her realise just how powerless and lonely she was. It was true that many of the servants were sympathetic to her plight, but she dare not ask anything of them, because if they were fired or worse as a result, she had no power to help them.

She also suspected that Raphael was denying her access to correspondence from her parents. The last letter she had received from them had been in June, when they had told her that they had been invited to Court and had asked her to pray that they would be successful in their attempt to gain royal favour. Since then she had heard neither from them nor from her sisters, but when she had brought the subject up with Raphael one evening as he was leaving her bedroom, he had merely said that if they had been accepted at Court they would no doubt be too busy to write to her, and would not say any more on the matter.

Harriet knew full well that no matter how busy they were, her parents would make time to write to her, and Melanie and Sophia would definitely continue writing regularly.

So for the moment the gnawing loneliness was banished by the problem now consuming her mind - how to get a letter to her family that would *not* be intercepted and read or withheld. If she could do that, she could invite them to visit her unannounced, as she knew Raphael would never have the courage to refuse them access in person, no matter how much he wanted to.

Hoping for an opportunity to get a letter past Raphael's eagle eye, she sat down one rainy evening at her writing desk and penned one, having sent Mrs Grave off on a fruitless errand to the other side of the house. She had written as quickly as possible, heedless of neatness, blots or accurate spelling, intending to hide it until a suitable opportunity to post it occurred. But Mrs Grave had returned quicker than she'd expected, and had seen her putting the finishing touches to it as she entered the room.

"Oh, you are writing a letter," she said, placing the jar of glass beads on the table next to her.

"Yes," Harriet replied crossly, scattering enough sand across the wet ink to conceal the words from her nosey companion, before picking up the beads. "I thought to trim my lilac satin with these. What do you think?"

Mrs Grave was not to be so easily deflected.

"If you have finished your letter, I'll ensure it is taken to the post for you tomorrow," she said.

Ensure it's taken to Raphael for scrutiny, no doubt receiving his thanks and a coin to add to your collection, Harriet thought. Any sympathy she might have once had for this woman's possible plight had long since vanished, following a frank conversation she had had with her a few weeks ago.

Harriet had asked her openly why she stayed, as she was clearly not suited to be a companion, having no conversational skills, and could not be happy being a spy. Stung, Mrs Grave had retorted that she was not paid to converse about trivial topics but to ensure that her ladyship behaved properly when Lord Hereford was not around to see her. She had been employed, she said, for her mature and sensible attitude, which the marquess had hoped might rub off on his wife.

Harriet had vowed then that the old bitch would live to regret that condescending comment, but it was not yet time for open hostility towards her. She did, however, find an awful lot of things she needed that just happened to be a great distance away, and which neither her ladies' maid nor her chambermaid could be spared to fetch, with the result that the woman spent a good part of her day running all over the house. She might dare to be impertinent, but she could not refuse a direct order of that sort from her mistress.

THE ECCENTRIC'S TALE: HARRIET

Now Harriet bit back the sarcastic retort on her tongue, and smiled up at the cold face of the older woman.

"No, I have not quite finished my letter yet," she said. "But when I do, I will give it to you."

Later, when Mrs Grave went to the privy, Harriet scrawled her name on the bottom, folded it and tucked it inside her pillowcase, and when her companion rejoined her she was watching some screwed-up papers burn to a crisp in the fire.

"I changed my mind," Harriet said. "I was not really in the mood to write. I'll try again tomorrow."

Now she just had to find a way to post it without involving any of the servants, if possible.

* * *

Harriet lay on her back with her legs open, staring past her husband's shaved head which loomed above her as he attempted once again to impregnate her. While he grunted and sweated she occupied herself by looking at the bedhangings and wondering which of the servants she could enlist to help her in the matter of the letter.

Two weeks had passed since she had hidden her missive to her mother in the pillowcase, and there had not been the slightest opportunity to get it to the post. Either she would have to give in, or risk a servant's job. But if he was successful, then she could ask her mother to employ him when she came to visit. Brian might be the best choice, because—

"For God's sake, it's like fucking a corpse," Raphael panted, interrupting her thoughts. "Can't you at least pretend to enjoy it?"

"No, I'm not that good an actress," she replied. "Why, how many corpses have you fucked?"

He stopped thrusting, his erection subsiding, and stared at her.

"To be able to make the comparison," she added.

The blow when it came shocked her, because although he had restricted her to the point where the only pleasure she still had was walking in the gardens, until now he had never struck her.

"Damn you, woman, you will *never* speak to me like that again, not even when we are alone," he said, clambering off her and going to the door.

"You wish me to lie to you then, even in private?" she asked, closing her legs and pulling down her nightgown. "It won't make you any more potent if I pretend to enjoy it, you know."

"I should never have married you," he spat. "I should have known that anyone as ugly as you was bound to be barren and useless." Before she could think of a retort he left the room, slamming the door behind him.

Well at least he stopped, she told herself, getting out of bed and washing herself thoroughly from the basin and ewer on the nightstand, as she always did after he'd finished and left her. She felt the blackness of despair rise up, and fought it back down, telling herself she would speak to Brian tomorrow, get the letter to the post. Further than that she would not think. Taking her life one day at a time was all she could do.

The next morning she took her time getting dressed, telling her ladies' maid that Raphael had hit her when she saw her observing but not commenting on the dark bruise on her mistress's shoulder where his blow had landed. She was not going to lie about his assault as women commonly did, saying that they had walked into a door. She had never walked into a door in her life, and was not about to start now. Let the servants gossip – more of them might turn against him as a result.

At the bottom of the stairs she turned toward the breakfast room and then stopped as the footman stood and made to open the door for her.

"Wait," she said. "Is my husband still eating? I am very late."

"He is, my lady," the footman said.

Oh to hell with it. She wasn't hungry anyway, and had no wish to meet him this morning, had no wish to meet him at all, in truth, but particularly not while her shoulder throbbed with every move she made, reminding her of his attack on her. She would go for a walk in the gardens first, calm herself, and by the time she came back he would hopefully have left.

She sent for her cloak, then trotted down the stairs and across the hall, and waited for the footman sitting by the front door to stand and open it for her. But instead he stood with his back to the door, facing her, and blushed scarlet.

"Whatever's the matter, Mark?" Harriet asked.

"Er…my lord…he…er…he…"

THE ECCENTRIC'S TALE: HARRIET

"He what? Tell me."

"He's instructed that you are not to leave the house, my lady," Mark said.

"What? I'm merely going for a walk in the gardens, as I do every day," Harriet said.

"I…he expressly said you were not to leave the house at all, that you are not allowed in the gardens any more, unless he expressly orders it," the footman said. Everything about him screamed his reluctance to perform this duty, and in spite of the rage rising in her at Raphael's pettiness, at his decision to deny her the last thing that gave her any pleasure, Harriet felt sympathy for this poor man. She could not vent her anger on him. It was not his fault.

She turned and walked across the hall and down the corridor into the chapel, which contained the first sash window that opened onto the outer part of the house. She presumed that the inner court with its fountain and flowerbeds would not be out of bounds to her, not least because the corridors that surrounded it were still not enclosed, and she could be continuously observed from the house if she was there.

It was the outer gardens that he was forbidding her access to, the gardens that she walked in every day, no matter the weather. The gardens that were her only comfort, in spite of the fact that she was not allowed any say in their design or maintenance. With the wind in her hair and the sun or rain on her face she could still pretend that she had *some* freedom, had some control over her life. She was not about to relinquish that.

Startling the maid who was placing flowers on the altar, Harriet strode to the window and standing on the pew opened it, then looked out. There was a drop of about six feet or so to the ground, which was no doubt why Raphael had thought she wouldn't attempt to leave the house this way.

She pulled herself up so that she was sitting on the windowsill, then swung her legs out, before twisting so that she could grip the edge of the outer sill and lower her body until she was hanging by her fingers from the sill. Then she let go, and landed safely on her feet on the path, having by this way only dropped a short distance, although her bruised shoulder protested at being forced to take her weight. Then she strode off across the lawns, not stopping until she reached the walled garden, where she knew she could not be observed from any of the house windows.

Once inside, she walked down the garden paths, breathing deeply, trying in vain to calm her temper, to push back the despair that threatened to overwhelm her, to weaken her. If she accepted this, he had won. She would not tolerate complete imprisonment, isolation and physical violence. To hell with him. To hell with the gossipy women he expected her to entertain. To hell with this marriage. She would die before she would let him destroy her. She might have no weapons, no power, but by God she would make an unholy noise as she went down.

She stood in the middle of the garden, fists clenched, staring up at the sky, and, remembering happier days lying on the grass with Jem while staring at the same sky, her eyes filled with tears of rage and misery.

"Fuck you, you fucking fucker!" she yelled at the clouds, determining that from now on she would use that word as noun, verb, adverb, adjective, at every possible opportunity, that word that he thought he could use to her, but which she could not utter in response.

"Er…" came a very small voice from below.

Harriet opened her eyes and looked down, to see an extremely small, extremely dirty child dressed in rags, standing in front of her. Or he was standing until she looked at him, at which he dropped to his knees as though she'd kicked him.

"Oh, stand up, for God's sake," she said, irritated. "I'm not the bloody king! I'm sorry," she added in a softer voice. "I'm not angry with you. Stand up, child." She bent down and put her hands under his armpits, intending to lift him to his feet, but instead lifting him right off the ground, as he was much lighter than she'd expected him to be.

He stood in front of her, head bowed, and muttered something incomprehensible, clearly overawed at being in the presence of such a great lady. A great lady who didn't even have the freedom to walk in her own gardens.

Pushing her rage away, she knelt down next to him.

"Come, child, look at me. I'm not angry with you."

He looked at her with a pair of wide brown eyes. His face was filthy, his hair lank and crawling with lice, his clothes mere scraps

THE ECCENTRIC'S TALE: HARRIET

of material, his feet bare. It was October, with a frost still on the ground although it must be ten o'clock at least, and he was almost naked. He was shivering.

"My da told me to look for you," he said. "He had a message."

"I see. Well, you have found me, so he will be pleased with you. What was the message?"

The child looked at her blankly.

"I…I forgot," he admitted, mortified.

"It's all right," Harriet said. "Let's go to your da. I'm sure he'll remember the message. Have you got no coat, child?"

He looked at her blankly, as though he had no idea what such a thing was.

"Or shoes?" she ventured. He followed her gaze and looked at his feet.

"They broke," he said.

"You must be cold," Harriet observed. She had three petticoats, a gown, stays, a shift and a cloak on, and was not particularly warm. "Are you cold?"

He shrugged.

Harriet stood, lifting him easily, although her shoulder protested. Settling him on her hip she wrapped her cloak around both of them, and set off to the far side of the garden where he was pointing to a tumbledown building which she presumed was his father's shed. On the way she talked softly to him, and, soothed by the warmth and her gentleness, he told her that his name was Jack, and that his da looked after this garden, and he didn't have a ma, but his da loved him anyway.

As she arrived at the shed, a man appeared in the doorway.

"Don't kneel to me!" she shouted as she approached. He staggered a little, having been about to sink to his knees, then stood.

He must have missed my servants' meeting, she thought. She certainly didn't recognise him.

Smiling reassuringly at him she opened her cloak, revealing the small, now excited face of his son.

"Little Jack here found me," she said, "and kindly showed me the way to you. He said you have a message for me?"

"I hope he ain't been no trouble, my lady," the gardener said, clearly astounded that the marchioness was actually carrying his

143

son. "Go on in now, boy," he said as she placed him on his feet.

"He hasn't been any trouble at all. I was just concerned at him being outside on such a cold day, without proper clothes. He was shivering, poor mite. Would he not be better at your house, by the fire? Where is it?"

The gardener looked distraught.

"I'm not angry with you," Harriet said, "I'm curious. Does he have no clothes?"

"I…them's all the clothes he has, my lady," the man said. "When I gets my new clothes, I'll make new ones for him from these," he added.

Harriet looked at the gardener's rough shirt and breeches, which had clearly already seen a lot of wear. A very lot of wear.

"When do you get your new clothes?" she asked.

"Er…Lord Hereford hasn't said yet, my lady," he replied.

Harriet pursed her lips, thought for a moment, then came to a decision.

"Where are your lodgings? I'd very much like to see them," she asked.

"They's here, my lady," he said, pointing behind him at the tiny hut Harriet had thought was a shed. "But they's not fit for you to step in. And my boy…your dress…" His voice tailed off.

Harriet looked down at her cream woollen dress, which was streaked with dirt from the boy's feet.

"I would still like to see them," she said, and walking past him, stepped through the doorway.

There was nothing in the single room other than a pile of rags in one corner, which Jack had burrowed into, and which Harriet surmised was where they slept, and one single shelf with two wooden bowls on it and a spoon. In the centre of the room was a round blackened space where the fire must normally be. But there was no fire now, and the room was very cold. She closed her eyes for a moment as a wave of shame washed over her. Until this second she had considered herself unfortunate, she, who lived in utter luxury. She had no freedom, but then neither did this man. He could not have, or he would not live here, surely. What hold did Raphael have over his servants, that they did not leave? It would not be difficult to find a better job than this! She could not ask the poor man such a question. He was already terrified. She

THE ECCENTRIC'S TALE: HARRIET

was the tyrant's wife, after all.

"You live here," she asked instead. "Just yourself and your son?"

"Yes, my lady. My wife, she died last year. It's not so bad. The roof don't leak, even when it rains heavy," he said unconvincingly. Harriet thought of Jeremiah and Jem, and the cosy cottage they lived in on her father's land. The cosy, warm, furnished cottage. She wouldn't keep pigs in here.

"You need to have a fire burning here, at the very least," she said, looking at the gardener's pinched features. "You look cold, and your son certainly is."

"I will, my lady. I'll buy some wood, as soon as I gets my wage," he said somewhat desperately.

"There are plenty of fallen branches in the woodland, just outside this garden," Harriet said. "Why do you need to buy wood? You can collect some from there."

The hunted look on the man's face should have given Harriet her answer, but she could not believe even Raphael would stoop so low, until the man confirmed it for her.

"We ain't allowed to take no wood, my lady," the man muttered.

"Not even the fallen wood?" she said. "There was plenty of it last time I was there, and I'm sure there's more since the recent windy weather. It's no use for anything else. It'll rot if it's not used."

"Yes, my lady," the gardener said politely.

"I'm sorry, of course you know that better than I do, being a gardener," she said. "Jack told me you look after this garden."

"I do, yes," he replied. "There's four of us as does."

"It's very beautiful," she remarked honestly. "It's one of my favourite parts of the grounds." It was. It was not as formal as the rest of the gardens, and there was always a profusion of flowers, even now with winter approaching, as the walls shielded the plants from the winds. "You're very skilled."

"Oh, thank you, my lady," the gardener said, smiling shyly and losing some of his fear of her, which was what she'd intended.

"In your work, do you ever use a wheelbarrow, and an axe?" she asked.

"Er…well, yes," he said.

145

"Excellent!" she responded crisply. "Could you fetch them here for me, please? Oh, and what was the message you had for me? I almost forgot."

"Oh! Lord Hereford wants you to attend him in the drawing room immediately."

Raphael knew she was not in the house then, if the gardeners had been instructed to search for her. Well, he could wait.

Fuck him, the fucking fucker.

Harriet smiled warmly up at the gardener.

"Thank you. I will. As soon as I've finished here, and seen your wheelbarrow and axe," she said. "So the sooner you fetch it, the sooner I can go back to the main house and attend my husband."

The gardener hurried off.

CHAPTER SEVEN

An hour later Harriet arrived outside her own front door and knocked on it. When the footman opened it, both his facial expression and the fact that he forgot to even bow, never mind kneel to her, told Harriet that she must look even more of a fright than she thought she did.

"We meet again, Mark!" she said brightly, walking past him into the hall. "I received a message that my husband wanted to see me in the drawing room. Is he still there?"

"Er…yes, my lady," the astonished footman replied. "But…er…my lord's oriental carpet…"

"Ah. Well spotted. Can't be leaving dirt all over the floors, can I?" she said cheerfully, noticing her muddy footprints. She kicked off her shoes, went to the drawing room, threw open the doors herself and walked in.

"You sent for me," she announced as she entered. Two of the three males in the room stood on hearing her voice, while her husband, sitting with his back to the door, offered her no such courtesy.

"Ah, Harriet, you have arrived *at last*. Our new neighbour, the Earl of Highbury has called to see us, and I wished him to meet you," he said.

Harriet walked forward, reaching out her hand to the visitor, then glanced down at it and withdrew it.

"Delighted to meet you, Lord Highbury," she said. "Better you don't kiss my hand though, eh, or even touch it at the moment. Same for you, young sir," she added, smiling down at the small boy next to him. "Have you called for refreshments yet, Raphael?" she asked.

147

"Dear God almighty!" Raphael cried as she came into his line of sight. "What on earth has happened to you?"

Harriet glanced down at her mud-smeared dress, at the torn lace dangling from the sleeve, at her scratched and dirty arms, and filthy stockinged feet, then smiled at the newcomers.

"Do forgive my slight disarray," she said to them with spectacular understatement. "I would have changed, but I was already late and did not want to keep my husband waiting any longer. His message to me did not mention that he had visitors. I was in the garden, Raphael," she continued, turning to him. "This morning I was informed by a footman that you have decided for some incomprehensible reason that I am forbidden to leave the house at all. I was sure this must be a misunderstanding, but the man was quite adamant, so I took the liberty of exiting the house by a different route than the front door." She turned back to the visitors. "I walk in the gardens every day – indeed it is my main pleasure."

"Did you exit the house via the chimney then?" Raphael asked coldly.

"No, of course not. If I had I would look like a chimney sweep and be black rather than muddy," she replied. "No, I climbed out of a window, far easier and more practical than climbing up a chimney then down from the roof, and was in the gardens when I met one of the gardeners' children. He was younger than you, my lord," she said to the child, whose eyes were brimming with amusement, as indeed were his father's, "but the poor thing was barefoot and almost naked, and shivering terribly. Imagine my surprise when I carried him home, to find that his father, who lives in the most appalling hovel, told me, upon me demanding to know why he had no fire burning there, that he is not allowed to take fallen wood from our forest!"

She looked at her husband, whose expression she would never, if she lived to be a hundred, forget. It was an expression that made her wish she had been this candid in front of guests years ago.

"Once again," she continued, "I was quite sure that there had been a misunderstanding, for I can see no reason at all why you would deny servants access to fallen wood, for which we have no possible use. The man is, I must say, an excellent gardener. Have

THE ECCENTRIC'S TALE: HARRIET

you seen our walled garden, Lord Highbury?"

"No, not as yet," Highbury commented. "We have only recently moved to the area. But I would very much like to."

"I would be delighted to show it to you! If my husband allows me to. So I took it upon myself to go and cut some wood for them, so that they would not freeze to death. I knew you would approve, Raphael, and I'm sure you will clear up the misunderstanding immediately so I do not have to collect wood every day for them, which I will otherwise be obliged to do. I could not possibly allow a small child to freeze to death because his father is so obedient to you. Oh yes, I also gave them my cloak, the red one."

The Earl of Highbury, on Harriet's gesture, sat down, his son following suit.

"The red one?" Raphael spluttered, looking far from approving about anything his wife had so far said. "But that was very expensive! It's fur-lined!"

"I know. But I thought that if I was not to be allowed in the gardens I would have no need of it, whereas he most certainly does, with no winter clothing and no access to firewood for either himself or his child. Far better used by them to save them from dying of the cold than hanging uselessly in my rooms, don't you think?" She smiled sweetly at her husband, enjoying herself thoroughly.

"Well, my lord," Highbury remarked, his voice somewhat choked. "It seems that whoever delivers messages to the servants needs to be severely reprimanded for a poor job. I can't imagine why anyone would deny their wife the innocent pleasure of walking in her own gardens, or indeed forbid the gathering of fallen wood by their outdoor servants. After all, it would keep the forest in better condition were it removed."

"Exactly my thoughts," Harriet said. "Shall I send for Harrison now for you to discipline him? It is he who delivers your orders, is it not?"

Raphael's face turned an interesting shade of red.

"This is clearly a misunderstanding," he finally muttered reluctantly. "Which footman denied you access to the gardens?"

"I have no idea. They all look the same to me. Isn't that the point of footmen? It's why they all wear the same livery and are of a uniform height and general appearance, isn't it?" she replied flippantly. "But I don't see why it matters who denied me, as it's hardly his fault if he is following Harrison's bungled instructions."

"I will deal with the matter later," Raphael said, clearly wishing himself anywhere but here.

"Excellent! Well, then," she said, "that is all settled. So we are now neighbours!

I do assure you I will be more presentable next time we meet, Lord Highbury."

"Your husband tells us that you are most accomplished on the harpsichord, my lady," Highbury said politely, his eyes dancing with laughter, "and that you might honour us with some music."

"Oh how kind he is!" Harriet said with transparent insincerity. "I do have some ability, although I'm sure you will have heard better. But I would be delighted to play for you. I hope it will compensate a little for my tardiness."

She went to the instrument in the corner, wiped her hands thoroughly on her skirt, then sitting, played a few pieces for them, during which time her husband seethed, the earl listened politely, and the child, who was certainly his son for he was an exact miniature of the adult, stared at her with an expression of wonder and admiration.

When she finished they applauded, and she returned to sit with them.

"You have some leaves in your hair. And a caterpillar," the boy said. "At the left side. It's about to walk down your neck."

Harriet reached up carefully, and captured a large extremely hairy brown specimen.

"How observant you are!" she said. "I would not have thought to see one at this time of year. I think he must have been keeping warm in the leaves for the winter. Would you like to take care of him?"

"Oh yes!" the boy replied eagerly, taking it from her and smiling as it crawled slowly up and down his hand.

"It is actually about your forest that we have come, as well as to introduce ourselves," Highbury said. "My wife also wished to accompany us, but is unfortunately unwell today. Nothing serious, however. She asked me to convey her apologies, and hopes that you would do her the honour of visiting her as soon as it is

THE ECCENTRIC'S TALE: HARRIET

convenient, my lady. I am sure you two ladies would get along very well."

"I would be delighted to," Harriet replied. "But I am afraid Raphael has ordered that I am not allowed out of the gardens. And that certainly is not a misunderstanding, as it has been in force since the day I married, over two years ago."

"How extraordinary!" said the earl. "You mean you have not been off your estate since you married?"

"No, you misunderstand me," Harriet said. "I have in fact not seen the estate at all, nor have I met any of my tenants as yet. I am not allowed out of the *gardens.*"

"Your concern for your wife's safety is quite remarkable, my lord," Highbury said to the marquess, "but I do assure you that Frances – that is my wife – rides out to visit her acquaintance regularly and has never had the slightest problem. Indeed now we are living here, she also travels to London alone, although then she does take an armed guard on the coach with her. If you cannot afford such a guard, my lord, I would be happy to lend you mine, so that your wife might travel a little and enjoy herself. Indeed I am sure my wife would appreciate your company on her London trips if you wish to accompany her, my lady."

Oh, this was wonderful! *He knows what I am doing, and approves,* Harriet thought. He was clearly too accomplished a courtier not to know he had just insulted the marquess abominably by implying he was miserly or poor. She smiled warmly at the earl, who returned the gesture. There would be hell to pay later, she knew that. But oh, it was worth it to watch the bastard squirm now.

"That will not be necessary," Raphael said irritably. "Of course you may visit the Countess of Highbury, Harriet, as she has so kindly invited you to."

"That would be wonderful. I accept your invitation, of course," Harriet said. "But you said you also wished to talk about the forest?"

"Ah, yes. William here is very interested in trees, and in wildlife, but our own woodland is but recently established, so he was hoping that with your permission, my lord, he might be allowed to visit your much more established woodland on occasion, to learn to identify different trees and other woodland plants, and perhaps go birds' nesting?"

"Yes, of course he may," Raphael replied.

"Indeed. There is a gate to the east of the forest," Harriet said. "So he may enter from your lands whenever he wants. In fact, as it is such a beautiful day, if you wish, I could show it to you now, along with the rest of the gardens, Lord William? I would think you have had enough of sitting politely in a room by now. I know when I was your age I found it extremely tedious to have to sit still and listen to adults talk about things I had no interest in. I am sure the men have important matters to discuss that would be of no interest to either ladies or children. With your father's permission of course."

William looked at his father, his eyes alight.

"May I, Papa?" he asked.

"We have ridden here this morning," Highbury said. "William is learning to ride and has his own pony now, so if you would accommodate him, I see no reason to refuse, if it please you, my lady?"

"I am sure you must have other duties today, my lord," Raphael said, clearly wanting to end this deeply embarrassing visit as quickly as possible. "It is really not the best time of year to see the gardens, either. Perhaps the spring would be better?"

"I assure you I have no other duties today," the earl replied, seemingly oblivious to broad hints. "And I am enjoying myself immensely."

"I am so glad to hear it," Harriet said. "In fact, as I have had no need to ride since I married two years ago, I am out of practice myself, so will ride very slowly and sedately. I need not change. This dress is quite ruined anyway, so will be suitable for riding through the woods. And then we can build the caterpillar a new nest of leaves for him to sleep in until spring. Shall we go?"

* * *

Later, father and son rode home slowly.

"Lady Harriet told me that I ride very well," the boy said, once he had settled to the walk of the pony.

"And so you do," the earl replied. "You will be a fine horseman one day. I am very pleased with your progress." William beamed. "I am very pleased with your conduct during the visit today as well. You behaved extremely well in quite unusual circumstances."

"Thank you, Papa," the boy replied. "I like Lady Harriet very well," he added after a few moments.

"Yes, she seems a most remarkable lady," the earl replied. "And what was your opinion of Lord Hereford?"

"Oh. I couldn't give an opinion of Lord Hereford, Papa," William said.

"Really? Why ever not?"

"Because you told me I must never speak ill of my elders, Papa."

Highbury burst out laughing, and his son looked across at him.

"I think I may make an exception this time, as we are alone, without even a servant to overhear us," the earl said.

"Then I don't like him," the boy said at once. "I think he's a cruel and spiteful man, and he thinks too much of himself and too little of others."

"Hmm. You take the lady's side then. Very chivalrous. But are you sure the Lady Harriet was being truthful?"

He always questioned his son's opinions, wanting him to be able to justify them. One day this boy, God willing, would inherit the estate and title, and when he did he would need to be able to make good, reasoned decisions. William, accustomed to this, thought for a moment, then replied at length.

"I think she was, yes. If his instructions really had been misunderstood Lord Hereford would have been angry rather than ashamed. And then she told us the truth when she said she hadn't ridden for two years, so I think she may have told the truth in everything. She showed me where she'd taken the wood from too, in the forest."

"How do you know she told the truth about not riding?"

"When we went to the stables to get Thunder," he patted his pony's shoulder affectionately, "the Master of Horse was very put out that she wanted him to saddle a horse for her, which he wouldn't be if she rode out regularly. He even said that they had no side-saddle. And Lady Harriet said she was very glad of it, for they were bloody awful things, and that she would get far more pleasure spreading her legs to ride a horse than she did spreading them for that bastard. I didn't really understand that bit, but the rest told me that she hasn't had a horse prepared for her before."

"Good Lord!" the earl said. "She actually said that?"

"Yes, Papa. I'd taken Thunder outside before she said it. I don't think she would have used the bad words if she'd thought I could still hear her. When the groom brought her horse out of the stable to the mounting post, his face looked like yours did when Lady Harriet walked in the drawing room this morning."

"Ha ha! I'm sure it did. Well, it seems we have interesting neighbours, William. Perhaps we should invite them to dinner so your Mama can meet them, when her tooth is not paining her so."

"I wish we could just invite the marchioness, Papa," William said.

"Well you must learn to be very cordial to everyone, whether you like them or not, you know, so this will be a good lesson for you."

"Yes, I suppose so," William replied unenthusiastically. "She knows a lot about plants and trees. I hope to see her when I ride in her forest."

"I'm sure you will, once Lord Hereford has sorted out the *misunderstanding* of his orders," the earl replied.

* * *

The little boy did indeed see the marchioness again, in fact the very next time he was in the forest, some days later. At first he heard her, so rode in the direction of her voice, finally emerging into a small clearing, at present populated by a number of very poorly dressed men, a large pile of wood, and Lady Harriet, clean and respectable-looking this time.

"Some of this wood has lain here for a long time," she was saying, "so it should burn well, once dry. When it's chopped you can store it in that temple to Diana that nobody ever goes in. The whole front is open, so the air will flow through and dry it nicely."

"Did Lord Hereford really say we could have all this wood?" one of the men said, then flushed scarlet, realising that he had just questioned her honesty.

"Ah, Lord William!" she cried as he rode into view, causing everyone to turn and look at him. "You have arrived just in time! This is the son of the Earl of Highbury, who is our new neighbour, and who was in fact present when the marquess

THE ECCENTRIC'S TALE: HARRIET

confirmed that his orders regarding the use of fallen wood had been misunderstood. My lord, I am sure you will confirm that and put these gentlemen's minds at rest?"

"Yes, of course," William said, pleased to be spoken to as though he were an adult whose views were of consequence. "He did indeed say that," he said to the men.

"Thank you, my lord." She came over to him. "I have no horse with me today, but if you will ride slowly, I will walk and show you a badger's sett if you like," she said.

"I will walk, and you may ride Thunder," William offered.

"What a polite child you are!" Harriet replied. "But I may be a little heavy for Thunder, and I like to walk. It is not far, near the gate between us. In fact part of the sett is probably on your land."

They went on together, leaving the men chopping wood in the clearing and piling it into wheelbarrows, until Harriet stopped in front of a hole in the side of a sloping part of the land.

"There," she said. "Badgers have a lot of entrances to their setts as they are quite social, but this one is in regular use. Have you ever seen a badger?"

"No," William replied. "I've lived in London since I was three. There are no badgers there."

"How old are you now?"

"Five."

"Only five! I thought you older by your attitude."

"How do you know it's in use?" William asked, dismounting and crouching down by the hole.

"It's very clean, and there's fresh soil there, from their digging." She pointed. "If it wasn't being used, at this time of the year there would be dead leaves drifting into it. They will be bringing bedding into it for the winter now. They come out in the evening to feed, but it might be a little dark by now to see them. Perhaps you would be better to come back in the spring with your father, when the evenings are a little lighter. You would have to sit up there, under the trees, very very quietly though, perhaps for a long time. Could you do that?"

"Oh yes! If it's for something so interesting," the boy said. "Would you like to come and see one too?"

"That would be lovely. But I think it better if we don't tell the marquess that there is a badger sett here. If we did he might send the gamekeeper to kill them, because they're thought to eat the game birds, you know, and to drive the foxes away. The marquess hunts regularly."

"Yes, Papa does too. I will join him when I'm a little older. Do you not hunt, my lady?"

"I used to, yes. But my husband forbade me to. In truth I preferred the fast riding around the countryside and the company to the killing part, but I do miss it."

"I won't tell anyone about the badger sett," William said. "Thank you for trusting me."

"What are you being trusted with then, William?" a voice came from nearby. Harriet and William, still crouching by the hole, looked up together, to see the earl leaning over the gate watching them.

"Lady Harriet was showing me a badger sett, Papa, and said in the spring we might come and sit and watch the badgers in the evening."

"I see. And would you like to do that?"

"Oh very much! Lady Harriet said she would like to do that too! But she said we must not tell the marquess, Papa, or he might have them killed."

"We will not, then. It seems you have made a conquest of my son, Lady Hereford," the earl remarked, smiling.

"Please, call me by my name, unless you want to stand on ceremony," she said. "I'm not one who feels I need to be reminded of my title all the time."

"Very well, Lady Harriet. Thank you. In which case, my given name is Daniel. I'm afraid I will have to deprive you of the company of my son. We have been called back to London, and must leave this afternoon."

"Oh. I hope there's nothing amiss," Harriet said.

"No, indeed, just Court business. The king and queen have moved to Hampton Court for the winter and are giving a ball for the king's birthday next month."

"You attend Court regularly, my lord?" Harriet asked.

"Yes. That's one reason why I bought this property, because it is in the countryside, which I do love, yet close enough to London for me to be there in a few hours if I ride hard. Of course I will be taking the coach today, for my wife and son are coming

THE ECCENTRIC'S TALE: HARRIET

too, so it will take a little longer."

"Are you acquainted with the Duke and Duchess of Darlington, by any chance?" she asked casually.

"Why yes! I would be so bold as to say the duke and I are friends. A most capital fellow. Are you acquainted with him, Lady Harriet?"

"You could say so, yes. He is my father."

The earl's eyes widened.

"Is he? Good Lord. Well, I will tell him tomorrow of my good fortune in finding that my neighbour is none other than his daughter! I shall give him and your good lady mother your regards, of course."

Harriet smiled.

"If you are willing, I would ask you to give them a little more than that, if you would be so kind," she said.

"Of course!"

"I would be very much obliged if you could give them this letter," Harriet said, producing a somewhat crumpled sealed missive from her pocket. "But I will be honest with you, sir. I have been trying to find a way to get this to the post for some while now."

"Can you not just give it to a footman to take?" the earl asked, puzzled.

"I cannot. If I could, I would not impose on yourself," Harriet said. "I have not heard from my parents in months. Raphael tells me he is sure they are too busy at Court to write, but we are a close family, and I find it hard to believe they would not send me at least a few lines, no matter how busy they are. I must confess that I believe letters between us are being intercepted, although I have no proof."

"Oh, you are a damsel in distress, as in *Le Morte d'Arthur!*" William cried. "I am reading it at the moment with my tutor. Papa, we must rescue her!"

The earl looked down at his son's earnest face, and tousled his hair affectionately.

"Indeed, my boy, I believe we must," he said, taking the letter from the damsel's hand. "But we must also keep this a secret between us. A noble secret. I am honoured to be entrusted with your correspondence, my lady. I will not fail in my quest," he concluded formally for the benefit of his son, who was ecstatic to be part of this adult intrigue.

"I am obliged to you, my lord," Harriet replied, curtseying deeply to both the earl and his son in keeping with the spirit of the moment.

She watched them ride away, then set off slowly back to the house. It took her half an hour to walk back, and it took that time for her to calm down and conceal the joy and excitement that would otherwise alert both her husband and his spy Grave to the fact that she had just won another victory.

Life was getting better and better.

* * *

November 1690

As Harriet had requested, her parents did not respond to her letter, but in the middle of November Amelia arrived unexpectedly and alone, informing the somewhat startled marquess that this was the first opportunity she had had to visit her dearest daughter, and that Stephen sent his apologies, but as he was now quite indispensable to the king he could not be spared, particularly at a time when the monarch was planning to travel to Holland.

"Melanie and Sophia send their love, my sweet," she said to Harriet, "they would also have come, but are waiting on the queen, so it is quite impossible!"

Having comprehensively conveyed just how very important and beloved her whole family was by the new monarchs, and thereby rendering the marquess incapable of raising objections to her visit, Amelia swept her daughter off upstairs, in the process taking in the character of Mrs Grave at one glance and slamming the door in her face as she was about to join mother and daughter in Harriet's private rooms.

"There," she said. "What a dreadful-looking woman. What is Raphael thinking of, employing her as your companion?"

"He's thinking of making me feel as restricted as he can, and of having someone who can report back every fart I make," Harriet replied. "Oh Mama, it is so good to see you!" And with that she burst into tears, which told Amelia more than any words could just how desperately unhappy her eldest daughter really was.

A few minutes later, Harriet, now sitting on the bed being warmly embraced by her mother as she wept, lifted her head from Amelia's shoulder.

"I'm sorry," she sniffed. "Whatever will you think of me? I didn't invite you here to bawl all over you."

"I think the same as I ever did of you, as you well know. Now, you must tell me what has brought you to this. You are really quite pale, child, and have lost weight too, I think."

So, after obtaining a promise from Amelia that she would not tell her husband, Harriet spent the next hour outlining the past two years of her life while her mother listened without comment.

"It doesn't sound as bad as it feels, now I'm telling you," Harriet admitted finally.

"It does to me, because I know you," Amelia replied. "You have always been full of energy and life, since you were a baby. What other women would find tolerable you will not. And it seems to me that the marquess is well aware of that, which is why he is able to make you so unhappy without doing the slightest thing that could justify a separation."

Harriet looked at her mother.

"I never thought of it like that," she said. "He seems hardly to notice I even exist. It never occurred to me that he's actually studied me enough to know what will make me unhappy. That makes him even more evil than I thought he was."

"You have not seen what men are capable of, sweetheart. Your father and I have been blessed in our marriage, and I had hoped you would be too. True, he did seem a little stiff and formal during your courtship, but I put that down to nervousness. I see I was wrong, or maybe I unwittingly chose to ignore the signs because we were so desperate for his money."

"Oh, Mama, you must not think like that! I know Papa would, which is why I made you promise not to tell him, but you are practical, as am I. It made sense, and the sacrifice seemed worth it. None of us could have known how spiteful he could be. Or that I would not get with child."

To Harriet's surprise, her mother blushed crimson at that. Yet she was not a woman to be embarrassed by *anything*.

"You are still trying?" Amelia asked after a moment.

"Yes, unfortunately. He is desperate for a son to inherit his estate *and* the dukedom. I used to think that if I managed to produce a boy he would let me have more freedom, but I don't think that any more. I hope I *never* have a baby."

"Oh, you must not hope that!" Amelia cried. "Babies are a great blessing. There is no joy on earth like that of holding your newborn child."

"I don't know. I think babies are boring," Harriet said. "They don't do anything interesting."

"But you must want children of your own!"

"*Children* are all right. I like them once they start walking and talking. Then you can do things with them. Highbury's little boy and I are becoming friends. We see each other regularly because he rides in our woodland. But he really is very mature for his age."

"Well, it's true that you can do more with them when they get older. But you will feel differently when you have your own baby."

"Maybe," Harriet said doubtfully. "But it's not looking as though I'll have the chance to find out, is it? After all, he could live for another forty years. Not that I would marry again, if he died. I hate being married."

"Marriage can be wonderful though," Amelia said. "I'm very happy."

"I know you are. But I think that's unusual. Most of the women I have to entertain while Raphael and their husbands go off hunting talk of nothing but how miserable they are. Unless they're spending hours talking about bloody fashion or destroying someone's reputation, that is."

Amelia laughed.

"You really haven't changed," she said.

"Oh, I have. I'm wiser now, and not as impetuous. I spent the first months actually being nice to the bastard, hoping that he'd soften in time, but now I've realised he never will, I'm working very hard to make his life as miserable as he's making mine. It's the only thing that kept me sane until I met the Earl of Highbury. At least now I get to teach little William about plants and animals, and I visit the countess from time to time. She's quite an interesting woman, and not a gossip, which is refreshing. We talk

THE ECCENTRIC'S TALE: HARRIET

about politics and articles in the periodicals."

"But you are still very unhappy."

"I won't lie to you, I am. But I will be happier if you can come to visit me, when your Court duties allow."

"I will be leaving Court soon," Amelia put in, blushing again.

"You have news of some sort. You keep going as red as a strawberry," Harriet said. "What is it?"

"I am with child," Amelia replied bluntly.

For a moment there was a silence as Harriet took this in.

"But…is it safe for you, Mama, at your age?" she asked tactlessly.

"Safe or not, it's in there, so it's a little late now to worry about that," Amelia pointed out. "But you make me sound like a crone! I'm forty-two, which is not young, but ladies older than I am have children quite successfully."

"In that case, this is wonderful news! Papa must be so excited!"

"He is, although he is also worried, but he was with all of you, because childbirth at any age is not without risk. And we were both very surprised. After all, it has been eleven years since your brother was born."

"And it was not for the want of trying, was it?" Harriet grinned.

"Harriet!" her mother cried.

"I'm sorry. Until I married Raphael I thought that all married people slept together all night every night. Then I found out that wasn't the norm at all. But I think it's lovely that you love each other so much!"

"I wish it could be the same for you," Amelia said.

"I wish he would die, and then I could be happy."

"Harriet!" her mother cried again. "You must not think that!"

"No, Mama. I must not *say* that, outside of this room. But I cannot help thinking it."

* * *

Amelia stayed for three days, during which time mother and daughter spent almost all their time together. On the second day the weather was sunny and unseasonably warm, and the couple decided to walk in the gardens. When they got to the front door,

Mrs Grave was waiting for them with their cloaks. She was already wearing hers.

"Thank you," Harriet said, taking the cloaks from her. "You need not come with us."

"His lordship has ordered me to accompany you on your walk, my lady," Mrs Grave said.

"You are not needed. Today my mother is my companion and I am hardly likely to have my virtue compromised in my own gardens."

Mother and daughter walked out on to the step, Mrs Grave following them.

"Are you hard of hearing?" Amelia said icily. "Your mistress has dismissed you for today."

"I answer to his lordship," Mrs Grave said, "and he told me—"

"Oh to hell with this," Harriet said impatiently, moving forward and stamping on the older woman's foot with her heel, so hard that all of them heard the crack of bone. Mrs Grave screamed in agony and crumpled to the ground, while Amelia looked on in horror.

"Paul," Harriet called calmly to a nearby servant, who had witnessed the whole incident, "Mrs Grave seems to have had an unfortunate accident. Would you kindly carry her to my room and ensure that the physician is summoned?"

"At once, my lady," he replied calmly.

"Excellent! Shall we go?" Harriet said coolly to her mother, then strode off down the steps.

"I can't believe you actually did that," Amelia said, once they were out of earshot.

"I am sick of her. She not only reports everything I do back to Raphael, but she delights in it, and delights in making me unhappy. I should have done it years ago. I think I broke a bone. If so, she won't be following me around the gardens for months."

"I do hope I never become your enemy," Amelia commented as they walked through the knot gardens towards the maze.

"How could you? I adore you, and you are family."

"Percy is family too," Amelia said dryly.

"He is. And that is why I only *threatened* to shoot him through the heart and didn't actually do it," Harriet pointed out.

Her daughter really was formidable, Amelia thought. How dreadful that that insipid, spiteful man had the legal power to control her.

"I hope you give me a brother," Harriet continued as they reached the fountain in the centre of the knot garden. "Raphael wants to redesign this, get rid of the dolphins and have a statue of Hercules or some such nonsense."

"Don't you approve?"

"It doesn't really matter whether I approve or not, does it? I'd change the whole place, if I had my way. I know all this clipped symmetry is the fashion, but I don't like it. I prefer natural-looking landscapes. Of course topiary gardens are a good way of showing how wealthy you are, as it takes an army of gardeners to keep them in shape, which is all that matters to Raphael. I haven't seen him walking in the gardens once, in two years. For him they are just a status symbol."

"He has so much land. He could allow you to have your own garden, to do what you wish with," Amelia commented.

"Yes, he could, but that would make me happier, so he won't."

"You *do* realise that if I have a boy, he will inherit the dukedom rather than any son of yours?" Amelia asked.

"Of course I do. That is why I want you to give me a brother. A boy would make you and Papa very happy, and Raphael very unhappy. What could be better? Although he will still want me to have a son to inherit all this. When are you going to tell him?" Harriet asked. "Or do you want me to?"

"No. I won't tell him at all. I'll just invite you both to the baptism," Amelia said. "Then try to find a way to keep you there when he leaves."

"He won't let me stay with you, if he comes at all. He'll probably make an excuse to decline. And he won't show you or anyone else his true colours. It will appear that I am being unfair to him if I try to leave him. And he can force me back to him, can't he?"

"Maybe we can get you a place at Court, although in truth you would probably be more restricted and bored there than here. Melanie is waiting on the queen and absolutely hates it."

They had still not found a solution by the time they got back to the house. It had started to rain, so they really had no excuse to stay out any longer. In truth there *was* no solution. Nothing Raphael was doing would be considered harsh by his acquaintance, by anyone in fact. He was very careful to see to that.

Which was why he did not deprive her of the things most women would want, such as clothes, jewellery, cosmetics, expensive scents, embroidery silks, music, tapestries for her rooms, and other things in which she had no interest. Instead he deprived her of archery, gardening, hunting, intelligent conversation, freedom.

It was a man's right to discipline his wife, even to strike her if he wished. She was his property, and he would have to behave with unspeakable brutality towards her for her to be justified in leaving him. Absolutely no one would think she was justified because he denied her access to pastimes that many people thought were masculine anyway.

When they got into the hall, they were informed that the marquess wished to have a private word with his wife in the library.

Harriet went to the library, accompanied by Amelia.

"Harriet," he said as she walked in, "I believe you have had a moment of insanity."

"My daughter has never had a moment of insanity in her life," Amelia said, following in behind Harriet.

Raphael inhaled sharply.

"Your Grace, I would have a private word with my wife, if it please you."

"Please continue," Amelia said, closing the door and standing with her back to it. "You cannot possibly object to my presence, my lord. After all, you ordered Mrs Grave to accompany us on our private walk today, and Harriet is clearly in as much danger here as she was in the gardens, so if you believed she needed the protection of that appalling woman there, you can hardly object to mine here."

Raphael was flummoxed. His expression told both women that he would like nothing more than to throw her out bodily. But he could not do that without causing a scandal. And she was in high favour with the queen, too.

"Well…er…Mrs Grave is quite badly injured, and I have had to summon a physician. She told me a remarkable story, that you maliciously attacked her without provocation! Really Harriet, this is abominable behaviour and I will not tolerate it," he said officiously.

Harriet coloured angrily and opened her mouth to respond.

"Really, I cannot believe you are so lax with your servants, Lord Hereford, as to allow them to slander your dear wife in such a pernicious manner," Amelia cut in. "I was present throughout the scene, and it was in fact an accident. I stepped forward at the same time as your menial and unfortunately trod most heavily upon her foot, although I did not realise until this moment how badly she was hurt. I actually felt sorry for her, but not any more! I do assure you that the woman, as well as being a liar, is clearly taking advantage of your trusting nature. I have no idea why she dislikes my daughter enough to wish to cause disharmony in her marriage. Perhaps she is enamoured of you, and hopes to become your mistress?"

Harriet managed to turn her involuntary snort of laughter at the thought of Mrs Grave and Raphael in bed together into a coughing fit, and sat down, turning away from her husband so as not to see his expression of utter confusion, as he tried to work out how to reply to the duchess's comment without offending her or losing face.

"I…er…I will investigate this further, when Mrs Grave has been attended to," he finally replied in a deflated tone.

"I am glad to hear it. May I suggest you dismiss the woman? I would certainly never employ a servant who was so mendacious. I am sure you can afford to employ a higher calibre of person than that, my lord," Amelia said, a duchess to the core.

Harriet had never loved her mother more than she did at that moment.

* * *

Amelia kept her promise to Harriet, not telling her husband how miserable their daughter was. It would only make him angry and unhappy, and there was nothing he could do to remedy the situation anyway. Harriet belonged to Raphael now, not to her parents.

She also kept her promise to visit as often as possible, and did so until the early spring, when her condition meant that she had to leave Court and retire to her house for the confinement. She told Harriet that she would write both to her and the Earl of Highbury when the child was born, and that he had agreed to call at the house and make sure he announced his delight at the birth at a time when Harriet was present, so that the news could not be kept from her.

In the end he did more than that, not only appearing at the most unsocial hour of dinner, when he knew Harriet and Raphael were likely to be together, but also apologising immediately upon being admitted to the dining room, and announcing that he was sure they would forgive him in view of the utterly delightful news. And of course all four of them must travel to the christening together, making a most happy party for a most happy occasion!

Once again Raphael was coerced into not only expressing his joy at the birth of the boy child that had destroyed his chance of getting his hands on both the title and estates of the dukedom, but into maintaining his joy at the birth for the two days it took to ride there in the earl and countess's coach. And he would now have to either attend the christening himself or allow his wife to do so without him, as he could not claim she had important business on that date when he didn't allow her to do *anything* relevant.

The Marquess of Hereford had one great weakness; he could not bear to be thought badly of in public. Both Amelia and Daniel, Earl of Highbury knew that. And both of them were willing to use that weakness against the marquess, in support of Harriet.

King Charles had been right. Friends (and loyal family) were true diamonds, and Harriet knew how lucky she was to have not only her family on her side, but her neighbour too. Her little war was progressing nicely.

That thought made her smile, something she did increasingly rarely nowadays.

CHAPTER EIGHT

By putting the fact that she would have to return to Hertfordshire with her husband in a week out of her mind, Harriet managed to have a wonderful time visiting her family and attending the christening of her new baby brother, named William in honour of the king.

There were a number of reasons for her having a wonderful time, apart from the obvious ones of her now considering the Highburys as friends and of spending time with her family. She thoroughly enjoyed watching Raphael pretending to be happy about the birth of the child who had cheated any son he might have of a dukedom. And because the Ashleighs were now riding high at Court and he was not, Raphael was on his very best and most unctuous behaviour, hoping to be recommended to the king and queen by his in-laws.

He didn't even have the chance to complain when alone in bed with her, because Amelia allocated them separate bedchambers on opposite sides of the house, giving Harriet her old room and saying somewhat puritanically that she was sure he would understand that it would not be seemly for one man to sleep among so many women, as Sophia's and Melanie's rooms were on either side of his wife's. Harriet could have kissed her.

A whole week without suffering one of his sexual assaults on her, which is what *she* considered them to be, even if the law did not. A whole week without hearing him tell her how ugly she was, how barren, how stupid, and how marrying her was the worst decision he'd ever made. A whole week without him belittling her in front of company or the servants. A whole week of being able to walk in the gardens alone at any time, of not seeing Mrs Grave, who had not accompanied them after the Countess of Highbury, wearing the same expression she customarily wore when in Raphael's presence, had made it quite clear that she could not bear the woman and saw no reason why Harriet would need a companion when she would be in the bosom of her family and friends.

The day after the christening, Melanie and Harriet went for a walk around the gardens together, arm in arm. Melanie was fourteen now, and seemed to Harriet, who had not seen her for two years, to have become a woman overnight. They talked about Court, and what it was like to have a duty that every noblewoman in the realm would kill for.

"I hate it," Melanie said as soon as they were out of earshot of the other christening guests, many of whom were taking advantage of the fine spring weather to sit outdoors. "I know I should be grateful to be a lady of the bedchamber, and the queen is really very kind, but she's in very low spirits, with the king being away fighting Louis of France at Mons. So Whitehall Palace is a gloomy place to be right now."

"Won't it be better when the king comes back, though? Then it'll be happy again, surely?" Harriet asked.

"I suppose so, but I hate it anyway, even when the queen is happy. It's so boring and constricting, as even when you're not actually on duty you have to be available at a moment's notice, so you can't go anywhere. I'm trying to persuade the queen to let Sophia take my place. It would make sense. She's older than me and loves the glamour and prestige of life at Court. She wouldn't mind standing around for hours or sitting in gloomy corners reading or embroidering on lovely days. Or knotting. I hate knotting. It's pointless and boring, but the queen loves it because it doesn't strain her weak eyes, and so every ambitious lady has to love it too. Sophia has convinced herself she really *does* love it, just because the queen does. Really, she's in her element there. And she'd be more likely to meet a handsome courtier too and get married if she was a lady of the bedchamber, which is what she really wants to do."

"And what do you want to do?" Harriet asked. Melanie looked at her sister, clearly undecided whether to tell her.

THE ECCENTRIC'S TALE: HARRIET

"You won't laugh if I tell you what I'd like?" she said finally.

"Why would I?"

"I want to live in the countryside with my family, and learn to bake beautiful cakes. I want to have my own animals; not a dog or a cat, but farm animals like cows. I really want a cow. And I want to learn to paint properly too, and have my own library, full of wonderful books that I like. I would sit there in the evenings all by myself and read for hours without being interrupted."

Harriet didn't laugh. Instead she considered seriously what her sister had said.

"What would you do with a cow?" she asked finally.

"Love it. I love their sad brown eyes. And I could make butter and cheese from the milk! But I wouldn't let her be killed for beef, because she'd be my pet cow, and would be called Buttercup."

"But you can surely paint and have books at the palace at least, can't you?" Harriet asked.

"Yes, but I want to be able to spend the whole day on my own somewhere painting, without having to rush off to attend the queen, or without having some stupid man telling me how wonderful my daub is and how beautiful I am, just because he thinks I have influence with the queen. And I want to have my own books, and read anything I want rather than what the queen thinks I should read. I know it sounds very silly, and I know I should be grateful to be able to live at the palace, but I'm not."

"It doesn't sound silly to me," Harriet said. "I think I'd hate attending the queen too."

"You would," Melanie agreed immediately. "You'd hate it even more than I do. I never met anyone who needed their freedom more than you. You're very unhappy with that cold fish you married, aren't you?"

"Yes, I am," Harriet said candidly. "But don't tell Papa, because he'll worry and he can't do anything about it. And like you, the complaints I have would sound trivial to anyone else. I wish the bastard would just die. I wish that every day, although I know I shouldn't."

"I don't see why you shouldn't wish it," Melanie said, "but you shouldn't *say* it. Because if he *does* die and everyone knows you wanted him to, you might be thought to have poisoned him. Like the women in Rome did."

"What women in Rome?"

"It was about thirty years ago. I read about it in one of the queen's books one day when I was bored. There was a group of women who had this poison called Aqua Tofana, which was colourless, odourless and tasteless and killed really quickly. They sold it to women who were unhappily married, so they could poison their husbands. It's said that it was impossible to tell if a person had been poisoned, because there was no trace left in the body."

"If no one could tell, then how do you know about them?" Harriet asked.

"The men died of terrible stomach pains and vomiting, but nothing could be proved because the poison was untraceable, so it could have just been a terrible flux of some sort. What gave them away was the *number* of men who died, and the surfeit of new and very happy widows in Rome. The poisoners were arrested and tortured until they confessed. And then the servants gave evidence against them and the widows too. If they'd been more careful they might not have been discovered."

"So what's in this Aqua…?"

"Tofana. I don't know. Arsenic, they say, because of the pains, but other things too. Why, would you really consider poisoning the marquess?"

"No, of course I wouldn't," Harriet said. "Poison seems a bit too obvious, anyway, to me. If someone's perfectly healthy today and then tomorrow is vomiting and bleeding, it would surely look suspicious? I don't think I'm a good enough actress to kill someone then pretend I was shocked and sad that they were dead. And it's one thing *wishing* someone was dead, but it's quite another actually *killing* them."

"You were going to kill Uncle Percy though," Melanie pointed out.

"No I wasn't. I was going to shoot him in the leg or arm and cause him a lot of pain, not kill him."

"Maybe you could shoot the marquess," Melanie said.

"No, I couldn't. I'm not allowed to practice archery any more, and even if I was, everyone knows I'm an expert. I could hardly claim to have shot him by accident. That's the problem with poison too – I would have to buy it from someone else, and then

THE ECCENTRIC'S TALE: HARRIET

that person would always have a hold on me, so I still wouldn't be free. We shouldn't even be talking like this, as you said."

"We're alone, though. And he makes me shiver. He's got cold, dead eyes."

"Even so, I'm not going to make the rest of him cold and dead too. I'm having fun making his life miserable, at least."

"He's *really* miserable right now, isn't he?" Melanie laughed.

"He is. Because our little brother has just deprived his unborn son of a wonderful future, and he's got to pretend to be glad about it."

"And you're depriving him of having a son at all!" Melanie added. "Which is a wonderful revenge for him depriving you of your freedom. You're denying him the thing he wants most in life, just as he's denying you."

Harriet hadn't thought of it like that before, but if she continued to be barren, then she was indeed depriving him of having any legitimate heirs at all. They were both young and could look forward to many years of unhappy, childless marriage together.

Could Raphael divorce her if she remained barren? She didn't think so, but if he could and did, she'd be very happy.

"Let's talk about something else," Harriet said. "I'm enjoying being here. I don't want to think about Raphael."

"One of the reasons I've brought you in this direction is so you can see Jem if you want," Melanie replied. "I know he's your friend, and I know Raphael is watching you like a hawk, but he can hardly say anything if I'm with you, and he's with Papa and Highbury anyway, trying to ingratiate himself with them. Here's Jem's cottage now. I'll go and sit over there, out of the way."

On impulse Harriet turned and gave her sister a bear hug.

"You have really grown up," she said. "You're far more observant than Sophia."

"That's because Sophia spends so much time thinking of herself that she doesn't notice others. I want you to be happy while you're here, and I knew you'd want to see Jem. Go."

Jem and Harriet sat on the grassy bank, as had been their custom as children and when Harriet was single. But this time he didn't show her how to whistle using a blade of grass or how to tickle trout. Instead they talked seriously, while Melanie sat in sight of them but with her back turned, reading a book that she'd brought with her.

"You're very unhappy, aren't you?" Jem observed.

"I just talked about that with Melanie," Harriet said, lying back and gazing up at the sky. "I don't want to talk about it again. How is it that everyone knows I'm unhappy, though? Can't I keep anything a secret?"

"Not from those who knows…who know you. You look different."

"In what way?" she asked.

Jem lay down too, and after a moment pointed up to the sky. "See the birds?" he said. "Before you met him you were like them, free and happy, and all glossy, like their feathers are. Now you're like those birds Lady Sophia keeps in a cage in her room. They're still singing and eating, so people think they're happy, but their plumage is dull, and they're always hopping from perch to perch, restless-like. And that's you. Even lying here with me you're not resting. You're tense, and it feels as though you're going to get up and walk away at any moment. You never used to be like that. When you was…were here, you were here, not somewhere else as well."

She had no answer to this, so both of them lay side by side staring upwards in companionable silence for a few minutes.

"Would it help if I came to live there?" he asked finally. "You could take me on as a gardener."

"No, I couldn't," Harriet said. "He wouldn't let me. But even if he would, I don't want you there."

"Ah. I see."

The tone in his voice made her sit up suddenly and look down at him.

"No, you don't, Jem. I'm sorry, I spoke without thinking of how it would sound. I'm not angry about what you said. You're right, I *am* like Sophia's birds. My marriage is a cage, and Raphael reminds me that I'm locked in it every chance he can. That's not why I don't want you there. I don't want you there because I don't want to see you having to kneel to him every time he passes, and be given the worst jobs because you were our gardener. He'd use you to take revenge on the family,

THE ECCENTRIC'S TALE: HARRIET

because he's too cowardly to say anything directly to Mama and Papa."

"I wouldn't mind if it would stop him taking revenge on you," he said, squinting up at her, his blue eyes deadly serious.

"It wouldn't stop him doing that. It would just make me more unhappy, knowing you were suffering. And once you were there, you wouldn't be able to leave."

"Why not?"

"Because if a servant wants to leave of their own accord he tells them that if they do he will go to the law about the money they stole."

"I wouldn't steal any money," Jem said, puzzled.

"Neither do they. He says it to keep them, because he wants to have complete power over everyone. They know that in a court of law the word of a marquess will count above theirs, and that they could hang. I always wondered why more of the servants didn't leave. After all, Papa is a caring master, but some of the servants still go. Raphael is a dreadful master. He pays them very little, the food they get is of the poorest quality and the accommodations I've seen are horrible. One of the footmen told me why no one leaves, and I believe him. He took a big risk telling me, because if I said anything to Raphael, he'd be very angry. So no, I don't want you there. How's Jeremiah?"

Jem took the hint, and told her that His Grace had paid for his own physician to examine Jeremiah, but that there wasn't really anything to be done.

"It's his heart, it's just weak. He sleeps most of the time now, but he's comfortable enough, and ready to meet his maker. It's just a matter of time. He is over sixty, and he's had a good life here."

"What will you do when he dies? Will you stay, or go on to somewhere else when you don't have to look after your da?"

"I'll stay, I think. His Grace is good to work for, and as you've just said, if I move I could end up in a much worse position."

"Yes, but if you stay here you'll never be head gardener, will you? Won't you regret it one day, if you don't at least try?"

"Well now, I might, but I'm young yet, and I'm learning the reading, slowly, and saving to buy the books I want. I'll wait yet awhile and see what happens."

"Wait for what?" Harriet asked.

But on that Jem would not be drawn.

* * *

Harriet took Jem's observation to heart, and for the rest of her time with her family she made a conscious effort to relax. For the first time she noticed that her brow was furrowed and her shoulders tense all the time. Her father knew her at least as well as Melanie and Jem, and if she was to stop him worrying she had to relax, or at least appear to relax. So she focussed on smoothing her brow and on lowering her shoulders, and at the end of the week as she rode out of the gates in the Highbury coach, her sadness at leaving was mitigated by the fact that her father hadn't commented on her being miserable at all, which he surely would have done had he noticed.

It was also mitigated by the fact that an hour before she'd left, Harriet had gone into Sophia's room and had let her birds go, watching them fly out of the window to freedom with mixed emotions of satisfaction and profound envy. They had been wild, had been trapped for Sophia, and so would know how to live in the wild again.

As would she, if she ever got the chance to.

Once the coach had disappeared round the bend in the drive, Melanie, Sophia and the servants went back into the house, but Stephen remained standing on the step, staring down the drive.

"Shall we go in?" Amelia suggested after a time. "It's going to rain, and she's not coming back, you know."

"No, I know." He turned to look at his wife. "So, do you know why she's so unhappy and why she's trying so desperately to hide it from me, rather than telling me as she should?" he asked.

Amelia sighed.

"I do. But she asked me not to tell you, because there's nothing you can do, and she doesn't want you to be unhappy too."

"Hmm. I never saw it before, but having spent four days with him, it's quite clear that there's something wrong with him," Stephen said, almost to himself. "It's as though he's a shell of a man, acting out all the emotions he thinks he should have. Well, you must keep Harriet's confidence, I suppose. Unless he's beating her, in which case tell me now, and I'll go and call him out. Although I feel that if I cut him he'd bleed sawdust rather than blood."

"Sawdust, or malice," Amelia said. "No, he's not beating her, although if he did in moderation it would be his right, as you know."

"To hell with his rights. If he was doing that, I'd call him out anyway."

"I know you would, and so does Harriet. Which is one reason why she was trying to hide her unhappiness from you, because she doesn't want you to react like that. And in truth he isn't doing anything you could reasonably call him out for." She stood for a minute, thinking. "You told him you'd mention him favourably to the king, didn't you?" she said.

"Yes. He's so eager to get back to Court it's pitiful. I hope I was never that pathetically sycophantic when I was out in the cold."

"No you weren't, which is probably one reason why we were out of favour for so long. But it's also one of the reasons I still love you as much as I did when we married."

He laughed, and put his arm round her shoulders.

"Let's go inside, and talk," she said. "I think I'm about to break a promise to my daughter."

* * *

Summer 1691

Harriet climbed out of the church window and went for a stomp around the gardens until her temper cooled, upon which she started to hear birdsong and notice flowers blooming, and the stomp became a stroll.

She didn't know how much longer she could carry on like this. Raphael had been bearable when they'd first arrived home from her parents, which had surprised her a little – she'd expected him to take his anger about her brother out on her. But until yesterday everything had carried on as normal. He still insulted her all the time and still came to her room every night, because if he couldn't have a dukedom for his son, he still wanted an heir for the marquessate. Also, as he had pointed out to her with relish, babies were so fragile, more of them dying than surviving infancy. There was a good chance that baby William would not survive to inherit his dukedom anyway.

But he hadn't denied her access to the gardens or stopped her seeing the Highburys, both of which she'd thought he might do, and she had started receiving letters from her family again, and had written uncomplaining replies, knowing that anything else would not get to them. So life had continued as normal, or at least as normal as it could be in a household where the married couple hated each other.

Until yesterday, when everything had changed. She still really didn't know why it had suddenly changed, although it was certainly to do with the paper he'd rolled up and brandished like a sword as he'd marched into her rooms, dismissing Mrs Grave with a flick of his hand.

"Don't think," he had said angrily, the moment the door was closed and they were alone, "that I can't get rid of you if I decide to."

Harriet put down the current piece of embroidery she was massacring and looked up at him.

"Please feel free to, any time you want," she said. "I'd be delighted if you divorced me. You might have trouble proving your case though. You can hardly accuse me of adultery, can you, when you pay that old bitch to shadow me all day every day? You could always dismiss her of course, and let me out of the grounds occasionally in the hope that I'll be indiscreet. Although I must admit, having endured your fumblings for the last years, the very last thing I want to do is fuck anyone else."

"No one would do it with you anyway," he shot back. "Do you think I would, if I didn't need an heir? It makes me sick just looking down at you while you're lying there like a corpse. I can't think how I've been able to finish at all."

"Put the lamp out next time then," Harriet said, who was so used to his insults she hardly registered them any more. "At least then I can just turn over and go to sleep as soon as you've finished. Have you finished now, or do you want to insult me a little more before you go?"

"I wasn't thinking about divorce," he said. "You're no use to me. You're ugly, barren, and clearly not in your right mind,

THE ECCENTRIC'S TALE: HARRIET

scrabbling around in the undergrowth with that pampered Highbury brat looking for insects. You are clearly unwell. If you continue in this way then I shall have no choice but to send you to a hospital for lunatics."

"A hospital for lunatics? Whatever do you mean? I am no more insane than you are, as you well know," she cried. "You cannot do that!"

"I can do what I want," he assured her. "You are my wife. An acquaintance of mine has just in fact committed his wife to such a place, for her own good, of course."

"If you think my family would let you do such a thing, even if it were possible," she said, fighting back the panic at the thought of such a confinement, "you are sadly mistaken."

"I am sure they would object. Indeed, that would be an added benefit. Your father has made it quite clear," he spat, brandishing the rolled-up letter at her, "that he does not intend to assist me in returning to Court, so I have no reason to care about his opinion of me any more, do I? Your parents cannot protect you from me. I think it's time you understood that I have complete control over you. We will start with the gardens. From this moment your access to them is denied absolutely, and you will disobey me at your peril, madam."

After he'd gone, she had sat in stunned disbelief for a moment, until Mrs Grave had returned, her supercilious smile telling Harriet that Raphael had either confided in her or she had been listening at the door. She adopted an indifferent attitude, picked up her embroidery and continued sewing as though nothing out of the ordinary had happened.

The next morning she didn't even attempt to leave by the door, instead just walking straight into the church, throwing open the window and clambering out, her only thought being that if Raphael was about to try such a thing as committing her to the hell of what was effectively a prison for mad people, she needed to make her family and her friends aware of it, and she could only see the Highburys by being outside. They would not let him do such a thing, surely? Did he *really* have the power to do that?

Of course he does, she told herself. *In law I belong to him completely. He has money, a lot of money. Money brings power.* But he did not have the favour of the monarchs, which her family had, and which brought power and influence. Even if they could stop him sending her to a hospital though, they could not stop him confining her at home.

She should not be defying him now, she realised. She should be accepting that she had lost, that her life would be better if she submitted, became the pathetic fawning rag he wanted her to be.

No. She could not do that. She could never do that. She would kill herself before she'd do that. She looked around, making a conscious effort to take in the beauty of the gardens in full summer, aware that in all probability, soon the only view she would have of them would be through the little square of window in her rooms. He would certainly nail up all the downstairs windows once he knew she was climbing out of them.

"Lady Harriet!" a youthful voice came, breaking into her gloomy panic.

"Lord William!" she replied, managing to sound happy with a huge effort. "I didn't expect to see you until I came to the woodland."

"I love the walled garden too, as you do," he said happily, reining his pony in beside her. "It's very beautiful, especially at this time of the year, when everything is in bloom. I didn't think you'd mind me straying from the woodland."

"Me? I don't mind at all."

"The marquess would though, I suppose."

"To hell with the marquess," Harriet replied vehemently, then caught the boy's shocked expression. "I'm sorry. Forget I said that. Is your father in the woodland? I would like to see him. Or your mother."

"Mama would never come into the woodland," William said. "She is afraid of beetles and spiders. She always stays to the gravel paths in the formal part of the grounds. But I'm happy to see you today, Lady Harriet. I found a mushroom I haven't seen before under the trees and I wanted to show it to you."

"Have you drawn it?" she asked. William's current obsession was with mushrooms and toadstools, and he had taken to carrying sketching equipment with him so that he could draw the ones he found. His parents were pleased, because although he had told them that drawing and painting were boring, mainly because he

THE ECCENTRIC'S TALE: HARRIET

had to sit for long periods indoors to learn how to do it, he would happily scrunch up on the damp ground outside for half an hour drawing the various things he found there.

"No, not yet," he said. "I thought I'd see if you were here first to tell me what it is."

William dismounted and they walked to the woodland together, the little boy chatting happily about the fact that he'd been allowed to gallop across the field for the first time last week, and had done very well, the Master of Horse had said, while Harriet listened, loving his enthusiasm for life, but saddened by the knowledge that this might be the last time they spent outdoors together.

They arrived at a big oak tree on the edge of the woodland, and William squatted down.

"Here it is," he said, pointing to a mushroom under the tree. It was mainly white, although the cap was pale green. She knelt down next to him to look at it, then very carefully brushed the leaf debris away from the bottom of the slender white stem to reveal a swollen base. "Do you know what it is?" he asked.

"Have you touched it?" she said, her voice suddenly serious.

"No," he replied. "Why?"

"You mustn't touch it. I think it's a Death Cap mushroom, and if it is, it's very poisonous. Are you sure you didn't touch it at all?"

"Yes. You told me not to touch any mushroom until I knew what it was last week when I wanted to pick the Fly Agaric because it was so pretty. Can it kill you?"

"Yes, it can," she said, sitting back on the damp leafy ground. "When I was a little girl, Jeremiah, one of our gardeners, showed me this, and I've never forgotten it. He said it's the most deadly mushroom there is. Just one of them can kill you, and there's no cure. He told me to look for the swollen base, see? And they grow under oak trees, so I really think this is one."

"Wow! How does it kill you?" William asked with boyish relish.

"I don't know," Harriet admitted. "Jeremiah wouldn't tell me. I think he thought I might try to poison Percy."

"Who's Percy?"

"Oh, he's my uncle, although he's nearly the same age as me, and we've always hated each other. He's a pompous prig, but I would never poison him. I was only a child at the time though, so I can understand why Jeremiah didn't trust me not to."

William nodded, and taking out his paper, began to draw it. Harriet watched him, smiling at the little brow furrowed with concentration, his tongue sticking out at the corner of his mouth. He was a lovely child, natural and unaffected. If she ever did have a son, she would want him to be like this little boy. But of course that would not happen, because Raphael would take him away from her, and bring him up to be cold and cruel like his father.

She sighed, and William looked up from his drawing.

"I won't be much longer," he said, misunderstanding.

"No, you must take the time you need. I'm not bored. I like to watch you draw."

He smiled and continued. The birds sang in the trees, the sun dappled through the branches and leaves, and Harriet concentrated very hard, trying to commit this perfect moment to memory, so that when she was confined to her rooms she could remember it, and it would comfort her.

Later, having waved goodbye to William and made him promise to have his father or mother invite her to some occasion Raphael could not refuse, she walked back to the house slowly, stopping under the oak tree again.

The memory would not comfort her. But the mushroom might. Could she do it? Could she poison her husband?

Yes, I could now, after last night, she realised. She could, and would not regret it for a minute, would take her chance on God understanding why she'd done it. But she did not think she was a good enough actress to hide what she'd done from others, and she could not endure either prison or death by burning.

Maybe, if Raphael *did* confine her to her rooms she could use them to kill herself, and make a deathbed confession that she believed he'd poisoned her because she was barren. That would be the ultimate revenge – she would escape him forever, and he would almost certainly be executed. He made no secret of his hatred for her, and had enough enemies among the servants for them to testify against him.

She took out her handkerchief and very carefully picked the

THE ECCENTRIC'S TALE: HARRIET

mushrooms, wrapping them and placing them in her pocket. Then, smiling, she set off for home.

* * *

Raphael did not come down for dinner that afternoon, which was very unusual. He enjoyed taunting her over the meal, belittling her in front of the numerous footmen who stood waiting to fill glasses, take plates away, or just look decorative.

Harriet enjoyed her meal without him, and afterwards she sat in the inner courtyard listening to the fountain and turning her face up to the last of the sun before it disappeared behind the enclosing walls of the house. He hated her freckles, so she always made sure to expose her face to the sun, which brought them out.

He did not come to her bed that night either, although he was certainly at home. Was he making plans to have her incarcerated, she wondered? Whatever the reason, it was still pleasant to spend a whole day without seeing him at all, and particularly the night part, which she always dreaded.

* * *

Harriet was shaken awake from a deep sleep by Mrs Grave, who never touched her normally. At first, still half in the grip of a vague dream about giant mushrooms, she had no idea where she was. And then her companion lit a candle, placing it on the table next to her bed, and Harriet sat up, wiping her eyes to try and wake herself. Something must be wrong.

"What, what is it?" she asked muzzily. Mrs Grave wore an expression of utter panic.

"Oh, my lady, the marquess is very ill!" she cried. For one insane moment Harriet wondered if, rather than dreaming it, she had actually chopped the mushrooms into his meal in reality. And then her sleep-drenched mind cleared, and she was awake.

"Ill? In what way?" she asked.

"He went to his rooms earlier, saying that he felt a little unwell, that was all, and that he wanted to lie down for a while. He told his man not to disturb him, because he wanted to sleep. But John just heard him calling out, so he went in, and his lordship has a terrible fever and is raving," she said, wringing her hands in distress.

Harriet managed with an effort to keep her expression sombre, and throwing a shawl round her shoulders she padded across the hall to her husband's rooms, the first time she had been to them in over two years. John was standing outside, looking very upset, but when he saw his mistress his relief was palpable.

"Oh, my lady!" he cried. "Lord Hereford is in a terrible way…I think perhaps we should send for the physician, but if I do and it's only a mild fever, he will be very angry with me. I don't know what I should do."

"Let me see him," Harriet said. She opened the door and walked in. Her husband had thrown off the bedclothes and was curled on his side, and even by candlelight she could see that his nightclothes were soaked with sweat, although it was a cool evening.

"Raphael," Harriet said. "John tells me you are ill and he thinks we should send for the physician. What is wrong?"

He turned his head to look up at her, his eyes bright with fever, although he was quite calm, not raving as Mrs Grave had dramatically claimed.

"No physician," he said. "I have a headache and my back is aching abominably, but I'm sure I will be well in the morning. Open the windows. This room is damnably hot!"

She leaned over and put her hand on his forehead, although she had no wish to touch him.

"The room is cool, it is you who are hot. Your skin is burning. You have a fever. I think we should send for the physician."

"No. I hate physicians. They kill more people than they save. Get out, all of you, and let me sleep. Open the window before you go."

Harriet went to the window, flung it open and then left. That was as much caring as she could feign in one evening.

"For what it's worth, John, I agree that we should call the physician. But you heard Lord Hereford's views, I assume?"

"I did, my lady," he said. "I will stay with him. I will open the door a little and sleep right outside it. Then I will hear if he calls."

"I cannot send for the physician without his permission," she said, hoping she looked distressed and indecisive, rather than happy and hoping the bastard wouldn't survive the night.

"No, you can't. He will be very angry if you disobey him,"

THE ECCENTRIC'S TALE: HARRIET

John agreed. "Go to bed, my lady. I will call you if he gets worse, I promise."

She went back to bed with apparent reluctance and lay there, thinking. What could it be? Raphael was, like her, never ill. He had looked dreadful, but any number of illnesses started with fever. Hopefully it was something fatal, but she could not be that lucky. It was probably just a touch of fever. No doubt he would be perfectly well by the morning.

She turned over and went back to sleep.

* * *

He was not perfectly well by the morning, and remained in bed, but refused to see the doctor, saying it was just a fever and he had no wish to have his blood drained from him, nor to be given a purge. When she went to him he told her to get out in no uncertain terms, and that John could tend to him.

She got out and was happy to do so, although she told John to come to her immediately if the marquess deteriorated, and she would send for the physician anyway. The last thing she wanted was for him to die and her to be arrested for not ensuring he had medical treatment. In fact, if she'd had her way she would have sent for the physician immediately, because she did believe, as had her friend King Charles before her, that they killed far more people than they cured. But she could not do it unless he agreed or became too ill to make the decision himself.

It was the third day before he became too ill to make the decision, when his fever became dangerously high, he *did* start raving, and refused to eat. Harriet sent for the physician, who arrived a couple of hours later, and having listened to John as he described the symptoms and looked in the patient's mouth, pronounced immediately that it was smallpox.

"Dear God," said Harriet, while John and Mrs Grave paled noticeably. Both of them had been with the marquess a lot, John because he was tending him, and Mrs Grave because she was nosey and was enjoying the prestige of updating the servants regularly about his illness.

Smallpox. The illness that wiped out whole families, whole towns. The illness that, if it did not kill you, often left you hideously disfigured, or blind.

"What can we do to stop it spreading to the rest of the household?" Harriet asked as the physician pulled his bloodletting tools out of his bag.

"I will stay here and look after him," John offered. "I've been washing and feeding him, so have been in contact with him the most. If I have caught it, it's God's will."

"I will pray that you haven't," Mrs Grave said. "I will go to the chapel now," she added, obviously desperate to be out of the room as quickly as possible.

"You've been holding his hand too, though, haven't you?" John said. Harriet watched with amusement as her companion blanched, and then felt immediately guilty. She had no sympathy for her husband, would be ecstatic if he died, but although she disliked Mrs Grave intently, she would not wish smallpox on her.

"You must both stay in his rooms and have no contact with anyone else in the household, until it is sure that you have not contracted the disease," the doctor said. "My lady, I cannot order you to confine yourself to your rooms of course, as you will have to manage the household until the marquess is well, but I would ask that you have as little contact with others as possible. Now, you must put out the fire, and the windows must be opened and kept open so the room is as cool as possible. That will help to break the fever. He cannot eat at the moment, as his mouth is full of pustules. These will spread and cover his body – it will be a rash at first, and then blisters. I will send my servant with some small beer, which is ONLY for the marquess, as it will contain spirit of vitriol. And he must be kept quiet. If you would instruct the household to pray for his recovery, my lady. Do not despair, a good number of people do survive this illness, and the marquess is young and strong, so has a better chance than many."

"Thank you, Dr Smith. That's very reassuring," Harriet lied. "I will order a day of prayer for him, of course." She would, because she knew she must now show no sign that she wished, with every fibre of her being, that he would die. If he did, absolutely no suspicion must attach to her.

She went back to her room, took out the pieces of mushroom she had collected, and threw them down the privy. On no account could those be found in her chambers. Then she went for a walk in the gardens to come to terms with the terrible news she had

THE ECCENTRIC'S TALE: HARRIET

just had, as she told the servants. In reality she wanted to make the most of the extension to her freedom, because while Raphael was so ill he could not order her to be contained in the house.

And if he died…

At the woodland she met the Earl of Highbury, who was standing at the gate between their properties.

"Daniel!" she cried. "What a pleasant surprise!"

"I have been here every day for an hour, as I know this is usually the time you meet William. He said you wished to see myself or Frances, and as the weather is so agreeable I thought to stroll around my grounds each day."

"Is William riding over?"

"No, he is a little unwell today."

"Unwell? In what way?" she asked, instantly alarmed.

"He ate too many strawberries yesterday. Far too many strawberries, although he was told not to. He will learn from it, as did I when I was his age."

"Are you sure? Does he have a fever? A headache?" Harriet persisted.

"No, not at all. He has diarrhoea and belly pain, that is all. What's wrong?"

Harriet closed her eyes for a moment and sent up a thank you to the Heavens.

"Raphael has smallpox," she said. "The doctor is with him now. That is why I am standing over here rather than coming closer."

"Dear God, that is terrible news," Highbury said.

"It is," Harriet replied with as much sincerity as she could feign. "You must all keep away. Tell William he must keep out of my grounds until the marquess has recovered."

"I will, of course. Did you wish to speak to me still, or would you prefer to return and tend your husband?"

"No, I would prefer to speak to you," Harriet said automatically then realised how that sounded. "That is…I mean…"

"I understand completely," said Highbury, who did. "The physician is with him, and talking to me will take your mind off this dreadful news."

"Yes! Exactly," she said. "Although what I have to say concerns the marquess."

He listened while she told him of her husband's threat to commit her to an asylum or confine her to her rooms, and then he nodded, as though this was something he had expected rather than a surprise.

"I think we must wait and see if the marquess recovers. If he does, I do assure you that I will do everything in my power to prevent him from inflicting such a cruelty on you. You are no more insane than I am. Have you written to your parents about this?"

"No," she said. "Such a letter would not get to them. Although I suppose I could write now, while he is indisposed."

"No," said Highbury. "It may not be necessary, and better that no one knows you have an immediate reason to wish him dead. People can be very malicious. If it becomes necessary, then I will inform them. We will not let you be sent to an asylum, Harriet. Of that at least I can assure you."

Later, in her room, blissfully free of the company of Mrs Grave, who was now confined in the marquess's rooms, Harriet realised two things. The earl was warning her that she should give no one reason to believe she might want to murder him, nor did he offer to pray for his recovery, even though that would be the standard response to news of such serious illness. And he had not said that he could prevent the marquess from confining her to her rooms, only the asylum.

Die, you bastard, she thought vehemently. *Naturally.*

* * *

For the next ten days Raphael fought the illness that was consuming him. As the doctor had said, the rash spread from his mouth to the rest of his body, and was most concentrated on his face and arms. He looked hideous, and Dr Smith, who visited daily, warned Harriet that if he survived, which as the illness raged and he grew weaker seemed less and less likely, he would probably be severely disfigured, although hopefully not blind, as the pustules were not near his eyes.

At least if he is disfigured, he won't be able to tell me how ugly I am any more, she thought but did not say.

As the steward and housekeeper were already running the household, apparently efficiently, Harriet spent the first seven

THE ECCENTRIC'S TALE: HARRIET

days walking in the gardens in the glorious summer weather, keeping the servants updated on the progress of the master's illness from a safe distance, and practising appearing to be upset that he was ill. On the eighth day John developed a fever, and Harriet packed him off to a nearby guest room and reconciled herself to caring for Raphael. She could hardly demand that any of the other poorly paid, maltreated servants risk their lives to nurse him, and she *had* been exposed to the illness already. She would just have to touch him as little as possible and pray that her strong constitution protected her.

As she didn't want to expose anyone else, she found herself looking after John as well, as Mrs Grave was as useless at caring for sick people as she was at being a companion, and spent most of her time in Raphael's closet praying and wringing her hands.

The next day, as she was washing his face with cool water and a cloth, Raphael woke, and looked at her sleepily but without delirium.

"What are you doing here?" he said thickly. "Where's John?"

Harriet put the cloth back into the bowl, and wrung it out.

"He's fallen sick," she said. "Dr Smith is with him now. I thought I'd bathe your face."

"No," Raphael said.

"Well, it's up to you. But it will cool you," Harriet replied indifferently.

"Not that. No doctor for John. He must leave, now."

"What are you talking about? He can't leave. He's ill."

"Throw him out. I'm not paying for his care. He has to leave, he knows that."

Harriet, who had been about to wipe his face again, dropped the cloth back in the basin with a splash.

"Raphael, he got sick because he was looking after you. I'm damned if I'll throw him out. He deserves the best treatment we can give him."

"It's not up to you," he said. "I'm not dead yet. He signed to say he'd leave. They all did. Throw him out, now."

She got up immediately and left the room before she told him exactly what she thought of him in no uncertain terms. If she did Mrs Grave would hear, and if he died she would report to anyone who'd listen that the marchioness had told her husband she hated him when he was on his deathbed. To hell with him. She was damned if she would throw a faithful servant out on the street, a servant who had risked his life to nurse his ungrateful shit of a master.

She went to John's room, and stood looking down at him as he slept. He didn't look as ill as Raphael had on the second day of his illness. Hopefully he would recover, and Raphael would die.

On the way back to her husband's room she met Mary, one of the kitchenmaids, coming with the master's meal, which she would place outside his door and then go away.

"I won't take the tray from you, Mary," Harriet said. "Just leave it there and I'll take it in myself. Can I ask you something?"

"Anything, my lady."

"When you started working here, did you sign anything to say that you'd leave if you fell ill?"

"Yes, my lady. Not if I got a cold, but if I got a bad sickness that would mean me not being able to work for a while, and would need treatment."

"I see. And is that normal? As far as I know my father never asked for such an agreement."

"I don't know. My last place didn't ask me to sign such a thing, but my sister, she's a maid of all work at Mr Royal's, she had to agree to that, yes."

There was a big difference between someone who could afford only one servant and someone who could pay footmen to stand around for hours just for effect though, Harriet thought later as she watched her husband sleeping. No doubt the Royals, whoever they were, could not afford the expense of treating a servant, whereas Raphael most certainly could. And agreement or not, to throw the person who'd become ill due to their devotion to you out on the street to die was evil. She would not do it, would claim that she'd thought him delirious if he asked her later about it.

She had never wanted him to die as much as she did at that minute. She looked at him with utter loathing. The illness had rendered him almost unrecognisable. His previously handsome face was just a mass of pustules, as were his arms and legs. He now looked like his personality was, loathsome, hideous. He would die. Surely he would die. His fever had raged for ten days, and he had lost a lot of weight. He had to die.

Two days later the pustules started to dry up and form scabs, and his fever broke.

"Well, this is good news, my lady," Dr Smith said when he made his daily call and saw the scabs forming. Harriet had been sitting in the closet with Mrs Grave while the doctor examined Raphael. "He is a little cooler, so the fever is breaking, and the fact that scabs are forming is a very good sign. It's true that he is very weak, so I cannot be certain yet, but it is now possible that he will survive, with a great deal of rest."

"Oh, that is wonderful news!" cried Mrs Grave. "Our prayers have been answered."

"Indeed," Harriet agreed. "This is amazing news."

"I do not want to raise your hopes too high, you understand," Dr Smith added. "But the case is far more hopeful than it was. I will be more certain tomorrow. I have used the treatment recommended by Dr Sydenham, whose success in treating smallpox is quite remarkable. He also invented an excellent medicine, called Sydenham's Laudanum, which induces sleep and relieves pain, which I will give to his lordship tonight. It will help him to sleep, which he certainly needs to do now to allow his body to recover. He is exhausted."

She was exhausted too, she realised, as she sat at her husband's bedside that night, watching him sleep by candlelight. His face was now becoming a mass of scabs, whereas John's rash was just appearing but was not as extreme as Raphael's had been. She had told Dr Smith to spare no expense in treating John, and that the marquess would be distraught if his loyal servant was to die.

Mrs Grave was asleep in the next room, and the house was quiet. She was probably the only person in the building who was still awake. She glanced at the clock. Two-thirty. In three hours the maids would rise and would start to light fires in the rooms, and then the other servants would get up to begin their chores.

And she would sit here and watch the man who was ruining her life recover, the man who was ruining the lives of the servants, and probably of all those who lived on his estate too who she had never met. Hundreds of people whose lives were being made miserable because this man was still breathing. Hundreds of people whose lives would continue to be made miserable because this man was going to recover.

And when he did he would throw John out on the street to die and then would confine her to an asylum or to her rooms, where she would exist until she went mad or died, or killed herself. She had now read the letter that her father had sent to him, the letter Raphael had brandished like a weapon the night before he'd fallen ill. In it Stephen had told his son-in-law that he would not recommend him to the king, that in fact he would do everything in his power to keep him out of Court, unless he treated his wife as she should be treated, with love and consideration.

And Raphael's response to that had been to threaten her with an asylum.

Her father could not stop him. All he could do was write letters for Raphael to ignore. Highbury could not stop him. Only one person could stop him, and if she was going to, she had to do it now, while the whole house slept.

She stood, walked round to the empty side of the bed and picked up the pillow. Then before her mind could analyse what she was about to do and stop her, she climbed onto the bed, straddled her husband's body and placed the pillow over his face, holding it down at both sides with all her strength.

She expected him to struggle more than he actually did. But he was very weak after ten days of fever, and was drugged too, with this laudanum that the doctor had given him to help him sleep. *I will help you sleep even better, you heartless, hateful bastard,* she thought.

She stayed there until he was completely still, and then stayed there a little longer. And then she removed the pillow from his face and replaced it on the empty side of the bed. After that she sat down on the chair at the side of the bed again, her mind strangely calm, pulled back the sheet and observed him. His chest was not rising and falling, not even slightly. When she put her hand under his nostrils, she could feel no breath on her skin.

She replaced the sheet, and then thought, coolly. She could not pretend that he had just died and feign panic. She was not that good an actress. So she would do as the doctor had advised, and once sure the marquess was soundly asleep, go and get some rest herself. The laudanum would ensure that he slept for a good few hours, and he could be left alone for that time, the doctor had said. No one would criticise her for following the doctor's orders.

Let Mrs Grave find him and have her final moment of importance, to be the one to tell the whole house and all her acquaintance, that she had found the Marquess of Hereford dead. What a tragedy. She would relish it.

Harriet felt no jubilation, no remorse. Instead she felt calm but completely and utterly exhausted. Very quietly she stood, and taking the candle with her went back to her own rooms, where she undressed herself, not wanting to wake Mrs Grave to ask her to, and not being able to have any other servants attend her so closely due to the risk of contagion.

Then she climbed into bed and fell asleep immediately.

CHAPTER NINE

September 1691

Harriet stood on the battlements looking across at the lands that her husband's ancestor had built this tower in order to stake his claim to, hundreds of years ago.

"I'm sorry," she said softly to the spirit of the long-dead ancestor. She had wiped out his line; the least he deserved was an apology, although in truth she was not sorry at all for what she'd done. That surprised her. After all, even though no one but herself knew it, she had murdered her husband, and even as she had sat on top of him coldly holding the pillow over his face, in the recesses of her mind she had expected to be racked with guilt about it later.

But here she was. More than a month had passed and in all that time she had not felt even the slightest twinge of guilt.

It hadn't seemed normal to feel no guilt at all for murdering someone, but standing here now she realised that she was no different from any of the thousands of soldiers who killed their enemies on the battlefield every day. They didn't spend their lives racked with guilt – in fact they boasted of how many they'd killed, and were praised and rewarded for doing so. Raphael had been her enemy, the house and grounds had been the battlefield, and she had seized the opportunity to rid herself of him, for her sake and that of all the people under his control. She couldn't boast about it and she would receive no praise if she did; but in a manner of speaking she had been rewarded for it.

She looked out across the lawns to the cream walls of the enormous house that was now all hers. It was beautiful, as would

THE ECCENTRIC'S TALE: HARRIET

the gardens be, when she had changed them. All this, and the estate she had not yet seen were now hers too, but it was not that that made her heart soar.

She was certainly rich, because Raphael had not changed his will before he died, which meant that she had inherited his whole estate. She was sure that given time he would have made a new will, but being as robust as she herself was he clearly had not expected to die at thirty-one.

Death can come at any time, she thought. True, she had assisted Death, but even so… You could never take life for granted, so while you had it you should live it to the full. And she fully intended to do just that. But slowly, one step at a time. For now she must be patient, and keep her eye on the prize.

The prize was freedom. Everything else, the house, the estate, the money, the title, were bonuses. Freedom was what was making her heart soar and her mouth smile whenever she knew she would not be observed. She was nineteen, a widow and free, and she was not about to risk that by rushing to embrace that freedom.

The moment Mrs Grave had informed her of what she already knew, she had plunged the household into mourning. She had done everything by the book. The whole house was draped in black cloth, mirrors and portraits had been turned to the wall, every servant had been provided with mourning costume, and Harriet had paid the fee of £5 to gain exemption from the Act that stated all corpses must be buried in woollen cloth. So Raphael had been buried in the family tomb in a costly gold-embroidered outfit, with all the trimmings society would expect from a grieving aristocratic widow.

He had not been in favour at Court, so King William and Queen Mary had not attended the funeral, but many other nobles including her own family had, and all of them had received a mourning ring from the heavily veiled widow. Heavily veiled because it allowed her the opportunity to show her true emotions for at least part of the time.

It was difficult feigning grief when all she felt was ecstasy. But she would take no chances, do nothing that might raise suspicion that Raphael had died of anything other than natural causes. True, there was absolutely no doubt that he had had smallpox, and the doctor had never expressed the slightest doubt that he had died of that and nothing else, but it *was* well known that theirs had not been a happy marriage, and his death had left her very wealthy. It was possible she was being over-cautious because she knew his death had been due to her rather than smallpox, but better to be over-cautious than risk arousing suspicion. She had no idea whether or not a close examination of Raphael's body would provide evidence that he'd died of asphyxiation, but she was taking no chances. Every day that passed his body rotted a little more, eradicating any incriminating evidence there might be.

One of the drawbacks of that was that both Mrs Grave and Mr Harrison were still employed by her. She had adopted the policy of not changing anything at all for at least six weeks after Raphael's death, partly to give the impression of being prostrate with grief, and partly because she did not want spiteful servants to spread malicious rumours, which they might do if she dismissed them.

However, the six weeks were almost up. She would continue to wear black for six months before turning to purple or white, as was customary, but it was time to start making changes.

At the funeral she had taken her father to one side and asked him if he could recommend a new steward to her. She'd admitted that she didn't get on with Mr Harrison and would like to replace him, but had no real cause to at the moment. Stephen had pointed out that she didn't *need* a cause to dismiss a servant, but he admired her for feeling she did.

"However," he'd added, "if he doesn't treat you with the respect and deference you deserve, that is reason enough for dismissal. Would you like me to have a word with him?"

"You're very kind, Papa," she'd replied, "but I won't command anybody's respect if I ask my father to discipline my servants for me. I need to do that myself. Otherwise, the moment you leave they will think they can walk all over me. Which I have no intention of letting them do."

"I'm sorry, darling," Stephen had replied. "I know you're capable of handling the servants, until you find a new husband. I have absolute faith in you."

Before Harriet could respond to this her father had offered her the services of Mr Noakes his steward for a week or two, to

THE ECCENTRIC'S TALE: HARRIET

go over the accounts and give Harriet an accurate figure of what the estate earned, and her annual disposable income. Stephen had told her that Mr Noakes was training up his son, who was doing very well, and showed signs of being as honest and conscientious as his parent. Perhaps he would be a suitable replacement for Harrison.

Harriet had arranged for Mr Noakes to call next week, and to bring his son with him if he wished. She intended to keep the prospective visit to herself, as she didn't want Harrison to have time to hide any incriminating papers, if there were any. If there were not, she would dismiss him anyway, but it would be easier to justify it to him and others if he was a thief.

Once she knew what she was really worth she could start making changes. She had not done it earlier, because she had had to wait until she was sure she had not caught smallpox from either Raphael or John. The last thing she wanted to do was to start her new life by killing off half her servants and tenants!

John was now recovering slowly, although he was terribly disfigured by the illness and had lost the sight of one eye. He had been very low in spirits about this, until she had reassured him that she was not about to dismiss him because he was no longer as handsome as he had been. When he had pointed out that appearances were a crucial part of the role of a footman she had informed him in no uncertain terms that for her, loyalty and dedication were crucial parts of any servant she employed, and he had proved himself to be abundantly possessed of those qualities. Then she had asked him how much Raphael had paid him, and had doubled his wages on the spot.

She could not make any such offers to the rest of the servants yet, but this was the man who had almost died due to his loyal care of his ungrateful master, and such dedication was worth rewarding.

What she could do now though, was dismiss Mrs Grave. That she had no qualms about doing, now she was certain the woman had not contracted smallpox either. Harriet cast another look across her lands, and then hauling her impractical and cumbersome skirts up, she carefully descended the crumbling spiral staircase of the tower and made her way back to the house.

It was time to start making the first of the many changes she hoped to make, now she was free to do as she liked.

* * *

When she got back to her rooms Mrs Grave was not there, so she made her way through to Raphael's apartments. Was it too early to start making a note of what he had that she wanted to keep for herself and what she could pass on to others? Possibly, but if anyone asked what she was doing, she could say that she felt comforted when surrounded by Raphael's things.

She was being ridiculous. It was not the servants' place to ask her what she was doing, and they wouldn't believe such bullscutter if she told it to them anyway. They had seen how he had treated her, and knew she had never had any comfort from him when he was alive. The only people who would believe such lies were her peers.

She realised that one of the tasks she had was to truly realise that for the first time in her life she did not have to answer to *anybody*. Not her parents, not her husband, nobody. All she had to do was to ensure that society knew that, and follow her friend King Charles' advice: Often it is necessary to be friendly to people who you don't like at all, or who don't like you, because you might need those people to help you achieve what you want.

With this in mind, and because she didn't as yet know who she would need, after Raphael's death she had endured a series of visits from fellow aristocrats, in which they expressed their deepest sympathy on the death of her dear husband. That was standard and expected, and Harriet had thanked them for their kindness. What she had not expected was the outpouring of apparently genuine belief that she must be completely heartbroken and bereft without Raphael. All of the people expressing this utter rubbish had seen him mocking her at every event they'd attended together, had listened as he had told her she was ugly and barren, could not sing, dance or utter a sensible opinion on anything.

Why on earth would they *really* think that she would be bereft at the loss of such a husband as Raphael had been? Or in fact give a damn what they, who had presumably agreed with him, thought? Because not one of them had spoken a word in her defence. And

THE ECCENTRIC'S TALE: HARRIET

yet it seemed they did think her bereft, and in need of their support. Presumably a woman was lost without a man, even when that man had been a complete bastard. Even her father, who knew her better than anyone, had assumed that she would take another husband in time, and might need support until then.

To hell with that. She had no intention of marrying again. Ever.

She opened one of the trunks that contained Raphael's clothes, took out a richly embroidered coat and sat on the bed, stroking the soft maroon velvet. It was beautiful. And far more practical than the layers of clothing she had to wear. Why did women have to wear such stupid restrictive clothes? You couldn't run in them, couldn't ride properly in them, they got caught on every bush when you were out in the garden, and the bottom of the skirts got covered in mud whenever it rained.

Men's clothes were far more sensible. On impulse she stood and put the coat on, then looked at herself in the mirror. It was a little long in the sleeve and loose in the shoulder, and as Raphael had been much taller than her, hung almost to her calves. Of course it looked ridiculous anyway, over a dress.

Still wearing the coat she rummaged in the trunk, looking for a shirt, the matching knee-length waistcoat and breeches, intending to try a whole outfit on. It would pass the time. She found a shirt, and was looking for the other items when she suddenly became aware she was no longer alone.

Turning, she saw Mrs Grave standing in the doorway, a shocked expression on her face.

"Ah!" she said, placing the shirt on the bed. "I have been looking for you. Please, sit down. We need to speak."

Mrs Grave looked around as though searching for a chair, although there were plenty in the room, then back at her mistress.

"Any chair," Harriet prompted. She took off the coat, because it was a warm day and a heavy coat, and dropped it carelessly back in the trunk. "Dr Smith has assured me it is certain now that we have not contracted smallpox, as I'm sure you know."

"Yes, thank God," Mrs Grave said.

"Indeed. So with that in mind, there is really no reason for you to stay here any longer, is there? You can terminate your employment immediately. I will give you your wages due, plus an extra three months, and a good character. You may stay until the end of the month or until you find a new post or accommodation."

In view of the woman's behaviour over the last years Harriet thought this to be extremely generous, but the expression on Mrs Grave's face said clearly that she did not agree.

"But my lady, now you are alone in the world, it is all the more reason for you to have a companion," she said. "I hoped to be that person, a comfort to you in your dark days."

Was the idiot serious? Or was she trying to provoke her into an indiscreet remark? Harriet thought for a moment. It was perhaps too soon in her widowhood for brutal honesty.

"Mrs Grave, let me be frank," Harriet lied. "We both know that you were not employed by Raphael to be my companion, but to spy on me for him. Now he is gone there is no need for you to do that. As kind as it is of you to offer your comfort to me at this sad time, I think we also both know that our personalities differ too much for you to be an appropriate companion for me. However, I hope you will be successful elsewhere, and the character I give you will assist you in finding such a place. I would not wish to add anything to that character that might render it difficult for you to obtain another post," she added.

There. That was much better than bugger off, you vicious, traitorous bitch, which was what she would have said, were she truly being frank.

Mrs Grave sat for a moment absorbing this, and hopefully taking on board the threat. Harriet gave her time to do so by folding the coat and replacing it carefully in the trunk. Finally Mrs Grave sighed, and stood up.

"I suppose there is nothing I can do to change your mind?" she asked.

"You suppose right," Harriet said, growing impatient now. "I won't keep you any longer, as you will be impatient to start searching for a new position."

Well, that was not too difficult, she thought after Mrs Grave had left. At least the woman hadn't burst into tears or made any ridiculous threats or insults. She had accepted defeat. It was a good start, although Harriet did not expect the next dismissal to go as well. But go it would.

THE ECCENTRIC'S TALE: HARRIET

She was the mistress here now, and intended everyone to know it. That evening she would write to her father and tell him it was time to send Mr Noakes.

* * *

Harriet stood five steps up on the staircase, looking across at the sea of servants' faces, as she had nearly three years previously when she had first declared war on her husband, a war she had comprehensively won. Now she was here to start establishing the peace, and to share the spoils as it were, once she knew exactly what the spoils were. She smiled at them, and a number of them smiled back, which was a start.

"I've called you all together today for a number of reasons," she said. "First of all, I would like to thank you all for helping me through the last weeks. Your expressions of sympathy and loyalty have been a great comfort to me in this sad time."

Right, enough of the sentimental bull. On to what mattered.

"First of all I'd like to address the topic that I'm sure is on your minds. As you will no doubt be aware, now that I am alone, I will not need as many servants, especially as many footmen, to serve only myself. I am not like Lord Hereford, and do not feel the need to have a huge number of idle liveried servants purely to show how rich I am. Having said that, I have no wish to dismiss people without good reason. I'm aware that some of you may wish to leave, and if any of you do, then I will pay your wages for the year and will give you a good character, of course. Please come and see me either today or tomorrow if you wish to go.

"If you don't, then depending on your current role, you may need to be adaptable and take on a new job. I am intending to make some alterations in the house and gardens in time, and if you have any relevant skills, or are adaptable and willing to learn new things and work hard, then I will do my utmost to find a place for you. Again, if you are interested in this offer, come to see me and we can discuss it.

"As I've just said, I intend to make some changes, but before I can do that I need to learn about the estate, and what needs to be done. I am relying on you all to be honest and trustworthy and to help me in whatever way you can. Such help will be noticed, I assure you."

In the background she saw Mr Harrison smile smugly, no doubt thinking he was one of the indispensables. *No one is indispensable, you bastard,* she thought. *You will find that out soon enough.*

"Over the next week or so I would like to see all your sleeping quarters, to see if anything needs to be done to make them more comfortable, so be prepared for me to come to them. However, I will make one change right now, and that is to say that from today I will allow all of you one scuttle of coal each day in the summer months, and two in the winter if you need it, to ensure your rooms are warm and dry. If you currently sleep in the corridors or other rooms, please let me know, and we will talk about that.

"If any of you have any worries, or wish to discuss anything at all with me, then I will be available to anyone in the library from eleven until one each day for the next two weeks."

"Excuse me, my lady, but eleven until one is the customary time for receiving visitors," Harrison called out.

"Yes, I am quite aware of the customary time for receiving visitors," Harriet replied coldly. "That is why I have chosen that time to receive the servants, who will be visitors."

"But—"

"Brian, Paul, I will leave it to yourselves to explain to any non-staff visitors who call that I am unavailable for the next two weeks. I am sure it is one of the tasks you undertook for his lordship," Harriet interrupted.

"But this is most irregular, my lady," Harrison persisted.

"Mr Harrison," Harriet said. "You are employed as my steward. As far as I am aware, it is not a steward's job to teach his employer society etiquette. If I felt the need for such instruction, which I do not, then I would approach my mother, who as a duchess is eminently qualified in such matters."

With that, she turned her attention back to the now grinning servants, ignoring his furious expression, and dismissing them all, she repaired to the library.

You will have to do a damn sight better than that if you wish to undermine me, she thought furiously.

The afternoon found her at the stables, where she informed the Master of Horse that she now intended to ride, a lot, and so would need a suitable mount.

THE ECCENTRIC'S TALE: HARRIET

"I know you haven't had the opportunity to see me ride," she said, "But I am an accomplished horsewoman, and have missed riding enormously. I will of course keep both the coach and a garden chaise for occasional visitors who wish to tour the gardens, but for myself, unless the weather is truly appalling, I will ride. Is there a particular horse you would recommend for me?"

Mr Evans was looking unaccountably uncomfortable, Harriet noticed, but due to the ignorance Raphael had kept her in, she had no way of knowing if the man was accustomed to brutal treatment from his employer, was hiding something, or if this was just his natural demeanour. She assumed the former was most likely, and continued.

"I will not hold you to account if you pick an unsuitable horse, but as you know their temperaments far better than I, your opinion would be helpful."

He looked behind her at a small pile of hay, as though wondering if a suitable horse might be found there, and then nodded slightly before leading her to the stalls.

"In truth, my lady, most of the horses have delightful temperaments, and if you're an experienced rider, any of them would suit. With the exception of Boxer, that is. He is one on his own, and I wouldn't recommend anyone to ride him, or even go in his stall alone," Mr Evans said.

"Really? Why ever not?"

"He's wild, my lady. Lord Hereford won him in a bet, I believe, and I'm sure the loser was happy to pay. He thought we could tame him, but he's very unpredictable."

"Well, then," Harriet said, eyeing a soft-eyed grey horse in the stall next to her, "I think over the next days I'll ride a number of them to see if there's a particular one I get on well with, and then I'll choose a regular mount. I will start tomorrow with this one. I intend to ride down to the villages and begin to meet my tenants."

"Tomorrow?" Mr Evans replied. "But you will need a side-saddle, and we don't have such a thing. One will have to be ordered for you."

"Oh bugger," said Harriet. "I will ride astride, then. I prefer that anyway."

Mr Evans' eyes widened, and then he blushed, presumably remembering the last conversation they'd had on the subject.

"But my lady, is that not a little…er…unseemly if you intend to meet people? It's not customary for such a great lady as yourself to ride astride. Do forgive me," he added immediately, blushing. "I didn't mean to tell you what you should do."

"Mr Evans, never apologise for giving me advice. I will tell you now, I am not my husband. I will always appreciate a knowledgeable opinion. And on equine matters you are knowledgeable, or you would not hold the post you do, which is why I value your opinion as to a suitable mount. And sadly, you are right. It would not do for me to shock my tenants on our first meeting. Very well, we will order a side saddle, and in the meantime I will ride in the chaise. But I will call in as often as I can so the horses can get to know me." Hmm…there, the uncomfortable look and the glance at the pile of hay again. She started to walk back towards it and the door.

"Will you not need more than one chaise, my lady?" Mr Evans ventured. "Not for visiting the tenants, but for when guests come to stay and wish to tour the gardens?"

It was on the tip of her tongue to say *I don't intend to have many visitors,* but he was right about that too. She couldn't change everything overnight. *Don't be impatient,* she admonished herself, *you can have it all, if you take it slowly.*

"Ah, of course. I had not thought of that," she said. "How many do we have at the moment?" She was right next to the pile of hay now. Was he hiding contraband?

"Ten, my lady."

"Ten?! Well, I suppose we should keep everything as it is for now, then." Suddenly she kicked out sideways into the hay. If he was hiding bottles of brandy or some such, she would feel it, or hear it clank.

Her foot came into contact with something, eliciting a squeak of pain, which was quickly stifled. Before Mr Evans could react, Harriet reached down into the hay and pulled a tiny, grubby child out of it. They looked at each other for a moment, Harriet with shock and the child with utter terror, and then, still firmly grasping the little girl's arm so she couldn't flee, Harriet turned her attention to the ashen-faced Horse Master.

"I hope you have a good explanation for why you are concealing a little girl on the premises, Mr Evans," she said. "It's

THE ECCENTRIC'S TALE: HARRIET

clear from your expression that you are up to no good."

Mr Evans' mouth dropped open.

"No, no, my lady…my lady. My God, it's nothing like that!" he replied, flustered.

"What is it like, then? I can see no reason why she would be here. None of you are married – I know that because Raphael never employed married servants. So she is not your child. Or is she your child, and you are concealing your marriage from me?"

"I….I…er…" Mr Evans stuttered, his face a mask of desperation.

"He ain't my Pa, Lady Hereford," came a small voice at Harriet's elbow. Harriet looked down, and seeing that the child seemed currently to be more capable of answering questions than the adult, she addressed her.

"What's your name, child?" Harriet asked.

"Claire," the little girl said. "Claire Morley. I'm one of the scullery maids, my lady."

"So, Claire Morley," replied Harriet, "If you're a scullery maid, why are you here instead of in the scullery?"

"I loves it here," she answered. "I loves the horses, I does."

"I'm very glad of it, but don't you have work to do in the scullery?"

"She doesn't normally come here in the day time, my lady," Mr Evans, who had now found his voice, said. "She brought my lunch today."

"If she only brought your lunch, why did you feel the need to hide her from me?"

"Because it's not the scullery maid's job to bring food, but the cook let her because she knows Claire loves the animals here. It was a kindness, but I didn't know if…er…"

"You didn't know if I'd be angry because Raphael would have been," Harriet finished. "You said she doesn't normally come in the day time. I presume you do in the night, then?" she said, looking back at the child and letting go of her arm, as she showed no inclination to flee.

"Yes, my lady. But only when it's time to sleep! I sleeps here, that's all, but I don't go in Boxer's stall no more, since Mr Evans gave me a row for it. I don't cause no trouble, and I does all my work in the kitchen, honest!" she said.

She had the same accent and way of speaking as Jem had

before Harriet had started correcting his speech to make him sound more educated. Harriet smiled at the thought, and both Claire and Mr Evans relaxed noticeably. She sighed.

"Let me say this to both of you, and anyone else listening," she said. "I will never be angry if people tell me the truth, even if that's an unpleasant truth. I will never be angry with people giving me advice. I *will* be angry with people who lie to me, however. I am nothing like my husband. I realise it will take time for you to truly believe that, but please start now. Claire, do you not have a place to sleep at the house?"

"Yes, I sleeps in the kitchen. But it's noisy, and it has lots of smells, and it's too hot. I likes to be outside, my lady, and so I comes here, where it smells of hay and horses, and Mr Evans, he lets me sleep in the straw, which is lovely. I sleeps better here than in the kitchen, and so I can work harder for you!" the child added somewhat desperately.

"Don't you like working in the kitchens?" Harriet asked.

Claire considered for a moment.

"No, I hates it," she said. "But Ma says I has to, as there's too many of us at home. She'll be mad if I has to leave."

"Well, that was honest," Harriet said, smiling. "I suppose you'd like to work with horses then."

"Oh yes! I'd like that more than anything!" Claire breathed.

"I've told her she can't be a stablehand, my lady, because they're all boys, but she loves being with the horses so much, and she's no trouble sleeping here, now she keeps out of Boxer's stall. I reckoned if anyone was to try to mess with the horses in the night, she'd raise the alarm."

"That's true. Boxer. Is he the wild horse you told me about?"

"He ain't wild, my lady. Just sad, he is, that's all," Claire piped up. "I told Mr Evans he won't trample me, because we's the same. Just been treated bad, he has. Don't trust no one."

Mr Evans snorted.

"He hasn't been treated badly here, but he kicks and bites anyone who comes near him. I found her in the stall with him one night, just standing stroking his nose and talking to him. I nearly died of fright, I can tell you. She was very lucky not to be killed."

"Have you been treated badly, child?" Harriet asked.

Claire blushed.

THE ECCENTRIC'S TALE: HARRIET

"He's gone now, my lady. My ma threw him out, she did. I'm well now. Boxer will be too, but animals takes longer, because you can't tell them with words that you ain't going to hurt them. They has to smell it on you, and learn by how you speaks, not the words you says."

"Can you show me how you speak to him?" Harriet asked.

"Not now, my lady. Because he don't know you, but can smell you's here, so he'll be upset, he will. Have to wait until you's gone for a while, or until you's been here a lot, so he knows you. Then I can."

Interesting. Harriet considered for a minute.

"Would you like to be a stablehand then, instead of a scullery maid?" she asked, and was rewarded with a brilliant smile.

"I'd love to! But I's a girl."

"You are. So am I. I don't see why a girl can't be anything she wants as long as she's strong enough to do the work needed. Do you think you're strong enough to do the work?"

"Oh yes! I's strong, because I has to carry big pots and water in the kitchens."

"Well then. You have a new stablehand, Mr Evans. I need to speak to the cook, though, Claire, because if she really needs you in the kitchen, you might have to stay there until I can find a replacement. Is there enough work for her here?"

"Er…yes, enough work. But…my lady, stablehands are always male."

"Not any more," Harriet said. "If cook can manage without you, you can stay here, and I'll check on you in a few days."

The expression on the Master's face told Harriet that he realised she was deadly serious about this.

"But she can't sleep with the other stablehands in the loft. It wouldn't be right," he objected.

"That's true. But she's sleeping here in the straw anyway, so she can carry on doing that for now. I'll be looking at all the accommodations soon, as I said, and I will think of a more permanent solution then, providing she proves she's a good worker."

"I will be! I promise, I will be!" Claire cried.

"How old are you?" Harriet asked.

"Eight. I'll be nine when it snows," Claire replied.

"Treat her as you would the other very young stableboys, Mr Evans. Let's give her a chance to prove herself. We all deserve that in life. Order the saddle for me, and in the meantime have the chaise ready tomorrow at ten."

She left the stables, smiling. God, it was good to be able to make decisions herself! And to give others a chance to have a happy life! Mr Evans might not be happy with her decision, but he seemed a fair, kind man. He wouldn't have let the child sleep in the stables if he wasn't kind. And the child had interesting ideas about animals, seemed to identify with them. It would be nice to let her explore that, see if she did have a way with them.

That evening she went back to Raphael's rooms, and this time took out all his outfits, laying some of them out on the bed. Then she called for Mrs Morton the housekeeper to attend her. The woman arrived a few minutes later and curtsied deeply.

"Have I dragged you away from some urgent duty?" Harriet asked, seeing the woman's flustered expression.

"Oh no, my lady! No duty is more urgent than a summons from yourself," Mrs Morton replied hurriedly.

"Hmm. Well, I won't keep you for more than a few minutes. I am thinking to have these outfits of my husband," she indicated the outfits on the bed, "altered. Do we have a seamstress here who would be capable of such work or do you think I should employ a tailor?"

Mrs Morton ran her hand across one of the coats.

"If anyone can do it, it would be Susan," she said after a moment. "She is very accomplished, and I know she's made alterations to livery occasionally when a new footman has been hired. Although of course these garments are of very high quality. I suppose it will depend on the extent of the alteration needed. Do I know the person they are to be altered for, my lady?"

"Yes. They would be for me," Harriet replied.

"For you?!" Mrs Morton said, deeply shocked.

"Indeed. I thought they would be just the thing for riding, which I now intend to do a lot of."

"Oh, you mean just the coats!" Mrs Morton said with obvious relief. "What a fine idea! Wearing a masculine coat over your riding dress is the height of fashion, and it would be an excellent way of keeping a little of Lord Hereford with you, as it were, when you are out riding. I beg your pardon for being so familiar, my lady."

And so wrong, thought Harriet, although it would do no harm if the servants believed she missed that bastard enough to want to wear his coats.

"Exactly." Harriet smiled. "I will need to see Susan, then."

"I will enquire as to whether I can still obtain dress material to match the coats exactly," Mrs Morton said. "Perhaps Susan can finish them in time for when you come out of mourning."

"Yes, but don't worry about the dress material," Harriet said. "I'm sure I have some dresses that are a similar, or complementary colour."

While she waited for Susan to appear, Harriet sat on the bed. It had been a long day spent dealing with people she didn't know at all, and Mrs Morton had been no exception. Over four years of marriage and she hadn't exchanged more than a few sentences with the woman. It was ridiculous to have to get to know so many people for the first time, when she'd been living in the same house with them for years. And it was exhausting.

She sat down on the bed, suddenly very tired, wanting nothing more than to sleep, then to wake up in the morning and spend the whole day without talking to anyone at all, as she often had when she'd lived with her parents. Being alone refreshed her. But she couldn't do that. Not yet.

There was a knock on the door, and Susan appeared. Harriet wiped her hand across her face and adopted a welcoming expression.

"Mrs Morton told me you just wanted the coats altering, my lady," Susan said when Harriet explained what she actually wanted.

"She seemed a little shocked even by that, until she remembered the current riding fashions," Harriet observed. "I didn't see the need to upset her any more. Especially as it won't be her doing the alterations. Can you do it?"

"I think so. The breeches I can certainly alter. The coats will be more difficult, because you being a lady, I'd have to alter them not just for size, but for shape too. But I'd like to try. It's only…"

"It's only what?" Harriet asked when it became apparent that

Susan wasn't going to finish the sentence.

"Well, I'm not *certain* that I can do it, and I'd be very afraid of perhaps spoiling the first one. They really are very costly," she said. "Perhaps if there's an old manservant's outfit somewhere that I could practice with?"

"Nonsense," Harriet replied. "Raphael's not going to wear them again, is he? And judging by what most of the servants are wearing, an *old* outfit would be nothing more than rags and no good to practice on at all. Apart from the footmen, of course. I intend to amend that state of affairs. Bloody ridiculous having half the staff dressed like beggars," she added to herself. "Anyway," she continued, remembering who she was talking to, "take the purple one to use for practice. I don't like that anyway, so it'll be no loss if you ruin it. I'm sure, given a little time, you'll be able to do it. And if you really don't think you can once you've tried your best, then you must tell me. I won't be angry."

"Will you be wearing them for masquerade parties, or for plays if you decide to put one on for your friends, my lady?" Susan asked, lifting the purple satin outfit from the bed carefully.

"God, no. Why would I do that?" Harriet said. "There's only one thing I hate more than a room crowded with people pretending they don't know each other because they're wearing a costume and a scrap of silk on their faces, even though it's bloody obvious who everyone is. And that's interminable plays acted by people who have no damn idea how to do it. Bloody dreadful. I hate them. No, I intend to wear them, once I'm out of mourning. Couldn't find a black suit, after all."

"You intend to wear them as your normal attire?" Susan asked, her expression now as shocked as Mrs Morton's had been. "Oh! I'm so sorry, my lady, I—"

"Don't apologise for asking a question, girl! Or for expressing a view," Harriet interrupted. "When I was a child, I was a great friend of the king for a time. King Charles, that was, the current queen's uncle. He told me that Queen Catherine, when she first arrived in England, often wore men's clothes when out in the private gardens, as they were not as restrictive as feminine fashions were. If it's good enough for a queen, then it's good enough for me."

Susan smiled, presumably reassured by the fact that a queen

THE ECCENTRIC'S TALE: HARRIET

had set the fashion. "I'll do my very best for you, my lady," she said. "I think people might be shocked, though, if they *do* happen to call when you're in the gardens."

"I don't give a damn if they are," Harriet said.

God, it was so good to speak the truth. Even if the hearer clearly didn't believe it.

"Oh, and Susan," Harriet added as the seamstress was leaving the room, purple satin draped over her arm. Susan stopped and looked back. "Don't be ruining your eyes sewing them by candlelight. Tell Mrs Morton that someone else will have to do your normal duties, so that you can sew by day. Be no use to me if you're blind, will you?"

"No, my lady. Thank you," Susan said, and left the room smiling.

* * *

The three people were sitting around the dining table, although they were not enjoying a meal. The table was instead spread with a plan of the estate which Harriet had found amongst Raphael's possessions. Her father's steward Mr Noakes and his son Harold, who had arrived the previous day, were listening as Harriet enlightened them as to what she hoped to do in the near future.

"The first thing I want to do is to improve the servants' accommodation. I'd also like to increase the wages of most of them, and provide the ones who are not seen by noble visitors with decent clothing," she said. "Raphael only cared about appearances, so the out-of-sight servants look like beggars. I really believe that if the staff is decently treated and comfortable, then the whole household will be run well. Raphael believed in using threats and fear to keep his servants working hard. I don't believe in that."

"You hold your father's view of household matters, then," Mr Noakes observed.

"I suppose I do. But really I just hold the view that if people are treated well, then they will be happy, and happy, well-treated servants are more likely to be loyal and trustworthy than resentful cowed ones will be."

"I agree. Although some would mistake such kindness for weakness. And you will always have some servants who are not loyal and trustworthy, no matter how well they're treated. That's just the way of the world."

"I know, but it's really important for me to have as many dependable trustworthy staff as possible, particularly the senior staff, if I am to manage the estate alone for the rest of my life."

"Hmm. Well, then, let us see what we can do to help you achieve that," Mr Noakes said.

"God, it is so good to speak the truth," Harriet said happily. "And to be believed."

"Why would I not believe you?" Mr Noakes said. "I have known you since you were a child, and you have always been honest, even when you would have made life easier for yourself by lying. If you say you have no intention of remarrying, then I have no reason to doubt you. Although if you fall in love, then everything will change, you know."

Harriet laughed.

"That's true. I will never fall in love with someone deeply enough to throw my freedom away, though. It's different for men, of course. They can fall in love and marry and still do what they want. I can't understand why so many women want so desperately to marry and be completely controlled by a man. It's ridiculous."

"Not all marriages are like that, though," Mr Noakes said. "I think you were unfortunate. And the lot of a lifelong spinster is not an enviable one. A woman gains respect by marrying."

"Bloody ridiculous, that is. I can't see why shackling yourself to some idiot man makes you respectable! But in any case, I'm not a spinster now. I've done the marriage thing. Now I'm a widow, and that gives me respect *and* freedom. I won't be giving that up for sweet words and kisses and such nonsense."

Harold Noakes looked at her admiringly, while his father laughed out loud.

"You have not changed, Lady Harriet…I beg your pardon, Lady Hereford," he said. "I pray you never do. I find such honesty truly refreshing."

"I prefer you to call me Lady Harriet. Thank you! However, I'm now constantly pestered by well-meaning people who don't find such honesty refreshing. In fact most of them wouldn't know honesty if I shot them with it. If I say anything that they don't agree with, or that is not 'acceptable' to society, then I'm either

THE ECCENTRIC'S TALE: HARRIET

stupid or infantile. And I've only told them a tiny fraction of what I actually intend to do. I can't wait to start showing people I mean what I say. Maybe then they'll stop giving me unwanted advice. Maybe they'll stop visiting me altogether. That would be bloody marvellous."

Mr Noakes smiled.

"Then let us make it possible for you to do what you intend," he said. "You want to know how much money the estate brings in?"

Harriet smiled.

"Yes, but I need to know more than that. I intend to dismiss Mr Harrison," she said. "He is disrespectful and arrogant, and as Papa said, that is enough. But I also think he may be stealing from the estate, and that he may have been doing so for a long time. And that is why I asked Papa if I could use your services. Any steward worth his salt could add up the figures and tell me how much I'm earning, but you are capable of finding out if he is falsifying the accounts. I dislike him intensely, but I'm sure he is very clever."

"What makes you think he's falsifying the accounts?" Harold asked.

"It's not just because I don't like him," she answered. "He's ambitious, and he thinks a great deal of himself. And yet he's been here for fifteen years and has never tried to improve on his position."

"He could not improve much more, though, could he?" Harold said. "A steward is the highest position in a household, and only dukes and royalty are above a marquessate."

"That's true, but I still think he would try. He has a great sense of self-importance. I believe that two things have stopped him from moving up. One of those is that Raphael gave him free rein to tyrannise the staff – indeed he probably encouraged him to, being a tyrant himself. And the other is that he is earning far more here than his salary. He has his own apartments in the east wing of the house, and a few days ago I paid him a surprise visit. He absolutely would not let me into even his sitting room, and when I asked to go in to discuss the matter, he actually came out into the corridor and closed the door, telling me he was thinking of my reputation, and that it was not appropriate for me to be alone with him in his rooms!"

"Good Lord!" said Mr Noakes. "He actually said that? Does he really think that you, a marchioness, would compromise your reputation with a servant?"

"No, I don't think he thinks that, although I don't think he believes himself to be a mere servant either. He was trying to keep me out of his rooms, and from the glimpse I got through the door, I believe that was because if I saw them I would know that he could not afford such luxury on his salary. I didn't insist that he let me in, because I didn't want him to suspect I might investigate him."

"He could say that your husband made presents to him, though," Harold pointed out.

"He could indeed. Which is why I need such an accomplished steward as your father to discover the truth. But your father is also utterly trustworthy and loyal to my family, as, from what Papa has said, are you. If after investigation you tell me there are no discrepancies, then I will know it is the truth, and not that you have been bought off by him. And that means a great deal to me. I would be obliged if you could start tomorrow. I will introduce you to him, and will make it very clear that he must show you absolutely everything you ask for, without question. If he does not, tell me, and I will dismiss him on the spot. In the meantime I intend to visit the villages on the estate, and the bakehouse, brewery, home farm and so on. I will be very observant, and then once you have examined his accounts we will compare what they indicate with what I have seen."

"If we do find irregularities, will you prosecute him?" Mr Noakes asked.

"Not for a few small things, no. I will tell you, Raphael was a cold, cruel man who cared nothing for the welfare of others, so Harrison could always say he had been ordered to bully and threaten the tenants. But if he has been majorly dishonest in keeping the accounts, then I would most definitely prosecute him. If I did, that would solve the other problem you mentioned too."

"Which problem was that?"

"That if I seek to improve the lot of my servants, some of them might mistake kindness for weakness. Prosecuting Harrison would send a clear message to *all* the servants that although I am a woman, I am not to be trifled with. Now, I will leave you to enjoy the rest of your evening."

THE ECCENTRIC'S TALE: HARRIET

After she had gone, father and son sat silently for a moment. Then Harold whistled softly through his teeth.

"I did warn you," his father said, correctly interpreting the gesture.

"You did. But I thought you were exaggerating. I mean she's only nineteen! I didn't expect her to be quite so frank. Or so formidable."

"Men of nineteen have led armies, in the past," Mr Noakes pointed out. "Alexander the Great was the same age when he became king."

"Well yes, but he was—"

"A man? Never underestimate women, my boy. Lady Amelia is another formidable woman. You will meet many of them in your life, and you will do well to recognise them. Lady Harriet is different only in that she is outspoken and makes no attempt to hide her strength behind a façade of femininity. Perhaps she will learn to do that when she is older, although I doubt it."

"I hope she doesn't," Harold said. "She's refreshing, as you said."

"That she is. And good to have as a friend. She is finding her strength, and when she does, I think you will not want her for an enemy."

"I don't want her for one now!" Harold replied.

CHAPTER TEN

January 1692

Harriet's guests sat around the dinner table, which sparkled with silver serving dishes and crystal glasses, reflecting the candlelight beautifully. Although it was only two o'clock, the sky was leaden with snow clouds and the wind howled around the house, but in the cosy dining room with a large fire and many candles burning you could forget the weather, unless you had to go out in it later.

Luckily, only two of the diners had to go out later, and they only had a very short distance to travel. The others had agreed to stay a few more days, in the hope that the weather would improve, and one of them had just agreed to stay here permanently as Harriet's steward. The dinner was being given as a thank you to Harold and his father, who had helped enormously to get Harriet's life firmly on the road she wished to pursue.

"So, there has been no word of Harrison?" her father asked, beckoning a footman to refill his wine glass.

"No. I suspect he's gone abroad," Harriet replied. "That's what I'd do, if I'd embezzled that much money from my employer. He'd certainly hang if he was convicted. At least by sneaking off in the night he saved me the job of dismissing him and prosecuting him."

"I can't believe he'd been stealing so much, for so long," Amelia said. "What was your husband thinking of to allow such blatant theft?"

"I don't think he knew anything about it. The accounts were very carefully kept. I find it amusing that he was so obsessed with money that he threatened the servants with jail rather than pay

THE ECCENTRIC'S TALE: HARRIET

them properly to stop them leaving, and yet the one servant he trusted was cheating him of a fortune. And if I hadn't taken the time to go round the estate and chat to the villagers in their homes, something Raphael would never have done, I wouldn't have known anything about it either."

"Is that how you found out, then?"

"Partly. The accounts showed payments for farming implements, thatch for the cottages, and various other things that should have meant the tenants were living reasonably well. But when I rode round the villages and went into the houses, they were in an appalling condition, as were the tenants. That angered me the most, that Harrison would allow people to live in such abject misery, allow children to die because their parents could not afford food or a physician, just so that he could have gold dishes to eat from and tapestries in his rooms."

"Are you talking about Raphael or Harrison?" Amelia asked.

"Both, in truth," Harriet said. "Raphael didn't care a fig about his servants. But he did care about getting a revenue from the estate, which was why he agreed to the new tools and repairs, I presume. It was Harrison who denied them the thatch and bought gold dishes, which even I don't have. And were it not for our guests of honour," she raised her glass to Mr Noakes and his son, who were flushed with pleasure at the honour of being invited to dinner with a duke and duchess as well as an earl and countess, "I would not have found that out. Harrison hid his tracks well."

"We cannot take all the credit, my lady," said Mr Noakes. "That was just the surface. It was yourself who discovered the serious theft."

"Maybe. But I can't tell you how happy I am that you have agreed to become my steward, Harold," Harriet said. "You are a credit to your father, and I have every confidence and faith in you. And that is so very important to me."

"How did you discover the serious theft?" the Earl of Highbury asked.

Harriet recounted how, after seeing the pages of expenditure for farming implements, thatch and furniture to a family by the name of Yale, she had gone to the farm in question and had dismounted to talk to the farmer's wife, who was standing in the doorway of a ramshackle cottage. She was very thin and dressed in ragged clothes, and when Harriet had openly asked her when the roof had last been thatched and whether she'd had a payment for furniture, the woman had invited her into the house.

Harriet had never seen such squalor in her life. The only furniture in the room was an ancient table and a home-made bench, along with a rough wooden chair by the empty grate. The wall at the end of the room was falling down and had obviously been patched with some mud, and there was daylight coming through the thatch. She remembered the entries she had seen in Harrison's neat hand, dated two months ago, for the roof to be re-thatched, a table, chairs and beds.

There was nothing in this house, and the woman was obviously hungry, as were the four young children who emerged from the recesses of the room to eye the richly dressed lady who had come to visit. And yet she clearly tried to keep it clean. The floor was swept, and the table was scrubbed and clean. This was no drunken slovenly housewife who had squandered the money on drink.

"I assume you know Mr Harrison?" Harriet had asked, and had watched with interest as the woman's face twisted with disgust before she remembered who she was with and schooled her expression to one of neutrality. "I see you do, then. I'll be honest with you, Mrs Yale, and I hope you'll answer me honestly, because God knows I value the truth and need it. I have been charged for a new roof for this cottage and for several items of furniture, just two months ago. Do you know anything about it?"

The woman had looked at her for a moment, clearly weighing her up.

"No," she replied. "I know my Seth asked for the roof to be done, because when it rains it leaks terrible. But Mr Harrison said that you had better things to do with your money than waste it on such things, and that Seth should be able to see to it himself."

"I see," Harriet had said. "Are you paying a reduced rent for the farm, then? Is Seth earning enough from the land to pay for a new roof himself?"

Mrs Yale had snorted with laughter at that, and then had bobbed a slight curtsey by way of apology.

"We aren't paying a reduced rent, no, my lady. And Seth works

THE ECCENTRIC'S TALE: HARRIET

very hard, he does, and the smith repairs the tools for nothing for us, for all the farmers, but…" Her voice trailed off, but she seemed to be thinking, so Harriet waited for a moment, only speaking when it was clear the woman was uncertain of the reception her information would get.

"Mrs Yale," she said after a minute. "I need to tell you this. I am not like my husband. I am interested in the welfare of my tenants, and the entries I am seeing in my books do not correspond with what I'm seeing here. My husband did not tell me anything about the estate, so I am in the process of finding out for myself how much it brings in. However, I would think it to be enough that the workers don't have to live like paupers. The land is good and there is plenty of it. I intend to make changes, changes for the better, but I can't do that unless I know what is happening now, and whether my steward is a trustworthy man or not. If you can tell me anything that will help me, I will be very grateful."

Mrs Yale had inhaled very deeply through her nose, and then had sent the children out of the house.

"This can't be known to come from me," she said, once they were out of earshot. "If it is, then my life will be worth nothing. And everyone knows you've come to see me."

Harriet had nodded.

"I can't swear not to act on whatever you tell me, if it needs to be acted on. But if you tell me what you know, then I swear to you I will never say who told me. After I've been here I will go to every other house in the village, if it takes me all day, and chat with everyone, so no one will know where my information has come from."

Mrs Yale had nodded.

"You've been good to my sister, and she thinks you're an angel from heaven. You had no reason to do that but kindness. And God knows she needs kindness, with what Ma's lodger did to her. So I'll take a chance and be honest with you."

She had then gone on to tell Harriet that not only had Harrison ignored all pleas for repairs on houses, but that the rents charged were exorbitant. He loaned money at high interest rates to farmers so that they could buy essential tools, and then insisted on taking twenty percent of everything they produced as well as the interest payments.

"So we're always in debt to him, and if we tried to do anything about it, he'd prosecute us," she said.

He's using the same tactics that Raphael used with the servants to stop them leaving, Harriet thought, and so believed the woman immediately.

"Thank you," she said. "I really need to know this."

"No, there's more than that. Some of the people deal in smuggled goods, and store them here when they come up from the coast."

"Everyone does that," Harriet said, who was no more a lover of paying customs duties than anyone else in the country. "I would not act against whoever is storing the goods, as long as they do it discreetly."

Mrs Yale had smiled.

"I knew you were a good'un," she said, "but that's not what I was telling you, really. Mr Harrison is paying for whole cargoes to be brought in though, and then he forces us, whether we want to or not, to head down to the coast and bring the stuff up here."

"Whole cargoes?" Harriet had said. "But that must cost an enormous amount of money!"

"I don't know about that. But I do know that I don't want my Seth risking his life unloading and transporting brandy and silk and suchlike, especially when he gets nothing for it, and loses a few days of work too every couple of months."

"Have any of you refused to do it?" Harriet had asked, already suspecting the answer but needing to hear it for herself.

"We can't. He said if any of us go against him, he'll inform on us, and that he's doing everything on the orders of Lord Hereford. Begging your pardon and God rest his soul, but his lordship was not a man we felt we could go to to discuss such things."

Harriet closed her eyes for a moment. Had Raphael really been behind this, or had Harrison been stealing huge amounts of money from him to pay for the cargoes and reap the profit?

"My husband has been dead for several months now," she'd said. "Has a cargo been brought in since then?"

Mrs Yale had nodded.

"Yes. And one's gone out too. He sends wool out across the channel."

"And did he say he was doing that on my orders?" Harriet asked.

THE ECCENTRIC'S TALE: HARRIET

"No, but he did say nothing had changed, that his orders were still the same."

Which was tantamount to saying that Harriet had ordered him to break the law. She had him. Not only was he stealing large sums from her, but he was committing crime in her name.

By God, she'd thought vehemently, *he will hang for this, the bastard.*

"But he didn't hang for it, because he disappeared in the night with the gold plate he loved so much," Harriet finished. "And good riddance. At least I know he'll never dare to show his face again. And now I know just how damn rich I am, I intend to enjoy it. Looking after the people who depend on me is just the start. I managed to get the essential repairs done to the cottages before the worst of the winter came, but in the spring I'm going to arrange for the other repairs to be done. I've written off all their so-called debt, provided them with food for the winter, and will provide them with whatever tools they need for the spring. And then they should be able to look after themselves."

"And you're also refurbishing all the servants' apartments," Stephen said.

"Yes. My theory, which I've really learnt from you and Mama, is that if you treat your servants well, then they will stay longer and work harder. And be happier too. I know there will always be *some* who take advantage, or try to, but that's the same everywhere, not just with servants."

"Can you really afford all this, though? It seems an awful lot to be doing so soon after Raphael's death," Stephen said.

Harriet reached across the table and patted his hand.

"Papa, you and Mama taught me well. I am not overreaching myself. Really, the estate is only a fraction of my income. Raphael had an enormous number of investments as well. I am richer than I ever thought possible, but I'm only saying that to you because I trust you all implicitly. And I have no one to leave it to, so I'm going to damn well enjoy it. And my family can enjoy it too! Except Percy of course. He can go to hell."

"What was it you did for Mrs Yale's sister, that made her trust you enough to risk her life?" Highbury asked now, before Amelia could comment on the continued enmity between Harriet and the uncle she never saw.

"Her sister was a scullery maid here, but I caught her hiding in the stables. It seems that she loves animals and horses in particular, so I said she could be a stable girl."

"A stable girl?" the Countess of Highbury said. "I didn't know there was such a thing!"

"Well, if there wasn't, there is now," Harriet stated. "Got a way with horses, she has, too. Quite remarkable. She's only eight. Raphael won this wild horse in a bet or some such thing, and insisted the Master of Horse should be able to tame it. Boxer, he's called, the horse, not the Master. Of course when he couldn't Raphael said he was incompetent, even though the man's never had any problems with any mount before, and the stables are run impeccably. Anyway, this Boxer made their lives hell because he wouldn't let anyone near him, so it was really difficult to clean out his stall, and exercising him was virtually impossible."

"Perhaps he should be shot, if he's that wild," Daniel said.

"I thought that. But Claire, that's the girl's name, said he wasn't wild, he was just sad. I thought she was a bit strange, and maybe she is, but strange or not, she's the only person who can go near him. When she's there he's completely docile, will let her lead him out of the stables, and will come to her when she calls."

"Really?"

"Yes. I wouldn't have believed it, but I've seen it myself. I asked her what she does, and she said she just talks to him, but she understands him and he knows she's suffered like him, and that she's damaged too, and so he trusts her. He does, that's clear."

"Even so, she can't be a stablehand if she's a girl, surely?" the countess said.

"Why not? If she can do the job, and she certainly can, then she can be a stablehand," Harriet said. "I don't believe in all this rot about girls not being able to do something because they haven't got a penis dangling between their legs. Never heard such rubbish. Don't clean stables with your penis, do you?"

A brief silence fell upon the table, and one of the footmen appeared to have a little coughing fit and had to leave the room for a moment.

"Harriet—" Amelia began tentatively after a minute.

"Yes, I know, Mama, I need to think about what I say," Harriet

THE ECCENTRIC'S TALE: HARRIET

interrupted. "But I consider you all friends. And family, of course, and so I should be able to say whatever I want to you, shouldn't I? In fact, I should be able to say whatever I want to pretty well anybody, because I don't really want friends who I can't be myself with, and I'm rich enough now not to give a damn what anyone thinks of me." She smiled disarmingly at everyone around the table. "A toast!" she said.

The glasses were filled and raised.

"To freedom," Harriet announced. "The most precious gift in the world."

"To freedom," her guests responded, with varying degrees of enthusiasm.

* * *

The next morning Amelia came to Harriet as she was enjoying her morning coffee in bed and asked to have a word with her.

"It's about my penis statement yesterday, isn't it?" Harriet said immediately. "I saw your face when I said it."

"No. Well, yes, in a way," Amelia admitted.

"I might not be quite that blunt if I was in different company," Harriet said. "But it's wonderful to have people I can say anything I want to, who won't judge me for it. I did learn a lot when I endured all those visits with you to learn to be a good wife. Not that it did me any good in the end. It did teach me how to behave in public though, so don't worry that I'll embarrass you at any social events I have to attend."

"I know you won't. I know you weren't happy with Raphael, darling," Amelia said. "But I'm sure your next husband will be different, and what you've learned will stand you in good stead as a wife then."

"There won't be a next husband, Mama," Harriet said. "I have no intention of ever marrying again."

"You can't mean that," Amelia said, aghast.

"Why can't I mean that?"

"You're still so young! You have your whole life in front of you."

"I know. And I'm a widow, so respectable in the eyes of the world, which thinks a woman has to have been married to be worth anything. And I'm very, very rich. Why would I want to give all that up to be married to another bastard?"

"Not all men are like Raphael was, sweeting. Your Papa and I are very happy, and we always have been," Amelia pointed out.

"I know, and I'm glad that you are. But a lot of married people are very unhappy, and even the ones who aren't, it's always the woman who has to give way to the man."

"That's just the way of things, Harriet. A woman's role is to support her husband, to help him to be successful and happy, and to give him children. That can bring great pleasure."

"I'm sure it can. But I don't want to spend my life supporting someone else to be happy. I want to be happy myself. I have everything I need to do that now, and can make all those I'm responsible for happier too. I can't think of *one* advantage of marrying again. Not one. If I do it, then he will get all my money, be able to dictate what I do and don't do, and I'll get nothing in return. Raphael once told me I was insane. If I marry again, I'll prove him right."

"But you must want to have babies! Every woman wants to have babies! And you have to be married for that."

"I don't know about every woman, but I don't want them. In truth I think babies are smelly and noisy. I certainly don't want to risk my life to have one of those, and there's no need for me to since you had my brother. I don't think I can, anyway. Raphael panted and fumbled over me enough, but I never got with child. I'd rather enjoy other people's children, once they're old enough to be interesting. Like Highbury's son, who's delightful. I know you love me, and you want what you think is best for me," Harriet said, seeing her mother's worried expression, "but really, I am happy."

"But you will need someone to help you manage the estate, which is an enormous responsibility. You can't do it alone. It's the man's job to run the outside servants, and the woman's to run the inside. You can't possibly do both. I worry you will overtax yourself."

"Mama, I've undertaxed myself for four years, because Raphael wouldn't let me do *anything*. He thought he could run the whole place himself. I can't do worse than him, and in fact I'm already doing better, I believe. I just need good senior servants, and I already have most of them. Harold will be an excellent

THE ECCENTRIC'S TALE: HARRIET

steward, I'm sure. Mrs Morton, though somewhat prim and easily shocked for my liking, is a very capable and fair housekeeper. Mr Evans is a wonderful master of horse.

"As for the gamekeeper, I found out he was shot last year by poachers whilst defending the game on our estate, and Raphael actually deducted the man's medical bills from his wages! Really, the more I hear about him, the happier I am that he's dead. The man told me he was going to leave as soon as he could afford to, but he changed his mind because I told him that I think such loyalty should be rewarded, and I paid his bills and raised his salary, so he's now staying. All I need now is a good head gardener who will be amenable to the changes I want to make in the grounds, which the current one is not. He seems to think the gardens should be a shrine to Raphael, whereas I cannot wait to make changes."

"You always did love the gardens, even as a child," Amelia said fondly, clearly remembering the time when Harriet had horrified the company by appearing among them covered in manure.

"Yes, and now I intend to indulge that love. I'd much rather grow pineapples and melons than babies. They'll be a lot quieter, and taste a damn sight better too, I'll be bound," she added dryly.

In spite of herself, Amelia laughed at that. But she had to bring her daughter down to earth.

"You do know that once you are out of mourning you will be besieged with suitors," she advised.

"I know. I can deal with that. I'll just say no. No one can make me marry them, except Papa until I'm twenty-one, and I know he won't force me to marry. I can do what I want now, and I intend to."

Amelia looked away for a moment, clearly unwilling to impart unpleasant news.

"If you know something I need to know, Mama, for God's sake tell me," Harriet said.

"The king can make you marry again, Harriet, whatever age you are," Amelia said gently.

"The king? Why should the king do that? I don't even know him! I haven't been to Court and hoped not to go, to live quietly in the countryside."

"You are a great heiress, darling, one of the wealthiest widows in the country. No matter how quiet you are you will not escape the notice of the king. He has already asked how you are coping with your bereavement, and has mentioned that you will be in need of another husband once you are out of mourning."

"Has he? Damn it," Harriet mused.

"If he has a courtier to whom he wishes to give a favour, he could command you to marry him. You could not just say no to that. It is a great honour, to be noticed by the king," Amelia added, seeing her daughter's mutinous expression.

"Not for me, not if he wants to marry me off to some sycophantic idiot. I hope the queen doesn't want me to wait on her too. I'll die if I have to do that. Can't you tell everyone I'm ugly and barren? Maybe that will put them off wanting to marry me, if I can't give them a precious son to inherit."

"Harriet, you are not ugly, and it could well be Raphael who couldn't give you a child. Certainly his family were not exactly fecund, which is why there's no one left to inherit the marquessate. But even if you were a hideous old crone, you would still be an attractive marriage prospect. King William will certainly offer you to a courtier, perhaps as a reward for great loyalty, or to attain the loyalty of someone who can help him further his ambitions."

Harriet sipped her coffee, frowning as she contemplated this.

"William's great ambition is to contain the French, isn't it?" she said finally. "He's afraid that the French will help James take back the crown he stole."

Amelia's eyes widened.

"Harriet—"

"No, I'll never say that in public, Mama. I know it's treason to speak the truth in this instance. But nevertheless William did steal the crown from James, and he has no hereditary right to it. He knows that, which is one of the reasons why he's so desperate to curb French power. And of course he wants to protect his Dutch territories. Don't look at me like that," she added. "I'm no Jacobite, you should know that. I'm no Williamite either. In truth I couldn't care less who's on the throne, as long as he leaves me alone to live the life I want."

"You're not saying that if William tells you to marry again, you'll try to help James take the throne back, surely?"

"What? No, of course not! I don't owe James anything, do I?

THE ECCENTRIC'S TALE: HARRIET

If he wanted to remain the king he should have stayed here and fought for it, not just run away and let his asthmatic son-in-law and milksop daughter take the crown from him!"

"Queen Mary is no milksop. She rules the country when William's away, you know. And it was a bit more complicated than that, Harriet, in fairness," Amelia said.

"I'm sure it was, but I didn't have access to the news then as I do now. As for the queen, she should have taken the power herself when she and William were invited over. After all, it was she who was the next in line to the throne, wasn't it? No reason why she couldn't rule herself, instead of that Dutch traitor. Well, I suppose they were both traitors really, to James, at any rate," she mused.

"Oh, God," Amelia said, clearly remembering her husband's equally disastrous faux pas when Harriet was six.

"Mama, we're alone. I wouldn't say this if there was the slightest chance of being overheard. Anyway, I don't have anything against James, but I don't support him either. Why should I? Just because you have the hereditary right doesn't mean you'll be up to the job, does it? Look at Raphael, for God's sake. Bloody awful marquess he was, letting his steward rob him blind."

"That's a relief, at least," Amelia breathed.

"You should know that I won't do anything that would jeopardise your position at Court. I know how much that means to you. If the king doesn't intend to leave me alone, then I think it's time that I came to Court too. I know Raphael was James' right hand man, but that was before we married. I think I should make it clear to the king that my loyalty is to him, not to James."

"That will not stop him commanding you to marry again, though," Amelia said.

"It might, if I word my feelings in the right way. Don't look so worried, Mama. I *can* be duplicitous if I have to be. And tactful."

Certainly she could, if her future and her happiness were at stake. And it seemed they were.

* * *

May 1692

As soon as she arrived home, Harriet did something she had desperately wanted to do for over a month; she got changed out of her sumptuous costume, walked down to the walled garden, lay on her back on the grass, inhaled the fresh sweet scent of the early roses and lavender, and stared at the sky. It was not a particularly warm morning, and the dew was already soaking through her clothes. Soon she would grow cold, but she didn't care. Right now she was alone, surrounded by growing things on her enormous estate, and, above all, she was free. Absolutely and utterly free. Her future stretched ahead, as cloudless as the blue sky above her, and as infinite in its possibilities.

She had done it. Hopefully.

She had waited impatiently until her period of mourning was over before going to Court, and had dressed with great regard for fashion and taste, remaining in black for a reason, although the heavy silk, expensive lace and sumptuous embroidery of her clothes announced how wealthy she was, as she intended.

Her mother had succeeded in obtaining an invitation for her to attend a soiree of Queen Mary's, as the king was away again. He certainly didn't seem to enjoy being in the country he'd worked so hard to become the king of, Harriet thought. He was hardly ever here. Having now caught up on current events and talked in depth with her family about the joint monarchs, Harriet was privately convinced that William had no love of either Britain or the British, and had become king merely so that he could finance his lifelong ambition of curtailing French domination of Europe, and in particular of his beloved Dutch territories.

It seemed she was not alone in thinking this; rumour abounded that King Louis was actively planning to invade England in an attempt to restore the exiled King James to the throne, and it seemed there was considerable support for this in parts of Britain. Whether the verbal supporters would actually risk their necks for James if he landed was uncertain, but for Harriet that was irrelevant at the moment. It seemed William was likely to be at war against one enemy or another for some time to come.

Her purpose was to convince the queen that she was a more

THE ECCENTRIC'S TALE: HARRIET

valuable asset to her as a widow than she would be as wife to an ambitious courtier. With that in mind she had learnt as much as she could about Mary, and had even mastered the numbingly boring knotting that the queen so loved. How the hell Melanie spent hours a day doing this was beyond Harriet. *Once I've secured my own future, I must rescue my sister,* she thought.

The first impression she'd had when she was admitted to the queen's chambers was that they were dark and gloomy, in spite of the luxurious furnishings and the enormous number of expensive beeswax candles which burnt in them. She had moved forward, focussing completely on her prey, ignoring the openly curious looks and murmurs of the ladies-in-waiting, and had curtsied deeply to the queen, who was sitting on a decidedly uncomfortable-looking sofa.

"I was sorry to hear of the tragic death of your husband, Lady Harriet," the queen said. "I hope you are recovering from your grief a little now?"

Harriet, who had not felt even a second's grief for the death of the man who'd made her life hell, stated that she was coming to terms with his loss slowly, but could not imagine that there was anyone who could ever replace him.

Or anyone who ever would, if she got her way.

"I cannot imagine how I would cope without my beloved husband," Mary remarked. "It is my constant fear when he is campaigning that he will be taken from me."

Harriet had not expected this outpouring of clearly genuine vulnerability from her monarch on first meeting, and paused for a moment, realising that her prepared speech of compliments on Her Majesty's appearance and generosity in agreeing to see her would not be an appropriate response to such a heartfelt utterance.

"I am sure he misses you greatly when he is away, Your Majesty. It must ease his mind to know that he has such a competent regent when he must depart on urgent business overseas." Would it be appropriate to add that the queen must take care of herself too? In truth she looked dreadful, pale and listless, her skin dull and lifeless in spite of the expertly-applied rouge, her eyes pools of utter misery. Having no idea whether the queen was ill or if that was her normal appearance, Harriet decided to err on the side of caution.

"You must be very busy, Your Majesty, all the more reason to thank you for making the time to see me," Harriet said.

"Nonsense! I am very fond of your family, and have wanted to meet you for a long time. But it was not…convenient, especially whilst you were in mourning. But now I hope that you will be a frequent visitor!"

Dear God. She would drown herself before she became a frequent visitor here. She'd only been in the room five minutes and already wanted to leave, or at the very least throw open the windows and let some fresh air into the stuffy, airless room. She was sweating like a pig in this bloody mantua and could only hope she wasn't flushed bright red. She resisted the urge to scratch her arm, which was itching abominably due to the starched lace ruffles that adorned her sleeves.

"You are too kind, Your Majesty, to do me such honour," Harriet said.

"Come, sit by me. Let us become better acquainted," the queen had said, patting the space next to her as though inviting a pet dog to sit by her.

Harriet, unaware of the extraordinary honour she had just been given, sat down next to the queen, and, for the next half hour, while the ladies-in-waiting strained their ears to listen to the conversation, uttered more lies than she had ever done in her life before, after which she was shown to her room, where she could refresh herself before supper.

She had lain on the bed, utterly exhausted, wondering whether it was going well or not and hoping that Melanie, who was present during the meeting, would come up to tell her how she had done so far. The queen certainly seemed to like her, seeing in her a tragic figure who had endured that which was utterly unendurable, but who had somehow survived. They were also both childless, which Mary clearly thought equally unendurable. Whatever William thought of Mary, Mary genuinely adored him, there was no doubt about that.

Harriet felt sorry for her, until she remembered that when she'd been offered the throne of Great Britain in her own right, with William having no power, she had refused absolutely, stating that the husband should not be obedient to the wife, but that

THE ECCENTRIC'S TALE: HARRIET

wives should be obedient to their husbands in everything. Why did women underestimate themselves so?

No. Queen Mary might feel that she had much in common with Harriet, and in fact it was important that she did feel that, but in reality they were chalk and cheese. This woman would not understand if Harriet were to say that she had no wish to marry again, that she wished to be independent and pursue her own life. She would not comprehend such views.

She would have to take a different approach. That was not a problem – Harriet had spent the last weeks planning multiple approaches to achieve her aims, but she had to move slowly. Impatience was her weakness. She had conquered that after Raphael's death though, and was confident she could quell the urge to just blurt out her heartfelt desires and have done with it. Duplicity and falseness were anathema to her. But her mother had taught her well, and now was the time to put all that learning into action.

And so she had, for an excruciating month. Over the first few days she had ingratiated herself with the queen, which in fairness was not as difficult as she'd thought it would be, because Mary was in fact a very likeable person in many ways. She was intelligent and gentle, and enjoyed walking in the gardens, in which she had a great interest. Harriet seized on that joint interest to endear herself to the queen, and by the end of the first week had become an expert on Dutch tulip bulbs, having been loaned some books on the subject by Mary, after which she had sat up late into the night reading up on the subject. *If I get my way,* she determined, *I will grow some of the rarest tulips in the world, and will present her with a huge bouquet of them by way of thanks.*

Now she lay in the garden remembering her promise, and resolving to keep it. Because she had indeed got what she wanted.

In the third week, after endless hours of listening to trivial gossip or illuminating religious sermons, both of which Mary was particularly fond, whilst tying fancy knots in yarn in a candlelit room while the spring sunshine beamed down outside, the queen had finally given Harriet the opportunity she'd been hoping for, by commenting on the fact that she found it commendable that Harriet still wore black, showing her grief for her husband's tragic early demise, although no one would blame her if she now wore purple or white, which would suit her complexion much better. Harriet had then abandoned her pointless yarn and had explained earnestly to the queen that she didn't think she could ever replace Raphael (which was certainly true), and felt that to marry again would be a betrayal of their unique relationship.

"All I desire," Harriet had said with genuine feeling, "is to live quietly in the countryside. It is all I have ever wanted." Her heart had lifted then as she'd seen the expression of empathy on the queen's face. Indeed, that was all the queen wanted to do as well, but birth and fate had decreed otherwise. Much of her unhappiness and poor health was certainly due to her having to be what she was not. Here was a woman who only wanted to be a submissive wife and mother, who instead had to rule the country during William's frequent prolonged absences. Which she did very well, but at great cost to her health, and who also struggled to accept that she was unlikely ever to bear a child. Wealth and power certainly had not brought happiness to the poor queen, although Harriet hoped they would to her.

With her disappointment no doubt in mind, the queen had sympathised deeply, but had gently remonstrated with the distraught widow, saying that she was too young to sacrifice her future to memories of the past. Harriet had agreed, but had then leaned in to whisper confidentially, ignoring the disapproving looks of the maids and the studiously downturned head of Melanie, who knew exactly what her sister was up to.

"In truth, Your Majesty, I have another fear too," she had confided. "I am aware that the king might wish me to marry one of his favoured courtiers, and of course if he does, I must obey him in that as in all things, for he is my rightful sovereign. But I confess to you, that I worry myself on his behalf about this."

"You worry yourself on the king's behalf! How kind of you. But why ever would you do that?" the queen had replied.

"I am sure you know how wealthy I now am, Your Majesty, and what a great prize I would be for any ambitious nobleman. But ambition is such a dangerous emotion, I feel, especially at the moment, when it is rumoured that your father, aided by the French king, is preparing to invade England.

"Of course, as you know, my loyalty and that of my whole

THE ECCENTRIC'S TALE: HARRIET

family is with you and the king, but I know many men who would, given wealth and a marquessate, have their heads turned and want to exercise that power. Kings know that nobles can desert them in a moment, if promised greater prizes elsewhere. If my new husband was so tempted I would be helpless to stop him, which worries me greatly. Being a woman, of course I have no wish for power, and would be happy to provide some financial aid to help His Majesty bring stability and happiness to the realm, and to preserve the Protestant faith. I have only modest aims, and desire above all to create a beautiful garden and grow exotic plants. I wish for nothing more."

Her Majesty had thought about this for some time, and Harriet had sat silently and respectfully, allowing her to.

"Your commitment to the true faith is very heartening, and gladdens me greatly. It is a great source of comfort to me, and I'm sure it is to you too, in your terrible loss. May I ask what degree of support you feel you could provide to aid my husband in his endeavours for the Protestant faith?"

Harriet had leaned in even closer and whispered a figure in the queen's ear which had brought natural colour to her cheeks and a sparkle to her eye, and in that moment Harriet had known that, as long as the king respected his wife as much as Harriet thought he did, her future was secure, at least as long as they remained King and Queen of Britain. They were both reasonably young, and even if William were to be killed in battle, as the blood heir, if not technically the *rightful* one, Mary could continue to rule after him.

Later Melanie had managed to sneak away, and the sisters sat in Harriet's room discussing the evening.

"I couldn't believe it when you mentioned James to her. I really thought she would reject you then. You certainly have courage. Or stupidity, I'm not sure which," Melanie observed.

"It seems to have worked, anyway," Harriet replied. "I know you and Mama told me not to mention her father because she was racked with guilt about her betrayal of him, but really, I needed to show just how fickle supposedly loyal courtiers can be, and there's no better example than all the shits who betrayed James, is there? Including Raphael. If I'd tried to get that across *without* mentioning James the omission would have been obvious, and would have made her think that I *did* blame her for throwing him off the throne. Better that I just talk about him with apparent innocence."

Melanie whistled softly through her teeth.

"I never would have believed you could be such an accomplished courtier. Not you. You *hate* duplicity."

"I hate bloody knotting even more. What's the point in tying hundreds of fancy knots in a bit of thread, for God's sake?"

"You can make fringes and tassels, or sew it onto clothes in fancy patterns," Melanie said. "Like this." She lifted her skirt to show a border of raised flowers on her petticoat composed entirely of tiny knots. Harriet observed it with distaste.

"Did you do that?" she asked after a moment.

"Yes."

"So after spending forever tying little knots, you then have to spend forever sewing the bloody things on your underclothes, which no one will ever see. I have to get you out of here as quickly as I can, before you go insane."

Melanie laughed.

"I'm serious," Harriet said. "If you can get away, you can come and live with me now. You can have your own apartments with that library you wanted. And cows."

"I only want one cow. Maybe two," Melanie said.

"You can have a whole field of them if you want. You know the queen better than I do. Do you think the king will listen to her if she says I shouldn't be forced to marry again?"

"Judging by her expression when you told her how much you'd pay to remain a widow, quite possibly. How much did you offer?"

Harriet named a figure, and Melanie's expression became very similar to the queen's.

"My God, Harriet! You offered to give that every *year?*"

Harriet nodded.

"You really did mean it when you said freedom was the most important thing in your life, didn't you?"

"Of course I did. I always tell the truth. Well, almost always. Not for the last few weeks. But if I get my way now, I intend in future to only lie when I absolutely have to. It's exhausting for

THE ECCENTRIC'S TALE: HARRIET

one thing, remembering all the rubbish you've told people so you don't catch yourself out."

"But if you bankrupt the estate you won't be able to grow all those tulips you want to grow," Melanie said.

"I don't really want to grow tulips. I will, so I can present them to the queen and remind her how grateful I am so that she'll do her best to stop William changing his mind and parcelling me off to some pampered fool. I want to grow fruit. Oranges, lemons, pineapples, melons. I want to find a fruit that no one's been able to grow here, and grow it. And I won't bankrupt the estate. I watched Mama and Papa grow old before their time because Grandpapa was an idiot. I won't make the same mistake. I can afford the amount I offered her. But don't tell *anyone* that. The last thing I want is some unprincipled fool trying to marry me by force to get his hands on it all."

Now, sitting in the garden, she remembered those words and realised that although Mary had promised to recommend she be left alone to William, when it came to unscrupulous suitors, she was on her own.

But she would worry about that this afternoon. Right now she would enjoy lying here, cold, wet, and unutterably happy, and enjoy being free to create her own future, her own happiness.

And thinking of that, it was nearly time.

She had a reliable and trustworthy steward, and a reliable and trustworthy, if somewhat prim housekeeper. The rest of the staff seemed to have settled in their jobs happily now, after a few hiccups. The servants' rooms had been renovated, and the rest of the house was already beautiful, only needing a few tweaks to make it her own.

Once they were finished it would be time to start remodelling the gardens.

* * *

"You want to do *what?*" the Earl of Highbury said.

"You heard me perfectly, Daniel," Harriet replied, lounging back against the cushions on his sofa. "This is much more comfortable than the queen's," she commented. "I can't think why she doesn't have something like this made for her instead of that horrible thing in her apartments."

Highbury, who had genuinely believed this woman was no longer capable of shocking him after two years of friendship, found that he was wrong.

"I could pay someone to teach me alone, but I thought it would be more fun if we learnt together, for both of us," she added.

"I'm sure William would be ecstatic, but it's not something women do, you know," Highbury ventured.

"Bloody ridiculous. Women need to defend themselves, after all. And they're not as strong as men, so all the more reason for them to learn to use a sword," Harriet said.

"Is this just because you wanted to do it as a child?" Highbury asked. "Because it's dangerous, you know. You could get hurt. Which is one reason why—"

"Women don't learn," Harriet finished for him. "When I was a child I wanted to learn sword fighting because I wanted to be a boy and run around in the fresh air, instead of sitting in a stuffy room learning how to embroider. Now I can run around in the fresh air all day if I want, and I will *never* embroider anything again. I'd still prefer to be a man though, just because it would be much easier to do what I want if I was. No. While I was lying in the garden congratulating myself on my success with the queen, it occurred to me that if some ambitious bastard decided to abduct and marry me by force, that would be legally binding, wouldn't it?"

"Well yes, if he…er…"

"Swived me straight away."

Highbury blinked. He was very relieved that Frances and William were visiting her aunt today. In the corner a footman stood with a very studied blank expression on his face.

"Is that why your…clothes are wet?" he asked.

"Yes. But they're drying now. Once the idea occurred to me I didn't want to waste time changing. And I wanted you to be the first to see my new mode of dress. I knew you'd give me an honest opinion of it."

Highbury pondered the proprieties for a moment, then dismissed the footman. The man already had enough gossip to entertain the servants for a month, without hearing Harriet's

THE ECCENTRIC'S TALE: HARRIET

response when he uttered his opinion of her fashion taste. Frances knew he would never be unfaithful to her, so he had no need of a chaperone.

"It's outrageous, Harriet," he replied when the door had closed. "Please tell me you only intend to wear it when at home alone."

"Why is it outrageous?" Harriet retorted. "Apart from the colour, which is bloody awful. Can't think what possessed Raphael to have a vivid purple outfit made. That's why I let Susan have it to practice with. She's done an excellent job of altering it, I must say. She's already started on his other suits."

"You can't seriously mean to wear such things in public?" Highbury said.

"Well, not at Court, no. And not if I'm at some interminable society ball or dinner, although I don't intend to attend many more of those. But otherwise, I don't see why not, when I'm at home or on the estate. Far more practical than trailing skirts, petticoats, tight stays and so on. I can move freely in this. And my body is actually more covered in this outfit than it would be in a dress, so I don't see why it's outrageous."

He had forgotten how difficult she was to argue with, because her reasoning had nothing to do with popular opinion, and everything to do with common sense. Even so…

"But it's acceptable for a woman to show the outline of her body, Harriet. Not her legs though, and yours are on public show."

"Only from the knee down, and even then they're covered. You'd see far more if I was wearing a dress in a high wind. Really, it's ridiculous to think a man will lose all reason if he sees a woman's lower legs, but won't if her breasts are on full display. I really believe that fashion is just another way of restricting women, and I'm not playing the game any more. Anyway, Queen Catherine wore men's clothes when she first came to Court. Charles told me that."

"Yes, but only in the gardens, in private. And it was only tolerated because her husband the king was so lenient. But that didn't stop people gossiping horribly about her."

"Well, I'll only be wearing them in private. More private than her, because her gardens would have been full of courtiers, which mine won't, because I don't intend to invite any. And I don't have a husband any more, thank God. And I don't care about gossip. People have been gossiping about me since I was six."

Highbury sighed. It was pointless. Unless he had a cast iron argument, she would not take his advice. And in truth, he admired her determination to be herself.

"So I assume you want to learn to use a sword so that if someone tries to abduct you, you can defend yourself," he said.

Harriet smiled.

"Exactly. And William told me that Mr Royce is going to teach him how to really fight, not just pretty moves. Which is what I want to do."

"Why not just employ some soldiers to guard you? You would be much safer then, with expert swordsmen. Because no matter how adept you are, you'll never be as good as an experienced soldier, you know."

"That's true," Harriet agreed, and for one moment he actually thought she was going to take his advice. "But I love being on my own. I don't want to have a troop of bloody soldiers following me everywhere. And if I learn to defend myself I'll have one great advantage over any abductor."

"What's that?"

"Surprise," she said. "No one will expect a woman to be able to use a sword. I'm going to learn to use a pistol, too. But I'll do that on my own, because William's too young at seven to learn to shoot yet, isn't he?"

"But you won't exactly be able to hide a sword about your person to produce as a surprise, will you?" Highbury pointed out.

Hmm. That was a good point.

"No. But I suppose I could have a short sword made, which I could carry under my dress in a scabbard. Or I could wear a normal sword when dressed as I am now. No one would think I'd know how to use it. And the exercise will be fun, and will strengthen my upper body at the very least. I'll need that for all the heavy garden work I intend to do soon."

Highbury managed to stop himself just before he pointed out that heavy digging was what garden labourers were for. He should know by now that this woman was a law unto herself. And in truth it was lovely to see her starting to blossom, even if she was looking to become a most unusual bloom.

Needless to say, William was ecstatic that his favourite adult in the whole world (after his Papa and Mama, of course) was going to learn to use a sword with him, and with the unconditioned mind of the child he didn't bat an eyelid when she turned up on the first day dressed in man's clothes, nor when she took off her coat, the day being warm, rolled up her shirt sleeves and joined in the stretching exercises the sword master taught them before they began to learn.

"Lord William has already spent some time practising with a wooden sword, my lady," Mr Royce said, his expression neutral, having been persuaded by a handsome tip from the earl to treat his new pupil exactly as he would any inexperienced youth. "I think it would be advisable for you to start in the same way, although you can practise the same moves as he will now be doing with a blunted blade. Once you've mastered the basics and your arm has become accustomed to the weight of the slightly lighter wooden sword, you can try a blade as well."

"Very sensible. I don't want to cut my own arm off, do I?" Harriet replied. "Or yours, sir!" She bowed to William, who giggled.

They set to work, Mr Royce teaching the importance of body position and foot placement, and for the first few sessions they did not actually use their weapons at all, although they had to hold them to become accustomed, not only to the weight, but to the change in balance that it caused. It was all very interesting.

And very tiring. The day after her first lesson Harriet couldn't even lift her arm to brush her own hair in the morning, and needed more help than usual in dressing. When she saw William in the gardens later that day, he told her that his arm was very sore as well, although from the way he moved it was clear to her that he was not aching as much as she was.

Some of that could be because she'd been holding the sword too tightly and herself too tensely, as the sword master had pointed out, whereas William, who already knew the basics, had not put as much effort into the moves as she had.

But most of it was because in the last years she had spent far too much time sitting around lifting nothing heavier than a pen or a needle, she realised. Even if it was painful, it was good to be active again.

CHAPTER ELEVEN

November 1692

The carriage halted by the large ornately gilded gates at the entrance to the driveway, and the coachman was about to get down from his perch at the front of the carriage when a small gate to the side of the main one was opened, and a liveried footman came out to ascertain the identity of the visitors. Once that was done the large gates were opened and the carriage continued down the long driveway that would eventually lead to the house.

"I don't remember those gates being here last time we came," Stephen commented. Amelia, sitting behind him, had turned to look through the small window in the back of the coach, from which she could see the gates being firmly closed again.

"Yes, they were, although the gilding is new. But they were open then, and looked as though they always had been, which is probably why you didn't notice them," she said.

They continued along the driveway, past the rows of perfectly clipped trees, the hedges of the perfectly clipped maze visible through them to the right. The young man sitting next to the driver outside the coach observed the topiaried landscape and the formal gardens which were just coming into view on the left with great interest.

"She doesn't appear to have changed much yet," Stephen said. "She disliked the style of the gardens so much and is so impatient, I imagined she'd have already had the whole lot dug over."

"I think she's been preoccupied with making sure all the repairs and alterations were done to the servants' quarters and estate workers' cottages," Amelia said. "And then of course she was at Court for over a month, remember."

"That's true. She did very well there, I must say. Knowing Harriet, I was worried that she'd say something inappropriate. But Her Majesty still asks about her regularly. I'm surprised she wasn't appointed as a lady-in-waiting."

Melanie, who had been allowed a rare week away from Queen Mary's side, was looking out of the window and took no part in the conversation. So it was that she was the first, as they came out of the trees, to see the boy and the youth in the distance at the far side of one of the lawns near the house, practising swordfighting. They were both in shirts and breeches, sleeves rolled up in spite of the chilly weather, and were fighting intently enough for Melanie to hope the swords were well blunted, the boy's at any rate, who seemed to be doing his best to kill the youth who had his back to the coach.

"Isn't that Highbury's son?" she asked.

Her parents stopped talking and looked out of the window. They were much closer to the combatants by now.

"It is," Stephen said. "He's coming on well! Still a little undisciplined though. It's just as well his partner is nimble enough to get out of the way quickly. Although he's deflecting the boy's thrusts pretty well. Needs to drop his shoulder a little though, or he'll tire quickly."

It was at that moment that the youth suddenly leapt sideways to avoid being skewered, as if demonstrating the truth of Stephen's comments. William ducked, bringing his sword under the youth's arm and then tapped him smartly on the chest to denote that in a real fight he would have killed him. The youth threw his arms out dramatically, dropped his sword, cried "Ah! I die!" and fell prostrate on the ground. William then proceeded to leap on top of his victim, which resulted in an impromptu wrestling match.

The young man who'd been so interested in the gardens laughed suddenly, then placing his fingers in his mouth uttered a piercing whistle, so loud that the driver sitting next to him jumped violently and the wrestling pair froze.

"Hell, man, what are you doing?" the coachman snarled. "Could have had the horses bolting, making a noise like that!"

"I'm sorry," the young man said immediately, his eyes dancing with merriment, although the apology was sincere. "I never thought of that. I'll not do it again."

The dead youth sat up and waved, then jumped up from the ground and set off running towards the coach, William following.

"Dear God almighty!" Stephen cried. "It can't be!"

But when the pair arrived at the coach as it drew up outside the house, it was very clear that it could indeed be.

"Papa! Mama! What a wonderful surprise!" Harriet cried. "Why didn't you send someone to tell me you were coming? And Mel! You got away from the gloomy palace! How long are you staying? John," she said to the tall, pockmarked footman who had trotted down the steps from the house, "will you ask cook to prepare a meal for an extra four people? Tell her we have unexpected guests, and to just do the best she can. I'm sure she'll come up with something wonderful anyway." She looked up at the front of the carriage, bestowing a brilliant smile on the whistling man.

"You came, then," she said.

"I did," Jem replied.

"Excellent! There's a lot to do. Well, you must all come in. Are you staying overnight? You're most welcome, of course. If you are, I'll get someone to—"

"Harriet," Stephen interrupted firmly. "What on earth are you doing?"

"I'm welcoming my family to the house," she said, a puzzled look on her face. "If you're staying I'll have fires lit in the guest rooms now, so they'll be thoroughly warm by tonight."

"I thought you were a young man, for God's sake!" Stephen persisted.

"Ah," she said, as understanding dawned. "Of course, you haven't seen me since I started wearing Raphael's old outfits. Very practical for swordfighting, though. Can't do that in a skirt, can I?"

"You shouldn't be doing that at all! And you can't dress like that in public! It's indecent!"

"Stephen," Amelia said, placing her hand on his arm. "Can we have this conversation indoors, where it'll be both warmer and more discreet?"

"Oh. Yes, of course," he said. The footman who had been standing uncertainly at the back of the coach, now jumped down and opened the door, placing the steps so the occupants could descend.

"If you and Bernard go to the kitchens, Alfred," Harriet said to the footman and coachman, "you'll be very well fed. Mama, are you staying for a few days, or just the one night? If so, I'll have rooms made up for them, too."

"We thought to stay for a couple of days," Amelia said.

"No point in riding all the way back to Ash Hall then, just to return straight away," Harriet said. "I've had some guest rooms for the use of servants' friends and family furnished, so I'll get those made up for you both. William, do you want to stay for dinner too?"

"No, Papa is expecting me home in an hour," the boy said. "Please excuse me, Your Graces." He bowed politely. "I'll ride back through the garden," he said. "Is it still all right for us to practice tomorrow?"

"Probably. But I'll send a message if it isn't. I need as much practice as I can, after all, if I'm to stop you killing me every day, don't I?" Harriet said.

Stephen opened his mouth.

"Inside," Amelia commented. He closed it again.

Melanie jumped down from the carriage and embraced her sister fervently.

"I didn't tell them," she murmured. "I wasn't sure whether you wanted them to know."

Harriet nodded.

"I set a room aside for your library when you can escape," she whispered in Melanie's ear. "And a field. For Buttercup. And for Daisy, or whatever you want to call the other one."

Melanie giggled. It was the first time Stephen and Amelia had heard her laugh in months.

"She's doing something right then," Amelia said softly to her husband as they followed their two daughters up the steps into the house. "Don't say anything yet, and not in front of the servants, or you'll undermine her. Be gentle with her. She's obviously happy."

In fairness to Stephen, he took his wife's advice and said nothing, instead going up to the rooms they were shown to to refresh themselves and change. When they came back down for dinner

THE ECCENTRIC'S TALE: HARRIET

he was pleased to see that Harriet was now wearing a gown, although she spoiled the gesture a little by stating that she'd had to change because her shirt and breeches had been soaked from her wrestling match on the grass with William.

He said nothing when instead of sending Jem to the kitchen with Bernard and Alfred, Harriet invited him to dine with them in the main dining hall. And he also said nothing when she arranged for guest apartments to be prepared for Jem in the main house rather than the servants' rooms.

"I'll have a cottage built for you in the grounds if you like, Jem," she said to him over dinner, which he was eating carefully and somewhat nervously, watching the others to see which cutlery they used for each course before following suit. "I wanted to wait until I was sure you were coming first though. And it'll mean you can decide how you want it laid out. In the meantime you can stay in the ruby apartments. They're red. Raphael named them all after jewels, and I haven't changed that because it makes sense, although I've had the sapphire and emerald rooms decorated in lighter shades of blue and green. They were so dark before I couldn't see a bloody thing in there. It was like being in a crypt."

Still Stephen said nothing.

"We have much to talk about, Jem," she said. "I want to make a lot of changes to the gardens. I was going to ask you to be head gardener, but then I realised that if I do that, the others may resent you, because they don't know you."

"And I've never been a head gardener," Jem pointed out.

"Well, no. But if we don't tell them that, they won't know, will they?"

Stephen opened his mouth again, then closed it.

"They will, my lady, because I wouldn't know what to do, and they'd see that. I hoped one day to become assistant head to one part of a garden, so the head could show me what to do, and then I could finally take over from him. But I can't take over ALL your gardens! They're enormous."

"Hmm. Good point. Hadn't thought it through, clearly. I don't dress like this in public, Papa. Not yet, anyway," Harriet said, unexpectedly changing the subject. "And I'm having an enormous amount of fun learning to swordfight with William. You wanted me to have friends and mix with people, so I don't see how you can object. I'm learning to shoot too. Not with William though. Daniel thinks he's a little young yet."

Now Stephen spoke.

"But you were out in the gardens, where anyone who drove in could see you! And God knows what the servants must think, seeing their mistress dressed indecently and rolling around on the ground!"

"I don't give a damn what the servants think. Why should I? I care for them, but they work for me, not the other way round. If they object that strongly to my clothing or actions they can leave. I don't give a damn what anyone thinks, to be honest. But if you noticed, the gates were closed, so no one's going to drive in without my express permission. The only reason the footmen let *you* in was because I told them my family are always welcome. Except for Percy, of course."

"I wondered why the gates were closed. I suppose that's something, at least, would give you time to get inside before they drew up, so you could change clothes before they saw you."

"Oh no, Papa, you mistake me," Harriet replied. "I keep the gates shut so that they can't get in at all. I spend a lot of time in the gardens, and if I let people drive up to the door, then I could hardly have the footman tell them I'm out or indisposed if they've seen me in the gardens on their way to the house, could I? Much easier this way. They give their card to the footman and bugger off. Then I can just relax when I'm outside and not worry that I might have to sit and endure hours of tedious gossip, when there are so many things I *want* to do."

"But you do give them a time when they can visit? And return the visits?" Amelia asked.

"No, of course not. I did at first, after I came out of mourning. I hoped that after the first few visits they'd realise that they weren't going to hear anything useful to gossip about, and stay away. But they didn't. So then I still saw them, and gave them food and drink, but made sure that the food was utterly disgusting and the wine sour. And I never had a fire lit in that room, so it was freezing and damp."

"Please tell me this is a joke, Harriet," her father said.

"No. Anyway, they *still* came, even though I didn't return their visits and answered all their conversation openers with one word and let the silences go on and on. Really, people *will not* take a hint. So, to avoid actually saying 'bugger off', which it seemed would be the only way to get rid of them, I just locked the gates and instructed the footmen not to let anyone in except you and Highbury. Oh, and the king or queen, but I doubt they'll visit. I bloody hope not."

Stephen looked about to burst.

"Do you at least return their cards with your own?" Amelia put in before he said something that neither servants nor gardeners should hear.

"God, no. Then I'd have to go and visit them! What a horrible thought. I can't understand why people want to spend their days travelling pointlessly from one person they don't like to another, having the same trivial conversation at every house. And they call the people in Bethlehem Hospital lunatics! I have much more pleasant things to do with my time. If I want to see someone, I'll invite them, or go to see them myself. Oh! I just had a thought, Jem. You could be assistant head gardener of exotic plants! How would that suit you?"

"I don't know anything about those, either," Jem said uncomfortably, looking from the horrified duke to the weary-looking duchess, and then to his new employer, who appeared completely unaware of her parents' disapproval of her actions. "Would the head gardener of exotic plants be happy to teach me everything?"

"Yes. That's why I asked you here now. I intend to build a hothouse over the winter, and you can spend the time reading and learning. You can read properly now, can't you?"

Jem blushed.

"I can. I'm a little slow, though. I hope the head gardener's patient with me!"

"I'm the head gardener of that, and I'll be very patient. It'll be fun. I've already ordered every book or treatise I can find about the subject. We can spend cosy hours in the library together, reading and discussing what we're going to plant, and you can see the hothouse being built. I can't wait to start!" She favoured him with a brilliant, happy smile, and Jem smiled back.

Stephen opened his mouth, and then closed it again. Then he wiped his hand tiredly across his face.

* * *

"You really don't give a damn, do you? You weren't just saying you didn't," Melanie asked the moment she'd entered her sister's room and closed the door behind her.

Harriet stopped brushing her hair and turned from the dressing table to face her sister.

"Of course I wasn't just saying it! What's the point in saying things you don't mean? I meant it about your library too. I've set aside a perfect room, and a whole suite of rooms around it for you. We can look at them tomorrow and if you tell me how you want them decorating and furnishing, I can make a start. Then they'll be ready when you can get away from Court."

Melanie smiled sadly.

"That would be lovely," she said. "I don't know when I'll be able to get away, though. Her Majesty has fallen out with her sister, which has made her terribly unhappy. She's ordered that no one is allowed to pay Anne any honours, none of us are allowed to visit her, and the minister of St James' Church isn't even permitted to place the day's text on her cushion before the service."

"That sounds very petty to me," Harriet said. "What's it all about?"

"The king doesn't like Anne's husband much and makes no secret of it, and Anne's friend Sarah, the Countess of Marlborough, has been spreading poison about it to Anne, because she's annoyed that *her* husband wasn't chosen to be a commander in Flanders. Anyway, it's rumoured that Marlborough made approaches to James Stuart, and then he tried to get the House of Lords to pass a motion that the king dismiss all foreigners from his service. When William heard of that, he dismissed Marlborough.

"Mary asked Anne to dismiss the countess, and Anne refused, saying that if she had to choose between her sister and her friend, then she'd choose her friend. And things just got much worse from then on, because the king's campaign in Europe went very badly too. But he arrived back in England last month, which is why I could come here."

"This is why I don't want anything to do with people in general, and the Court in particular," Harriet said. "I have no patience for all this lying and gossiping and people saying nasty

THE ECCENTRIC'S TALE: HARRIET

things to each other behind their backs, to try and get in favour. You're my sister. If you do something I'm annoyed about, I'll ask *you* about it, not listen to nasty gossip about you from others. Anyone who gossips about you or Mama and Papa to me would be out of favour so fast their arses would be burning."

Melanie laughed, and at that moment Amelia tapped on the door and walked in.

"It's good to hear you laugh," she said warmly to her daughter. "That's twice today. I miss it."

"Doesn't sound like there's much to laugh at at Court, that's certain," Harriet said. "Can't you persuade the queen to let Sophia take Mel's place, Mama? She'd be much happier as a lady-in-waiting, and then Mel could come and live with me."

"No, I can't. Your father's hoping that Sophia will be appointed to attend the queen as well as Melanie, not instead of her! The queen was very taken with you. It would be a great coup for us if all three of you were attending on the monarch. He can't understand why she didn't command you while you were there."

Harriet and Melanie exchanged a quick look, and then Harriet sighed.

"She didn't ask me, and the king is not going to command that I marry some sycophantic courtier either, because I appealed to her not to. All she ever wanted was a quiet life, so she sympathised with me when I said I wanted the same thing. Of course the fact that it seems her husband has also just used thousands of pounds of my money to have his arse kicked by the French also had a lot to do with it."

"What?!" Amelia cried.

"Mama, I wish you and Papa would believe me when I tell you I have no intention of ever getting married again, and want nothing to do with Court life. I would pay a lot more than I have to be excused that, but please don't tell the king or queen. God knows I'm paying a fortune now, but it's worth it if I'm left alone."

"Your father will have an apoplexy if he finds out," Amelia said, sitting down on the edge of the bed.

"He won't find out unless you tell him. I'm certainly not going to," Harriet said. "He was shocked enough by seeing me wrestling with William today."

"He's worried about you, because he loves you and wants the

247

best for you," Amelia said defensively.

"I know he is. But he wants what *he* thinks is the best for me – a place in royal circles and marriage to some wealthy courtier. And that's absolutely not what I want. I don't want him to be unhappy, or you either for that matter. But I'm not going to be miserable for the rest of my life just to make you both happy. I don't think that's what either of you really want for me."

Amelia was rendered silent by this heartfelt remark, and Harriet sat next to her and took her hand.

"I know I haven't been an easy daughter, and I know I'm different. When I come to Court, and I will, because the queen has invited me to and I really can't afford to displease her, then I'll wear proper clothes, I won't use bad language, wrestle in the grass or fight with swords, and I'll conform to what's expected of me. And I'll hate it. But I'll do it, partly because I'll then be left alone to live my own life quietly here for the rest of the time, and partly because I don't want to cause you any problems, as I know how important it is for you to be in royal favour. But when I'm here, I'm not going to pretend to be someone I'm not to you and Papa, or to Mel and Sophia either for that matter. Because you're my family, and I love you and accept you as you are and hope that you'll accept me as *I* am, because you love me. Can't you both do that? I don't give a damn about anyone else. I don't have many friends, and don't expect I ever shall, because friends will have to accept me as I am. But that's all right, because I have you as my family. If I can't have your support and understanding, then I'll be very unhappy, and lonely too. But I won't give up my freedom and live a false and unhappy life, even then. I've done it for the last four years, and wished I was dead for most of it. And I never, never want to feel that way again."

Amelia kissed her, and then stood up.

"I'll go and talk to your father," she said.

* * *

"I'm just trying to stop her from being mocked and insulted at Court, and from having her reputation dragged through the mud. Did you talk to her about our concerns regarding Jem?"

"No, I didn't, because what she said stopped me from doing so. And you're not listening. She doesn't *care* what people at Court

THE ECCENTRIC'S TALE: HARRIET

think of her. She genuinely does not care about it."

"But you heard her talking to Jem about spending cosy hours with him in the library reading! That's not acceptable behaviour for a marchioness!"

"I don't see why not. It would be acceptable behaviour for a marquess to spend hours reading and consulting with his staff about improvements to the gardens, wouldn't it?"

"Yes, but she's a woman, and he's a man! It's different."

"That's exactly the point. Our daughter is different. She thinks differently. Her closest friends have been a king, a gardener, and a seven-year-old earl's son. She doesn't care about status, age or gender. She cares about personality. And, to be honest, I admire her for that. It's refreshing to listen to someone honest and open, after months of enduring the lies and deceit of backstabbers at Court."

"I'm just worried about her. I want her to be happy, not steeped in scandal," Stephen said miserably.

"So do I. So it's time we let her be. Let her be who she is, whatever that is, and love her anyway. I think that will be easier to do than you think. She's going to go her own way anyway, and when she does she'll need our support, as you pointed out a long time ago. And in truth it's the least she deserves from us after what she did for us in marrying Raphael. He could have lived another thirty years you know, and if he had, I'm sure she would have endured it. For us. The least we can do is repay that love by allowing her the one thing she craves more than anything."

"Her freedom," Stephen said.

"Exactly. And trust that we've brought her up well enough to deal with that freedom. I think we have. And if she does cause herself problems, we'll be in a better position to support her if we haven't alienated her by criticising her all the time. We just have to accept that we have a very strong, independent daughter, and let her live. We want her to be happy, and really, that's the only way we're going to do it."

* * *

January 1693

Jem sat in the garden, as had been his habit of an evening while Harriet was away at Court. He loved this time of day, had always loved this time of day, when everyone had finished working, the gardens were deserted and he could go and find a spot to sit in where he could be alone for a while, knowing he would not be disturbed. As a child he had hidden in the woodland if the duke had visitors exploring the grounds, or on the bank of the river if he didn't. It had given him a little time to let his mind calm before going home to an evening with his father.

Not that evenings with his father had been an ordeal, not even when the old man was sick, in his final days. Jem missed him every day. It was just that he needed to be alone to refresh himself, whereas most people, as far as he could see, needed to be with other people to refresh themselves. He had always been like that. It was just who he was. In fact he could be alone most of the time, would rather be alone most of the time than with many of the people he knew.

Harriet was the only other person he had met who was like him in this. Or at least the only other person who admitted to preferring her own company to that of others, to finding endless chatter exhausting to listen to, to loving the wind and rain on her face, to needing time to be silent, to think. And because of that, she was the only person with whom he could enjoy spending endless hours, because being with her was like being alone; it refreshed him. She did not treat silence as an enemy, did not try to fill it with small talk; they could sit for hours together quietly, reading, thinking, staring at the fire, completely relaxed. It was glorious.

It was cold tonight and frosty, and the moon, rising from behind the maze, shone on the frosted stems and evergreen leaves of the bushes, so they appeared bedecked with glittering diamonds. It was very quiet, the only sounds those of nocturnal animals, and few of those in this formal, artificial part of the grounds. The sooner Harriet changed them the better, and now he knew why the head gardener was so resistant to the change he could tell her when she got back and let her deal with it wisely, as he knew she would.

In the distance was the dark shape of the house, numerous windows showing yellow lamplight, little shadows passing back and forth as the servants prepared the mistress's rooms for her return this evening. They would be warm and cosy when she arrived.

THE ECCENTRIC'S TALE: HARRIET

He shivered, and drew his coat closer around him. He didn't normally feel the cold, but he had been sitting still for a while and it was *very* cold tonight. He could, of course, have retired to his own warm and cosy apartments instead of sitting on a frosty log, but he could never find complete peace surrounded by walls and a roof, not like he could in the fresh air. His apartments were extremely luxurious, extremely comfortable, more so than he could ever have imagined he would live in. But even so, his little cottage was nearly finished now and he couldn't wait to move into it, away from the bustle of the house, from servants walking in on him at all hours of the day to clean, lay fires, even close and open curtains and light candles, as though he was incapable of doing even the simplest tasks himself. He found it invasive and could never relax completely because of it.

In this Harriet was not like him. She barely noticed the entrance of servants, was not inhibited by their presence, and did not change her behaviour in the slightest when they were there. Because she had grown up with this constant intrusion, did not think it insulting to have candles lit for her, curtains drawn and opened, chairs pushed under her as she sat down to dinner. Because she was a duke's daughter, and a marchioness.

And he was a gardener's son, and a gardener. Which although not the reason why he was sitting in the garden, *was* why he had been sitting here for so long. She was like him, enjoyed growing things, being outdoors, time alone, speaking her mind freely, being completely and utterly true to herself. All those things drew them together, had made them friends as children and kept them friends as adults. He told himself that every day. Many times. They were friends, and it was a privilege to be the friend of such a delightful, natural woman.

It was not a privilege to be the friend of a marchioness though. Because he knew, if she didn't, that things could not carry on like this, for two reasons.

The servants were already talking. He hadn't heard them talking, but had felt the initial puzzlement when a gardener, an outdoor servant, had been allocated aristocratic apartments rather than a room in the servants' quarters. That puzzlement had turned to resentment when Harriet had ordered that they cook and clean for him, that they do his laundry, make his bed, light his fires. He had felt the waves of hostility towards him as he'd walked from room to room in the house, passing servants who had no wish to bow or curtsey to a fellow menial, but were unsure of what her ladyship would expect, and so resentfully compromised by dipping their heads to him. He had felt it when Harriet had ordered meals to be served for both of them in the dining room or refreshments in the library where they had spent so much of the last rain-sodden month, reading books and planning the new exotic gardens.

But that feeling had soon been eclipsed by others, feelings he had long ago quenched, considering them no more than a youthful infatuation, but which had now risen like a demon from hell, stronger than ever. As he had ridden in on the duke and duchess's coach two months ago, he had told himself firmly that their relationship would be professional only – servant and mistress.

Harriet had doused that conviction immediately on his arrival by smiling so brilliantly at him, so openly happy to see him that his heart had soared. Then she had led him into dinner so naturally that he had thought nothing of it until he had seen the duke's pursed lips and the vast array of unfamiliar cutlery, and the meal had become a torture to him, a two hour reminder that he was not, and never could be, the equal of anyone else at that table.

It was clear to him then and had been made clearer to him since, that Harriet paid no heed to the opinions of anyone else, neither her servants nor her family.

He was her friend, and that overrode everything, every tradition, every convention, every viewpoint. And she had treated him as a complete equal, blithely indifferent to the atmosphere, to the feelings of the servants, to the concerns of her parents.

Blindly indifferent to his feelings too, he hoped. God knew he had done his best to hide them, to hide the thrill that shot through him when she sat next to him on the couch, their legs touching, when she patted his arm to get his attention (although she had no need to; he was only too thoroughly, burningly aware of her presence every second of the time he spent with her).

He loved everything about her; the way her forehead crinkled when she was thinking, the freckles across her nose and cheeks, her habit of wearing her dark blonde hair unfashionably loose, of combing it with her fingers and tying a ribbon carelessly around it to keep it from blowing all over her face on a windy day. He loved the way she sat when reading, her long slender legs curled up on the sofa, the shape of them clearly visible in her masculine attire of breeches and shirt. He loved the way the tip of her tongue poked out of the corner of her mouth when she was concentrating.

He loved her.

He had always *liked* her. As a child he had liked her because she had been interested in the same things as him, had liked him for who he was, had thought his opinions worth listening to. But when she had fought her father with every weapon she had to save him and his father from starvation, and had won, then his like had transformed to love.

And, he realised now, nothing had diminished that love, not her nobility, not her marriage to the marquess, not the years spent apart. Nothing ever had, and nothing but death ever would, and probably not even that. He just had not realised it until now.

He had loved her as a child, simply and honestly. But now he loved her as a man, and that was a completely different matter.

If she was his own class, he would already have asked her to be his sweetheart, to marry him. But she certainly only saw him as a friend, and of course would never think of him as any more than that. Confessing his love for her would kill that friendship stone dead, and he did not think he could live if that happened.

He had never had position and wealth, which, like most poor people, he had always thought automatically brought happiness, security and freedom. But now he realised that although the rich would never die of hunger or cold, in reality wealth and nobility just brought a different kind of prison and insecurity.

She might not care about the opinions and hostility of others, but he did. Not because he wished them to like him; he had no more time than she did for gossips and backstabbers. But because he knew, as she did not seem to, that the king would not allow the richest noble in his country to pursue a close friendship, no matter how innocent, with a mere gardener. The servants would talk, probably already were talking. The aristocracy would talk, and the king would hear about it. And no one would believe that their friendship was pure, because what on earth could a female aristocrat and a male gardener have in common, except lust?

Noble blood and common blood could not be allowed to mix. Bloodlines could not be sullied. And if that meant destroying the idyll Harriet had created, they would do it.

He had to make that clear to her. He must talk to her, make her listen somehow. And then he must begin to distance himself from her. For his sanity, and for her future.

There was no time to lose. He would make a start tonight, he resolved, when she got home.

Because he was already outside and because his hearing was very good, he heard the coach coming long before those in the house did and made his way over to the entrance of the house to meet it as it arrived. The door opened and footmen came down to unload the luggage and assist the mistress down from the coach, but before they could get there she had thrown open the door and jumped down herself, tripping on her skirts and almost falling face first on the drive.

"Bloody thing," she muttered. Then she moved forward to the front of the coach, reaching up to lift down the child who had been sitting on one of the horses.

"Well, what do you think then, child?" she asked. "Do you think you'll like being a postilion?"

"Oh, yes!" the little girl, for she was a girl, in spite of her boyish clothing and hat, said. "I think I'll like it more than anything in the world!" Her face was glowing both with cold and ecstasy in the light of the lanterns the footmen had brought down to light their mistress's way into the house.

"How did she do, Aaron?" Harriet asked the coachman.

"In truth I didn't have much hope for her, in spite of what you said about her way with the animals, begging your pardon my lady, but she's a natural with them, so she is. She talked to them when we stopped too, and they were very calm."

"I's been practising, I has," the child said. "Mr Evans let me ride Summer, but only when he was there to watch me. He told me how I should sit and suchlike, so's I moves with her, rather than jolting. It's a bit different with these horses though, they's so big and my legs is too short yet for stirrups."

"That's why you had the strap round your waist fastened to the saddle, so you wouldn't fall off or pitch over his head if he stumbled," Harriet said.

THE ECCENTRIC'S TALE: HARRIET

"Yes, but Louis knew he had to look after me, so he stepped carefully. We's friends, we is. All the horses is my friends," she said happily, her face alight with joy.

"Even Boxer," Harriet replied.

"Especially Boxer. He's not so sad now. One day he'll let me ride him. But I won't until he wants me to, and you says yes, my lady."

"I'm glad to hear that. I don't want my new postilion killed before she's even learned her job!"

"Boxer wouldn't kill me, but I won't do nothing to him that he don't want me to. Friends don't do that to each other. I wants to be a coachman when I grows up!" Claire said with conviction.

"You're not strong enough," Aaron put in. "It's very hard work, and it takes strength as well as skill to control the horses, especially in treacherous conditions. You won't never be a coachman, girl. Will she, my lady?"

"You're right, Aaron," Harriet replied. "We'll never make a coachman of her, that's certain."

Jem, standing to one side seemingly unnoticed, had never seen anyone plunge from joy to utter despair as quickly as Claire did at these words. The light in her face was quenched, her lower lip trembled and tears filled her eyes, sparkling in the lantern light.

Harriet put her finger under the child's chin, so she had to look up at her mistress.

"But we will make a coach*woman* of you, if you continue working as hard as you are," she said, winking. "Now go and get yourself warm, and tell Mr Evans I'm very pleased with you."

Claire sniffed, wiped her sleeve across her eyes and ran off happily, her joy restored.

"Jem," Harriet said, stopping the coachman from raising any objections to her last remark and proving that she was as observant as ever. "You've been sitting outside for a time. Your face is pinched and red. Are you too cold to go for a turn round the gardens with me? I have much to tell you, but after sitting for hours today and being mainly indoors for weeks, I need to use my legs and smell the fresh air."

"No," he said. "A walk will warm me up, anyway."

"Capital!" she replied. "We won't need the lantern, Brian, the moon's full and will light us, and we'll not be out too long. If you take my luggage in and ask cook if she can make something hot for us…have you eaten dinner, Jem?"

"I did, yes, earlier."

"…something hot for me then, in half an hour. Come on," she said.

They set off, walking slower than normal because of the heavy formal dress Harriet was wearing.

"I should have gone inside and changed," she said after a minute, "but I really wanted to get some clean air straight away. Did you miss me?"

"How was your time at Court?" he asked, avoiding answering her question.

"Bloody awful, for the most part. The king is still upset about his defeat in August, but even more upset by Parliament and this whole Marlborough thing. And to top it, the Lords then advised William that they believed the commanding officer of the British forces should be an Englishman, and that the army left in England when he went off fighting should be all Englishmen commanded by an Englishman. William took it as a personal insult because he's foreign, which it was, I suppose. So he was in a foul mood for much of the time, stomping about, and Mary, although she looked happier than the last time I saw her, was still miserable because her beloved husband was. And I couldn't get Mel away from her as I'd hoped to. Mama says that the queen is very unlikely to part with her, as Mel has a quality rarely found in ladies-in-waiting."

"What's that?"

"Discretion. The queen can tell her anything, no matter how juicy a piece of gossip it would be, and Mel will keep it completely to herself, won't even tell Mama. She told me that the queen really needs her right now because she's so unhappy about her sister and husband, and that she wouldn't leave her even if she could at the moment."

"Oh, that's a pity. So your visit was a waste of time then?" he said.

"In that respect, yes. But I had to go anyway, really, and I did meet the king. And he thanked me for my assistance, so I could assure him that that assistance would continue, and that I was very content living a quiet life and trusting him to deal with affairs I

THE ECCENTRIC'S TALE: HARRIET

couldn't comprehend – being a feeble woman of course. Which he accepted, even though his bloody wife rules the country for most of the time while he's off killing everything that moves. He seems hardly to notice her, poor woman. I'm sorry. I didn't mean to tell you all this. Boring anyway. How's everything gone here?"

"Well. My cottage is nearly built, and will be finished by spring. I've spent a lot of time reading about melons and cucumbers, and a little about orange and lemon trees, because you said you want to grow those."

"Excellent! You'll have to tell me what you've learned. What else?"

"I spent some time in the gardens, helping the men to dig. I had a talk with Mr Hornbury about why he doesn't want the gardens to be redesigned. It felt good to be outside, working with my hands again."

"Yes, well there'll be plenty of work of that kind to do when we've built the hothouse," Harriet said.

"The foundations are dug, but we stopped when you wrote to tell us to," Jem said. "Why didn't you want us to carry on?"

"Why doesn't Hornbury want me to redesign the gardens?" Harriet asked, evading the question as adroitly as he had hers earlier.

"He's worried that a lot of the men will lose their jobs if you do. Keeping those hedges and trees clipped needs a lot of labour."

"Of course it does. That's why Raphael had them. Didn't give a damn about the gardens, just wanted to show that he was rich enough to have hundreds of people clipping leaves all day. Hornbury should know me better than that. I didn't get rid of any of the ridiculous number of footmen Raphael had standing about all day doing nothing, did I? Only those who wanted to go. Found work for all the rest." She frowned.

"You'll have to talk to him about that. It took me a week to get him and the others to relax around me at all. I think he only told me because he thought I might be able to persuade you to leave the gardens as they are."

"I'll see him tomorrow. So, let's start by growing white cucumbers, melons, and oranges and lemons. Oh, and tulips, of course. Have you read anything about pineapples?"

"Pineapples? No. Why, do you want to grow them?"

"Yes, definitely. It's why I told you to halt the building of the hothouse. I wanted to find out if it would need to be adapted for the plant. But in fact it can continue now. The pinery will have to be a separate thing."

Jem frowned. "I don't know anything about pineapples," he said. "I don't even know what they look like!"

"Apparently there is not a nobler fruit in the universe! To taste it is so appetising a thing, so delicate, that words fail to give it its true praise for this."

"Really? Who told you that?"

"The king. Or rather Oviedo, originally. It's in a book he wrote about natural history. I've seen a picture of one too, although I find it hard to believe they really look like that. They're like a big pine cone, with a crown of leaves sticking out of the top, and they grow on a stem, just one fruit on a plant."

"They sound more difficult to grow than melons would be then," Jem pointed out.

"They do. And they probably are. But it's really important that we grow them successfully."

"Why?"

She stopped then suddenly, and turning to face him, took his hand impulsively and squeezed it.

"Because as well as promising William a supply of cucumbers, melons and oranges to delight his guests (and grapes if we can), I've told him he can have my first successful pineapple," she said. "And he told me that he's happy to let me stay a widow if I can achieve such a great feat, because it would be a fine prize for him if he could serve them to distinguished guests at Court. I don't know if he was joking or not, but he's not a very humorous sort of man, so I don't think he was. I think he wants to put Louis' nose out of joint."

"Louis?"

"The king. Of France. Really, kings are no different to any other men – they're all little boys, showing off to each other, boasting that they've rolled the hoop across the lawn the fastest, that they've got the biggest marble. Unfortunately kings have also got the power to ruin other people's lives if they don't get what they want."

"Or make them successful if they do. Is the money you're

THE ECCENTRIC'S TALE: HARRIET

giving him for his wars not enough then?"

"Kings can never have enough. It will do no harm to give him more, and in truth I don't care about giving huge dinners to show off my success in the garden. I just want to be left alone to grow the damn things. He can take the credit if he wants. There's another reason I want to grow them, though, apart from the challenge."

"What's that?"

"Quite a few people in England have tried growing the plants – indeed there are plants at Hampton Court. The king has promised me some when I have a place to put them, but getting them to fruit is another matter entirely. It takes about three years to produce a ripe fruit."

"Three years? And they need to be kept warm for all that time?"

"They do. So it will be a great challenge for us. But while I'm trying to ripen a fruit, I think he'll leave me alone to do so. Really he has no need to force me to marry, as I'm financing a good part of his wars for him, but if he can tell people he's allowing me to stay a widow on condition I produce exotic fruit for him, it heightens his prestige too, telling others that he has no need to buy loyalty by bribing his courtiers with rich wives."

"We need to grow pineapples then," Jem said with conviction.

Harriet smiled and squeezed his hand, touched by his desire that she be free and happy.

"We do. I need to do other things as well, rather than put all my eggs in one basket as I have been doing. I've been thinking about it, and remembering what Charles told me. But about pineapples. If we can do it, I'm going to call it the freedom fruit, because for me that's what it will be. Come, let's go back to the house. You're shivering, and I've walked enough to shake off some of the Court staleness."

They walked back in silence, she still holding his hand absentmindedly, and he committing the warm softness of her touch to memory, to last him when he distanced himself from her.

"Am I like that too?" he asked softly, just as they reached the house. She looked up at him, puzzled. "Boasting that I've got the biggest marble?"

She laughed then, and squeezed his hand again, then let it go.

"No, you're not. Not at all," she said. "Which is one of the reasons why I love you so."

And then she lifted her skirts and ran up the steps, to where John was opening the door for her. She stepped into the hall then turned and looked back down at him standing at the bottom of the steps, mouth open, unable to believe he'd heard her correctly.

"Come on," she said. "We need to study! Tomorrow we go to Chelsea Physic Garden, where there is a pinery you can see, and I've arranged for you to meet with the Earl of Portland next month."

"Me meet with the Earl of Portland?" Jem asked, alarmed. "Why?"

"Hans is an expert in pineapples, and will impart what he knows to us because the king will ask him to," Harriet said happily, "so we need to learn as much as we can about pineapples before then, to show we are serious. This is a great opportunity for both of us. I will be free for at least three years, and if you can successfully grow a pineapple, you will be the most sought after gardener in the land. It will be the making of you! And then we shall both be free!"

She was so happy, so enthusiastic, so concerned for his future as well as her own. How could he distance himself from such a woman?

He found that he could not make a start tonight after all.

CHAPTER TWELVE

May 1694

"So, do you think we will have a success this time?" Harriet asked. The two of them were crouching over several small, but healthy-looking plants in the pinery. Jem took out his kerchief and wiped his brow. How the men who fed the stoves survived was beyond him. He'd only been in here for five minutes and was already sweating. And he wasn't engaged in heavy physical labour shovelling coal into the stoves in the cellar underneath the pinery, as they did for hours every day. He pushed the thought of them from his mind. They were very well paid; maybe the thought of that kept them cool. He knelt down, placing his hand on the soil in which the pots containing the small plants were plunged. It was warm. A sign that the stoves underneath, rather than in the same room as the pineapples, were working to keep both the soil and air warm, while the flues were dispersing the choking smoke that had probably helped to kill the last batch of plants.

"It's impossible to tell," he said. "But at least they *are* growing well now, which is more than we've had before. Now we must look after them very carefully. We won't get good-sized fruit if the soil is too cold, or so I've read."

Harriet sighed.

"You were right," she said, "and I was wrong."

"About what?" he asked, still examining the plants carefully. They looked really healthy, all of them. Eleven. With luck at least one would survive. Whether it would produce fruit was another matter.

"I should have accepted the offer of a mature plant from the

Netherlands when Caspar Fagel died and the king bought his collection. I accepted tulip bulbs, after all," she said. The tulips in question were now blooming in the hothouse adjoining the pinery, and a large bunch of them was on its way to the queen in the hopes that it would cheer her, as her husband had now left England for the summer as he did every year.

"Yes, but you wanted to grow your own," Jem said. "If it had fruited, like the one at Oxford Physic Garden did, you could not have claimed to have *grown* it."

"No, but at least I would have seen what the bloody thing looked like," Harriet replied. "I find it hard to believe they really look like the paintings of them. How can the stalk support such a big heavy fruit? And do you really think it has leaves growing out of the top of it?"

"Carrots have leaves growing from the top of them," Jem pointed out.

"Yes, but they're root vegetables. Pineapples have leaves under the stem. I can't see why they need them on the top too. I must make sure I'm invited to William's next dinner where he has one on display so I can see what it really looks like."

"Doesn't make any sense to me, to keep displaying it at your dinners until it rots away," Jem said. "You could make a wax one instead, and no one would know the difference if it was well made. You would think people would want to taste it. Surely that would make a greater impression than just looking at it?"

"People, or nobles at least, are bloody stupid, the majority of them," Harriet replied bluntly. "Everything's about impressing others by showing how rich you are. Even the king thinks I'm growing pineapples just to impress him. I couldn't care less about impressing him. I'd grow them anyway, just for the challenge of doing so. They're all like Raphael was, don't give a damn about what the thing tastes like. They don't even care about how it grows. They only want it because it costs a fortune to grow – as much as a new coach would to buy - and takes three years to do it, so having one shows that you're rich."

"It would be nice to taste one," Jem said wistfully. "But I don't suppose we'll ever do that anyway, even if these grow."

"Of course we will!" Harriet replied, brushing her sweat-dampened hair back off her forehead. "That's why I'm praying that at least two survive. Because I've already promised William the first one. But the second one I'm going to cut up and share with everyone who has worked to make it happen. It's only fair that they should have something to tell their children about for all their hard work."

"Let's hope you have three, then," Jem said.

"Why? Do you want one for yourself?"

"No. Then you can put one on your table every month for those dinners you have," Jem replied, grinning.

"I could. The people at them are just the sort who'd be impressed by a rotting fruit sitting in the middle of the dining table." She sighed. "Don't remind me of that now, though. The next one's tomorrow, but right now I just want to enjoy tonight. Let's get out into the fresh air and take a walk. Then we can go back to the house and toast our success in getting the damn things to start growing."

They left the building, emerging into the cool evening air gratefully, and then set off for a walk around the gardens as they often did, chatting about the events of the day.

"I hope the tulips arrive safely this time," she commented as they strolled down the path towards the walled garden, still one of her favourite places. It had remained as it was in Raphael's time, whereas the rest of the gardens were now a work in progress.

The previous tulips had been ruined when the axle on the cart taking them to London had broken after just a few miles, scattering them across the road. They had not exactly been ruined. But they had been damaged, and therefore were not fit for a queen.

Harriet had put them in vases all over the house, and had given bunches of them to the maids for their rooms, to their utter delight. Not many mistresses would give exotic, prohibitively expensive blooms to their servants. They would give them to their aristocratic friends instead, to impress them. But Harriet was not interested in impressing her fellow aristocrats, would rather give them to people for whom they would be special, who would really appreciate them.

She was unique. Jem had never met anyone like her, and in eighteen months had not found the will to distance himself from her, and now knew he never would. If he did not have her in his life, he would die. It was not a dramatic statement. It was the simple truth as he saw it. Life without her would be inconceivable. He was her friend, and would never be any more than that. That much he had accepted completely now, and had largely succeeded in subduing his inappropriate feelings for her.

In that she had unknowingly helped him. Once his cottage was finished he had moved into it, and not once since then had she called on him there, or asked him if she could visit him. Instead all their meetings and conversations took place either in the main house, or in the gardens. That was a huge relief to him, and, perversely, a disappointment.

Indeed, to be her friend was a great honour, more than most servants would ever have with their noble employers. Many employers cared for their staff, adopted a semi-parental attitude towards them, and often had a friendly, somewhat informal relationship with their senior servants. But there was always a clear division between them, and a servant, no matter how senior and longstanding, must understand that or risk dismissal.

That was not the case with Harriet and Jem. He could speak his mind to her, be completely honest, tell her when she was at fault, and she would listen, weigh his opinions as if they were of great value. He could laugh and joke with her, tease her even, and she took it all in good part. She treated him as an equal.

But not as a man she could love. Never as that. For which he was grateful, as it made it easier for him. And apart from weak moments when he reflected on what could never be, he was happier than he had ever been in his life.

How could he not be? The last year had passed in a whirl of learning, activity and new experiences. No longer did he feel deeply embarrassed at a dinner party. He now knew which cutlery to use for which dish, how to moderate his drinking so as to appear to be keeping up with the others, how to engage in small talk and to sound intelligent. As well as being able to speak about exotic gardening, he could engage in conversation about politics and other topics of interest to the nobility. He no longer needed to be corrected when he spoke, and although he still had a slight rural accent, his diction was cultured, as were his manners. He did not pretend to be noble, or anything other than the marchioness's servant, but he was an educated, cultured servant, and it was

THE ECCENTRIC'S TALE: HARRIET

generally assumed that his parents had been country gentlefolk rather than paupers.

Harriet had patiently and painstakingly taught him all of that, and had taught him how to appear relaxed and confident, even when he wasn't.

"Because if you show even slightly that you're overawed or feel inferior, they'll pounce," she'd told him. "But if they do, I'll intervene, so don't worry."

That promise had galvanised him into ensuring she never had to intervene on his behalf, because he knew she would do, and he also knew that in doing so she would incite vicious unsavoury gossip that could put her whole future in jeopardy if the king heard about it.

So now he could hold his own, and was increasingly confident in his abilities, the proof of which was growing profusely in the main hothouse, and hopefully would grow in the pinery too. As well as tulips, in the last year they had grown vines, planted outside so the roots could grow deeply into the soil as they needed to, the tendrils trained carefully through purpose-built holes in the lower wall of the hothouse, so that the vines could enjoy the warmth and light they needed to produce grapes, which they should do next year, or maybe in two years, some of which would then be sent to the king.

They had orange and lemon trees in large pots, which were placed outside on warm days and moved into the hothouse when the weather was cool. These were now starting to fruit, and would hopefully provide something for the royal family this year.

They had also grown cucumbers and, to their great joy, melons from Cantaleupe, with which the king had been very impressed, and which had reminded him that Harriet was keeping her promise to provide him with exotic produce to impress his guests, and that he must therefore keep his side of the bargain too. Their next endeavour, apart from pineapples, was to attempt to grow a water melon, of which it was said the fruit was red and very refreshing. Harriet had searched unsuccessfully for information on how to grow one, which made it even more of a challenge. They were using the same method that had worked for the Cantaleupe melons, and would refine this as needed.

Jem was happy. Very happy, and to the best of his knowledge,

265

while some of the servants were undoubtedly jealous of his special relationship with the mistress of the house, no one was spreading gossip of a sexual nature, maybe because whenever they were together there were always servants within sight or hearing. That was probably why she didn't come to his cottage. If there were rumours her parents would certainly hear of it and would visit to chastise her, which they hadn't done until now. So all was well, and there was no reason to think it would not continue so.

"At least this bad weather we've had did some good," Harriet said suddenly, pulling him out of his contemplation.

"What was that?"

"It kept William home to celebrate his wife's birthday at the end of April. Really, if he cared about her at all, he'd delay going abroad *every* year until after her birthday. The poor woman does everything for him, and he can't even make such a simple gesture. I have no idea why she thinks he loves her."

"Maybe he does, in his own way," Jem ventured. Harriet made a rude sound in her throat.

"Bloody peculiar way, then. If he feels any love at all for her, it's only because she allows him to spend most of the year doing what he wants – going to war and living in his precious United Provinces. Really, I'd never say it in public, but I don't think for one minute that he pushed his father-in-law off the throne because he was concerned about the Protestant souls of Britain. I think he did it because he knew it would give him a huge amount of resources to protect his precious Netherlands from the French."

"I'm glad you wouldn't say it in public. You'd be called a Jacobite if you did."

"Ha! There's only one 'ite' I'll ever be," she replied.

"What's that?"

"A Harrietite."

Jem laughed.

"That sounds selfish," she mused. "I suppose I *am* selfish. But I don't really care. No one else will look after me if I don't."

I would look after you, he thought, then pushed the thought away immediately, before it became words.

"You're not selfish," he said instead. "You look after all your tenants and us servants really well, and your family too."

THE ECCENTRIC'S TALE: HARRIET

"Hmm. Not sure my family would agree with you. Not Papa at any rate. He still thinks I should marry again, even though it's clear I don't need to, that I can manage the estate perfectly well alone. But the tenants, yes. And 'the' servants, not 'us' servants. You're not a servant."

"I work for you, and you pay me my wage. Gardeners are still servants, you know."

She halted so suddenly that he'd walked a few steps ahead of her before he realised. He stopped and turned. She was standing in the middle of the path, frowning.

"Is that how you see yourself?" she asked quietly.

It's how I have to see myself, he thought fiercely, *or I'll go mad.*

"It's what I am," he said, achieving a matter-of-fact tone with an effort.

"It's not how I see you at all," she replied. "I see you as my friend. Don't you feel the same way?" Her voice was soft, and he thought he detected a tremble in it, as though she was on the edge of tears.

He was imagining things. Harriet never cried. She was practical, strong, self-sufficient. Even so, the thought that he might have upset her, even slightly, tore at him.

"Yes, of course we're friends," he said immediately. "I just meant that I'm your servant too, which is as it should be."

"Is it?" she said, so softly that he hardly heard her. "If I didn't pay you wages, would you leave?"

"I would have to, whether I wanted to or not," he said. "I must earn money, to live."

She wiped her hand across her face, suddenly looking very tired. "Yes, you're right, of course. I think I'll go back now. It's been a long day," she said. "I'll see you tomorrow. Goodnight."

And without waiting for a reply she walked away, leaving him standing there feeling suddenly bereft, although he had only spoken the plain truth.

* * *

Harriet sat at the head of the dinner table, her food largely untouched, deep in thought, although she kept an ear open in case the conversation, currently lively, went into a lull. Soon the final course would be brought in and then the gentlemen would be left to enjoy their brandy and chat for a while, whilst she retired with their wives to a luxuriously appointed room nearby. At that point she would definitely need to focus on her guests, so she allowed herself to think now.

She gave one big dinner and entertainment like this every month. This one was for specially selected nobles. Specially selected because they were all men who had some influence in society and whose ambitions were larger than their purses. The purpose of the evening was to show to everyone how wealthy their hostess was, how privileged they were to be invited to the house of a noble who was renowned for her reclusive nature, and to give them hope that she would assist their ambitions. Which she would, if it put them in her debt. She was accumulating favours, and, where possible, rendering her guests' futures dependent on her continuing goodwill.

She could afford it, and did not want her freedom to be dependent solely on the monarch's whim. Monarchs were fickle, and when they died they were replaced by new ones who wished to assert themselves. Neither William nor Mary were in particularly good health, and Harriet could not ingratiate herself with the heir Anne without incurring the enmity of the current queen. Nor did she wish to spend months fawning at Court; that would defeat the object altogether.

Better to endure these monthly dinners. One day in thirty was a small price to pay for her happiness. The next event would be for lower-ranking office holders; Anglican ministers, magistrates, lawyers, some judges, MPs. People who had a remarkable amount of influence in a smaller way, perhaps, but no less important to gain favour with. Those dinners were easier for her, as the guests were more easily impressed and remained on their good behaviour throughout rather than growing drunk and disorderly as this privileged lot were more likely to do.

The final courses, of fruit, tarts, syllabubs and a sugar subtlety of an enormous bouquet of roses arrived at the table.

She would ride to her solicitors tomorrow. Better that than have him visit her, where they might be overheard. She could not imagine why she hadn't thought of this before. It was obvious. Now she had, she felt there was no time to waste, and would have gone to see him today but for this bloody dinner.

THE ECCENTRIC'S TALE: HARRIET

"How delightful!" the baronet by her side announced, breaking into her thoughts. "Is this a representation of the beautiful blooms you grow in your hothouse, Lady Hereford?"

Startled out of her contemplation, she almost responded as she felt. *No, you bloody idiot. Why would I spend thousands of pounds building a hothouse to grow things that will thrive in a normal garden?*

"No, sir, I sought merely to see if my new sugar baker could match the beauty of the real thing," she said instead. "What do you think, everyone? Has she succeeded or should I send her on her way?"

Everyone looked from the exquisite sugar roses to the real thing, bouquets of which were placed at intervals in crystal vases on the table.

"Your sugar baker is a woman?" someone asked.

"Yes. Women have smaller fingers and a more delicate touch than many men, I feel, and are every bit as capable as their male counterparts of learning the trade," Harriet replied.

"I have read that sugar bakers work naked, as the work is so hot. It stops their clothes from sticking to their bodies and pulling out their bodily hair when removed," a man down the table remarked, leering. Several people laughed, and a wish to observe the baker at work was expressed.

Harriet shot the instigator a look which rendered him instantly crimson with embarrassment, and quenched the conversation.

"I think it is an exquisite work, my lady, although nothing can match the perfection of God's creation," the crimson bishop's wife put in hurriedly.

Good, she thought, relishing the speed with which the subject had been changed. *This shows how afraid they are of offending me. Long may it continue.*

Because of that, and because she had just come to a decision which pleased her, she did not comment that she was glad the bishop's wife remembered how a man of God should behave, even if her husband did not. These dinners were held to inspire loyalty, not to gain enemies. She certainly had enough of those already.

Instead she told them that they could each take a sugar rose home with them if they wished to do so, and the convivial atmosphere of the evening was restored.

* * *

Jem sat outside his cottage on a little stool, while the sun went down in a blaze of red, pink, lilac and gold. The book he had been attempting to read lay on his knee, forgotten, and the glory of the sunset was completely wasted on him.

He had not expected to see Harriet yesterday, as it was the day of the dinner, which usually occupied all her time, between dressing appropriately, ensuring that everything was as it should be, and then actually attending the event. He had not expected to see her early this morning either, because the music and card playing often went on into the early hours, so she would sleep late after them.

But he had not seen her all day. He had been tempted to fabricate an excuse for needing to speak to her, so that he could apologise for upsetting her, although he had no idea why she had been upset by what was the plain truth, and upset enough to keep away from him. Harriet was not one to sulk or mope; she was far more likely to march down and tell him bluntly how he had offended her, to want to talk it through and set things right.

Or at least that's what he assumed. In truth they had never had a cross word in all the time that he'd worked for her. But whatever she was doing, he could not enquire as to her whereabouts without risking the servants laughing and commenting that he could not manage for even one day without seeing her, which would not do.

So instead he had worked hard all day, helping the labourers to dig what was being called the new pond, although lake would be a more fitting description of it, from the size of the hole. Then he had stuck his head under the water pump to refresh himself and gone home, intending to read and absorb the book that now rested on his knee unopened. The sky darkened, and still he sat outside, until the stars twinkled above him. She would not come now.

He stood, intending to go inside, go to bed although he doubted he would sleep, when he saw a figure striding across the grass toward him. Instantly his heart soared, and he waited for her to reach him. Should he ask her inside? Maybe not. They had got this far without arousing scandal.

"Here," she said as she reached him, holding out a sheaf of papers. "These are for you. Take them, and read them." She

THE ECCENTRIC'S TALE: HARRIET

looked at the dark windows of his home. "Have you candles to do so?"

"Yes," he said. "I've been sitting outside, as I often do of an evening when it's dry."

She nodded.

"Well then," she said briskly. "I'll see you in the morning, and if you have any questions, you can ask me then. Goodnight to you."

She was so brisk, so businesslike. He had seen her like this before, many times, with traders, with officials, with builders. But never with him. His heart sank. He glanced down at the papers. It was too dark to read them but he could feel the thickness of the parchment, the lump of a wax seal, and knew they were official.

"Harriet," he called, as she started to walk away. She stopped, but did not turn back. "What are they?"

"Your freedom," she said. And then she walked away, and did not look back.

He went inside and put the papers on the table, then lit a candle, his hands trembling. Surely she would not dismiss him so coldly, without giving him a chance to explain? Although he had no idea what he would say, given such a chance. She had said they were friends, just two nights ago. What had changed?

He could not read these now. Cursing his own cowardice, he left the papers on the table and walked out, hoping a walk around his beloved gardens would calm him.

He walked, for a long time, but when he finally returned to the cottage he felt no calmer. They were not his gardens. It was not his cottage. Nothing was his, except the clothes on his back, which he had bought with the generous wages she paid him. Even his heart was not his, for she had stolen it long ago.

The last time he had felt this vulnerable was when his father had been dismissed by the duke, so many years ago. No, he had not felt as vulnerable then, because he had been a child, had known that his father would look after him.

Now he was a man, and must look after himself. But still he put off reading the papers, instead pouring himself a cup of beer. Then he sat down. For the first time he felt the helplessness and resentment of the working man, dependent for everything on the

JULIA BRANNAN

whims of their employers. And he understood fully the helplessness of women, dependent for everything on the whims of their husbands. It was unfair.

Life was unfair. He drained the cup, poured another, braced himself and sat down, pulling the candle closer to the documents. Then he began to read.

* * *

In the morning he was woken by a knocking on the door. At first he was disoriented, having been roused from a deep slumber. And then he looked through his small unshuttered window, saw that the sun was high in the sky, and shot out of bed. Opening the window he called down to the unknown visitor, who he could not see from this angle, that he had overslept, and would be but a minute.

Then he pulled on his shirt and breeches, combed through his hair with his fingers, looked in the basin and ewer in the corner of the room and saw they were empty, then stumbled downstairs, rubbing the sleep from his eyes. He opened the door.

"Good morning," Harriet said. "I didn't mean to wake you. I thought you'd have risen hours ago."

"I…I didn't sleep until very late," he said.

"And I didn't sleep at all," she replied. She glanced past him to the papers, which were still on the table next to the snuffed-out candle. "Did you read them?" she asked simply.

He nodded. There was a silence, while she tried to interpret his reaction from his nod and he wondered whether he should invite her in or not. Keeping her standing outside seemed rude, but inviting her in…he looked past her, saw no one in this part of the garden, and then stood back from the doorway, allowing her to make the choice.

Being Harriet, she walked in immediately, and looked around.

"I have often wondered how it would look inside," she said. "It's very much yours."

He had no idea what she meant by that. It was basic. Table, bench, settle by the fire, two shelves on the wall, on one of which were his books, on the other his eating implements. There was nothing ornamental. No tablecloth, no pictures on the wall, no ornaments. But it was tidy, clean, the floor swept, the fireplace clean of ashes.

272

THE ECCENTRIC'S TALE: HARRIET

"I don't spend a lot of time indoors," he said.

"I know. That's what I meant."

There was a moment of silence. Not the comfortable silence that often fell between them, but a tense one, as each waited for the other to address the elephant in the room.

"You should not have done that," he said finally. "There was no need."

"Yes, there was," she answered. "I should have done it a long time ago. Freedom is as important to you as to me. I feel privileged that I could choose to give it to you."

"I can't accept it," he said.

"Yes, you can. In fact you can't refuse it. This cottage is now yours. And the allowance will be paid to you every year. If you leave without giving an address it will be held for you, accruing interest, until you take it. It will be paid to you until you die, and then to any heirs for ten years afterwards. Mr Hanson is redrafting my will so that if I die you will still be paid. So you have to accept it!"

"You did not need to do this to keep my friendship," he said. "That is yours for life."

"If I needed to do this to keep your friendship, I would not have done it," she replied.

"Then why? Are we not happy as we are?"

"Yes," she replied. "No. Let us sit down to talk about this, instead of standing awkwardly. Not outside," she added as he turned to the door. "This conversation is not for others to hear. I am not as oblivious to malicious rumour as you think I am."

She sat down on the bench at the table, and after a moment he closed the cottage door then came to sit next to her, leaving as much of a space between them as he could.

"I cannot believe I didn't think of it before," she said. "I have always thought of us as friends, since we were children."

"And so we have been."

"Yes, but when you referred to yourself as a servant, I suddenly realised that it was true, and that there would always be a distance between us while you were, as there must always be between mistress and staff. I do not want that distance. I do not want any distance between us. So now you are no longer my servant. Now you are free to do as you wish, and I hope you wish

273

to stay here with me. Now we are equals."

"Harriet, we will never be equals. You are a marchioness, and I am a—"

She turned suddenly, and put her fingers on his lips.

"No," she said. "You are a man, and I am a woman. That is all the difference between us now, and all there ever will be." Gently she stroked his lips, then she moved towards him and cupping his face in her hands, she kissed him.

Her lips on his were feather-light, but the effect was not. For the briefest of moments he stayed there, unable to believe that she had done what he had ached to do for so very long. Instinctively his arms came up to embrace her.

Then he remembered where he was, and who he was, and that in spite of her desire, they were not equals, would never be equals, and he recoiled, standing so quickly that he almost overturned the bench they were sitting on.

"No!" he cried, his tone harsh with desire, with distress. "No," he repeated, softer now, but the damage was done.

Still sitting, she looked down at her lap for a moment, and then she straightened, and stood, bracing herself on the table with her hands, as though afraid her legs would not support her.

"I'm sorry," she said. "I should not have done that. I…you must not think for even a moment that with this," she gestured at the papers, "I was trying to buy your love. My intentions there were honest. Let us forget this happened, and remain friends. I will go, will see you in the hothouse later."

She made to leave, and he should have let her go, *would* have let her go, if he had not seen the tears in her eyes as she walked past him. Harriet, who he had never seen cry.

"Harriet," he said.

"No," she replied, "I cannot think what came over me. I know I am ugly, that men are repelled by me, though they pretend they are not in the hopes of winning my estate. I esteem you even more for your honesty in showing your revulsion, truly I do."

She took another step forward, and then he moved, taking her by the shoulders and turning her to him.

"God help me, for your sake, for both our sakes I should let you leave here believing that," he said. "But I cannot, because it would be a lie. You are not ugly, I have never thought you ugly.

THE ECCENTRIC'S TALE: HARRIET

You are the most beautiful woman I know."

In spite of the tears that stood in her eyes, she smiled at that.

"I am not beautiful," she said. "I have always known that. Raphael—"

"To hell with Raphael," Jem interrupted, his voice rising. "Raphael was evil, and said such things to diminish you, because you were worth more than he would ever be, and he knew it. But I will tell you true, you are not conventionally beautiful. Your skin is golden from the sun, not white as snow. You are slim and strong, not fat and curvy. Your eyes show intelligence rather than languor. Maybe the Court would not call you beautiful, but I do. I have wanted you for years," he added, unable to stop himself now the gates had opened, "and I pulled away from you because it isn't right for me to want you. It's too dangerous."

She smiled again, this time brilliantly, a smile that lit her eyes, that made his heart race just to see the happiness and vitality, the love of life that she radiated, that made her irresistible to him.

Then she stepped forward, and cupped his face again.

"I love danger," she said simply, "as I love you."

She kissed him again, and this time he did not recoil.

CHAPTER THIRTEEN

December 1694

Jem woke first, and glanced out of the window. It was twilight, so about four-thirty. He turned over in the bed slowly so as not to disturb his companion, although he knew really he should wake her immediately, as she would have to dress and return to the house before supper was served. Footmen would go to look for her if she did not appear for that. But he wanted to watch her sleeping. It made him so happy, and a few more minutes would do no harm.

He propped himself on one elbow and looked down at her, her features soft in the light of the single candle they had lit before they had undressed, trying not to tear each other's clothes in their hurry to make love. Rips would be noticed, would have to be repaired. But the time they managed to steal alone together, truly alone together, was so rare and precious, that it was hard to maintain control.

She looked so lovely when asleep, so fragile, so vulnerable, which she never did when awake. When awake she exuded confidence, privilege, and that, along with the male attire which she wore more and more often now, made her appear masculine to many, he knew.

Not to him. Never to him. To him she was the most beautiful, feminine, desirable woman in the world. Her body was perfect, soft, supple, sweet-smelling. No one who saw her naked could think her masculine; but then no one else *would* see her naked, which thought made him smile. She was his, as he was hers, and he would never love another. How could he? No other woman could ever come near to her. He could not get enough of her, nor she of him.

He thought back to the first time they had made love, how clumsy it had been, a world away from now, now they knew each other's bodies so intimately. When they had finished kissing that first time he had not known what to do next, torn between his overwhelming desire for her, his utter lack of experience with women, and his nagging awareness that in a manner of speaking they were about to leap over a cliff.

He had stood, frozen with indecision, and Harriet had taken command.

"Come on," she had said. "I've seen downstairs. Show me your bedroom." He had led her upstairs politely, as though her request was innocent, and once inside the room his shyness had overwhelmed him.

"I…er…I have never lain with a woman before," he had admitted, his face scarlet with embarrassment.

She had smiled, had taken his hand and kissed it.

"I have never lain with a man before," she said. "Only with a monster. I know one thing. Whatever happens here now, it will be done with love, and we can learn together, for in lovemaking I am as virgin as you."

That had reassured him a little, and they had carefully undressed each other, wanting to get the most from an experience that neither of them had enjoyed before – that of making love to someone you truly desired. It had been clumsy, fumbling, with various body parts colliding painfully and humorously, and to his utter mortification he had climaxed before he had even managed to penetrate her, after which they had both lain for a while, just caressing and kissing each other's bodies, starting to learn about each other, until he had been ready to try again. This time he had moved slowly, captivated by the feel of her body under his, her obvious delight when he entered her. They moved as one instinctively, slowly at first, then faster as their passion flamed, and he had known then that even if he lived to be very old he would never experience anything as perfect, as wondrous as this glorious moment when he became one for the first time with the woman he had adored for so long.

It had been the most wonderful experience of his life, and he had committed every second of it to memory, sure that this one experience of making love to her would be all he would ever have, would have to last him for the rest of his life.

Afterwards they had lain together for a while silently, just wanting to be together, both feeling that no words could express the wonder of what had just happened. Instead they had held hands and, finally, had slept a little.

Afterwards he had helped her to dress, brushed her hair and then had gone for a seemingly nonchalant walk in the gardens to make sure no one was around, after which she had kissed him once more and then left, leaving him flushed with renewed desire, very, very happy and utterly bereft, all at the same time.

There had not just been one experience after all. In the six months since then they had met intimately as often as possible, which was not as often as they would have liked. Now they had finally admitted their attraction to each other and had enjoyed each other's bodies once, nothing could stop them. But this was much more than just physical attraction. This was love of body *and* soul, deep, passionate, all-consuming.

Dangerous.

Jem reached down and gently stroked Harriet's hair back off her face, smiling as she sighed, screwed up her face, and started to wake. For him the hardest thing was keeping the attitude expected between an aristocrat and her gardener during their numerous meetings about the hothouse produce. He wanted to touch her all the time, not sexually but tenderly, affectionately. Because everything about her entranced him, and on occasion, when they looked at each other and her love for him shone clearly in her eyes, it was all he could do not to reach across and stroke her cheek.

As he did now, watching as her eyes slowly opened. She smiled sleepily up at him, and he leaned down and kissed her gently on the lips.

"What time is it?" she asked.

"A few minutes before five," he said. He had no watch or clock, and refused to have one, saying that if he did he would lose the ability to know the time instinctively, would become

THE ECCENTRIC'S TALE: HARRIET

constrained by artificial instead of natural time, which he never wanted to be.

"Damn," she said, coming fully awake now, and sitting up. "I didn't intend to stay this long. I need to be back and dressed appropriately before Thomas arrives."

"I'm sorry. I'd have woken you earlier had I known you expected visitors," he said. She smiled and reached across, pulling his head to hers and kissing him.

"You know I'd much rather stay here with you," she said. "But this is important." She stood up and started to retrieve her clothes from the floor where they had been scattered in the throes of passion earlier.

"Thomas who?" Jem asked.

"Tenison," she replied. "The new Archbishop of Canterbury," she added, when his expression made it clear he was none the wiser for knowing the surname. "William appointed him against Mary's wishes after Tillotson died. She wanted Stillingfleet, but William refused her. He's someone I want on my side if possible, so I invited him to stay overnight on his way to Kensington."

"You must go then. No one will be on your side if they see you sneaking out of here." He got up, picked up her stocking and rolled it expertly down his hand. "Sit down," he said, "I'll help you dress."

She did as he bid, pulling on her shirt while he rolled the stockings up her leg and gartered them at the knee.

"I can't wait for the day we can be open about our relationship," she said. "I hate all this sneaking around. It was fun at first, like when Melanie and I used to tiptoe down into the kitchens at night and steal cakes, then eat them under the bedcovers. But I'm tired of it now. As I'm sure you are. Neither of us enjoys subterfuge."

"We'll never be able to be open about it," he said. "I don't like it, but I've accepted it now. As long as you love me, I can cope with it."

"I will always love you," she said, pushing her feet into her shoes and standing up. "And we *will* be open about it. There must be a way, and if there is, I will find it. I must go."

After she had gone and he had recovered from the momentary wave of loneliness that always engulfed him at such times, he poured himself a cup of mulled wine, in keeping with the approaching festive season and the bitter weather, and went outside to sit on his bench.

He could see no way that they could ever proclaim their love openly. If they did, then the powers that be would stop it. Neither of them gave a damn about the opinions of others, of the mockery, the gossip, the scandal that would spread like wildfire if it were known that the Marchioness of Hereford, probably the richest woman in England, was fornicating with her gardener. It was not fear of that which kept them quiet.

It was true that Harriet did not want to hurt her parents, but she had said that even that would not stop her from having an open relationship with him.

"My parents love me and would come to terms with it," she had said when they had discussed it seriously last month. "But if the king finds out, he might banish them from Court. And he will not let us stay together, no matter how many pineapples I grow for him. He will force us apart, maybe marry me off to some idiot."

"How can he do that? We are both over twenty-one."

She had laughed bitterly.

"Easily, is the answer to your question. Because if I say no to giving you up, or to his choice of husband, he could accuse me of…anything he wants, really. Insanity. Treason even. Kings can always find someone to fabricate evidence. Then he could take my whole estate for himself."

"He could do that anyway, couldn't he?" Jem had asked. "Then he could fund even more wars!"

"No, he couldn't, not without good reason. Because if he did, he would undermine the trust of the whole of the aristocracy, which is never a good thing for a king to do, especially one who spends more time out of the country than in it. He needs their support to survive. Every king with sense knows that, and he knows that he holds the throne only through his wife. If he brought me down just to access my wealth, every other noble in the country would wonder when it was their turn, and rise against him. James Stuart would certainly fan the flames of discontent."

She had reached out, stroked his cheek.

"But if it is discovered that I am openly sleeping with my

THE ECCENTRIC'S TALE: HARRIET

servant, then he would be justified in reining me in. Blue blood cannot be tainted you know, and fornication is a sin against God – for women, at any rate. It seems men can sleep with whoever they want and no one gives a damn. No one would defend me."

"We could…" His voice trailed off.

"We could what?" she asked softly.

"I…if we married, then we could not be accused of sinning against God, at least," he had said, his heart plummeting as he had seen her expression instantly harden at his suggestion.

"I will never marry again. You know that," she had said firmly.

He had looked down at his hands resting on his knee. His workman's hands, calloused and brown.

"No, of course," he had said. "I shouldn't have been so forward. Forgive me."

She had looked at him then, had understood the emotions behind the words, as she understood everything about him, and her hand had come into his line of sight, had rested on his.

"It's not because of what you are thinking," she said. "I couldn't give a damn about 'blue blood'. Bloody ridiculous. My blood's as red as yours, and if you go back a few generations we Ashleighs were certainly commoners too. The only difference between your ancestors and mine is that one of mine was in a position to ingratiate himself with the king or queen at the time, and seized the opportunity. One day you might grow a twenty-pound pineapple for the king and be knighted for it or some such nonsense, and all of a sudden your blood will start changing colour too."

He had laughed then, in spite of his despondency.

"If I was ever going to marry again, it would be to you, that much I will say," Harriet continued. "But I won't do it. I will never put my whole life in the hands of a man again. It would damage our relationship, destroy the purity of what we have. I would feel the loss of freedom, and you would feel the pull of power. No, don't shake your head. I know you believe you would not, but you have never had power, and have no idea how corrupting it can be. I *have* been insecure, helpless, and I will never be so again. No. We must find another way."

"You have never been helpless," Jem remarked.

"Ha! I have. I fought back, yes, but I had no real weapons, not against the law, which favours men. We are free, you and I, and freedom is everything to us. Let us keep that freedom. We can do it, if we are careful."

He had not agreed with her then, although he had not said so, and he did not agree with her now. It was not freedom to be sneaking around, her coming to his cottage only when the weather was too foul for any outdoor servants to see, him sneaking furtively up the back stairs in the dead of night to her bedroom. It was not freedom for him to be terrified that she would get with child, even though she had reassured him that she was certainly barren, and in six months had not quickened. He wanted to be with her, openly, legally, as any man would, give her children, rear them together, grow old together. They could not, would never do those things.

He did not believe he would be corrupted by wealth and power if they married. He cared nothing for power, nothing for money, as long as he had enough to feed and shelter himself.

Seeing how hurt he was, she had explained that even if they were to marry, the king could and would have it annulled in a moment if it suited him, have both of them incarcerated or worse. And it *would* suit him to do so, rather than allow the son of a pauper to become the richest man in England.

So, they would continue as they were. Because for him there could be only one thing worse than losing her, and that would be being locked in a cell, never to feel the sun and rain on his face again, never to smell green things. Even the thought of that rendered him cold with terror.

And in thinking that, he realised that he could understand her horror of relinquishing her freedom to the whim of a man, even if that man were one she loved.

He went inside, got his coat, because it was very cold, and set off for a walk around the gardens. He could not be indoors now. Not until he had shaken the horror of a prison cell from his mind. Better stay as they were than lose everything.

* * *

Late January 1695

The coach made its way slowly along the road, partly because it was a moonless night and so very dark, but mainly because it was

THE ECCENTRIC'S TALE: HARRIET

bitterly cold, the road was icy, and to add to that it had just started to snow again.

Aaron huddled deeper into his heavy coat and sighed, remembering with longing the fire in the servants' quarters, to say nothing of the hot toddies. He would give a lot for one of those right now. He was frozen, his fingers stiff and awkward on the reins, even with gloves on.

"You all right there, girl? It's fearful cold. You can come and sit with me if you want," he called to the vague blob sitting on one of the front horses.

"No, the horses is a bit nervous, on account of the ice. They's calmer if I's here with them. And this blanket's keeping the worst out."

Aaron sighed again. He had hoped Claire would accept his offer so he could put her blanket across both their knees. In truth it was probably warmer there than where he was, as at least she had the warmth of the horse's body to keep her from freezing to death.

What had possessed the mistress to decide to go home on such a night was beyond him. No reason that he could see why she couldn't have stayed until the thaw set in. The passengers were out of the wind, but it would still be damn cold in the coach.

At least one of the inhabitants of the coach shared the driver's feelings, and was making her views known.

"I can't think why we had to leave tonight," Sophia grumbled. "I can't see why we had to leave *at all*. It's not even as though we can take off this dreadful black once we get home, is it? His Majesty has ordered all the nobility to wear it, wherever they are."

"I've already told you why," Harriet replied, somewhat impatiently. "Not everyone thinks the Court is Paradise. I bloody hate it, and Melanie's been hoping to leave for years. William said she could, so I wanted to get out of there quickly, before he changes his mind."

"I'm so cold I can't feel my feet any more," Sophia said sulkily. "I don't see why I had to come as well."

"I can stop the coach if you wish, and you can walk back. That'll warm you up a bit," Harriet said.

"I've never seen anyone so grief-stricken," Amelia put in before Sophia could complain again. Harriet was fast losing her temper with her sibling, who had moaned incessantly for the whole journey, and Amelia wouldn't put it past her throwing Sophia out on the road. "I thought he was going to die as well for a time. We all did."

"He loved her so much," Sophia said.

"Ha! Loved her so much he buggered off to Holland for months every year," Harriet said, "even though he knew she hated ruling in his stead. He's just upset because he won't be able to spend six months of the year there any more."

"Harriet!" Amelia cried. "He spent every moment with her when she was dying. He couldn't sleep or eat. He was truly distraught."

"I don't doubt it. But if he loved her that much, he should have shown it to her when she was able to enjoy it, shouldn't he? And he never did. Or he never did when I saw them together. I can't think of any reason why he'd be different when I wasn't there."

"He was not a demonstrative man," Melanie said quietly. "But I do believe he loved her, in his way. She adored him, that's certain. I think he just took her for granted, as men often do."

"I still don't see why we had to leave," Sophia said sulkily. "Papa stayed. I could have stayed with him."

"Oh, for God's sake!" Harriet shouted. "Papa stayed because he's one of William's close friends. The king said that he wanted the ladies-in-waiting to retire for a time after the funeral, because they remind him of his loss. I don't see what's difficult to understand about that. But you can go back tomorrow, whether the king wants you there or not. In fact I *insist* you go back tomorrow, because if you continue like this I'm going to be arrested for fratricide."

A short if somewhat hostile silence followed this heartfelt comment.

"Are you sure you want to live with Harriet, Melanie?" Amelia said after a minute or so. "You're very welcome to come home with me, you know."

"I know that, Mama. And I will of course visit you and Papa often. But I would really love to spend some time with Harriet, to keep her company."

"Harriet doesn't like company. She hates everyone," Sophia said malevolently.

THE ECCENTRIC'S TALE: HARRIET

"Only if they're less than five years old. Or act as though they are," Harriet replied.

This time the silence lasted longer, and was finally broken not by Amelia, but by a man shouting something outside the coach.

"Was that your driver? I expect he's cold too. You didn't even think about him, did—"

"Shut up!" Harriet hissed, so venomously that Sophia's mouth fell open in shock. "That was not Aaron's voice," she added, reaching up and opening the lantern door. She snuffed out the candle with her fingers, plunging them into darkness.

"Why did you do—" Sophia began, and then stopped as the voice called again, closer this time. The coach came to a halt.

"Is it someone in trouble, do you think?" Melanie said. "Perhaps they need assistance." She leaned forward, but Harriet's hand captured hers as she reached for the handle of the coach door.

"No, wait," she whispered. "It could be a highwayman. Aaron is armed, and is a good—"

A shot rang out in the night, cutting off the rest of Harriet's sentence. The carriage jerked forward, then stopped again. Sophia screamed.

"Oh fuck!" came a deep voice from outside the coach door. "What did you do that for?"

Another man replied from further away, but they didn't hear what he said.

Harriet let go of Melanie's arm and reached down to her side, feeling for her fur hand muff and slipping it onto her left hand.

"Dear Lord preserve us," Amelia murmured. "Have they shot Aaron?"

Harriet closed her eyes momentarily, took a deep breath to steady herself, and then spoke.

"We are ladies alone, and beg your mercy," she called. "We wish only to continue on our way. If I may step down to speak with you." Very slowly she opened the coach door. "Stay here," she whispered fiercely to the others.

Amelia, realising that her daughter was about to jump out of the coach, lunged forward to stop her but was too late. Harriet leapt to the ground, staggered slightly, then shut the coach door behind her. She looked around as if in terror. Next to her was a

285

horse on which sat a man dressed in dark colours, his face covered with a kerchief.

Even criminals are in mourning for the queen, she thought ridiculously, then stepped to the side, ostensibly to look up and speak to him, but in reality to get out of the way of the horse so she could see to the front of the coach. Another man stood holding the reins of the horses, who were very restless, spooked by the shot. A dark shape lay on the snowy road, presumably Aaron. There was no sign of Claire. And no sign of anyone else.

The man on the horse courteously lifted his hat and dipped his head to her.

"My lady," he said. "We will not harm you or your companions. We seek only a little something to warm us in this bitter weather."

Whether he meant gold to buy food and a warm room or sexual favours, she never found out. She shook the fur muff concealing one of her pistols off her left hand, letting it fall to the ground, then raised her arm and fired straight into the horseman's face. He fell backwards in the saddle as the horse first shied then bolted, the rider's feet jolting out of the stirrups so he fell onto the ground almost at Harriet's feet. Ignoring both him and the fleeing horse she stepped forward, took her right hand out of her deep pocket, cocking her second pistol as she did, and shot the other man, who had been pulled off balance by the horse he was holding rearing at the first pistol shot.

Turning back she kicked the man who had fallen off the horse in the groin area. There was no response, which meant he was probably dead, or deeply unconscious. Then she ran to the other prostrate man, and reversing the pistol, hit him as hard as she could on the side of the head. It was too dark to see the finer signs of life, and she was taking no chances. She was a good shot, but pistols were notoriously inaccurate at distance. If he was not dead, he would now certainly be unconscious for a time.

She grabbed for the reins, pulling at one side of them with all her might to bring the horses' heads round and stop them bolting, then waited a moment, listening, but heard no sounds as of other ruffians coming to their friends' rescue. Just the two, then.

"Claire!" she called softly.

A muffled noise came from the direction of the horses and a

THE ECCENTRIC'S TALE: HARRIET

moment later Claire's legs appeared between the two front horses.

"I slid down the side between them, when I heard the man shout," she said shakily.

"Well done, girl. Are you hurt?"

"No, my lady," Claire said, her voice high-pitched with incipient hysteria.

"Good. Now I need you to calm the horses for me. They've had a shock. Can you do that?" Harriet said.

"Oh yes! They's well trained, my lady. They'll do well for me."

"Excellent. You do that, then." Having given the child something to occupy her mind, Harriet closed her eyes for a moment, took a deep steadying breath, and then opened the carriage door.

"You can come out now. It's safe," she said. "Can one of you light the lantern? I need you to help me get Aaron into the carriage."

The three women climbed out, Melanie reaching up as she did so for the lantern. Amelia stepped forward and seized her eldest daughter in a strangling embrace.

"My God," she sobbed, "I thought he'd shot you! I didn't know who to try and protect, you or your sisters. Oh, God! I thought you were dead!"

"Mama, I need you to hold yourself together, please," Harriet murmured. "I'm fine, but I need you to be strong for me."

Amelia took a shuddering breath, then another. Then she released her daughter and stepped back, just as Melanie succeeded in lighting the lantern. She raised it and looked around.

"You shot both of them?" she said in shocked admiration.

Sophia looked down at the now illuminated gory mess that had been the head of the man, lying on the ground a couple of feet from her, and fainted, sliding down the side of the coach to the ground.

"Bloody useless," Harriet commented. "Bring the lantern."

The two sisters moved round to Aaron, who was lying on his side on the ground. Very gently Harriet turned him over to see where he had been shot, and as she did he moaned softly, to her relief.

"Aaron," she said urgently. "Where did he shoot you?"

"I'm sorry, my lady," he murmured. "I should…my hands were too cold."

"Never mind that, man. Where did he shoot you?" Harriet replied, her tone harsh. "I'm not angry with you," she added. "We need to get you to a doctor. Where are you hurt?"

"Side, right side," he said faintly.

"Can you stand, if we help you? You have to, I think. It's your only chance. I could ride for help on the highwayman's horse, but you'd freeze to death before I got back. You have to get in the coach."

Very, very slowly they succeeded in getting him to his knees, and then he crawled to the coach, holding his side with one hand, and with the help of the three conscious women, finally managed to get in, slumping across one seat. She could not see how much blood he'd lost, as all servants had to wear black mourning livery, but she could see by the lantern light that the hand holding his side was bright red, and his face was deathly pale.

"You must lie very still," Harriet said. "Mama and Melanie will care for you."

She jumped down again and looked at Sophia, who was starting to come round now.

"You ought to be ashamed," she said. "My eleven-year-old postilion is calming the horses, and all you could do is faint. Get in the coach, and if you say one more word of complaint, I swear I'll throw you out."

Harriet walked forward and climbed up onto the front of the coach, then flexed and massaged her wrists, which were hurting due to the kick of the pistols as she'd fired.

"Are the horses calm now, Claire?" she asked. "They seem so."

"Yes, my lady. They doesn't like being next to a dead man though, scares them, it does."

"Good. Let us get them away from the dead man then. Now I need you here next to me. Put your lovely blanket over both of us. I need you to help me drive the coach. Can you do that?"

"I ain't never drove the coach, my lady. Aaron says I's too young yet. When I's fourteen, maybe."

"But I'm sure you've watched him closely when he's been driving, haven't you?"

"Oh yes! I wants to learn quick when I's fourteen."

"Well, I'm older than fourteen, so I think with my age and

THE ECCENTRIC'S TALE: HARRIET

your knowledge we can do it. In truth we have to. And if we get home safely, maybe we can start your training a little early. We're only a few miles away."

They set off, very slowly but steadily.

"What will you do about the bad men?" Claire asked after a minute.

"I think they're dead," Harriet said. "If I had not shot them, I think they would have harmed us, as they harmed Aaron. I must think of Aaron first, for he's alive, and I would have him stay so. But I will send some watchmen out to arrest them if they're alive and bury them if they're dead, I suppose."

"Better if they's dead. They'll hang else, and that's a bad way to go. I seen a hanging once. My ma took us and bought us gingerbread. We had a lovely day, but I didn't like the hanging bit. Took a long time to die, they did. Ma said we should learn, and never do nothing to get us up on the end of a rope."

"I don't think there's any danger of that, child. I should think you'll be my coachwoman one day. But I would like to keep my coachman alive, if I can."

She kept her coachman alive, but only just. Instead of going home she rode straight to the physician's house and, ignoring his comments that he was about to go to an important recital, demanded he attend her servant immediately.

"Or do you think attending a concert worth my eternal enmity should my man die as a result?" she asked coldly.

Aaron was immediately taken to the physician's best bedroom while he went to get his bag. She left him there, saying she would return in the morning personally to see how he was, and to compensate the doctor for his ruined evening. Then she paid his servant a sovereign to run and inform the watch that two highwaymen were lying, probably dead, on the road to London, not five miles away. After that she went home, made sure that her mother and sisters were well cared for, that a huge fire and a meal was prepared for Claire in one of the guest rooms for the night as a treat for her bravery. And then she retired to bed, saying that she had a terrible headache and wanted to rest undisturbed until the morning. If the watch came, she said, she would see them tomorrow.

She waited a few minutes before sneaking down the back stairs and running across the lawns to Jem's cottage.

He held her as she trembled, as she broke down and cried, as she explained between sobs what she had done. Then he took her to bed, not to make love, but to warm her, to comfort her, which was what she needed now. With him she had acted as she would not with any other, not even her mother, aware that she could not show weakness to her parents in case they thought her incapable of managing the estate alone. He knew that, and was deeply honoured that she trusted him so, with the very heart of her.

"I think they would understand, though," Jem said. "It's not an easy thing to kill another person, even if you were right to do so. And you were. I'm glad you learned to shoot properly."

"So am I. Have you killed someone?" she asked. She could not imagine her gentle lover killing a human being. He hated even to kill vermin, did it only because there was no alternative. *I cannot create life,* he had said, *so I should not take it, if I don't have to.*

"No. I never had cause to. But Hal, he came to work at Ash Hall after you left, he was a soldier, and he told me that even in battle your first kill is a terrible thing, and makes you sick. You get used to it eventually, he said, but the first one is bad."

This was not my first kill, she thought, but did not say. Not even to Jem would she say that.

"I had to," she said instead. "If they hadn't shot Aaron, and had just wanted money, I would have given them that. They were probably soldiers too, home for the winter and needing money. Highway robbery always increases when the army is discharged."

"They should pay them a pension when they're not fighting," Jem said. "It's not right to expect a man to risk his life for his country, then leave him to starve until he's needed to fight again."

"Did Hal tell you that too?" she asked.

"No. But he told me how he nearly starved to death one year, because he'd been wounded, a musket ball in the shoulder, and he couldn't get any other work to see him over the winter. And it struck me that that's not right."

"I agree with you. But it's no different really to when Raphael wanted to throw John out because he had smallpox."

"You didn't let him though."

THE ECCENTRIC'S TALE: HARRIET

"No. And I would have given the highwaymen money, then waited until the morning to tell the watch, to give them time to get away. But not after they shot Aaron. And not when he said that to me. I was not about to let them rape us all, nor to let Aaron die while they were doing so. Do you think that's what he meant?"

"Yes," Jem replied. "He would have said, 'we want your money and jewels' otherwise, surely? It's a strange way to ask for them. You did right. And you were very brave. No one will say otherwise."

She turned into his side, and snuggled into him. He kissed the top of her head.

"Thank you," she said. "I don't know what I'd do without you. I wish that…" Her voice trailed off. He waited a moment, but she didn't speak further.

"You wish that what?" he asked.

"I wish that I could stay here forever with you," she said, although that was not what she had been about to say. She could never say what she had been about to say. That was her secret, and she would take it to the grave with her.

"You shouldn't rightly be here at all," he said. "Not with your family staying. If they find out, they won't understand."

"I had to be with you. But you're right. I'll go soon," she said. "I just want to stay with you a little longer. It's very cosy in here."

He smiled. In the last months he had whitewashed all the interior walls to lighten the rooms, and had bought curtains for the windows, and needlepoint cushions for the settle. Not that he cared about such things. The outdoors was his real home, the cottage only a shelter when the weather was very bad, a place to be alone, and a place to sleep. But now it was a place to be with the woman he loved, and he wanted to make it pleasant for her. It seemed he'd succeeded.

"Oh! I meant to tell you! I forgot with what's happened," he said.

"Meant to tell me what?"

"While you've been at Court at Her Majesty's funeral, one of the pineapple plants has started to fruit."

"Has it? In this weather?"

"The weather doesn't matter. It's as hot as hell in there. I expect the men working in there are happier at the moment than in the summer though, at least. It's very tiny, but definitely a little rosette in the centre of the plant."

"Oh that's wonderful! Let's go and see it!" she cried.

"We can't. You have a headache and have to rest alone all night, you told me. If we go to the hothouse you'll be seen. With me."

"Damn it," Harriet said.

"It will still be there tomorrow. Or you could go alone, I suppose, say you were unable to sleep."

"No. I want to see it for the first time with you. I'll wait. And thank you."

"I haven't done anything, except make sure the temperature stayed as constant as possible," Jem said.

"Not for that. For being here for me. For loving me as I really am, good and bad. For being you. Tonight I killed those men to protect myself and my family. But I'd do the same for you."

He wrapped his arm tighter around her.

"You did protect me tonight," he said. "Because I could not live without you, you must know that."

She did. Because she felt the same way for him.

* * *

February 1695

"How on earth can that idiot be related to me? To us," Harriet said, throwing herself down into a chair. "Oh, that feels so much better. You don't mind, do you?"

Melanie looked at her sister.

"I don't mind what? You calling our sister an idiot?"

"No. I'm quite sure you agree with me. Me wearing breeches and a shirt."

"Why would I care what you wear? As long as you don't expect me to wear them."

"Of course not. You should try, though. It's remarkably liberating not to wear stays and have heavy skirts tripping you up all the time."

"Uncle Percy's related to us, you know," Melanie commented, "and he's an idiot."

"True. But not as directly as Sophia. He could have inherited

THE ECCENTRIC'S TALE: HARRIET

his pompous idiocy from his mother's side. We can't say that of Sophia."

"Percy's mother is our grandmother," Melanie pointed out. "They do have one thing in common though."

"What's that?"

"They've been indulged a little too much, I think, Percy because he was the youngest child, and Sophia because she was so docile. Mama and Papa didn't need to discipline her as they did you and I. And because she's so pretty and childlike the queen and all her ladies treated her like a little pet at Court, feeding her sweetmeats and suchlike. I don't believe it's good for children to get everything they want."

"I never really thought about that. I don't want children myself, so how to rear them is not something I concern myself with."

"I don't know if I want them or not. If I meet the right man, maybe I will. But I won't be bereft if I never do," Melanie said. "I don't feel as pressured to get married and have children now our little brother's growing so strong and healthy."

"As long as you have your cows."

They both laughed.

"We must go to a cattle fair in the spring, and you can choose a calf or two," Harriet said. "We can take Barnaby with us. He has a good eye for healthy stock. And we must finish your library. Now you're here we can order the rest of the furniture. And the books you want."

Melanie smiled happily.

"I'm really looking forward to filling all the shelves with books I want to read. And then actually having time to read them," she said. She looked around at the numerous empty shelves. Only one was already full. "I looked at those earlier," she said. "Why have you put all those horticulture books in here? And why have you relocated my library to the other side of the house? I'm not complaining, the view from the window here is lovely, or will be soon. I can paint it when the weather doesn't allow me to paint outside. But was there something wrong with the room you allocated before?"

To her surprise, Harriet blushed. Harriet never *blushed*. She flushed red with anger at times, but blush? No. Melanie waited. This was going to be interesting.

"I have a favour to ask you," she said after a moment. "But I wanted to wait until the others had gone home before I did. And you'll realise when I tell you what it is, that this must remain in confidence."

She went on to explain about her relationship with Jem, and then waited in silence for a minute while Melanie digested the information. She was ready to have to justify her reasons and feelings to her shocked sister if necessary.

"I can't say I'm too surprised. You have been very close since you were children, after all," Melanie said after a minute. "You're very well suited. Apart from your class, of course. I assume that's why you're not telling Mama and Papa."

"It's why I'm not telling *anyone*," Harriet said.

"Except me. I'm honoured. But can't you do what you like now, really? You don't care what people think of you, after all. What can anyone do if you marry him? You don't care about being ostracised from society, which is what would certainly happen."

"No. I'd be happy to be ostracised from society. But I'm quite sure the king would not let his richest noblewoman do such a thing."

"The king is so bereft right now, that I think you could do anything short of declare war on him and he wouldn't care at all," Melanie said. "You deserve happiness. Why not marry Jem and just sink into obscurity? True, it would be a source of much gossip, but only until the next thing came along."

Harriet stood suddenly, and went to look out of the window. The snow lay heavy on the ground, blanketing the landscape work in progress. It would look beautiful when finished, but now it looked horrible. She couldn't wait for the spring, when she could be out and really active again. At least she could still care for plants in the hothouse.

"The pineapple is growing well," she said suddenly. "And another plant is showing signs of fruiting too. But the water melon plants have died."

Melanie knew her sister well, so did not respond to this attempt at a change of subject. After another few minutes' silence Harriet sighed and turned from the wintry view back to the cosy room.

THE ECCENTRIC'S TALE: HARRIET

"I can't marry him," she said. "Not because he's my gardener. I can't marry anyone. I will never marry again. Even the thought of it makes my blood run cold."

"Harriet, you had a terrible experience with Raphael. I know that. The man was inhuman. But most men are not like that. Look at Father and Mother, for example! Or Uncle John and Aunt Marion. They are happy."

"They *seem* to be happy. No, that's unfair. I know Mama and Papa are happy. But they're happy because Mama has devoted her life to Papa's concerns. She's never known anything else. I know they were in love, and she defied her parents to marry him, but since then she's had to accept his views and actions and live with the consequences of them, whether she agreed with them or not. It's an unequal relationship, as every marriage is."

"Do you think that if you married Jem he would start to lay down the law?" Melanie asked. "I don't think he would, but you know him better than I do."

"No, in truth I don't think he would. But if he *did* I would have no comeback, no power to go against him. Right now I am free. I have power and my power is growing, because although as a woman I can't be a Member of Parliament, a Justice of the Peace or hold any other official position, if I can render the men who do hold those positions dependent on me for their places, then I can influence what they do. I'm doing that."

Melanie nodded.

"It's a shame you were not born a boy," she said. "You would be a wonderful duke."

"Maybe. And if I was a man, and Jem a woman, then I would marry him. Because I don't care about his background, and because although people would disapprove, no one would have me committed to an insane hospital for doing so, and in time they would come to terms with my marriage. But if I was a man I could marry Jem and retain my freedom. As a woman I cannot. And I know myself too well. If I marry him then that will eat at me, whether he takes advantage of it or not. And it will destroy our love. I cannot do it. God knows I've thought about it a lot, but I cannot."

"I think if Jem was a woman he would not marry you either. He feels as you do about his freedom, I think, except he is dependent on you for his keep."

"No, he is not any more. I have given him his cottage and an allowance for life, which he will be paid regardless of what he does. I wanted him to be free too. In that way I know his love for me is as pure as mine for him."

Melanie nodded.

"You cannot choose between freedom and love," Melanie said. "Because both are as important to you. As they no doubt are to him."

Harriet laughed.

"You always had a way of getting to the heart of things. Yes. That is exactly my problem."

"And I always wanted to remain single but be free and independent," Melanie said, "something that unmarried women rarely are. They usually end as unpaid, despised servants to various family members. You, with your generous settlement on me, have just given me both the things I desired most. I think the least I can do is help you to have both the things you desire. So tell me why you have moved my library, and why I need to become interested in horticulture."

Harriet sat down.

"Have I ever told you that you are the most wonderful sister anyone could ever wish for?" she said.

"No. But you are right, of course, and you can tell me as many times as you wish."

"You don't need to become interested in horticulture," Harriet explained. "What I do need is a way to meet Jem as often as I want without all the servants knowing about it. They know we spend a lot of time together, but that can be attributed to my great interest in gardening, and to the fact that we are trying to grow exotic flowers and fruit for the king. It is natural for us to spend a lot of time together over such an important task, and we always leave doors open so no one can accuse us of impropriety.

"At the moment either I am sneaking off to his cottage in the dead of night, or he is creeping up the back stairs to my bedroom, which is frankly ridiculous, and risky. It's only a matter of time before we're discovered, and then the servants will do everything they can to spy on us. You know what people are like. I don't care about them, but they must never have any evidence of us having a carnal relationship. No matter how bereft the king is, he will not

THE ECCENTRIC'S TALE: HARRIET

let me create a scandal for the nobility. And it would damage our family's status with him too, which would be terrible. I cannot let that happen.

"This library is directly beneath my private chambers, and there's a narrow spiral staircase behind that panel at the side of the fireplace that is not generally known about. When I found the key and opened it, it was thick with cobwebs and had clearly not been used for many years. If Jem is given permission to use your library to quietly study, no one will connect him with me. And then he can come up to see me without anyone being any the wiser, come back down and leave from the library."

"Will people not think that perhaps he and I have a relationship then?" Melanie asked.

"Not if he is only allowed in here when you're not here. I can state that I conduct official private business in my library, which I do, being honest, and so it will be better for him to study here. Your private rooms are on the other side of the wing, so no one will think anything of it. It will just make life a lot easier for us."

"Climbing up a spider-infested secret stairway is a lot safer than climbing up stairs the servants use, I agree," Melanie said. "But you are still playing with fire, you know that. What will you do if he gets you with child?"

"I'm barren," Harriet said. "Raphael tried for years without success. Mama said that was probably down to him rather than me, but I show no sign of quickening with Jem either."

"That doesn't mean you're barren, though. What will you do if you do get with child?"

"I don't know. I don't want children. I think babies are ugly, and boring. They're certainly not worth risking your life for. I can't understand why so many women do it."

"They do it because most women have as much of a passion to have babies as you and I do to be free," Melanie said. "Mama and I have talked about it, because I also don't really want to have children. If I was married I might enjoy having babies, but I don't have the desperate desire to have them that it seems most women do."

"I don't want them at all, married or not," Harriet said. "I truly think I'm barren. There has been no sign at all, in over four years. And as for playing with fire, I've done that my whole life, to survive, to remain who I am. But this is worth it, because now I'm truly happy. I have never been so happy in my life. I have everything I've ever wanted. And I will do *anything* to keep it, and I will do a great deal to keep my family happy too. But I won't involve you, if you don't approve. That would be unfair."

"How can I not approve of you being happy?" Melanie said. "And in truth, Jem is a good man, I think, and worthy of you. I care as much about rank and status as you do. I just haven't the courage you have to stand up for yourself. I never have had, and I don't think I ever will have."

"You don't need to have. I will stand up for you now. Just enjoy your life. I certainly intend to carry on enjoying mine."

CHAPTER FOURTEEN

They enjoyed their lives. It was much easier for Jem and Harriet to meet now, and they did so with increasing frequency, spending most nights together. Not always making love, although they did do that frequently, but being together naturally as lovers do, not worrying that loving glances and gestures might be intercepted by some nosey servant, simply behaving as any young couple in love would, spontaneously, teasing each other, laughing at nothing, just for the pure joy of being together and in love.

It was wonderful, intoxicating. And the more they were together, the more they wanted to be together. They did not tire of each other, as Harriet had feared they would, as, in truth, Jem had feared they would. They just grew closer with time, and the extremes of emotion, of joy, of sexual passion, of desperate longing for the night to come so they could truly be together, settled into a happiness, a peace, a deep contentment at being able to share their lives with the person they truly loved, the person who truly accepted them as they were, who did not wish to change them, in fact who thought they were perfect as they were.

Melanie bought a calf in the spring, and then another, and finally a third, and Buttercup, Daisy and Violet became her passion. On fine days she would paint, sitting happily outside for hours. It was she who painted pictures of Harriet and Jem's first full-grown pineapple before it was carefully transported to grace the king's dining table until it rotted. She also painted the second pineapple, this time cut into segments, which was eaten by every servant who had shovelled coal into the fires, sat up at night guarding the precious plants from would-be thieves, who had tended them, and who had moved tons of manure over the three-year growth cycle of this king of fruits, crowned with a circle of stiff leaves.

But mostly she enjoyed painting her beloved cows, and the beautiful gardens in which she spent so much of her time. She painted the lake, now finished, the nearby river diverted to fill it. Moored at the jetty was a spectacular boat, with an open cabin which could be covered with an awning should the weather be inclement. Carved figures of Grecian gods decorated its rear, and a gilded dragon coiled along the prow. In the centre of the lake was an island, to which Harriet and Jem would sometimes swim in the evenings when the gardens were deserted. Melanie had visited it by boat, but had not yet been persuaded to learn to swim, saying she could think of more interesting ways to risk her life.

Now Harriet was extending the woodland in which she still walked and chatted regularly with Highbury's son. If the earl needed his son for some reason and he was not to be found, invariably he would be in the gardens with Harriet, practising swordplay, archery and shooting as he grew older. Sometimes they would climb into a tree and sit together reading poetry aloud, giving their opinions on the verses. And increasingly they would be planting new trees together, digging the holes themselves while the gardeners looked on with amusement.

It was a gratification to Daniel that his naturally reserved, even shy son had such a friend as Harriet. When they had moved from London for the sake of Frances's health, which had deteriorated with alarming rapidity in the city, Daniel had worried that William would remain too shy to assert himself as he would one day have to when he inherited the earldom. The Marchioness of Hereford was not someone he would have chosen as a bosom friend for his son at the age of five, and had thought it would be a passing phase: William would grow and want friends of his own age and gender, and Harriet would quickly tire of such a young companion.

But their friendship had gone from strength to strength, and Harriet's unfeigned interest and confidence in the child's qualities and abilities had given him confidence, as his mother had imbued in him all the social conventions, society manners and rituals, which Harriet never would, not giving a damn about them.

She was a remarkable woman, Daniel thought as he strode through the gate leading to his neighbour's woodland. It was a

THE ECCENTRIC'S TALE: HARRIET

shame that Harriet and Frances had never moved beyond polite acceptance of each other to become friends. They were too different, though.

Once in the woodland he stopped and listened for a moment as he always did, hoping to hear his son and his neighbour. Silence. A drop of water landed on his nose, then another. He looked up at the sky, which was a cloudless late August blue, and frowned, puzzled. Then he wiped his hand across his face and looked at it. No, it was not bird droppings. Definitely water.

More water fell on his head, this time a trickle, accompanied by a hastily smothered giggle, and Daniel looked up into the leafy branches of the tree he was standing under.

"I cannot see you, but I know you're up there," he said. "Shame on you, William, this is no way for an earl's son to greet a visitor!"

There was another smothered giggle, and then Harriet, dressed in green breeches and waistcoat, swung lightly down from one of the lower branches.

Highbury bowed elaborately.

"Madam, you are corrupting my son, I believe," he said.

"I admit my guilt," Harriet replied unconcernedly. "But I'm not doing it very well. I told him to sprinkle drops on you, to see how long it would be before you realised that it could not possibly be rain, but he became a little over-enthusiastic. Come down, you rascal, and share your father's disapproval, before I wither under it."

William clambered down the trunk and landed on the ground in a flurry of leaves.

"Papa, you have to see the willow tree!" he announced. "It's wonderful, and when you stand—"

"Shh!" Harriet replied, and the boy immediately stopped. "It is a surprise. I have invited my family to visit me in a fortnight for two days, and I would be delighted if you and Frances, and William of course, would join us. It's to celebrate the completion of part of the gardens. We will have fishing, boating on the lake, a tennis tournament, ride around the completed gardens, and lunch in the Temple to Flora."

"And the willow tree," William put in.

"And the willow tree," Harriet agreed. "Then there will be music, cards, dancing, fireworks, all the usual things in the

301

evening. I haven't seen some of my uncles and cousins for a long time, so I thought it would be a good idea. Far more fun than those damn monthly dinners I have. And there will be enough going on that if some of us don't exactly get on well together, we can amuse ourselves elsewhere to avoid argument. So it should all be very pleasant. Will you come?"

"I think we have to, if only to see the mysterious willow tree," Daniel said. "William, the tailor has arrived to fit you for a new suit. You must go home."

After William had gone, Daniel and Harriet walked in the gardens together for a time.

"So there is no breath of it?" Harriet asked, once they were sure the child was out of earshot.

"No. I would hear if there was. They talk of your ridiculous attire, of your generosity to your servants and tenants which is sure to give them ideas above their station, and now Melanie is living with you, they say that you are encouraging her to be as wayward as you are. But there is no talk of you and your gardener. I don't know how you do it, in truth. Even the most loyal servants cannot resist gossip."

"They can if you pay them extraordinary wages, and if they know that when they grow too old to work they will receive an annuity to ensure they don't starve," Harriet said. "Or most of them can. But of course you are right. Jem and I go to great lengths not to arouse suspicion. Or rather, if we arouse suspicion, not to provide any meat to the bones of a potential scandal. In truth, though, my senior servants are loyal, which is good, because they are the ones who would be listened to and taken seriously."

"Even so…but I won't lecture you again. It is your life, not mine, and you must live it as you will. William tells me you are thinking to go to Spain with Jem."

"I am thinking to, yes. We cannot get the damn water melons to fruit. It's quite ridiculous. We've managed to grow all kinds of plants that are 'impossible' to grow in England, but for some reason the melons refuse to oblige us. They grow well in Spain, so I thought to go there and observe for myself the natural conditions they need, then see if we can emulate that in the hothouses. I have not decided yet, though. I'll decide after the family party."

"Oh, I must tell you, the pineapple was a great success!" Daniel said. "It still is, for that matter, although it's looking somewhat decayed now. The king was complimented hugely on it."

"Ha! Was he? No doubt he took all the credit for growing it."

"No, but he didn't deny it, either. Does that bother you?"

"Not at all, as long as he leaves me alone to enjoy my life. When do you go back to Court?"

"In two weeks," Daniel replied. "Why?"

"I will give you another one to replace the rotting one he has," Harriet said. "Have you ever tasted pineapple?"

"God, no. It's far too precious to actually eat!" Highbury declared.

"What rot. I don't see the purpose of growing edible plants if you don't actually eat the bloody things. Come to my party in two weeks then, and you can all taste it. I will be serving it at dinner."

* * *

September 1696

It seemed that someone was smiling down on Harriet on the days of her party, because the weather was glorious, perfect for outdoor activities. Whether that someone was God or Satan depended on how you viewed the hostess's eccentric lifestyle. Certainly the newly completed gardens were eccentric, with serpentine paths winding along meadows leading to groves of trees, fountains, huge beds of flowers or little temples at which food and drink were served. It was all very different from the straight lines, severely clipped hedges and symmetrical tree plantings that Raphael had laid out. In fact it was very different to most aristocrats' gardens. This was something of a departure from the norm.

"It feels more as though I'm out in the open countryside than in a garden," Aunt Susanna commented, eyeing with some apprehension a small group of cows who were gazing intently at her across the field. "They are rather large," she added.

"Oh, don't worry about them. They're Melanie's pets, and not at all vicious. Cows are rarely aggressive anyway, unless they have calves and think you're threatening them," Harriet reassured her.

"But I'm gratified, because that's exactly the feeling I was aiming for, to have the gardens appear more natural."

"It's very unusual, Harriet," her Uncle John said, coming up behind aunt and niece as they strolled along. "Who have you emulated?"

"Emulated? No one. I'm just doing what I want to do, that's all. I don't like gardens that look too artificial. It took the gardeners endless hours to clip all those trees, and must have been incredibly boring for them to do. Now they each have time for their own plots where they can grow vegetables to feed their families, but there is still plenty for them to do in the gardens as well, just a little more varied than clipping leaves. There's a lot of scything of grass though, to have such neat lawns, which is why I now have these wildflower meadows interspersed with the lawns. It's wonderful to just lie in them on a fine day and watch the insect life!" It was fun to lie in them with Jem too, but she did not mention that.

Susanna and John exchanged a look. Lying in the grass and watching insects was not something aristocrats did, or certainly not something they did when they were twenty-four years of age.

"Surely as long as they're paid, the servants won't care what they do," Aunt Susanna said.

"They won't *say* anything, no, but that doesn't mean they won't care, does it? I'd hate to have to, for example, embroider a rose for twelve hours every day for the rest of my life, no matter how much I was paid to do it. Wouldn't you?"

"Yes of course, but the lower orders are different to us," Susanna said.

"In what way? Apart from being poorer."

"Well, they are not as intelligent, not as ambitious, of course. They are more suited to repetitive tasks that do not tax their minds, only their bodies."

"What bullscutter," Harriet replied rudely. "I know some very intelligent paupers and some particularly stupid nobles, as I'm sure do you, Aunt."

"I say, Harriet, you've made a mess of the gardens, haven't you? Why didn't you just sell up and go to live in the wilds of Scotland, where it already looks ugly? Would have been a lot cheaper!" came a voice from behind the three.

THE ECCENTRIC'S TALE: HARRIET

"Oh, and here's a perfect example of one," Harriet said to her uncle and aunt. "Percy. Have you ever been to the wilds of Scotland?"

"No, of course not. But I'm led to believe that it looks as uncivilised as this. And the women there dress indecently as a matter of course too, showing their legs up to the knee, or higher at times. You'd feel right at home."

"I see nothing indecent about Harriet's dress at all," John retorted, who disliked his younger brother almost as much as Harriet did. "She is dressed most becomingly."

"For a change. I expected to find you rolling around on the grass naked. Nothing would surprise me. Who are you trying to impress?"

"No one," Harriet replied coolly. "But I know how easily distressed you are. Had I worn my usual shocking attire I was concerned you might faint at my feet. Again."

Percy flushed instantly scarlet.

"Ah! So, this is what I have brought you to see," Harriet said, changing the subject and in doing so dismissing him. "At the top of the slope is my Temple to Flora! But we must wait for the others to join us. There are a number of steps leading up to it, but that will only whet our appetites for lunch. The views are quite extraordinary." Harriet turned back to see how far away the rest of her family and the Highburys were. "They'll be here in just a moment," she said. "The gardeners worked incredibly hard carrying the stones up the slope and building the water tank, but now, as you'll see, there is a lovely waterfall, which I will start when we get there. It's truly a relaxing place to eat lunch. We will have musicians too. And then later—"

She stopped as Stephen and Amelia appeared, accompanied by the Highburys. Frances, leaning heavily on her husband's arm, looked up at the steps ahead with trepidation.

"Anyone who feels that they have walked quite enough – I know that even the small part of the gardens I have changed means that some of the walks are in excess of two miles," Harriet said, "are quite welcome to be taken up the steps by chair. In fact we all can if you like. I'm told that Chinese Emperors, or is it Japanese, are carried everywhere in this way! Hence the Oriental decoration on the chairs. You will see."

"Why have you left this dead tree here?" Percy asked, looking up into the leafless branches of the tree he was standing under, Harriet having carefully manoeuvred him there. "It looks horrible. Were the gardeners too tired to chop it down after you'd made them carry hundreds of rocks up the hill for your pointless fountain?"

"Waterfall, not a fountain," Harriet replied.

"Is that—?" William began excitedly.

"As I was saying," Harriet continued, cutting William off, "after lunch and music, we could have a game of tennis, Papa, if you wish to challenge me. I have an outdoor and indoor court, so you can't use the weather as an excuse to refuse me. I was thinking to have a tournament if enough of you wish to play. Who is interested?"

"It's a few years since I've played, but how can I refuse such a gauntlet thrown down?" Stephen said smilingly. Several other men agreed. It would be a pleasant way to spend the afternoon, when the weather had cooled a little.

"Good. Now, as I was saying," Harriet continued, raising her hand in the air in an uncharacteristically elaborate gesture, "above us you see the Temple of Flora—"

The rest of what she was about to say was drowned out by an unearthly screech from underneath the dead tree, which quite remarkably seemed to have suddenly come to life and was squirting rather a large amount of icy cold water from its branches, soaking the unfortunate individual standing beneath it.

"That, Percy," Harriet said coolly, "is a fountain. I'm sure you will not confuse it with a waterfall again. Shall we go up, and then you can see the difference between them?"

Percy, who had come alone, his wife being too large with her fourth child to travel, refused Harriet's offer of a water feature comparison and went home immediately. The rest of the family, along with the Earl and Countess of Highbury and their eleven-year-old son, who was virtually prostrate with laughter, ascended to the temple, either by chair or on foot.

The building was truly magnificent, circular and flanked by stone columns carved with vines hiding in which were small, beautifully carved animals and birds. Urns filled with flowers were

THE ECCENTRIC'S TALE: HARRIET

placed between the columns, and a quartet of musicians played while the food was served. To the rear of the temple was a large double door, now open, showing a wonderful view across the countryside, and when the music was not playing the refreshing sound of water rushing over rocks floated in to the diners.

"Thank you for accompanying Frances in the chair," Highbury murmured to Harriet as they sat. "She is most sensitive about her frailty."

"Not at all," Harriet said. "I've walked all day and also appreciated not having to climb the steps."

"I take it that was the famous willow tree," Daniel continued.

"Indeed it was. Probably even more famous now. Or infamous, as far as Percy's concerned."

"You are incorrigible. I thought my heir was going to die of mirth on the spot. Remind me never to incur your enmity."

"You need have no fear, Daniel. When I love, I love for life. When I hate, likewise. But you would have to do a *lot* to turn me from one emotion to the other."

"Why do you hate him so?"

"He has always tried to ridicule me, to undermine me, since we were tiny children. I think he resents the fact that my father inherited the dukedom and I was his heir. And now he resents the fact that his brother John is an earl, whereas he is not. He hunts for your weakness and then exploits it. He enjoys hurting others."

"Which is why he mentioned countless times today to John that his wife fell immediately with child directly after the last one was born, I presume."

"Yes. I walked carefully edging him to stand under the tree today, but if he hadn't I'd have made damn sure he went in the lake at some point, vicious bastard. Aunt Marion has had five miscarriages now. She doesn't need that spiteful idiot to keep reminding her how inadequate she is. I knew that once I baited him he would focus all his spite on me. You'd really think he'd have learned by now though."

"Learned what?"

"That I have no weaknesses. Or none that he will find."

Let us hope he never does, then, Highbury thought.

The party was a resounding success, such a success that no one raised any objections when Harriet changed into breeches, shirt and waistcoat and took part in the tennis tournament, reaching the semi-finals. Or maybe they felt unable to object after Harriet informed them that the king had given her her first lesson. Certainly no one objected to the treatment of Percy. In fact Uncle John made a point of catching her alone that evening while Marion was busy playing cards, to thank her.

"Don't thank me for what was an absolute pleasure. He's a complete bastard."

"Even so, Marion has relaxed visibly now, and I'm sure she'll enjoy the rest of her stay. She so needed a change of air to pull her from her melancholy. I am worried about her."

"Maybe she'll carry the next child to term," Harriet said, knowing how desperate they both were to have children.

"I hope so. But the doctors are not hopeful. And it is a worry to me, as she almost died the last time. But she so wants a child, she wishes to continue trying. It is the only argument we have. I am for accepting our childlessness. We can still enjoy life together, which I could never do if I were to lose her."

Harriet fell silent, clearly troubled.

"I'm sorry, I didn't mean to burden you with our problems. This is a wonderful party. We do not see enough of you, as you do not come to Court."

"I hate Court," Harriet said. "You know I like living quietly. But I would very much like to come and see you. I have something to discuss with you, something which might assist both of us greatly."

"Really? Well, you are always welcome. What is it that you wish to discuss?" he asked, intrigued.

"Something private," she said. "I will call on you in a few weeks."

* * *

"On my own?" Jem said.

"Yes. You can do it alone. I have every confidence in you."

They were sitting on red and white striped chairs in Harriet's apartments. In the hearth a large fire burned. The curtains were drawn, the candles lit, and the room was warm and cosy, made even more so by the sound of the hail battering against the windows. The weather had turned in the last days and it had

THE ECCENTRIC'S TALE: HARRIET

rained almost ceaselessly. Luckily most of the crops had been harvested, so there should be no food shortages this winter. Certainly not on Harriet's estate, anyway.

In spite of the comfort of the room and the large glass of brandy sitting on the small table by his side, Jem felt neither warm nor cosy. Instead he felt cold with horror.

"But you said you wanted to come with me. You were so excited about going to Spain with me!" he said.

"I was. And you told me it was a really dangerous thing to do."

"I don't think you coming with me is dangerous. It's the way you want to do it that I'm worried about."

They sat for a moment, both remembering the night in July when he had come up to her room to find, to his shock, a man in there. Even when the man had turned to face him Jem had not immediately realised that it was Harriet. She had worn breeches, stockings, a long waistcoat and a heavy coat with wide sleeves. At her throat was a Steinkirk cravat. She had also worn a sword, an elaborate dark wig which curled over her shoulders, a wide-brimmed hat trimmed with feathers which shadowed her face, gloves, and shoes with heels that added a couple of inches to her height. Jem had realised then that although Harriet often wore men's clothing, she had never before attempted to be masculine; she was always undoubtedly a woman dressed in masculine attire.

But now she was a man. Not just in clothing, but in the way she stood, the way she walked across the room to him, her attitude. Even her voice was deeper when she spoke. If he hadn't known her so intimately, hadn't been expecting to see her, he would not have guessed her to be anything other than a somewhat diminutive man.

When he told her that she had been delighted, had told him she'd been observing all the men she knew closely in the past weeks, had practised their mannerisms, had read books aloud in her room in a deeper voice. And had done it all because she intended to come to Spain with him as a man.

"We can go as two gentlemen who are interested in gardening," she'd said excitedly. "We can share a cabin, which is quite normal. During the day we can be friends, and at night we can be lovers. Quiet lovers," she added.

He had expressed his doubts that she could keep up the façade for such a long time, and had said that if she was discovered, nothing would stop the scandal rocketing straight to the palace.

"I don't see why I can't manage," Harriet had said. "Catalina de Erauso did."

"Who?"

Harriet had gone on to explain that she'd been reading a play, *Comedia Famosa de la Monja Alferez* to practise her Spanish ready for the trip, which was about a woman who lived as a man, who was even a captain of the army invading Chile, and who had won battles.

"She was sent to be a nun as a child, but escaped. She had lots of adventures, had a business, fought duels, and only revealed she was a woman to avoid execution when she was arrested. I thought it was just a play, but it seems that it's actually a true story! Even her brother didn't recognise her. There's a painting of her by Juan van der Hamen. I would love to see that."

"Why can't you just go as a woman, but not as the Marchioness of Hereford, and I could be your husband?" Jem had suggested. "Then we could share a cabin and wouldn't have to pretend to be male friends during the day."

"I would be recognised," Harriet said. "The whole of the aristocracy knows what I look like. There would be a much higher chance of us being discovered if I did that."

"So why have you changed your mind?" Jem asked now. "Is it because you've realised how dangerous the idea was?"

"No," she replied honestly. "I would love to do it one day. I really think I can, perhaps with more practice. But I need to stay here. My uncle and aunt need my help, and I have to visit some of my other estates to make sure all is well with them. That's long overdue. When we both return, you from Spain, and me from my estates, we can concentrate on finally growing a successful water melon."

"I could wait," he said. "I could wait here until you get back from your estates, and then we could go together. Or I could come with you to your estates. I would much rather do that. I don't want to be away from you for so long."

"But we would be apart anyway. I can't take you to my other

THE ECCENTRIC'S TALE: HARRIET

estates. I have no plausible reason to do that. And if you wait until I get back to go to Spain the weather will be too bad for us to sail, and we'll have to wait another year at least before we can try the water melons again."

"Could you not go to your estates when we return from Spain? We could make a short trip instead of the long one you've planned. We don't need to go to the Hortus Botanicus as well. Then I could start the water melons growing for you while you were away," he suggested.

"No. Or at least, I could delay going to the estates, yes, but not to my aunt and uncle. That's more urgent."

He fell silent at that. He never asked her to elaborate on family matters. She watched him as he stared into the hearth, the firelight gilding his blond hair, painting his strong, handsome face with a ruddy glow, and she felt a pain that was almost physical at the thought of being apart from this man who she loved so deeply. Even a week would be unbearable, and she would be away from him for much longer than that, *had* to be away from him for much longer than that.

"Have you fallen out of love with me?" he asked suddenly, pulling her abruptly out of her unhappy thoughts. "If you have I'd much rather you just told me, than prolong it. That would be much worse for me."

"No, never!" she cried, so vehemently that he could not doubt her sincerity. "I cannot imagine life without you. I love you completely, and always will. You must know that!"

"I did. I do," he said. "But you were so excited about us travelling together, and have changed your mind so suddenly…I…I had to ask, or I would have worried about it, made it into something real."

"It's not real," she said. "That will never be real. I swear that to you on my life. I have always loved you. I will always love you."

He smiled then.

"And I will always love you. I will go alone, if you want me to. But I'm afraid to do so, I admit. I don't want to disappoint you."

"You won't disappoint me. I think it will be good for you to go without me, as my representative. It will prove to you that you can command respect in any company now. It will give you the confidence to truly believe what I keep telling you - that you are respected in your own right for your vast knowledge and experience in gardening. It will allay any gossip that might be brewing, too. And you can write to me, as I will write to you."

* * *

He had gone at the start of October. And letting him go, knowing she would not see him for months, was the hardest thing she had ever done. After he'd left she had gone to her rooms, and although not overly religious had prayed fervently for him to come back to her safely. Already, after only a few hours without him, she was missing him. Which seemed ridiculous, because they often did not see each other for hours, even for a day or so. But she always knew he was there, on the estate, that she could be with him within a few minutes if she needed to.

But now she would not be with him for months, would not see his wheat-gold hair fall over his face, his merry summer-blue eyes as he laughed, as he looked at her with love, always with love. She would not feel his arms around her, holding her, protecting her. He was the only person in her life who knew that in spite of her independence, her confidence, her ability to kill without hesitation if threatened, still she needed protection, comfort, reassurance. Now there was a great empty space on the estate, a dark, cold chasm where he should be.

She lay awake all night, desolate, desperately lonely. Then in the morning she got up, dressed, pulled herself together, and sent for Melanie.

Melanie sat quietly and did not interrupt as Harriet, after dismissing her maid and locking the door so they would not be interrupted, told her why she had sent Jem to Spain alone, why she was going to visit Uncle John and Aunt Marion, and why she would then be visiting her estates until March.

When Harriet had finished, still Melanie didn't speak, but sat, looking at her hands which were folded neatly in her lap, until Harriet could bear it no longer.

"Say something, for God's sake," she begged. "Tell me I'm an idiot, tell me the plan is impossible, tell me you warned me and I didn't heed you, which is true. Just say *something!*"

Then Melanie looked up, her eyes bright with tears.

"Oh sweetheart," she said. "I could say all of those things, but

THE ECCENTRIC'S TALE: HARRIET

I won't. Come here." Then she opened her arms and Harriet accepted her sister's embrace, awkwardly at first, because they were not normally physically demonstrative. But then Melanie whispered, "I am so, so sorry," into her ear, and Harriet realised that, after all, she did need comfort, needed to know someone was there for her, would support her.

Because she could not seek support from the person she normally would go to. Not about this. Never about this.

Finally they separated, but sat together on the sofa, still holding hands.

"You cannot keep this from Jem, you know," Melanie said gently. "After all, it's his baby too. He has a right to know about it. And you will struggle to keep it from him, I think."

"I will. We have no secrets from each other. But I cannot tell him this. If he comes back before the child is born, then he will think I am on my estates. In fact I will go to my estates, but will return to John and Marion's before the birth."

"If they agree."

"If they agree. I cannot tell Jem. If I tell him, he'll want to marry me, want us to keep the child and bring it up together. Or he'll insist on keeping it himself, if I won't marry him, which I won't. I can't allow that. If that happens everyone will know it's mine, especially if it looks like me."

"Have you thought that maybe this is a sign that you should abandon all this pretence and just be with him openly?" Melanie asked. "I still can't understand why you're so very afraid of everyone knowing, you, who couldn't care less about being cast out of society. Their opinions mean nothing to you. Why do you care what they think about your relationship with Jem? In truth, what can the king do about it? I don't really believe he would fabricate treason charges or declare you insane for falling in love with your gardener."

"I can't do that!" Harriet replied hotly. "If I have the child and bring it up as the bastard child of a servant, it would never be accepted in any society, either noble or common. I might not care what anyone thinks of me, but I would not condemn my child to a shadow world."

"If you marry Jem, the child would be legitimate," Melanie pointed out.

"The king would not allow that."

"Why not? I know Jem is the son of a garden labourer, and that his grandfather was hung for theft, but God knows our own ancestors have done some very unsavoury things too. What could the king do? I don't think he could make your life any more difficult than it is now, when you're constantly worrying about being discovered and denounced. Are you sure you're not using the king as a scapegoat because you're terrified of marrying again, after the way you suffered with Raphael? Jem would never treat you like that, and you know it. You do him a great injustice to think he might."

Harriet sat, shocked into silence for a moment by her sister's unusual display of passion and disapproval. Was that true? Never one to defend herself against criticism on principle, Harriet considered what Melanie had said. Was she right? Melanie, knowing what Harriet was doing, allowed her the time to think.

"No," Harriet said finally. "There is some truth in what you say. I *am* afraid of relinquishing control, but my worries are not unreasonable. No monarch would allow a gardener to be richer than he is. William only allows me to be because I'm a woman and he underestimates me, believes I could never threaten his crown. Which I could not, directly at least. But my husband could. That is why William allows me to remain unmarried. The pineapples help," she added, smiling wryly, "but only a little."

"You're richer than the *king?*" Melanie said. "Do you mean because he has to ask Parliament for money to pay for his wars?"

"No. I mean I am richer than the king. My personal fortune is more than his. A lot more than his. I couldn't overthrow him, but if I put my mind to it, I could cause him a lot of difficulties. I suppose if I decided to support James Stuart wholeheartedly I maybe *could* overthrow him, or ensure that James could. If he wasn't so bloody incompetent."

"You're not serious," Melanie gasped.

"Mel, I have large estates in five counties, all of them profitable. I have expanded them, and employ excellent stewards to look after them for me, so that I can grow pineapples and grapes and spend time with my gardener. I have the money to control the election of twenty-seven members of Parliament, whose voters live on my estates. I also control Justices of the

THE ECCENTRIC'S TALE: HARRIET

Peace, magistrates, churchmen, and a number of other influential people. Because after Raphael died I decided to make myself as powerful as I possibly could, so that if anyone ever tried to make me do anything I didn't want to do, I could make their lives hell. I have been very successful in doing that. And, ironically, it's because of that that if I did something as drastic as marrying again, I would stop being a ridiculous figure of fun and gossip, and instead would attract the king's serious attention. If he investigated, which he certainly would, he would discover just how powerful I am. And even though I am a mere woman, he would bring me down. He would have to. I would do the same, were I him. I cannot come to his attention in that way, neither by marrying my gardener nor by openly giving him a bastard child."

"So your striving to retain your freedom has actually had the opposite effect," Melanie said softly.

"Yes," Harriet replied. "Amusing, isn't it?"

"No. It's stopping you living openly with the man you love. I think that's tragic, not amusing."

"It is what it is. I have made my own bed, and now I must lie in it as comfortably as possible. If Uncle John and Aunt Marion accept my proposal, it will solve a lot of problems for all of us. She has been told by the physicians that she's unlikely to carry a child to term, that she could die if she tries."

"Childbirth is dangerous for every woman," Melanie said.

"I know." Harriet sighed. "But especially for her. John said he is terribly worried, but Marion is desperate to give him a child."

"She will want to give him her own child, though, not yours."

"I know. No plan is perfect. But if they accept, then the child, boy or girl will be legitimate, will inherit the earldom, or marry someone who will. And I will ensure he or she never lacks money."

"Will you find it so easy to give up Jem's baby?" Melanie asked.

"I haven't changed, if that's what you're thinking. I still think babies are ugly and boring, and no, I don't want one. Let's not pursue this line of conversation," she added when Melanie went to speak. "I'm going to see them next week, and I'm telling you because I need your support. I need you to watch over the household for me, write to me if there are any problems. And not tell anyone ever what we have spoken about today. You are one of the very few people I can trust completely, and I will never tell *anyone* else about this. So you must not even tell Uncle John and Aunt Marion that you know, if they accept."

"I won't. And I will be here for you, should you find this harder to do than you think it will be," Melanie said. "It's a huge thing you're asking, of Uncle John and Aunt Marion, but also of yourself. And before you ask, no, I will never breathe a word of how rich and powerful you are, either. But I'm glad you told me. I understand your behaviour far better now."

* * *

October 1696

"It's a huge thing you're asking of us, Harriet," John said, unconsciously echoing Melanie's sentiments of the previous month.

"I know. But it seems to me that we have a problem, and this is the way to solve it, for all of us."

The three of them were sitting in Marion's private chamber, Harriet having said that the conversation she wanted to have was not fit for drawing rooms and for the ears of servants. As they walked to the chamber, Harriet had glanced about with an expert eye. The house was very grand, but the tapestries were worn, some of the curtains were a little moth-eaten, the rooms could do with redecoration. There had been weeds growing in the driveway too. All signs that her aunt and uncle were economising to some extent.

"I cannot believe you are with child. You are the *last* woman in the family I would expect to be telling me this. Now if it was—"

"John," Marion said gently, the first word she had spoken since Harriet had outlined her dilemma.

"Don't worry, Aunt," Harriet said. "I'm not sensitive. I know that I am not a woman men find attractive."

"What? No, that's not what I meant at all!" John protested. "I meant that you seem so practical, not the sort to let your heart rule your head. There's nothing wrong with the way you look!"

"Hmm," Harriet replied. "Now if it was Sophia, were you going to say? Is she making a fool of herself over some man?"

John reddened, but did not deny that.

THE ECCENTRIC'S TALE: HARRIET

"Does she know you're with child?" he asked instead.

"*Sophia?* God, no. She's the last person I'd tell. It would be all over the country in a day if I did. I know she's my sister, but she's a bloody idiot. I agree with you. I wouldn't be at all surprised if she ends up with a bastard child, or having to marry some dashing man in a uniform who will beat her and then abandon her when the next war comes along. No one knows. Not even Papa and Mama. No one ever will know, unless you tell them."

"What will you do if we refuse?" John asked.

"In truth I don't know. I'll think of something though. If you decide to take the baby as yours you must do it wholeheartedly, and love it as you would your own. That is the only condition I would put on you."

"Marion," John said softly, turning to his wife. "You must give your opinion on this. I cannot make a decision on something so important to all of us without knowing what you think."

Marion bit her lip, her eyes filling with tears.

"I so wanted to give you a child of our own," she said after a moment. "I have tried so hard. I feel that I've failed you as a wife. If we accept this baby, then that confirms I have."

"No," John said. "You have been the best wife any man could ever wish for. It is no fault of yours that we do not have our own children. You have been so careful each time you were with child. I truly believe it is God's will that we don't have them, and it is not for us to argue with Him. You know I don't want to risk your life any more, which we certainly will if we carry on trying to have an heir. If you died in childbirth I would never forgive myself, whether the child survived or not. I wish to grow old with you."

"And this is a way for you both to do that, and have an heir as well," Harriet said, who had felt distinctly uncomfortable at witnessing this emotional scene between her uncle and aunt. "The child will at least have Ashleigh blood, through me."

"What of the father?" Marion asked. "Who is he? Will he not perhaps object, wish to claim the child later?"

"No. The father is gone. He's no longer in the country, and he doesn't even know I'm with child. There is no danger from him. He is not someone you are ever likely to meet in company. More than that I will not say, except that he is healthy and strong, and handsome, so if the child looks like him it will not be hideous."

While Harriet walked around the gardens an hour later, John and Marion sat together and discussed the issue. They had asked for some time alone to consider it, and Harriet had agreed, knowing that this was an enormous thing she was asking of them, and something that would not be easy to accomplish in secret. They would certainly be breaking laws too, although she didn't give a damn about that.

"You want to accept her proposal, don't you?" Marion said.

"I will be honest, yes, I do. I am so afraid that you will die if we try to have another child, and this is a way for us to have a child and each other."

"I wondered…I have wondered…"

"What have you wondered? I will not be angry, whatever it is," John prompted.

"I thought to suggest that if you could not have children with me, perhaps you could have them with someone else," she said.

"What, you mean divorce you and marry again? Never."

"No, I meant perhaps have a child with a serving maid, and take it as ours. Then at least it would be your child by blood, which this one will not be, not directly."

Knowing how much it had cost his wife to say this, John gave some thought before he replied.

"No, I could not do that, for several reasons. One is that we would then be open to extortion, because the maid would almost certainly want money, a lot of money to remain silent. We would never be able to rest. And the other is because although I know it is considered normal for men to have mistresses, I have never had one, and do not intend to. You are the only woman I want in my bed, and I will never take another."

He took her in his arms then, because she started to cry in earnest, having been on the brink of it since Harriet had first outlined her proposal. Some time passed, and finally she had calmed enough to speak.

"You are the best husband anyone could ever have. I have been so blessed. And I am sorry—"

"Never say sorry to me. I too have been blessed in you. I have never regretted marrying you, and never will."

THE ECCENTRIC'S TALE: HARRIET

She smiled weakly because of her tears, but it was clear that he meant it.

"Then we must say yes, for if we say no I think we may both one day regret doing so," she replied.

* * *

Once the decision was made, they sprang into action. Harriet could not consult a doctor, but Marion, having carried five babies, two of them almost to full-term, estimated that she had perhaps five months before the child came. They decided that Harriet would go to her estates as she'd planned, but in a coach, not on horseback, and that she would wear ladies' clothing from now on, because it was so much easier to conceal her pregnancy in a dress than in breeches. In three months, John and Marion would visit their niece on one of her northern estates, and would stay until after the birth.

In the meantime Marion would announce that she was once more with child, but that this time she was going to take every precaution, and live quietly. She would dress herself, which, if she refused to wear stays in case the constriction damaged the child, she could do. The household would think she was eccentric, but John would tell them that the mistress was delicate and somewhat prone to hysteria at this emotional time, and that the servants must indulge her in everything or answer to him.

"Marion will have to attend you at the birth, because we cannot call a midwife," John said worriedly. "That is a concern to me."

"We can say that the birth happened very suddenly," Harriet said. "No one will question why we didn't send for one. And the servants will not know us intimately, so there is less likelihood of them commenting on our uncharacteristic behaviour."

"No, I'm concerned for the risk to your health," John said.

"Nonsense!" Harriet replied. "I'm as strong as an ox. I have no faith in bloody doctors, and don't see that midwives would be so different. Kill more people than they cure. We'll do the job, between us."

They had to. There was no other choice, so Harriet put the possible dangers to the back of her mind and set off to tour her estates.

* * *

The baby, a boy, was born in early March, and Harriet had never known such pain in her life. If she had never wanted babies before the birth, afterwards she swore that she would kill herself before she went through that hell again. How women had baby after baby for upwards of twenty years and actually considered them a blessing, was beyond her.

She did not say any of this to John or Marion, however. In the two months that they'd spent reclusively together, the three of them had grown very close, and Harriet understood just how important this child had become to them. Once they'd agreed to adopt the baby as their own, they had begun to feel a closeness to it, as though it really *was* theirs and that Harriet was just the vessel carrying it on behalf of Marion.

It felt strange to be a 'vessel', but Harriet, realising that it was her uncle's and aunt's way of accepting the child completely, made no objections. She just wanted rid of this thing that was causing her constant discomfort, sleepless nights, was making her waddle about like a fat old crone. She couldn't wait for her body to be her own again, free of this unwanted parasite.

She did not say any of this to John or Marion either.

So it came as somewhat of a surprise to her that, when the birth was finally over and Marion had cleared away all the mess single-handedly, had washed both the baby boy and Harriet and then sat down at the side of the bed with him in her arms, Harriet had wanted to see what she had produced.

"Can I see him?" she said after a moment. "Now he's clean, and I'm not screaming in agony."

"Yes, of course! I'm sorry," Marion said instantly, placing him in Harriet's arms.

She had taken one look at him, and had seen with relief that he looked nothing like Jem. Nothing like her either, for that matter. He looked like all the other babies she'd seen, sort of crumpled, cross and red, with no distinct features. He was ugly, like all babies were.

And she fell in love with him immediately.

* * *

THE ECCENTRIC'S TALE: HARRIET

May 1697

Jem and Harriet lay on the riverbank together. This was a little different to the one they had lain on as children, as that had been her father's riverbank and this was hers. But the sky was the same, the sun was as warm on their faces, the bees buzzing in the flowers sounded the same, and the couple lying side by side still loved each other, just in a different way than they had as children.

But everything else had changed irrevocably. She had a secret from him now, not a secret like the one she would never tell anyone, but a secret that involved him, a secret he had a right to know.

She couldn't tell him. She couldn't *not* tell him either.

She'd come back only the day before, deliberately arriving late in the day so she wouldn't have to see him immediately and would have some time to prepare herself to meet him. It had taken her longer than she'd expected to feel well enough to come home. The birth had utterly drained her, left her emotionally as well as physically weak, which she hadn't expected. It had imbued in her a new respect for women who bore children every year, and who had to rise immediately and return to their chores. She, who prided herself on her fitness, had been depleted, and to her surprise, had been desperately unhappy.

At first she had put it down to her physical weakness, but even after she had recovered from that, for weeks her whole world had seemed pointless, all her normal optimism and love of life overlaid by a grey fog that drained the colour from her life.

After that first night, when she had fallen asleep with her baby in her arms, she had told them to take him away from her, that she needed time to rest. But the truth was that now he was born she did not want to give him up, wanted to keep him with a ferocity that shocked her. If she kept seeing him she would not be able to let him go.

She *had* to let him go. She told herself a hundred times a day that in letting him go she was doing the best thing for him as well as for her aunt and uncle. He would have a wonderful life, would be dearly loved, would one day inherit an earldom. And she would be able to see him, once she was over this ridiculous emotional insanity she appeared to be suffering from.

She could see him. As his cousin. Never as his mother.

Three days after the birth, in spite of still feeling absolutely dreadful, she had left her estate, telling John and Marion to stay there as long as they wanted, and had headed to another of her houses in the midlands, where she had given herself a good talking to. It had helped a lot. She still did not want babies, she realised, once she was away from him and once she was over the strange melancholy that had afflicted her following the birth. She had never had that drive that most women had, that led them to willingly risk their lives to procreate. But this baby was part of Jem, and it was *that* she had not wanted to relinquish.

It was over, she told herself. Almost over. There was just one thing left to do, and then she could put the whole episode behind her. And make sure she did not see her aunt and uncle until it truly *was* behind her.

So now they lay on the grass, together again, and he told her about Spain.

"It's hotter there than it is here, which we knew of course. But it was very strange to be outside in November and feel as though it was the height of summer! Of course in the summer it's very much hotter, which is why we need a hothouse even then, not just in winter. It's drier too, because it doesn't rain as much as in England. They plant the water melons on hills, as with the Cantaleupe, but much further apart. I think that's one thing we've done wrongly – planting them too close together. And then I was told that they don't fruit if you water them too much. They need to be kept drier than we have been doing. Also of course, we have to grow them from seed instead of transplants as we do with Cantaleupe melons. I have brought a lot of seeds back with me. I was told that they do not like to be transplanted, so that also could be a reason why we haven't been successful. If we plant the seeds where they are to fruit, that might help."

She loved listening to him talk about plants. He was so enthusiastic when he did.

"Oh, the soil has to be sandy and light, too," he added.

"What does it taste like?"

"It's very strange. I brought seeds from two kinds back. The

THE ECCENTRIC'S TALE: HARRIET

flesh on both is red, and the seeds are black, but one is completely red inside, and the other looks a little like a pomegranate when you cut it, red segments surrounded by white inedible flesh, only the melon is larger and the red is a different consistency to a pomegranate. The flesh is very sweet, but light, refreshing. I've never tasted anything like it, so it's very difficult to describe."

"I thought it would taste like a Cantaleupe," she mused.

"No. It tastes nothing like that. Hopefully one will grow and you can taste it yourself."

"What of Spain itself? Did you enjoy it?" she asked.

"Not without you," he replied, with such sincerity her heart lurched in her chest. "I tried to avoid social invitations, although I had to go to some events."

"Why did you avoid invitations?"

"Not because I was afraid to go alone, as you're thinking," he said, grinning suddenly at her. "I *was* nervous, but it wasn't that. It just felt wrong, being in the fields all day talking to the poor people, who are *very* poor because they are taxed terribly. The Church tells them that they are blessed to be poor and that they will get their reward in Heaven, and many of them truly believe that. But it doesn't make their suffering any easier to see. And then in the evening, to drink with the nobles, who pay no taxes at all, and who will drunkenly spill a bottle of wine that cost more than the peasant I've spent the day with earns in a year. No, I could not in conscience enjoy that."

"The same happens here. I am obscenely rich, and many people are obscenely poor, you know," Harriet pointed out gently.

"I know. But you look after your tenants, and you pay land tax. I know not everyone does, but it was different there. The poor are much poorer than here. Most of the churchmen are aristocracy, so of course they will tell the people who are working for them that it's a blessing to be poor, as it makes them even richer. It was the hypocrisy that I hated. And I saw it directly, mixing with both peoples. I felt more at home with the peasants. Did I do wrong?"

"No," Harriet said. "You were yourself, as you should be. I maybe would not have noticed that in the same way as you, because I've been brought up with wealth. It would have been interesting to be there with you, and have this conversation at the time."

"I wish you had been," Jem said fervently. "I will say this now. I learnt a lot in Spain, and the Leiden Hortus Botanicus was wonderful too. I would love to see it in summer, but it was still fascinating. But I never want to travel to such places again without you. Not because I'm afraid. You were right, I am respected and was treated with honour, and being there alone made me realise that. But there's no joy for me in seeing such wonders if you are not there to share them with me."

"I will not be separated from you for so long again," she said, reaching across and taking his hand. "I missed you terribly. It was almost impossible for me to feign indifference when your letters arrived."

"Letters are strange things to me," Jem said. "I know you're accustomed to them. But for me it's very strange to write down your half of a conversation, and then wait weeks for the other half of it to come back to you."

She laughed then. She had never thought of letters like that before.

"I was told about another fruit, too, although it doesn't grow in Spain, but in some islands near Africa which belong to Spain. It's called the banana. One of the peasants said he has eaten one, and that it's a wondrous thing. You can cook them too. I would love to try it."

"I've heard of them. Some people say that it was the fruit that Eve tempted Adam with in the Garden of Eden, and not an apple at all," Harriet said. "Papa told me that there were some in London, a long time ago, before he was born even. Grandpapa told him about them. But I've never seen one. Maybe we can go to these islands together one day and learn how to grow them! That would be a great challenge."

"Greater than growing water melons," Jem agreed.

They lay for a moment in silence then, as they often did when together, each in their own thoughts, each enjoying the company of the other.

Now. Do it now. Have it over with.

"Jem, I have to tell you something," Harriet said. Her serious tone made him turn on his side, look at her with curiosity. He waited for her to continue, patiently, as was his way.

"I…while you were away I discovered that I was with child," she said.

THE ECCENTRIC'S TALE: HARRIET

His eyes opened wide and he sat up, his face a catalogue of emotions: hope, joy, fear, confusion.

"The baby is lost to us," she said softly, praying he wouldn't notice her strange way of speaking. She could not tell him the baby was dead, could not lie to him so baldly.

He closed his eyes tightly for a moment, and swallowed hard. His mouth twisted as though he was in great pain, and then he pulled himself together, with a great effort.

"Oh God," he said. "And you went through this alone? Why didn't you write to me? I could have come home!"

His first concern was for her. *What a bitch I am,* she thought.

"I don't deserve you," she said without thinking.

He leaned across then and put his arm around her, pulling her in to his side.

"Don't ever say that, for it's not true," he said. "We agreed that we could never have children together. How could I be angry with you for losing one? It's not your fault. It was a shock to hear of it, that's all. But it must have been terrible for you. I should have been with you, to share it with you."

"No, you could not have been with me in any case. I was on my estates in the north, and everyone would have known if you had come to me. As it is, no one knows. Except you, and me. But I...my body looks different, ugly. Luckily I don't need a maid to dress as a man. Otherwise she would surely know what has happened."

"So, you lost the baby late. Was it a...I'm sorry. It doesn't matter," he said. "You could never be ugly to me, my love. Oh, I am so, so sorry."

"It was a boy," she told him, knowing the question he had wanted to ask. *Francis. Lord Francis Ashleigh. One day to be Earl of Tisbury.*

"Are you well now?"

"Yes, of course. It's new for you, but it happened two months ago, and I am well now, in every way. It's you I'm concerned for. And it has made me think."

"I will be fine. I'll walk in the gardens, and think, and maybe spend a few days alone, if you don't mind, and I will come to terms with it. But we cannot let this happen again, I understand that. Now we know that you *can* conceive, we must ensure you don't. I...I think it will be difficult, but we must do it. Perhaps I should not come to your room at night, until we have good control," Jem said.

"What? No! I have been reading a lot. I had little else to do while I was recovering. There is a thing, called a 'condom', which is used by men who visit whores to stop them getting the pox, but doctors and churchmen say that they are immoral as they stop babies too, which are the will of God. I'm damn sure that if men had babies instead of women they'd take a different view, though. We could use those. I think that would work. And then there is a way where the man withdraws just before he comes off, which we could try. And there are herbal tinctures I can take, to make my monthly blood flow well, because I noted that before the baby quickened my flow stopped. But when my flow is regular, I have never got with child. So I think a tincture to keep the monthly blood regular will stop me getting with child."

Jem, to whom much of this was a mystery, looked doubtful.

"But these are all just thoughts. If a man does not lie with a woman, then for certain she cannot get with child," he said. "So perhaps—"

"No," Harriet said. "Unless you don't want me any more."

"Of course I do! There's nothing better than for us to show how much we love each other, and that's the most wondrous way. But there are other ways too. Being together, holding each other as we are now, knowing that everything we do is important to the other, that we wish to be together all the time. We are neither of us people who feel lonely when alone – we *need* to be alone. But we can be alone together. That is a precious thing I never felt with anyone before, and will never feel again."

He was right. But the thought of never feeling him inside her, of never again truly completing physically, as they already did emotionally, was unbearable to her. Almost as unbearable as having to give away another child, as having to lie to him again. As having to give him up, which she would certainly have to do if it was known that she had had a bastard child with her gardener.

"I…I don't know if I can make such a sacrifice," she said.

"You won't be doing it alone. We will do it together, as we do everything else," he said.

"Do you want children?" she asked suddenly, surprising herself.

THE ECCENTRIC'S TALE: HARRIET

"I won't lie. A child of my own would be a great joy to me," he said. "But I want you much more than I will ever want a child. And that is all there is to it."

He saw things so clearly, made sense of things by going straight to the crucial matter. He always had.

She smiled, and turning to him, kissed him.

That night he came to her room, and they lay the whole night together. They caressed each other, kissed every inch of each other's bodies, and they even brought each other to fulfilment, as they had learned they could do by accident in the past as they had explored the delights of lovemaking. It was not the same as true copulation, but it was still a wondrous thing, as it was wondrous to sleep in each other's arms, to wake together, and for the first thing you saw on opening your eyes to be the person you loved most in the world, the person who loved you most in the world.

It would have to do.

CHAPTER FIFTEEN

For a long time, life passed by in a haze of happiness for Harriet, Jem and Melanie. Or at least any problems were minor and either short-lived or solved by Harriet throwing money at them, or wielding the considerable behind-the-scenes power she had so carefully accrued.

The gardens continued to be remodelled in unique and fascinating ways; Harriet had now had a canal built around the perimeter of the grounds, which Jem jokingly called The Moat. The few guests she invited to visit could, if they wished, stay on a luxuriously appointed boat and tour slowly around the grounds, the boat pulled by a horse which walked along a path at the side of the canal. At various points along the way were items of interest – fountains, a maze, summerhouses, statues. It was all considered to be very exciting or ridiculous, depending on whether you were the aristocracy in general, or Percy and Sophia, who seemed now to have banded together in their dislike of Harriet.

Jem had told Harriet that although he would say nothing regarding the mutual enmity between Harriet and Percy, partly because it was something that had been going on since they were babies and partly because it seemed that *everyone* disliked Percy, Sophia was a different matter.

"For one thing," he said to Harriet as they lay in bed one summer morning, "she's your sister and it doesn't seem right for such close relatives to be enemies, and for another thing, in truth you were harsh with her after you shot the highwaymen. Most women would have fainted at the sight of a man with half his face shot away."

"Melanie didn't. She helped me get Aaron into the coach and

THE ECCENTRIC'S TALE: HARRIET

pressed his wound hard with her hand to stop the bleeding until we could get to the physician," Harriet replied defensively. "Neither did Claire, and she was only eleven at the time. She calmed the horses, *and* helped me drive the coach home, while Sophia swooned and moaned that she would never recover from the shock."

"You and Melanie are quite extraordinary women, though. Sophia is not. And you said she's been indulged by your parents, and by the queen as her prettiest lady-in-waiting. It's not really her fault she's a fragile bloom. I wish you would try to reconcile with her."

Harriet had sighed. But he was right. The estrangement was causing Stephen and Amelia some distress as well. And of course Percy now had an ally in the family, which would never do.

So she had tried. She had asked her parents to bring Sophia with them on their next visit, and had arranged for her to tour the canal in a particularly lavish boat with two of her silly giggly friends. She had arranged a theatrical evening, and had held three balls in a week, which completely exhausted her capacity to be with people. Sophia loved being admired and dancing in that order, and so Harriet had invited every eligible bachelor who was not a rakehell she could think of. With luck Sophia would find a suitable partner and would be thankful to her older sister for introducing them. Or at least would be too busy being in love to hate her any more.

By way of gratitude Sophia had complained that it had rained while she was sailing round the grounds, that the statues were boring and the summerhouse too hot, that not one of the men at the balls had danced as well as Harry, whoever the hell he was, and that her breakfast chocolate was cold in the mornings.

Gritting her teeth, Harriet had gone to her sister's room on the final morning and had said she'd like to sort out the differences between them if she could.

"I know I spoke harshly to you on the night of the robbery," she'd said, "I was somewhat distraught and took it out on you, which was unfair of me."

"It wouldn't have happened at all if you hadn't dragged us away from the palace after the queen's death," Sophia had commented sullenly. "We could have stayed."

"I didn't drag us away," Harriet said, with an effort keeping her voice calm, "and we couldn't have stayed. The king had expressly said that he wanted the ladies to leave for a time."

"I think that if we'd stayed anyway, he would not have made us leave. Life is so boring in the country," Sophia replied. "There's nothing to do."

"You're in the country now," Harriet pointed out, "and you've been constantly occupied since the moment you got here."

"Oh, so that's why you've come to see me. You want me to grovel at your feet in thanks for all the effort you've made. I'd have thought you'd enjoy having something useful to do for a change. It's not as though you have anything else to do, is it, apart from making your gardens look stupid, growing cabbages and pretending you're a man?"

Harriet had left the room before she compounded things by pouring Sophia's chocolate on her head, and the enmity had continued unabated, from Sophia's side at least. Harriet decided life was too precious to go to war with such a fool, so after an angry stomp around the gardens she put the whole incident to the back of her mind, and continued making her gardens look unique, not with cabbages, but by growing a beautiful lemon-scented jasmine inside the hothouse and the heavily scented sweet pea outside it, both newly introduced into the country, very rare and very expensive. Along with Jem she also finally managed to successfully grow a water melon, which was presented to King William in September of 1701, along with more pineapples, at which they were now adept.

For her part Melanie had filled all the shelves of her library with books, and was considering expanding it to include the next room. She was also now a very accomplished harpsichordist, and as well as playing at Harriet's monthly dinners and occasional other social events, would often play on summer evenings for the entertainment of anyone who wanted to listen, and the particular enjoyment of Harriet and Jem, up to whom the exquisite notes would drift as they enjoyed precious time alone in Harriet's apartments.

She now had a whole herd of cows, all named after flowers, along with a dairy which provided the house with butter, cheese

THE ECCENTRIC'S TALE: HARRIET

and milk, all of which Melanie had spent a good deal of time learning to make herself, with the help of two dairymaids. Periodically she would visit her family for a time, and on her return would regale Harriet with all the family gossip.

So it was that Harriet learned that Uncle John and Aunt Marion's son Francis was growing rapidly, and at the age of four could already read and had his own pony, which he loved riding.

"Does he look anything like Jem?" Harriet had asked when the sisters had spent an emotional evening together on Melanie's return home.

"Do you really want to know this?" Melanie had said. "I know it must be distressing for you even to hear about him."

"It's not distressing! Well, yes, it is, but only a very little, and it's wonderful too. It's a lot of things. But I can't pretend he doesn't exist. And it's inevitable that one day we'll meet. So yes, I want to know."

"He looks a lot like you," Melanie said. "But he has Jem's straight nose and chin…in profile he does look like Jem. But otherwise, no. Except his hair is the same colour, that lovely wheat-gold. No one would remark on it. They might if he lived here, or if Jem was a nobleman instead of a servant. But you're safe. No one will look for resemblances to anyone anyway, because he's Uncle John and Aunt Marion's son. He's happy and healthy."

Harriet smiled, but her eyes were sad.

"The king loved my water melon," she said, changing the subject. "He wrote personally to tell me, and to ask me if there were any more."

"Were there?"

"Yes, but we've eaten them all. Except one, which is for you."

"You can send it to the king if you like," Melanie said.

"Bugger the king," Harriet replied rudely, venting her emotions through bad language, as was her way. "I'd far rather you had it. Bloody delicious. Nearly as delicious as those cakes you make. I've missed those, while you've been away."

* * *

Harriet had given up worrying about the king dying and disrupting her happy isolated existence. He had so many ailments, from gout to asthma to swollen legs, and yet just kept creaking on and on, that not only she, but the whole nation thought he would continue into senility, by which time hopefully his heir Anne would have a living child, although after eighteen pregnancies and only one child surviving to the age of eleven before dying, this looked increasingly unlikely. Indeed it seemed more likely that Anne herself would predecease her brother-in-law, as her health was also very precarious, and she was dreadfully overweight.

So when the news came in February 1702 that the king had fallen off his horse and broken his collarbone, no one was particularly alarmed, including Harriet. But he deteriorated rapidly, contracting pneumonia and then dying in March, leaving the Jacobite supporters of the exiled and deceased King James' son to toast the 'little gentleman in the black velvet waistcoat' who had helped to finish William off by building the molehill over which the horse had stumbled.

Harriet resignedly draped her home, servants and herself in black and in April prepared to go to Queen Anne's coronation, hoping against hope that the new queen would be as amenable to her remaining widowed and reclusive as her sister Mary had been, so many years ago.

* * *

May 1702

On the evening of their return from London Harriet and Melanie invited Jem to join them in the library, where they had a cosy chat about the events of the past week.

"Anne seems to have made a great effort to reassure people that she doesn't intend to make a lot of changes from William's reign, although there is a general feeling of relief that the monarch is now English and won't be draining our resources to benefit a foreign country," Harriet said.

"She sent Marlborough to Holland almost immediately to reassure our allies that England is still willing to go to war with France, just in case they thought that being a woman, she lacked courage," Melanie added.

Jem snorted.

"Having known Harriet for most of my life I would never

think a woman lacked the will to fight!" he said.

"I fight for what is important to me," Harriet said. "I think most people would do that."

"Maybe, although I'm not so sure," Melanie commented. "I would have to be in a dire situation to fight the way you do about minor issues. I think it comes more naturally to you to stand your ground than it does to most women."

"And to some men," Jem said. "I don't understand why men are expected to enjoy challenging each other to duels over ridiculous points of honour, or putting on a dashing uniform and then slaughtering each other because some king wants to have a bit more land. I would hate to do such things. They make no sense to me." He was sprawled on a sofa, thoroughly at ease, a glass of brandy in his hand. The sight warmed Harriet; it had taken Jem so long to relax completely in front of anyone of the nobility, excepting herself of course. He was still very much a servant with any other aristocrats than herself and Melanie, but that was now for show, to avert any suspicion, not because he felt he was inferior.

"They do it for the glory," Melanie said.

"I see no glory in butchering your fellow men. I see no glory in war at all. I would much rather live quietly, in peace with nature, than fight it."

"You are a creator, not a destroyer. That is one of the things I love about you. Being with you makes me feel calm and contented," Harriet commented.

Jem smiled.

"And I love that you will fight so fiercely for what you believe in, but only for what *you* believe in, not because others say you should," he replied.

"You're very well suited," Melanie said. "I think it a tragedy that you cannot openly declare your love."

"It wouldn't make it any stronger if everyone knew about it," Jem said.

"It would make life easier for you, though."

"No, it wouldn't," Harriet countered, "because then people would stick their noses into what is not their business, and some of them have the power to cause a lot of problems."

"I'm content as I am," Jem said, and clearly meant it. "Was her husband, Prince George, is it? Was he crowned king with Queen Anne then?"

"No. There was a lot of talk of it, all the more so because William was crowned king even though it was the queen who was the rightful heir, and this is the same situation. In fact William insisted on being king, saying he would not be subordinate to his wife, and Mary agreed with him. But George says he is happy as he is."

"Most people seem to think him an ineffectual fool," Melanie said. "But I think it takes courage to admit you have no wish for power, and that you are content."

"Of course all the bloody men are now trying to find a way to reconcile themselves to being a woman's subjects, comparing her to Queen Elizabeth and suchlike," Harriet said. "The same men who thought nothing of being ruled by Mary for ten years while William was off trying to get himself killed in battle."

"They believed he was directing her, though, so thought she was just his mouthpiece," Jem pointed out.

"Then they're even more stupid than I thought. Did it not occur to them that she often would have had to make decisions on her own, without waiting weeks for letters to go back and forth finding out what her husband wanted her to do?"

"It seems to me, looking on the nobility from the outside, that much of the power and reputation is really like a painting," Jem remarked, his eye on a half-finished landscape of Melanie's sitting on an easel in the corner of the room.

"Like a painting? Why?" Melanie asked.

"Because a duke is a man, just the same as me," he said. "But whereas I am just me, and only become respected through what I do, a duke already has a positive image around him, like your painting. It makes the corn look more golden and the sky look more blue than they usually are. You show the countryside as it would be if it was perfect. You don't show the caterpillar eating the leaves, the cowpats in the meadow, the clouds coming in. So a duke or a lord has a tinsel around him from birth of fine clothes, a fine name, house and so on. He might be a worse man than me, but people don't look at that but at the tinsel and are dazzled by it. So if these dazzling lords, who believe themselves greater than anyone, especially women, suddenly have to accept direct rule by

THE ECCENTRIC'S TALE: HARRIET

a woman, even a queen, it demeans them. If they can pretend that the woman is just doing what a man told her to do, it keeps their tinsel sparkling."

"That's true," Harriet said. "I'd never thought of it in that way before."

"You would if you were not one of the nobility yourself, perhaps," Jem replied.

"So am I covered in tinsel too?" Harriet asked.

"No. You don't care about that, which makes you stronger. The power you have is real. That's admirable, but it's why others hate you," Jem said.

"Maybe George doesn't care about it either. Certainly he's not William. In truth, he's interesting to me, because a lot of people treat him with contempt, but I find him likeable. And the queen loves him – he has influence with her."

"Not as much influence as Sarah, though," Melanie said.

Harriet's mouth twisted.

"Who's Sarah?" Jem asked.

"Marlborough's wife. She's the one who caused Anne and Mary to become estranged years ago. Marlborough is an asset to the queen, that's certain. But his wife is a first-rate bitch," Harriet said. "I can't abide the woman. It took me all my patience to be pleasant to her for two minutes when we were introduced. She has far too high an opinion of herself, and seems to think everyone else beneath her, even the queen. Bloody obnoxious woman."

"And a very bad enemy to have," Melanie pointed out.

"I did nothing to make her dislike me," Harriet said defensively. "I listened meekly enough to the woman telling me how important she was. I doubt I'll see her again, anyway. I'll do my best not to. If I have George on my side, all should be well. And in truth, I think the queen has enough to keep her busy, setting up her parliament and trying to get the Whigs and Tories to stop hating each other enough to remember they're supposed to be helping her rule the country. I believe we're safe, for now at least. Mama and Papa are at Court. They will write to me with any news."

"Anne is shy and retiring as well," Melanie said, "so hopefully we will not be invited to too many balls. Sophia is hoping to

335

become a lady-of-the-bedchamber, once she's married."

"Good luck to her. Personally I'd rather shoot myself in the head."

"Your sister is getting married?" Jem asked.

Harriet stood, threw another log on the fire, retrieved the brandy bottle and poured the three of them another glass of amber liquor.

"It feels so good to be able to relax again, wear comfortable clothes, and say what I think instead of having to ponder every word before I utter it," she said, throwing herself back down on the sofa blissfully. "I missed you terribly, Jem. The nights were lonely without you."

Jem coloured slightly, then seeing the amused smile on Melanie's face as she observed this, took too large a gulp of brandy, resulting in a coughing fit which left him as red as a tomato and both sisters wearing amused smiles.

"Who is she marrying?" he asked when he could speak again.

"Lord Fairley. Although that's not who she wanted to marry. She seems happy enough now with Fairley, but she likes me even less, if that were possible," Harriet said.

"Why?"

"Because the man she thought she was in love with, and who Mama and Papa were going to allow her to marry, mainly because they made such a mistake in choosing Raphael for me, was a wastrel."

"Mama and Papa didn't know he was a wastrel, though," Melanie added quickly in defence of her parents.

"What? No, of course they didn't. Wouldn't have agreed to let her marry him if they had. Neither did Sophia, for that matter, although everyone except her could see he was a buffoon. If that's all he was she could have married him with my blessing."

"What has that got to do with you?" Jem asked.

"I put out the word, because when I married Raphael he seemed like a good choice. I know the servants didn't think so, but my parents wouldn't have taken servants' gossip seriously at the time. Actually, I'm glad that servants' gossip is often disregarded now! So when I heard about Arenton I investigated and discovered that he's gambled half his estate away, has killed four men in duels that he provoked because he can't control his temper, and already has three mistresses set up in apartments across London. One of the benefits of having ears everywhere," Harriet said. "When I told Papa, I thought he was going to challenge the bastard to a duel himself. Needless to say, the betrothal was cancelled, and Sophia told me that I did it to ruin her life because I'm too ugly to find any man who would want me, let alone a handsome one like dear Harry. At least I found out who Harry is."

"I think Fairley is as handsome as Arenton, maybe not in such a dramatic way, though," Melanie said.

"Could Sophia cause trouble for you at Court?" Jem asked, frowning.

"No. As I said, the queen will be too busy trying to control parliament, and Sophia will realise she had a lucky escape once she's married to Fairley. He really loves her, and I'm sure he'll shower her with attention and presents, and then babies. She'll be too busy to worry about me as well, I'm sure. She'll probably tell Percy I'm a bitch, but I don't care about that. Whatever she does, I couldn't let her marry such a complete bastard. She might be a fool, but she's still my sister, and I care for her."

"She should be grateful to you," Melanie said. "I'll tell her so if she says anything to me."

"No, let's leave it. All I want to do now is continue living as we are. Sitting here like this with two of the people I love most in the world, knowing that tomorrow I don't have to do one damn thing that I don't want to, is making me realise just how blessed I am. Long may it continue."

She raised her glass, and the other two joined her in a toast to their precious, perfect lives.

Their precious, perfect, fragile lives.

* * *

September 1704

Harriet was too enraged even to wait for the footman to open the door to the apartment at Windsor Castle that she was sharing with Melanie during her royal visit to join in the celebrations for the Duke of Marlborough's outstanding victory against the French at Blenheim. Instead she beat him to the doorhandle, threw the door open so violently that it hit the wall, then turning, grabbed it on the rebound and slammed it shut in the startled servant's face, before kicking a small table to the side of it over, smashing an ornate expensive vase in the process.

She stood for a few moments facing the door, palms on the gilded wood, arms braced, breathing heavily, trying to regain control of herself. Then she turned and saw that Melanie was not alone in the room. Sitting on a sofa staring at her were Stephen and Amelia, books open on their laps. Melanie had leapt up, sending her book to the floor, and was standing, eyes wide, frozen.

To hell with it. To hell with considering their feelings, Harriet thought as she glanced at her parents.

"So, which one of you told my fucking bitch of a sister that Jem and I were having an affair?" she said harshly.

Melanie took a step forward as if to comfort Harriet, then stopped, recognising that she was not ready for that yet.

"Harriet!" Stephen cried, clearly shocked, but whether he was shocked by her language, her description of his youngest daughter, or the fact that she appeared to have admitted to fornicating with a gardener Harriet neither knew nor cared.

"She's too young to know what she told me just now," Harriet said, standing with her back to the door, "and too self-absorbed to notice I was in love with Jem even if she'd caught us fucking on the floor in front of her. So one of you has told her. Because no one else knows, and few even suspect, and none who would discuss it with her. Which of you was it?"

"How could it be us?" Stephen replied, his tone as cold as Harriet's was hot. "Even we didn't know until this second! I admit I was concerned about the closeness between you, but what the hell are you thinking of, having…relations with Jem?"

Now she strode forward to stand in front of her father. They locked gazes.

"I'll tell you what I'm thinking of," she said. "I'm thinking of actually enjoying my life, after nearly four years of hell with the man *you* chose for me. The man who raped me every night, who made my life a living hell, who insulted me and degraded me, and who, if he hadn't died, would have put me in a hospital for lunatics! Oh, but he was a fucking *marquess,* so that was perfectly

THE ECCENTRIC'S TALE: HARRIET

acceptable! Now I am in love with the man I chose, who is tender, gentle, who makes every day a joy, who loves and respects me. But he's a *gardener,* so of course that's completely unacceptable! Well fuck acceptable, fuck unacceptable. I have spent *years* behaving carefully to stop other people sticking their noses into my business. I've spent thousands and thousands of guineas sweetening first William and now Anne, just to be left alone. That's all. Just to be left alone.

"And now that pampered little bitch is threatening the life of the man I love, out of spite because I saved her from a marriage that would have been even worse than mine. And I swear to God, I will kill her if she succeeds in her vicious plot. Which one of you told her?"

Melanie turned and looked at her parents expectantly, which gave Harriet her answer.

"Both of you. It was both of you, wasn't it?" Harriet said.

"I didn't know myself until this second!" Stephen shouted. "How could I—"

Amelia had remained silent until this moment, but now she looked up, her eyes full of tears.

"We didn't tell her," she said. "We didn't know. Or we weren't sure. But we have discussed our concerns about you and Jem together."

"In front of her?" Harriet said. "In front of how many servants as well?"

"None," Stephen said icily. "We have been very careful who we say *anything* in front of since you told King James he was a royal papist arse-cloth to Louis."

"Don't try to attack me with that," Harriet retorted. "That debt was paid in four years of hell with Raphael. So," she said, turning to look at her mother, "you discussed your concerns with Sophia?"

"Not with her, no. But she may have been within earshot. What's happened?"

"What seems to have happened is that our daughter, rather than behaving respectably, has been having sexual relations with—"

"Stephen, will you shut up?!" Amelia shouted, stunning her husband into silence. "Harriet, sit down. Or go and walk around the gardens for a time until you've calmed enough to speak rationally, and then we can discuss this."

Harriet closed her eyes for a moment, and then opened them again. She took two steps towards a chair, then changing her mind, turned, and throwing open the door again, strode out.

* * *

She returned an hour later, drenched, as she'd been caught in a shower which had thankfully cleared the gardens of other courtiers, ensuring that she only snubbed two or three before the rain started.

This time she allowed the footman to open the door for her, which the other Ashleighs took as a good sign, although the expression on her face was no less angry than it had been earlier. She threw herself down in a chair and pulled her sodden ribboned headdress off her head, then pushed her hair back over her shoulders. She looked at her family. Melanie was pale and distraught; Stephen tight-lipped and sullen; Amelia cool, conciliatory.

Amelia sat down opposite her daughter.

"Tell us what has happened between you and Sophia, and we'll see what can be done," she said calmly.

What had happened was that Sophia had invited Harriet to her private rooms, which she had as she was now a lady-of-the-bedchamber to Queen Anne, and it seemed a favoured one, judging by the expensive furniture and rich tapestries that adorned the room Harriet was shown into. She looked around, impressed.

"You have done well for yourself, sister," she said, smiling, hoping that Sophia had summoned her here in a spirit of reconciliation, and wanting to do nothing that might threaten that. "Are you happier now that you're back at Court, and with such a prestigious position?"

Sophia had not stood to greet her sister, but Harriet chose to disregard that lapse in manners for the sake of family unity.

"I am much happier now than I was when you dragged me away from Court to be robbed on a windswept common, yes," Sophia said. "But I've called you here to discuss something that is making me most unhappy, indeed is making our whole family unhappy." Her tone was imperious, and Harriet sighed inwardly.

340

THE ECCENTRIC'S TALE: HARRIET

She sat down without being invited to, because it seemed Sophia had forgotten her Court manners, and although Harriet was willing to let her indulge in a little pomposity for the sake of family peace, she was not about to stand and be lectured to.

"What is this thing you wish to discuss?" she asked. *Let's get it over with,* she thought. Maybe she would have time to go riding before the evening's concert.

"I wished to discuss the fact that Mama and Papa are terribly worried that you are about to drag the Ashleigh name into the gutter again, as you did when a child. Of course then it was innocent, but now it's far from that," Sophia said.

"I have no idea what you're talking about," Harriet replied.

"Oh come on, don't prevaricate with me," Sophia replied. "You know exactly what I'm speaking of. I'm talking about your ridiculous sordid affair with that gardener's brat. It's absolutely disgusting."

"Which gardener's brat is this?" Harriet asked coldly. "I employ over thirty gardeners. Only four of them have children, and all of them under five years of age."

Sophia leaned forward then, her eyes sparkling with malice.

"I'm talking about Jem. The one you've been close to for years. The one you locked horns with Father over. The one you pretend is your 'exotic plants' gardener, so that you can swive him."

Keep calm, Harriet told herself as she felt her temper rise.

"If you spoke to him for more than five minutes, you would see how ridiculous your accusation is. He's an extremely knowledgeable gardener. It's because of his knowledge that Her Majesty enjoys such delicacies as pineapple, oranges, limes and water melon so regularly."

"You don't deny that you're swiving him, then?" Sophia said.

"I won't even dignify that with a reply," Harriet answered. "If Mama and Papa had any concerns about my behaviour at all, I'm sure they would approach me directly, not discuss their concerns with you. What would be the point in that?"

"Why wouldn't they discuss things with me?" Sophia asked, thrown off course for a moment by Harriet's contemptuous tone.

"Why *would* they discuss any concerns with the least intelligent member of the family? They're hardly likely to get any practical suggestions from you, are they? If they have concerns, they can speak to me themselves. Have we finished now?" It was clear that Sophia had had no pacific intention in inviting Harriet here, and she didn't need to listen to this.

"As it happens, you're wrong," Sophia said. "I have a *very* practical suggestion. And I have made it. And it has been very well received."

She was bluffing, trying to make Harriet confess her relationship with Jem. She was an idiot.

"Has it? Well, I will ask Papa later at dinner what it was. Now, if—"

"Oh, I did not make the suggestion to Papa. I made it to Her Majesty. She at least thinks very highly of me, as you noted when you came in. She thinks my suggestion an excellent one, and is most concerned by the possible smirching of the Ashleigh name, even if you are not."

Harriet, who had been about to stand, subsided back into the chair.

"And are you going to share this remarkable suggestion with me, or keep me in suspense?" she asked icily.

"No, I will tell you. You would not be in suspense for long, anyway. The queen has told me she will discuss it with you tomorrow. I have told her I think it would be wise if another husband was found for you, a strong man who can keep you in check."

Harriet had, just an hour ago, received an order to attend the queen in her chambers tomorrow at eleven. Sophia was not bluffing. God, was she really *that* vindictive?

"I am a widow, sister," she said. "And I will remain so. I am not about to be told by you that I should remarry, or who my husband should be. You may be in the queen's favour for now, but I will give *you* some advice. Do not attempt to rise above yourself. You will fall if you do, and hard."

"*You* dare to threaten *me?*" Sophia cried, her voice rising as she lost her temper. "You, who the whole family is ashamed of? How dare you!"

"The last time I looked, Percy was not the whole family, merely the least liked. You look to be taking second place to him. It does not please me to marry again. I'm done with this conversation."

THE ECCENTRIC'S TALE: HARRIET

Now she did stand.

"You will go to the queen tomorrow, and you will accept her suggestion of a husband," Sophia said imperiously. "Because if you do not, then I will tell her that your gardener is preying on you as a vulnerable widow, that he seeks only to marry you in order to gain your fortune. That is bad enough, but when I tell her he is a Jacobite who intends to give all of your fortune to the Pretender, she will certainly command you to marry. And your precious 'exotic' gardener will no doubt be executed for treason."

She sat back, crimson with emotion, her face twisted with hatred, with malice.

"My God," said Harriet. "I thought you were just a foolish, silly girl. But you're not, are you? You're a selfish vindictive bitch as well. You don't give a damn about the family name. It's revenge you want."

"Why shouldn't I have revenge?" Sophia cried. "You poisoned Papa and Mama against Harry, just because you hate anyone to be happy!"

"I *told* Papa and Mama what Harry really was, because I didn't want you to make a terrible mistake and end up even more unhappy than I was!" Harriet replied. "I used no poison, only facts. Surely you didn't still want to marry him, once you found out what he was like?"

"I loved him!" she shouted. "I told him what you'd said about him, and he didn't deny it. He was honest, admitted that he'd lived a misguided life!"

"Misguided?" Harriet snorted. "The man was a rakehell. Of course he didn't deny it, because he knew that there was proof of what he was. He only wanted you for your name, and for the dowry that—" she stopped herself just in time from saying, *the dowry that I provided for you,* "that would have paid off some of his debt. The man had three mistresses, could not control his temper and had no sense of responsibility! How could you possibly think he would make you happy?"

"He was going to change, he told me that himself. He told me that falling in love with me had given his life new meaning, and that he was going to reform, once we were married!"

"And you believed that bullscutter?" Harriet said. "If he was going to reform, why was he waiting until you married? Why was he waiting until you found him out, for that matter? Why didn't he do it straight away?"

"Well I'll never know, will I? Because you killed him!" Sophia cried dramatically.

"I did *not* kill him, you bloody fool!" Harriet said. "His latest mistress's husband did that, in yet another duel. I can't believe he had the sheer cheek to actually challenge his mistress's *husband* when he found out they were having an affair. Any man with a shred of honour would have apologised profusely and ended the liaison, not challenged the rightful husband to a duel!"

"He wouldn't have done that, if I'd been allowed to marry him!" Sophia screamed, beside herself now. "I hate you! You've ruined my life, and now I'm going to ruin yours. You will marry whoever the queen wants you to marry. If you don't I'll watch that gardener of yours hang, and I'll laugh as they disembowel him."

"If she tells you tomorrow that I tried to strangle her then, she won't be lying, for once," Harriet said to her shocked parents and sister, after she'd related all this. "How I refrained from actually killing her, I'll never know. But I'll tell you this, and you all know me well enough to know I'm not making an idle threat when I say that if Jem ends up in gaol or on the scaffold, or is harmed in any way because of her, I will make her life a living hell. And I can do it."

"Harriet, she's your sister," Amelia said.

"No. She's not my sister. Not after today. I tried to save her from a miserable marriage to a man who would have neglected her and made her a pauper. I wish I'd never spoken, because they deserved each other. My mistake. I thought she was only young and silly. Now I know my enemy, and by God I will fight her. And I will win. I don't expect you to take sides though."

"What will you do?" Melanie asked quietly, her face pale and drawn. "You can't defy the queen."

"I can turn down the queen's suggestion of a husband," Harriet said. "If I do it carefully, I can. The queen is malleable."

"And much influenced by Sarah Churchill, who is, at the moment, very friendly with Sophia," Melanie remarked.

"Is she?" Harriet said. She smiled at Melanie, recognising the warning. She had one ally then. "I don't know what I will do, not yet. I need to calm down. I will think about it. Mama, will you do one thing for me, and then I will ask for nothing more?"

"What is it?" Amelia said warily.

"Please make my excuses to the queen tonight. Tell her I have a terrible…no. I won't give her that satisfaction. It doesn't matter. I have had few true friends in my life, but I value the advice they have given me, and will take it. I'm going to change out of these wet clothes and prepare for the concert."

And with that Harriet stood and went into her bedroom, closing the door quietly behind her. The three remaining members of the Ashleigh family sat in shocked silence for a minute.

"She doesn't mean it," Stephen said finally.

"Who doesn't?" Melanie asked.

"Harriet. I know Sophia can behave a little wilfully at times, and she certainly spoke out of turn, but Harriet will come to see reason, to see that she can't possibly continue such an inappropriate relationship. We have accepted her eccentricities, but this affects all of us. She must of course give him up, and consider this proposal of the queen's. Do we know who is suggested?"

Melanie stared at her father disbelievingly.

"I realise now that I've been under a misapprehension for most of my life," she said quietly. "I always thought that you loved Harriet more than the rest of your children. I was even a little jealous of her when I was a child because of it. But now I realise that you don't love her at all. She is worth a hundred of that vicious fool that you have created, and if you cannot see that, then I can. She doesn't expect us to take sides, but I can see you're taking Sophia's, so I'll tell you now, I am with Harriet."

"I'm not taking Sophia's side!" Stephen said.

Melanie smiled, bitterly.

"Of course you are if you think that Sophia is merely 'a little wilful' for trying to ruin Harriet's life and condemn an innocent man to death. And you truly think the Ashleigh name is worth destroying the life of a daughter who has raised this family from poverty and disgrace – a disgrace brought on us not by her, but by your indiscretion when she was a child? She has brought us back to royal favour. She has improved not only our lives and our name, but the lives of countless of her servants and tenants. As for Jem, you could learn a lot from him, Papa, for he cares about the things that matter in life, not the tinsel that you think is so important.

"I have always respected and loved you, Papa," she added, standing, her voice trembling with unshed tears, "but that was another misapprehension, for you don't deserve my respect. My love you have, because I cannot switch that off as easily as it seems you can. I will see you at the concert tonight, and I will be civil, for the sake of all of us, and because I do not want Sophia to know that she has split this family in two, as that would give her great pleasure. But I am done with her. And if you truly believe what you've just said, then I am done with you, too."

It was the longest speech she had made in a long time, and the only truly defiant one she had ever made to her parents. Until now she had always shown them the deepest regard and respect. And so it was that when she stood and walked out without saying another word, they did not try to stop her, or remonstrate with her, but merely left for their own rooms, silently, and somewhat ashamed of themselves.

CHAPTER SIXTEEN

The following morning Harriet had her interview with Queen Anne, which Her Majesty kindly allowed her to have in private, to Sophia's disgust, who had wanted to witness her sister's humiliation personally. After the interview the ladies of the bedchamber returned, but the queen did not comment on what had taken place, and pointedly ignored Sophia's attempts to winkle anything out of her, merely saying that Lady Harriet had been most respectful and gracious.

Sophia doubted this was true, because the very next day Harriet abruptly left Windsor and returned home, leaving the rest of her family to wonder what had transpired. At the end of the week Melanie also returned to Broadfields Hall, responding with a look of contempt to Stephen's request as she left that she inform them by letter regarding what Harriet was doing.

She arrived home, repaired to her room to change out of her formal wear into something more casual, then went in search of Harriet. After being told by an unusually subdued footman that Lady Hereford was in the hothouse with the new gardener, Melanie headed across the gardens to the largest of the glass houses, which was now a glory to behold, grapevines studded with tiny bunches of fruit trailing across part of the ceiling, orange and lemon trees in pots along one wall, soon to be placed outdoors as the weather warmed, and a riot of rare and beautiful flowers colouring and perfuming the warm interior of the building delightfully.

Harriet was standing with a nervous-looking dark-haired young man by the melon bed, but as they were both intent on their activity, Harriet talking, the young man listening attentively, neither of them noticed Melanie until she was close enough to hear what they were talking about.

"Now," Harriet was saying, "the most difficult part of growing them, now we have them established, is knowing when the bloody things are ripe, because they're not like other fruit – they don't ripen after they've been picked. So if you get it wrong, then the whole season has been wasted."

If Melanie had not thought the young man could look any more nervous than he already did, she now realised she was wrong. The poor thing looked terrified.

"Some idiots say you should thump the things, because they sound different when they're ripe, but that's absolute bullscutter. Best way to do it is by looking at that." Harriet bent over and pointed at something. "Got eyes like a bloody hawk, have you?" she asked, looking back up.

The young man flushed scarlet.

"Er…no, my lady," he stammered.

"Thought not. Kneel down then, man, so you can see what I'm talking about!"

The young man dropped to his knees as though felled by an axe, and peered at a little tendril Harriet was pointing at.

"See that?" she said. "When that goes brown, then the fruit's nearly ripe. And then if you very carefully lift the melon up and look at the underneath, it should be a sort of yellow-cream colour. Not light green. When it's yellow-cream, you can pick it. Now, have you got that?"

"Yes, my lady," he said obligingly.

"Excellent! Tell me how to grow melons, then. Pretend I don't know how…ah! Melanie! Welcome home! Melanie, this is Patrick. Patrick is my new exotic head gardener, or will be when he knows what the bloody hell he's doing. Very good with flowers, not with fruit and vegetables, so I'm training him. Patrick, Lady Melanie knows nothing about melons. You tell her how to grow them, and then I'll take you outside and show you the celery plants."

Patrick bowed deeply to Melanie, clearly wishing that he could take the nearby spade, dig a great hole with it and bury himself. She took pity on him. Harriet had no doubt deluged the poor man with information.

"Why not let Patrick have a moment to compose himself and get

THE ECCENTRIC'S TALE: HARRIET

his thoughts in order, Harriet?" she suggested. "Is Jem unwell?"

"Jem is dismissed," Harriet said. "Gone. Patrick has replaced him. I have to go abroad soon, which is why Patrick needs to learn everything somewhat faster than normal."

"Jem is dismissed?" Melanie echoed in shock. "Why? Where's he gone?"

"I've no idea," Harriet replied indifferently. "Left yesterday, packed his bag. I neither know nor care where he is. Now, Patrick—"

"Give him another minute or two," Melanie said, now as distressed as the gardener. She looked wildly around, then pointed to some greenery off in the corner. "Let's walk over there and see how those…er…green things are doing."

"Bell peppers," Harriet replied, amused.

"Yes! I'm very interested in them."

The sisters walked across the hothouse until they were out of earshot of the unfortunate Patrick.

"You don't give a damn about peppers," Harriet said. "About any plants, unless you're painting them. Or eating them."

"No. I do give a damn about Jem, though. What's happened? Have you really dismissed him?"

"Not here," Harriet said softly. "Every servant in the place has their ears on sticks now. Later. Yes, I've dismissed him," she continued more loudly. "Excellent gardener, but some things just cannot be tolerated. Now, peppers."

Every servant did indeed have his or her ears on sticks, but in spite of that no one seemed to know why her ladyship had suddenly dismissed her most valued servant, the one who half the household had believed she was having a romantic liaison with, although no one had ever actually caught them *in flagrante delicto*. Even those who didn't believe their mistress would actually either sexually or romantically consort with a mere gardener had to admit he was a very close friend. So his sudden dismissal after twelve years had taken the household by storm. For three days the subject had been dissected at every servants' meal.

Jem himself had given no information, walking tight-lipped and ashen-faced out of his meeting with her ladyship, then heading straight to his cottage and locking himself in. He had

349

appeared the following morning with a bag and had ridden off on the horse Lady Hereford had given him a couple of years previously, saying only that he would not stay with a family that had treated him so badly, and him having given so many years faithful service. He would seek new shores, where his talents would be appreciated.

"Do you think he means to go abroad?" Mrs Morton asked the senior servants.

"I'm sure I don't know," Mr Noakes said. "New shores could mean that, or could just be a figure of speech. But he's certainly gone, and that's all we need to know."

"True. But I can't believe Lady Hereford would dismiss him, of all people!"

"If she'd dismiss him, then none of us are safe," one footman remarked. A number of the other servants made noises of agreement.

"For my part, I don't believe Lady Hereford would dismiss anyone without very good reason, so I don't think you need to fear. Unless you're doing something disloyal," John said.

"Why do you think she dismissed him, then?" Mrs Morton asked. A silence fell as everyone waited for John's thoughts. Her ladyship had effectively saved his life when the master was dying, had kept him on as a footman even though his face was badly scarred from the smallpox, and always entrusted him with tasks which required discretion. He knew the marchioness better than any other servant, except Jem of course. His opinion was worth listening to. He was also unfailingly loyal to her, but it never occurred to the others that he might withhold information because of that. He was one of them, after all.

"I don't know, in truth," John replied. "But I always knew this – Lady Hereford's friendship with Jem was a professional one, no more. True that they'd known each other since they were children, but I've never believed for one moment that she overstepped the bounds. Respectable, she is, and anyone who says different to my face will regret it."

"Oh of course!" Mrs Morton said a little too hurriedly. "No one would think *that!* Even so…"

"If you ask me, maybe *he* overstepped the bounds, tried to kiss her, assumed that she felt more than she does for him," John said

THE ECCENTRIC'S TALE: HARRIET

with great conviction. "An understandable mistake, perhaps, but not one someone as respectable as Lady Hereford would be able to ignore."

"No, of course she wouldn't," Mrs Morton agreed.

"So then. I think John is probably right. We should accept that, and get on with our duties," Mr Noakes added with a finality which silenced everyone.

In Harriet's bedroom, the doors and windows firmly closed, all servants dismissed and the outer doors of the apartments locked, Melanie was also silenced, not by Mr Noakes, but by her sister, who had just explained some of what she intended to do.

"Dear God, Harriet, you can't do that!" she said finally.

"Of course I can! I haven't made a detailed plan yet, but I'm almost certain I can obtain the queen's permission as well, in view of what I'm going for. That will put the bitch's nose out of joint." Harriet smiled grimly. "It will be excellent if I can actually get her to agree to me going to the Leiden Hortus. Then I'll stay away until everything dies down."

"But people will report back if they see you with Jem," Melanie said.

"Jem? No they won't, because I won't *be* with Jem there. He isn't going to Holland."

Melanie sat for a moment staring at the embers of the fire, which they were allowing to die down as it was a warm evening and the windows had to remain closed while they conversed.

"If you know he's not going to Holland, then I assume you do know where he's going," she said finally.

"Jem is going to go to London, and then he'll disappear. London is an easy place to disappear from, especially when you're not known and you have money, which he does, because I've given him a lot of it."

"So where is he going to disappear to?"

"Why would I know that?"

"Because you love him, and you would not let him just go to London and then disappear without knowing where he was going. I've known you my whole life. Your indifferent attitude might fool the servants, and the queen for that matter, but not me. If you knew you weren't going to see him again, you'd be distraught. Don't treat me like a fool."

Harriet sighed then, deeply.

"I'm sorry. I'm not trying to treat you like a fool. I'm trying to protect you. I need to get Jem out of the way, because I have no intention of marrying anyone, whether the queen tells me to or not. Maybe ten years ago, even five I would have given way, but not now. I'll die before I submit to anyone now. But even if I can persuade the queen to leave me as a widow, I have no doubt that Sophia will carry out her threat. Jem warned me that she could be dangerous, but I ignored him. I underestimated her, and overestimated her loyalty to family. I won't make that mistake again. And I will not let Jem be arrested as a Jacobite. So he has to disappear."

"For how long?"

"Until I can get the measure of the queen and undermine her relationship with Sophia. I knew how to get my way with Mary, and with William, but I couldn't establish a relationship with Anne while they were alive without making enemies of them. I suspect I know how to do it, but I'm not sure, and I won't play with Jem's life in the meantime, even if Sophia will."

"What makes you believe Anne will let you go to Leiden rather than marry?" Melanie asked. "Is there a new fruit you want to grow for her? It would have to be amazing for her to abandon her idea of you marrying, particularly with Sophia *and* Sarah pouring their poison in her ear."

"Hmm, well, I need to do something about Sarah too," Harriet said, but did not elaborate. "And of course Her Majesty will not be *abandoning* the idea of me remarrying, merely postponing it. There is a new fruit I'm interested in, but it's not in Leiden. In Leiden is Herman Boerhaave."

"Herman Boerhaave? I've never heard of him," Melanie said.

"He's the lecturer in medicine there, very respected, and very interested in plants that can heal people. Can heal people of such ailments as gout, for example. What better than for an expert in exotic plants to go to speak with him, to obtain recommendations for healing plants, and then to grow the bloody things purely to relieve Her Majesty of her affliction?"

Melanie's mouth fell open.

"My God, and you say you haven't thought this through?" she said. "So Jem is going to Leiden then, incognito?"

THE ECCENTRIC'S TALE: HARRIET

"No, he isn't. I've told you that. I'm the expert who's going to Leiden. I'll send assorted plants back, hopefully, which Patrick, who really isn't as stupid as he appeared today, he was just a little overawed, will nurture."

"And then?"

"I need you to look after the estate for me, Mel. Would you do that for me? I'll make all the arrangements so that you can, and really, it's easy, as Mr Noakes and Mrs Morton are completely trustworthy and very efficient, although I wouldn't trust Mrs Morton not to gossip about me. It would be a huge relief to me if I know you'll be keeping an eye on things."

"How long do you want me to do that for?" Melanie asked.

"But if you want to go back home to Papa and Mama's, of course I'll understand. You must tell me if you do, and I'll make other arrangements for the estate."

"How long do you intend to be away?" Melanie asked.

"Do you think you'll want to go back to—"

"How long do you intend to be away? It doesn't matter how many times you try to avoid it, I'll keep asking the question until you answer."

"I don't know," Harriet admitted.

Melanie looked at Harriet, who avoided her gaze.

"There's a whole lot you're not telling me. Why? Don't you trust me?" she said.

"What? Yes, of course I trust you!"

"To run your estate, yes. But you don't trust me enough to tell me what you're intending to do after you've been to Leiden. Do you think I'll go running to Papa to tell him?"

"No. I don't think that. I'm not telling you because I don't think it's fair to you. I know how important family is to you."

"It's important to you, too," Melanie said.

"Yes. It is. It's just that I've chosen a new family to be loyal to now, as my loyalty to the Ashleighs, or some of them at least, seems to have been misplaced."

"Jem. He's your new family."

"Yes. And you, always you. But I don't expect you to take my side. I don't want you to. So it's better if you don't know exactly what I'm doing, because then when you visit the family and they ask you, you can tell them honestly that you don't know where I am. In fact you can tell *anyone* who asks that you don't know where I am."

"Harriet, I've already taken your side. I burned my bridges very comprehensively after you left the room at Windsor and Papa told me that Sophia was behaving 'a little wilfully'. I have no intention of going to visit the family for some time, and if I do see them I'll refuse categorically to tell them anything about you. I can deal with you leaving me for a time, even a long time, if I have to. But I cannot deal with you shutting me out completely. Please don't do that to me. Please." Her eyes filled with tears, and she looked down at her lap, trying to blink them away.

"Mel," Harriet said softly, moving off her chair and kneeling on the floor in front of her sister. Reaching out, she took Melanie's hands in hers. "I don't want to leave here. I definitely don't want to leave you, you must know that," she said earnestly. "But I cannot bring Jem back. Not while Sophia and Sarah are friends and in the ascendancy, maybe not while the queen lives. And in truth, life without him is worthless to me."

"You love him that much," Melanie said.

"I love him that much."

"So you *are* intending to go to Jem. Tell me what you're going to do, then. If I know, then maybe we can find a way to communicate with each other while you're away. That would make life bearable for me."

Seeing Melanie was deadly serious, and very distressed, Harriet gave in, and told her what she really intended to do. Melanie listened without interrupting until Harriet had finished.

Then she gently took her hand from her sister's, pulled out a handkerchief, blew her nose, wiped her eyes, then reached out and cupped her hands around Harriet's cheeks, kissing her on the forehead.

"You deserve happiness, you, who have given it to so many others," she said. "And now I have come to know Jem, I believe he's worthy of you. How can I help you in this? Apart from not saying a word to Mama and Papa, of course?"

"I don't like you having to take sides like this," Harriet admitted.

"I choose to take sides, because Papa is so blind to Sophia's faults. When I was a child I believed that he loved you best of all,

THE ECCENTRIC'S TALE: HARRIET

and I still believe he did. But when you married he transferred that love to Sophia, and he cannot admit that he was wrong to do so."

"I don't think he was wrong to love her, although I think he should have disciplined her more. But in truth he never was good at discipline, which is why I ran so wild for so long. I don't hate Papa, and I feel truly sorry for Mama, because she is in a terrible position. But I cannot trust either of them any more, and I cannot confide in her because she will tell Papa. Even if she didn't, it would put her in an even worse position than she's already in, and I would not do that to her. I don't want you to distance yourself from them, though, because once I am gone, they will be all you have."

"Bullscutter, as you're so fond of saying," Melanie replied, her voice still shaky, her eyes still tearful. "I have my cows, my painting, my library – all the things you've given me. And I have Uncle John and Aunt Marion, and little Francis to remind me of you both. Promise me you'll write to me, and I will manage if you do."

"I will write to you," Harriet promised. "Although I won't be able to confide everything in you, not by mail."

She stood up then, and going to the table, poured herself and Melanie an enormous glass of brandy each.

"I think we both need a drink," she said. "And I think we both need company tonight. Will you sleep here?"

"Yes, absolutely," Melanie said. She swallowed, then raised the glass.

"To freedom," she said, "and love."

They clinked glasses.

"And to the freedom *to* love," Harriet added.

They drank, deeply. And then refilled their glasses.

* * *

For the next couple of months life continued as normal. Or at least it appeared to continue as normal. Harriet had a slight reshuffle with the servants, which resulted in several moves, including John the footman now going to the post each day and bringing letters safely home, and Claire, who had been training for some time, now becoming her coachwoman, sharing the duties with Aaron, who was now growing old, and since being shot had grown more frail in any case.

Harriet continued to spend a lot of time with Patrick. She had promoted him on Jem's recommendation, that last tearful evening they'd spent together.

"He's got a way with flowers, he has," Jem had told her. "They just grow for him. The other gardeners think he's mad because he talks to the plants, but mad or not, it seems to work. Even I can't grow blooms as well as he can. I don't know if he'll be as good with fruit and vegetables though, but he's got a gift, and he's dedicated."

Now that Harriet had got the measure of Patrick and realised that he was shy, timid even, but indeed very passionate about plants, she had softened her attitude towards him, realising that part of her abruptness at the start had been because she was so upset that Jem had left. But that was not Patrick's fault, and it was not fair to take it out on him.

Harriet could be extremely gentle and considerate when she put her mind to it, and Patrick blossomed under her patient tutoring, soon proving that he was as talented with edible plants as he was with flowers. Good. Give him another month or so, and he should be able to be left alone to care for the plants. She could not leave it longer than that or she would have to wait until spring to sail to Leiden, which she had no intention of doing.

He could not ensure that the other hothouse gardeners did their work though, as Jem could. Patrick was not at all a commanding man. So she employed Will, one of the other experienced gardeners, a popular and confident man, to ensure that there was no slacking while she was away.

When she was not instructing Patrick about melons, pineapples, asparagus and celery, she spent most of the rest of her time instructing Melanie about managing the estate, secretly in the library. And she had some new outfits made, long-trained mantuas of beautifully patterned bizarre silks, in green, red and yellow, designed to impress, to declare that the wearer was a confident woman of power and wealth, as Harriet wished to make it clear she was.

In time the servants' gossip died down, starved of any more information, as Harriet had known it would. She continued to visit the Highburys periodically, more than she had previously in fact, as Frances' lungs were now failing and she was confined to

THE ECCENTRIC'S TALE: HARRIET

the house. Harriet liked Frances, although they had few interests in common so she found it difficult to keep a conversation going normally.

But in truth she had few interests in common with the pitifully shy Queen Anne either, but would soon have to not only make a good impression, but endear the monarch to her, so she could get her way. So Harriet thought of her afternoons with Frances as preparation, and chatted about her new outfits, about the latest Court news, played endless card games and listened with genuine interest as Frances talked about William's progress at university.

"He is such a serious young man," she said. "I worry that he doesn't know how to enjoy himself. Not that I would wish him to be a drunken rake, you understand, but I would have him be lighthearted from time to time."

For a moment Harriet didn't know how to respond, because this was not at all how she saw William, having played numerous practical jokes on him and had them returned on her, having acted as his confidante, as his playmate since he was a small child. It made her realise that he was actually more relaxed with her than he was with his own delicate, sickly mother. And that made her feel both honoured, and sad for Frances, that she was missing the fullness of her son.

"He *is* serious, that's true," she replied finally. "He thinks deeply about things, looks at all sides before making a decision, which is a commendable way to be. And he loves you very much, and is very considerate towards you. I think that is maybe why he is not too exuberant when with you, because he does not wish to overwhelm you. But you know, it is the way of all children, I think, as they grow older, to be one person with their parents and another with their friends. I'm sure he's as lighthearted as the next young man. But he is well brought up enough to know the appropriate time and place for frivolous acts. He is truly a credit to you and to Daniel."

"Oh! I had not thought of it in that way! Of course you are right. I suppose I was more giggly and silly when with my friends than with my parents, as I became a woman. I'm sure you were as well!"

Harriet agreed, although she had never in her life been giggly and silly, either with her parents or her very few friends. She had, however, been herself, in as far as she could be. Suddenly she felt unutterably weary. Why couldn't people just accept you or reject you, for what you were? Why did they continuously have to try to impose their idea of happiness on you, instead of leaving you alone to find your own way? A great wave of tiredness and despair washed over her. She was so sick of fighting, not for more wealth, not for more power, just to be herself, just to live in the way she wished, without disturbing others.

God, she hated people, on the whole.

Not Jem, though. Or Melanie. Or this gentle, fragile woman, who was now looking at the alarming expressions crossing Harriet's face with some concern. Harriet pulled herself together.

"I'm sorry," she said. "I was just thinking about a family problem. Nothing to do with William! I have a private audience with Her Majesty next week, and was hoping I could call round tomorrow with my maid and my new outfits for your opinion, which I would very much appreciate."

"Oh of course!" Frances cried. "That would be delightful! I will look forward to it."

It was always easy to stop someone pursuing an awkward subject, if you threw a glittering prospect into the conversation. Another thing she had learned from her mother, in her formative years.

She did not hate her mother, either. She missed her, terribly.

* * *

The gowns having passed inspection, the following week Harriet headed off to Court, more nervous than she had been for a long time, although you would not have known it from her confident manner. Jem would have known it, and so for that matter would Melanie, but they were not at Court, and neither was anyone else who knew her well enough to see beneath the relaxed and confident mask.

In the end it was very easy to persuade the queen to postpone all ideas of a marriage for a time and instead let Harriet travel to Leiden to meet the remarkable Herman Boerhaave in the hope of finding some new way of relieving her crippling gout. Indeed Anne was both enthusiastic about the idea and very touched that Harriet was willing to undertake such a long journey purely in

THE ECCENTRIC'S TALE: HARRIET

order to try to bring relief to her monarch.

She is starved of genuine affection, Harriet realised. It was obvious that Harriet had no wish to promote either a relative or herself to a prestigious position, that she wanted no money, nor a place for herself at Court. Indeed she had made it clear at the last interview that she wanted quite the opposite – merely to live quietly in the country. So what other reason could she have for this trip, than merely a desire to bring relief to the queen?

What other reason indeed?

All this made Harriet feel somewhat guilty, but not guilty enough to disabuse the queen of her notion. Her freedom and Jem's future were at stake, and she would do far more than hoodwink a queen to secure those. And in truth she *would* try to find and grow plants that would help this poor woman have less pain in her life.

In the end the audience exceeded the time allotted, which would certainly annoy Sophia, as the only possible reason for it was that Harriet was making a good impression.

As indeed she was. Harriet told the queen that it seemed someone was spreading scurrilous rumours that she was having an affair with her gardener, an absolutely ridiculous idea! It was true that she had spent a good deal of time with him, as she was extremely dedicated to growing the wonderful fruit and flowers that Her Majesty enjoyed at the palace, but to suggest that she would have an illicit relationship with a *servant* was utterly appalling. As a result she had felt compelled to dismiss the man, although it was most inconvenient to do so, as he was extremely proficient in his job, but she valued her reputation above everything, and would not have vicious gossip by people who saw scandal in the most innocent situations, threaten her good name.

"Indeed," Harriet added, "I would otherwise have taken him with me to Leiden, as I'm sure he would have been extremely useful there. He would certainly have understood any complex care arrangements for the plants, both during transportation and further cultivation. But it cannot be helped."

"Oh!" Anne said, reddening a little. "How unfortunate. Really, there are people who will read the most disgusting meaning into the most innocent of friendships. I assure you that I would pay no heed to such pettiness. Could you not recall the man, and take him to Leiden with you?"

Interesting, the flush on the queen's cheeks. Had sexual rumours been passed around about her too? It would seem so, judging by her expression of sympathy.

"I cannot, Your Majesty. He took his dismissal very badly, I'm afraid, which is of course understandable, as he is a most upright and dedicated man. I have no idea where he has gone. But certainly if I discover his whereabouts, I could request that he return to nurture your future cure! But of course I would not do that were I to lose my good name because of it."

"You will not lose your good name with me, Lady Harriet," Anne had assured her, patting her hand reassuringly.

"Then that is all that matters to me, Your Majesty," Harriet had said, curtseying and kissing her monarch's hand in gratitude.

After the interview she had repaired to the rooms provided for her and had lain down for a while, before changing out of her dress, which was soaked with nervous sweat, into another. Her ordeal was not over yet. But that interview had gone better than she could have dreamed possible. Not only had she received the permission she wanted, but she had managed to raise herself enormously in Anne's estimation, and by broaching the subject of Jem in advance, she had greatly diminished the chance of Sophia's weapons causing any damage were she to use them. There was still the threat of Jem being exposed as a Jacobite, but perhaps Anne would dismiss that too. It had been a good ploy to defend herself before she was attacked – it indicated she had nothing to hide, and made her case so much stronger.

She crossed her fingers while her maid was dressing her, and prayed the next interview would go as well. The outcome was not as crucial as this one had been, but it was still important to Harriet to achieve a second success if possible.

* * *

After saying her piece, Harriet sat back and allowed the Duchess of Marlborough to absorb it, watching as a variety of expressions crossed the woman's face. The woman who until now had called Lady Sophia Ashleigh her friend; the stubborn, strong-minded woman whose view Harriet had to change.

"So why are you telling me this? There must be some benefit

THE ECCENTRIC'S TALE: HARRIET

for you in it," the duchess said suspiciously.

"There's no monetary benefit for me, no position at Court that I want. In truth, I want nothing but to be left alone to continue living quietly in the country as I have done for many years. But yes, you are right, I *do* want something from you. I think you are a woman who has strong, intelligent opinions, and who speaks honestly."

"Indeed I do, and hope I always will."

"So do I. It is most refreshing. But we have that honesty in common, so I will be honest with you," Harriet said. *Partially honest, at least.* "I have obtained the queen's permission to go to Leiden and meet with a distinguished physician who is very knowledgeable about healing plants, in the hope that I can find something that will bring Her Majesty relief. If I do, then I will be happy. You have much influence with the queen, and I believe you can convince her that it is a good idea that rather than remarry, I may return home and live my days out quietly in widowhood, as I wish to. That is all I would like you to do, but if you do not wish to speak for me, I will understand."

"The marquess must have been a remarkable husband, for you to wish to mourn him perpetually," Sarah said, somewhat sarcastically.

"The marquess was indeed remarkable," Harriet agreed. "But I merely wish to live life as I want to, without a man telling me how to live it."

"John does not tell me how to live!" Sarah replied.

"No, it's clear to me that you have a most rare and wonderful marriage, and that you are both quite remarkable people, who respect and love each other completely. I doubt that I would be so lucky, and indeed I am now settled in my widowhood, and barren too, so marriage holds no attraction for me. I wish to be left alone. You can help me to be. But for that you must still *have* influence with the queen."

"And you truly believe your sister is trying to reduce my influence?"

"No, I think she is trying to do far more than that. I think she is trying to replace you in the queen's affections."

"Really? If you think she is capable of that, then you underestimate me," Sarah replied haughtily. "And Her Majesty," she added as an afterthought.

"In truth, perhaps I do," Harriet agreed. "I certainly underestimated Sophia. I thought her a pretty, foolish, spoilt child. A child who sought attention and who would do no more than stamp her feet and throw a tantrum if she did not get her way." She paused as though thinking of how to word her next sentence, but in reality she was watching Sarah, seeing by her expression that this was how the duchess saw Sophia too. "But then, when it was too late I discovered that she is far more than that. She is malicious and ambitious, and will stop at nothing to get what she wants. She wants attention above all, and praise, and what better way of getting that than to replace you as the queen's premier lady? I am not saying she will succeed. But she will try her utmost. I am warning you in advance, that is all, as I wish I had been warned."

"She is your sister, though. If she *was* successful that would benefit your whole family, surely? Why are you trying to work against her?"

"In honesty, my sister is working against me. She is angry that I gave our parents information that prevented her from marrying the man she was infatuated with, and is bent on revenge. It will be of no benefit to me if she replaces you."

"Which man was that?" Sarah asked.

"Lord Arenton."

"Harry? My God, the man was horrible! Handsome, I admit, but a thoroughly despicable character!" Sarah waved at a chair, and Harriet sat down, Sarah throwing herself down on a seat opposite. Good. This was going well. "He's dead now, anyway," Sarah added.

"Yes. Sophia blames me for that. Apparently he told her he was going to reform after he married her."

Sarah laughed disdainfully.

"If she believed that you were right in thinking her a fool," she said.

Harriet smiled.

"Yes. She is a fool. My mistake was in thinking that was all she is. That's why I'm warning you not to believe the same. For my own sake I do not want someone who is so bent on revenge to be able to pour her poison against me into the queen's ear. And for Her Majesty's sake I believe you are a true friend to her, and she needs those. Sophia is not."

Sarah smiled with genuine warmth now.

"You truly care about the queen," she said.

"Yes. She is a gentle woman who has had much misfortune in her life. I believe you are a great support to her, and she needs such support."

"That seems very kind of you. But how do I know you are not maligning your sister purely in order to win favour with me? Or to use me as the instrument of your revenge?"

Oh well done. Intelligent indeed.

"You don't, because I would be a fool to tell you if that was indeed the purpose of my interview with you. But there is a way you can discover for yourself what Sophia is, if you have someone at Court who can observe for you."

Sarah's forehead creased.

"What is that?"

"Make an excuse to leave the queen for a short while, to spend time with your children, to deal with important business while your husband is on campaign. Sophia is ambitious, but she is young, and very impatient. If you are gone, I'm certain she will seize the moment immediately, and begin to try to turn the queen against you. If she does, you will know I am right and can then act as you wish. If she does not, then you have merely had a few days or weeks at home, and nothing is lost."

Sarah observed Harriet intently for a few moments while she thought, her blue eyes intent, her forehead furrowed as she considered. Really, the woman was quite remarkably beautiful, and had an incredibly smooth English rose complexion. *Oh well,* thought Harriet, *at least she can't be jealous of my looks!* The only feature they had in common was their hair colour, which was the exact same shade of golden blonde. Sarah could be jealous of Sophia's looks though. And of her youth. Sarah might look far younger than her forty-four years, but that didn't mean she wasn't constantly aware of them. All female courtiers, and most women in general, for whom looks and allure were their only power, dreaded ageing.

"I must think about this more deeply," Sarah said. "But I thank you for your warning, and if I find you speak truly, I will repay your kindness in telling me."

"Thank you. I would beg one more small kindness, but not for myself," Harriet said. "I would ask that if I am proved right, you would endeavour to ensure that my parents do not suffer as a result of Sophia's ambitious spite. They are good people, innocent in this, and ignorant of Sophia's ambitions. They seek only to remain at Court in the positions they now hold. I would have them do so."

"That is an easy request to grant," Sarah said, "for I hold the duke and duchess in high esteem, and they have always been respectful of my position. Indeed, it is my regard for them that led me to take Sophia to my bosom. I will not act against them."

Back in her room, her dress only damp with sweat rather than soaking this time, Harriet resisted the impulse to dance around the room for joy, in part because her maid was in the room, and it would not be seemly. Not at Court, where everything you did was scrutinised and reported on. Although hopefully not the meeting with the Duchess of Marlborough, which Harriet had taken some pains to keep secret so as not to warn Sophia in advance. She had done all she could here, and the year was growing old.

Now she could go home.

Now she could go to Leiden.

* * *

Both the captain and his crew agreed that the ship's passenger was somewhat of an enigma. Mr Waters was certainly a very personable and affable young man, handsome and athletic, and obviously a gentleman by his clothes and manner, and was well spoken, although his accent had a very slight rural intonation.

And yet the man had no servant with him, and when the captain offered to delegate a crew member to serve him, Mr Waters had politely but firmly declined, saying that he could dress himself, but if he *did* need any assistance, he would make it known.

Mr Waters, although friendly when approached, was otherwise extraordinarily reserved, spending most of his days standing on deck gazing out across the ocean, watching the crew as they moved about their business with interest.

He suffered from no sea malaise, and indeed seemed not to notice the weather unless the rain was torrential and the waves washing over the deck, in which case he would reluctantly go below and sit in his small but adequate cabin, reappearing as soon as the storm had passed.

To add to that, he spent no time with his fellow passengers. Admittedly, as it was primarily a trade ship, there were only three other passengers, all of them much older than Mr Waters, and all of them thoroughly disagreeable sorts, their conversation exceedingly tedious, as the captain found out to his cost each night at dinner, which, at the start of the voyage he had rashly invited them all to join him for.

But at least they *had* conversation; Mr Waters ate well, drank sparingly, listened politely but spoke very rarely, which the captain at first put down to the fact that he was a gentle, soft-spoken man, whereas his fellow passengers were loud-mouthed and garrulous, prone to interrupting and quarrelling. But even when he tried to engage Waters in conversation if he encountered him on deck, the man answered in polite monosyllables for the most part, or asked a great many questions about ships and sailing, so that when the captain later returned to his cabin he would realise that while he had imparted a great deal of information, he had in fact learned nothing whatsoever about his passenger. Indeed, even at dinner the man cleverly deflected questions about his own life and reasons for travel by expressing an intense interest in whatever his neighbour wished to speak about.

So it was that when the ship finally docked in Cadiz and Mr Waters disappeared into the throng on shore, the captain and his crew knew no more about him than his name and that he was interested in horticulture. As that was a respectable hobby for a gentleman with more money than sense, the captain accepted it, dismissing his crew's suggestion that the man might be a spy for the Duke of Marlborough as ridiculous. A spy would certainly have sought to discover shipping routes, the cargo and suchlike, not the names of particular sails, what that rope was for and how to tie fancy knots!

Mr Waters, hindered by his lack of Spanish but aided by a goodly sum of money, succeeded in renting a small but clean suite of rooms near, but not too near the port, so that it was reasonably respectable. He also arranged for meals to be delivered to his rooms each day, and ventured forth only to secure a passage to his onward destination, and to engage a tutor who would instruct him in the rudiments of the Spanish language until such time as his ship sailed.

In truth, he would very much have liked to go and explore the local area, the strange buildings and the exotic plants which grew everywhere. But he was very aware that his fair hair and blue eyes marked him out as foreign immediately, and as English the moment he opened his mouth. Although Spain itself was not actually directly at war with Britain, the whole continent was fighting over the question of the highly contested Spanish succession, and an Englishman stood out like a sore thumb.

Added to that the country had been financially depleted by a series of wars with France, and whilst that meant his gold was very welcome, it also made him a target for robbers, and although being a gentleman he wore a sword, it was merely part of the image he needed to cultivate - he had neither the skill nor desire to use it. Because of this, while he waited for his ship to sail he remained almost permanently indoors, and threw himself into learning as much Spanish as he could. It would certainly come in very useful later.

So it was a great relief to him when the ship he had booked passage on finally departed, taking Mr Waters to his new life in the Americas, as he had told his landlord, his Spanish tutor, the woman who cleaned his rooms daily, and anyone else he happened to converse with.

When the ship docked at Gran Canaria, Mr Waters expressed a desire to stretch his legs and take a short walk, while the ship was being loaded with provisions. The captain warned him not to go out of earshot of the ship's horn, which would announce when they were sailing, and he promised he would not.

The ship was loaded, the horn sounded, the horn sounded again, and then once more, after which the captain ordered the ship to sail, assuming the young gentleman had either got lost, been attacked, or was in a tavern or whorehouse, too preoccupied to note the warning. Whichever way, it was not his concern. The gentleman had already paid his fare to the Americas, which was the important thing; it was not the captain's or the crew's job to act as nursemaid to an idiot. If the man was well, he could take the next ship.

Anchor was weighed, the ship sailed, and the unfortunate Mr Waters, abandoned in Gran Canaria, was forgotten about.

CHAPTER SEVENTEEN

February 1705

The last thing James Waters expected to see when he opened the door of his house in the morning was a somewhat diminutive gentleman standing in his courtyard admiring the view. It was true that the view was quite spectacular, as the *casa* was built partway up a hill, and the courtyard overlooked the rooves of the village below and the beautiful turquoise sea. But it was also true that it was in a somewhat isolated situation, and Mr Waters was not accustomed to visitors. Before he could comment on this intrusion, the gentleman turned, puffed on his long white clay pipe, then removing it from between his lips, used it to gesticulate at the house.

"Damn fine place, this. Well chosen," he said.

"Thank you. How did you get here?" Mr Waters replied.

"On a ship of course! How else would I get to an island? Oh, and a mule, to come up the hill. Bloody uncomfortable. Think I'd rather have walked. Wondered why you'd rent a place half way up a mountain, but now," he waved at the panorama, "I understand."

"It gives us some privacy, too," Mr Waters explained. "I thought you'd appreciate that."

"Hmm. Yes. Well thought out."

"I didn't expect you until the spring," Mr Waters said, moving to stand beside the visitor and looking up at the white-painted house. "There's an even better view from the balcony up there." He pointed to a beautiful, elaborately carved wooden balcony on the second floor. "I often stand out there in the evening before I go to bed. If I turn that way," he pointed out across the sea, "I'm facing England, I think. I fancy I am anyway."

The visitor turned and gazed in the direction he pointed.

"Maybe we can stand there together tonight, and you can show me where England is. Although I've had enough of the damn place for now."

"I don't need to now you're here. But yes, I would like to stand there with you," James Waters said. "I thought to spend another few months alone."

"Yes, well. I thought it better to sail while all the armies of Europe are in winter quarters. Marlborough's back in England now, and they won't fight without him, so it was unlikely we'd be attacked, whereas if I'd waited for spring…and I missed you terribly. The voyage was still interesting though. I think the weather was on the side of the French. That's why I took to this pipe – the captain told me it calmed the spirits. I needed to. There were times I thought it would have been better to risk being sunk by the French than by God. But I wasn't and I'm here now. Don't plan on sailing anywhere for a while."

"I never tried that," James said. "Don't like the smell of tobacco myself. I prefer my lungs to be full of the smell of fresh air and green things."

His companion immediately turned and threw the pipe over the courtyard wall.

"You didn't have to do that!" James exclaimed.

"If you don't like the smell, then I won't smoke. I don't need it anyway now. I'm here, with you."

They looked at each other, and smiled. The air seemed to suddenly become a lot warmer, although it was already warm.

"This is a Catholic island," James remarked casually.

"What of it?"

"Everything Protestant foreigners do is remarked on, and much of it reported to the authorities. I've managed to keep my head down so far, although I had to dismiss my maid, who set her eyes on me and wouldn't take no for an answer, even when I told her I was waiting for my wife to join me. If I'd given in to her I'd probably be rotting in a dungeon now for ruining a young woman's virtue and attempting to pervert her to the devil's ways."

"I'm glad you didn't give in to her then," his companion said. "Were you tempted?"

THE ECCENTRIC'S TALE: HARRIET

"No," he replied without hesitation. "There's only one woman for me, always has been, always will be. But I can't imagine what will happen if I'm discovered to be a seducer of young men, which I will be if you stand outside in full view for one more minute."

A broad smile appeared upon the diminutive gentleman's face, and moving forward he entered the house, disappearing into the cool interior.

After a moment Mr Waters followed, closing the door behind him and barring it to ensure they would not be disturbed.

They did not open the door again that day, although, dressed only in silk dressing gowns, they did make an appearance on the balcony outside their bedroom that evening, where they stood hand in hand to watch the sun set and to gaze in the possible direction of England.

"Do you miss it?" Harriet asked softly, as the sky turned from crimson to lilac and then to midnight blue. It was still warm, as warm as a summer day, which felt strange to her, it being February. "Home, I mean."

"I do, yes. But I missed you a lot more. It will be easier now you're here. You're staying with me?"

"Of course I'm staying with you! The only time I'll go back to England is if I can take you with me," Harriet exclaimed.

"I'm sorry. It must be hard for you. You have so much over there, so much to lose," Jem said.

She put her arm around his waist and squeezed.

"None of it means anything to me," she told him. "I thought it did, really, until my stupid sister threatened you, and then I realised that if I had all my estates and was free to stay a widow forever, none of it would matter if I didn't have you. Sometimes it takes such a threat to make you realise what's truly important and what isn't."

When he didn't answer she looked up at him, saw the tears in his eyes shimmer in the light from the candle they'd placed on the balcony.

"I'm sorry," she said. "I didn't mean to upset you."

"I'm not upset. Not in a bad way. That's the most wonderful thing anyone's ever said to me. I feel the same way, although I haven't got anything to lose, really, not like you have. But without you, I can't imagine seeing the beauty in *anything*. These last months have been hard."

"They're over now. Melanie will look after the estate. I've brought enough money with me for us to live here for the rest of our lives, if we need to. But I'm hoping we won't need to – unless we want to, that is. Melanie will write to me if my plan works. She's the only one who knows where we are. Everyone else thinks I'm in Leiden."

"What's the plan?"

"I'll tell you tomorrow," she said, squeezing his waist. "Not tonight. Tonight let's just be together. Completely together. We have the rest of our lives to talk."

"We have the rest of our lives to be completely together, too," he said, and bending his head, he kissed her. Then he reached out and picked up the candle, and still embracing, they went back to bed.

* * *

"So this is it," Harriet said, eyeing the bright yellow crescent-shaped fruit sitting on the tray along with a cup of coffee and a beautiful orange and blue flower.

"That's it. It's not your whole breakfast though, but I thought if you eat it first, you'll appreciate it more than if you have other tastes in your mouth."

She nodded. She was sitting up in bed, hair tousled from sleep and their early morning lovemaking. The doors leading to the balcony were open, and a warm breeze drifted into the room. She would have suggested they sit on the balcony to eat in the warmth of the sun, but they were both naked and she was enjoying the sight of his slender muscular body almost as much as she had enjoyed the touch of it for the last few hours. It would be a shame for it to be covered, as it would have to be if they went out.

"The flower is beautiful," she said, stroking its petals. "I've never seen anything like it! It doesn't look real!"

"It's a Bird of Paradise flower," he said. "I picked it from the courtyard this morning."

"You're growing it in the courtyard? I didn't notice yesterday! Did you pick the banana from there too?" Harriet asked.

"No. The banana isn't fruiting yet. The leaves on the Bird of Paradise plant look a lot like small banana leaves. They're like distant cousins. You were too busy looking at the view to notice

THE ECCENTRIC'S TALE: HARRIET

my plants though. I'm glad of it, because it meant the flower is a surprise as well as the banana."

"I can hardly remember the view either, to be honest," Harriet said, picking up the banana. "I was too busy being aware of your presence. I have missed you so very badly since we've been apart."

He blushed a little, which was so endearing that Harriet dropped the banana on the tray and leaned across to kiss him. After that, for a time both the flower and the fruit were forgotten, as Harriet and Jem had more interesting things to focus on.

Much later, the coffee now stone cold, Harriet picked the banana up again.

"You have to break the top, there, and then peel it," Jem advised. "They grow in bunches, like a hand, and each banana is a finger."

"A finger. It looks more like something else I've just been enjoying," she said. This time he blushed a lot, and she laughed out loud with the sheer joy of being here with him, of knowing that she would be staying here with him for as long as she wanted to, with no more sneaking about. She broke the top, and peeled it.

"Oh!" she said. "I thought it would be yellow, but it's cream-coloured! It smells wonderful. Do you like the taste? You must have tried them."

"I have, but I'm not telling you until you've eaten it."

"I hope you're worth it, little fruit," she said. "You've cost us a lot of time and money getting here to see you!" She put her mouth around the top and bit off a piece, chewing it slowly. After she'd swallowed it, she looked at Jem, her eyes alight.

"This is wonderful," she said. "I've never tasted anything like it. It's not juicy at all like most fruit. It's incredible!"

"It's worth it, then," Jem said.

"Yes, of course. It would have been worth it even if this tasted horrible. Because you're safe and we're together. But if we *can* return to England and grow this, it will be a sensation, I'm sure."

"There are different types. This is the one that I think will be popular in England, because it's sweet, easy to peel and eat. There's another one called the plantain, which the people here eat a lot. It looks the same but the skin's a lot thicker, and it's not sweet – it's a bit like a potato, it doesn't have a lot of taste. We can try them too later. You have to cook them," Jem said.

"It hasn't got any seeds," Harriet noted. "Where do you get the seeds from?"

"You don't. When the plant grows, it puts lots of little plants out at the bottom, like rose bushes put out suckers. You grow a new plant from those, but you have to cut them away from the main plant at the right time."

"You've been learning all about them," Harriet noted, taking another bite.

"Yes. There hasn't been a lot to do here, once I'd found the *casa*. I've been learning Spanish, and going for long walks. We can go down to the beach later, if you like. I often go swimming at night, because the sea's really warm, and it's so quiet then."

"I would love that," Harriet said. "I want you to show me everything you've discovered. And then we can discover new things together too."

"Do you think we ever will be able to go home?" Jem asked, and she noted the trace of longing in his voice.

"I hope so."

Then she told him about her visit to the queen and to the Duchess of Marlborough, and what had happened.

"Melanie knows everything," she said finally. "She's the only one who does, and she'll write to tell me if Sophia is banished. If she is, then yes, I think we can go home, if we wait until the gossip dies down, and until we know her banishment is not just a temporary thing."

"You did that for me?" Jem said, aghast. "But she's your sister!"

"No, she isn't. Not any more, not to me. But even if she was, you're more important than she is to me. More important than *anyone* is to me. Surely you know that?"

He sat for a moment, thinking.

"You've told me I am, and you've always been honest. But I know how important family is to you, so knowing that you would put me above them…yes, I really know it now."

"You are my family now," Harriet said. "You and Melanie. And before you ask, no, I have no regrets. I'd do the same thing all over again. I love you."

"And I love you."

THE ECCENTRIC'S TALE: HARRIET

"I know. Aren't we lucky? A lot of couples like each other, or learn to love each other, eventually. A lot hate each other but stay together because they must, or because they're afraid of scandal. But what we have…that is worth fighting for, worth any sacrifice. Or it is to me. And I think it is to you, too."

He smiled, that beautiful radiant smile that lit up his sky-blue eyes, and always reminded her of lying on the riverbank with him on cloudless summer days. She always loved those times with him, lying there, listening to the river and the wildlife.

"Is there a riverbank here we could lie on?" she asked.

* * *

They found a riverbank to lie on, although there were not many rivers on the island, and the riverbanks were not gently sloping, lush and cool like the English ones, although the sky was certainly summer-blue and cloudless. It was still pleasant, but they both soon learnt that doing the things they'd loved doing together in England, and noticing how different those simple activities were here, just reinforced their knowledge that they were strangers in a foreign country, which then made them miss England.

So they did things that they didn't do at home.

They walked together along the beaches, and, on beautiful starlit nights when everyone else was in bed, they would swim naked in the warm sea, their clothes laid in neat piles on the sand. Sometimes they would make love in the sea too, Jem standing, Harriet's legs wrapped round his waist, her head thrown back as she spiralled into orgasm, the diamond stars sparkling in the heavens above. Afterwards they would dry themselves with a cloth brought for the purpose, dress, and then lie on the beach watching the stars and listening to the soft susurration of the waves against the sand. Those were special nights, nights she would remember and treasure for the rest of her life. They could not do that at home, and that was one of the few things they would truly miss if they ever did return to their native land.

They also sat outside to eat all their meals, except on the rare days when it rained. Even when it was cloudy it was warm, and pleasant to sit outside. Jem told Harriet that when he arrived he had travelled around the island looking for the best place to live, and had chosen the north because it was so much greener than the southern part of the island, where the temperatures could get unbearably hot and it was almost always sunny.

"But it's brown and arid," he told her. "We can go there if you want, but I couldn't live there, and I didn't think you would be able to either. Although it's always warm here, at least it rains sometimes, and I could grow flowers and fruit. If I had a garden."

"We should move, to somewhere where we can have a garden. I miss that more than anything," Harriet said.

But the house they had was beautiful, with a lovely view, close to the town of Las Palmas with all its provisions, but still isolated enough that they were able to stand outside on their balcony naked at night, and, once the servants Harriet had employed went home at the end of their working day, Harriet could change out of her respectable dress into her comfortable breeches and shirt. It just seemed pointless to uproot and move, when they might not get a chance to establish their garden before they could go home.

And that, in the end, was the canker in the beauty of their new life together. The island was beautiful, a paradise even, but it was foreign to them. The language was different, the religion was different, the traditions were different, the people thought differently to them, and even though they didn't want to make a lot of friends, they missed the casual conversation with people who thought as they did, the jokes, the turns of phrase, even the food. It was hard to explain, but it was pervasive.

They were both dreadfully homesick, and in spite of the fact that they knew they might have to stay here for the rest of their lives, they wanted it to be a temporary stay so much that they were incapable of putting down the roots that would have allowed them to adapt to the new culture and to feel at home.

They *did* visit the south, partly because it was a small island, and partly because they needed to fill their days. When they'd lived in England Harriet had had the estate to manage, and Jem had had the hothouses as well as his own cottage and garden where he'd grown vegetables and fruit. They'd both been busy all the time, and didn't realise until they were here, with just a house and a courtyard to manage, just how incapable they were of doing nothing.

So they visited the arid, desert-like south, travelling around the tiny villages, and they travelled into the rugged mountains,

THE ECCENTRIC'S TALE: HARRIET

climbing up to see the volcanic craters, hiking down into the village of the Caldera de Bandama, where they refreshed themselves with delicious Canary wine. They went to the caves, where it was said the original inhabitants of the island had lived before Spain had conquered them and killed or enslaved the natives.

Back in the north of the island they wandered around the narrow cobbled streets of Las Palmas, drank rum made from the sugar which had once been the main crop of the island, but which, due to the cheaper sugar grown in Spain's Caribbean conquests, had now in the main been abandoned in favour of vineyards which grew the grapes for the ever-popular Canary wine.

They saw the *drago* trees. It was said that Dragon's Blood, the red resin from the tree, helped wounds to heal very quickly and cleanly, and if that were true it would be a wonderful tree to grow in England. But they took too long to grow, and were too tall even for Harriet's large hothouse to accommodate.

Bananas, however, were not. Although the plant was tall, it would just about fit in the hothouse. They spent a lot of time learning as much as they could about them, in the hope that one day they would be able to return home and grow them there. To the best of their knowledge, no one *was* trying to grow them in England.

"Well they seem quite easy to grow," Harriet commented. "I think the reason no one *is* growing them in Britain is because of the size of the plant, not the difficulty in growing them. Not many people can afford to build and maintain a hothouse big enough to grow something the size of a tree in."

"But you can," Jem said.

"Yes. And I have conscientious gardeners, who truly care about growing them. That's as important as the building. I'm very lucky in that."

"Luck has nothing to do with it," Jem said. "The reason you have such good gardeners is because you care about them. You pay them well, and when they're successful you share the fruit with them. I don't know of any other noble who would do that. You inspire loyalty in your staff, and in your tenants, because you're a wonderful person."

Harriet felt a great wave of happiness wash over her, partly at the thought that she had an estate full of allies, and partly because he had not included himself among the gardeners as he'd spoken. Which meant he now truly accepted that he was her equal. She squeezed his hand, and he smiled at her then dropped a little kiss on the end of her nose. Then he turned back to the plants, totally absorbed in them. *He needs a garden so desperately,* she thought.

"At least we don't have to worry about the wind blowing them over or the lack of water, in England," He said. "And they need a lot of feeding, but we can get plenty of chicken manure. They're not as difficult to grow as pineapples. We just have to keep the temperature warm. We can do that."

Of course one of the things they didn't do at home, which they did here all the time, was walk about hand in hand or with her arm tucked under his. When they stood together she would sometimes rest her head on his shoulder, and he would embrace her, pulling her in to him, revelling in the sheer joy of being able to openly express their deep love for each other. They could do that here, because here they were Mr and Mrs Waters. Here they were married, in the eyes of the people.

CHAPTER EIGHTEEN

March 1706

For the first few days on board they thoroughly enjoyed themselves. Unlike all the other passengers, neither Harriet nor Jem suffered from sea-sickness, so for nearly all of that time they had the ship to themselves, apart from the crew of course. They spent that time sitting on deck looking out at the ocean, watching the crew about their work, with Jem sharing some of the information about their tasks that he'd discovered on the way out, or making plans for when they arrived back in England.

"Melanie should have my letter by now, but if my carriage isn't waiting for us, then we can always take the mail coach. We could ride, which would be lovely, but I'm not sure if you could make such a long journey."

"I'll try if you really want to, although I've only ridden into the village and around the estate before," Jem said.

"No. You'd be too sore. In truth, so would I, probably, because I haven't ridden properly since I arrived on the island. I think the carriage will be there for us, though."

"You really believe that Sophia's threat is irrelevant now?" he asked quietly, his forehead creasing. "I can take any censure, can accept if the servants take against me, if your family takes against me. It would be pleasanter if they don't, but it doesn't bother me. But I can't take being in a prison. I couldn't take that."

"You won't have to. She's gone from Court, in disgrace, hiding in the country with her husband, who is none too pleased with her. She has no power any more. I made sure of that. I, on the other hand, do, and the little plants down in the hold will add to that, if we can make them grow. We are safe. I wouldn't come back, bring you back if I had any doubts."

"Yes, but…what we talked about. I know you love me, know you trust me. You've proved that many times," Jem said.

"As you have to me. You're proving that by coming back with me now, accepting that you're safe."

He nodded.

"So, when we get back we can carry on as before, if you like. We had a good arrangement, and if we go back to that, then we won't cause any scandal, won't attract attention to ourselves."

She had been standing next to him, holding his hand, but now she turned to face him.

"Don't you want to marry me, then?" she asked.

"Yes, of course I want to marry you! You're the only woman I'll ever want to marry. But you're still a marchioness, and I'm still a gardener, and our marriage will still be unacceptable to society, won't it?"

"Not as unacceptable as a marchioness fornicating unashamedly with her gardener in an ungodly relationship, no. It might be acceptable for a man to openly have a mistress, even to take her to balls and the theatre, but it's not for a woman. Bloody hypocrites, can't see what difference it makes. But it does."

"I know. That's why I said we can continue as we were, if you want. You don't need to prove your love to me."

"Jem, look at me," she said gently. He turned his troubled gaze from the ocean then to her. "I didn't suggest we marry to prove I love you. I know I don't need to do that. And I trust you, know you well enough now to know you are probably one of only a handful of men who will not be corrupted by wealth and power. You're not interested in it, at all. I want to marry you because you make me happy. All the time you make me happy, and I don't want to have to sneak around in my own house using secret stairs, to have to pretend that our relationship is professional only. To hell with that. That's not freedom. I thought it was, but I was wrong. Freedom is marrying the man you love and to hell with anyone who doesn't like it."

"But—"

"I've had a year of knowing what it would be like to be openly married to you, and I won't settle for less, not when I know how

THE ECCENTRIC'S TALE: HARRIET

glorious it is to stand here holding hands as we are now, without worrying that we might be seen and reported on. Bugger the queen, bugger the aristocracy and their hypocrisy, their duplicity. Bugger everyone who thinks they know better than us how we should live our lives."

He smiled then, and enfolded her in his arms.

"You put the argument too well for me to argue any more," he said. "Let's marry then, as soon as we get home."

"I'd ask the captain to do it for us now, if we hadn't already told him we were married to get a cabin together," Harriet said into his shoulder.

"No, it will be good to marry at home. Lady Melanie has done a lot for us. It's right that she should be a witness. And I'd like John too, if you've no objections."

"John? The footman John?"

"Yes. He's a good man, and I know he's stood up for me a few times when servants have spoken about me, or aired their suspicions about us. And he cares for you very much too."

"John it will be then. Oh, I can't wait, now the decision is made!" she said.

They stood for a good time in silence then, wrapped in each other's arms, just enjoying being alive, being still quite young, being in love. Being so very much in love.

Then they went for dinner in the cabin with the captain, which was a pleasant affair, as the captain was a gregarious man with some interesting stories to tell of his travels to foreign climes. Added to that, the less agreeable or bombastic passengers were all retching weakly in their cabins, which, coupled with the utter joy and enthusiasm for life the couple exuded every moment of the day, made for a very pleasant evening indeed. It was wonderful to see a couple so in love, the captain remarked after a few glasses of wine, at which the couple blushed and said that they were indeed very lucky to be so blessed.

"How much longer do you think it will be before we reach England?" Harriet asked that evening.

"It's always hard to tell. We're having unseasonably fine weather right now though, and if it holds up, then maybe another ten days. But of course the weather could change that in a moment."

Ten days…two weeks then to get home, and then get the licence. So in three weeks they could openly declare their love.

Whatever Jem's reasons for wanting to be legally wed, for Harriet there was one reason only: she was sick of hiding her love for this wonderful man. She was done with deceit, with furtiveness, forever. And not just in love, but in everything. From now on she would be open, honest, as she had always wished to be, and to hell with anyone who didn't like it.

Marrying Jem was just the start of her new life in which she would be, totally, herself.

* * *

It was still dark when she woke suddenly, and she lay for a moment, disoriented, listening for what had disturbed her. Hearing nothing, she turned over, and was just drifting off when it came again, a smothered moan. She sat up immediately and looked around, although she could see nothing, it being pitch-black in the cabin.

"Jem? Are you well?" she asked.

"I'm sorry," he answered in a strangled voice. "I didn't mean to wake you."

"What's wrong?" She threw back the covers and swung her legs out of bed, feeling for the tinderbox.

"I ate something that disagreed with me, that's all. Go to sleep."

Ignoring him she managed to light the candle, and then looked at the narrow bunk across from her where he slept. He was curled up in a ball on the bed holding his stomach, his face twisted with pain. She stood and leaned over him, placing her hand on his forehead. It was not a warm night, and the cabin was cool, but his skin was on fire, and the sweat was pouring from him.

"Where's the pain?" she asked, trying to keep her voice calm so as not to worry him. He was never ill. Neither of them were ever ill.

"My guts," he said. "I need to…oh…"

She got the bucket that they used as a chamberpot to him just in time. After he had finished and had fallen back into his bed, she reached for her shawl and pushed her feet into her shoes.

"Where are you going?" he gasped.

THE ECCENTRIC'S TALE: HARRIET

"To throw this overboard. It smells terrible. And to get the ship's doctor."

"No, it's the middle of the night. I should be well, now—"

He retched suddenly, and she held the bucket and stroked his hair while he was very, very sick. Then he lay back, gasping, still clutching his stomach, and before he could protest again she left the room, heading up to the deck. She would dispose of the disgusting contents of the bucket, then find out where the doctor slept and wake him. To hell with the time.

She did not need to wake the doctor. When she got on deck she met him there, about to go back to bed, looking tired.

"I need you to see my husband," she said without preamble. "He's very sick."

He wiped his hand across his forehead, and then looked down at the bucket she held.

"Is that from him?" he asked.

"Yes. I was going to throw it overboard, and then come to find you."

He raised his lantern and inspected the contents, then nodded.

"Take me to his cabin," he said.

The doctor examined his patient cursorily, then sat on the edge of Harriet's bed.

"He has the bloody flux, my lady," he said.

"Are you sure?" Harriet asked, sceptical in view of the mere glance he'd given Jem, and the same hand on the forehead she'd done.

"Yes. God knows I've seen enough of it in my time. And when you saw me I was just coming from another case of it."

"What can you do for him?" she asked. "Is it caused by bad food?"

"No. There are a number of causes. In the young it is often caused by drunkenness and lascivious behaviour, which weakens the body and leaves it open to an excess of bile and humours."

The last thing Harriet wanted now was a moral lecture. She was consulting a doctor, not a priest. But she needed his help, so she bit her tongue a little.

"We are both of us, sir, in our thirties, hardly in the flush of youth. Nor are we drunkards," she said a little acidly.

"Oh! I confess I had thought you both much younger," he said. "It is also caused by noxious air."

His attempt at flattery sailed over her head unnoticed.

"An excess of bile and humours. What can you do to balance them?" she asked.

Jem groaned again, and the bucket was put to further use.

"This is a good sign," the doctor said. "The body is purging itself of the excess humours. Now the best way to do that is through sweating, which he is also doing. But we must keep him clean so the sweat can flow freely. I will order warm water and vinegar sent down for you to wash him regularly. It is vital that we encourage him to purge the body of all the unwanted matter, so I will give him impecacuanha and tartar, to encourage further expulsion. I will order another bucket to be sent down as well. They must be emptied immediately to avoid a build-up of noxious air, which will endanger you too, should you breathe it. And I will bleed him immediately, to relieve the heat of the fever. Then we are in God's hands." He smiled encouragingly and opened his bag.

* * *

In the next days she washed Jem regularly, talked gently to him, and sat with him as he voided his bowels and stomach, which he did very frequently at first, then less and less as time went on. He could not eat or drink anything – when he tried he could not hold it down for more than a minute. And he was in torment, at first moaning and then later, as the illness overwhelmed him and he no longer had the strength to attempt to hide his distress from her, he would scream with the agonising pains which racked his body. And Harriet, who *did* have the strength, would fight the tears, forcing them back so he would not see how terrified she was as she watched him waste away with a rapidity she had not thought possible, his skin losing its natural freshness and becoming dry, and his eyes developing dark shadows under them.

On the third day she told the doctor that she did not want him to give any more purges, as it was causing Jem a great deal of pain to strain and retch, with no result. He was no longer sweating either, and although the doctor had bled him each day, he was still intermittently burning with fever and shivering with chills, regardless of the temperature.

THE ECCENTRIC'S TALE: HARRIET

She stayed with him, sitting on the end of the bed, his head on her lap, disregarding the doctor's warnings of contagion by breathing the noxious air from his lungs, not caring about anything except that he must live. He must live, but she had no way to cure him if the doctor could not, and no other medical man to consult. She had never felt so helpless in her life before.

So she washed him, because that comforted him, and talked to him about the wonderful life they would have in England, about the bananas they would grow, and other exotic fruits that no one had ever seen in the country. About the walks they would take together, hand in hand, no longer hiding. And when he slept, as he did increasingly as time went by, she would rest her head back against the wall of the cabin and doze, waking at the slightest movement of this man she adored, this man she would give anything, anything to save.

On the fourth day the doctor came to tell her that his other patient was recovering. It was clearly an attempt to give her hope, and would have succeeded had she not seen the expression on his face when he looked at Jem, now sleeping restlessly.

She thanked him and waited impatiently for him to leave, sensing on a subconscious level that every second was now immensely precious, and not wanting to waste even one of them on anyone other than this man who was her life. When the doctor had gone, closing the door quietly behind him, she sat, stroking Jem's hair, needing to have constant contact with him. She settled his head back on her lap, smiling as he sighed softly in his sleep, and then she leaned back and closed her own eyes.

She had no idea how long she'd slept, but when she woke Jem was still asleep, his face contorting now and then with the pains which still racked him, but not enough to wake him, which she grasped at as a good sign.

After she'd carefully lifted his head from her lap onto the pillow, she stood, stretching her legs to ease the cramp in her muscles. Then moving to the cabin door she opened it, hoping to let in a little fresh air, as the air in here was stale. She wedged it open with a shoe, but as she turned back she saw that he'd woken and was watching her. She went back to him, sat on the edge of his bed and felt his forehead, hoping the fever had broken. But he was still burning up.

"Not here," he said, so softly that she didn't hear the words, so she bent her head closer to his.

"Not here," he repeated. "I don't want to die here."

"No, you won't die here," she reassured him frantically. "You'll die at home, or in our gardens, when you're an old, old man."

He looked at her then, and knew what they both knew, what he had accepted but she could not.

"On deck," he whispered painfully. "Take me on deck. I want the last thing I see to be the sky, not this. Please."

She closed her eyes for a second, fighting back the tears that she could not give in to now, and then she ran up onto the deck, and five minutes later Jem had been carried up, with great care and tenderness, by some of the crewmen, who laid him in the sunlight on his mattress. Harriet covered him with a blanket, because although the sky was a bright summer blue, the blue of his eyes, there was a stiff breeze and a chill in the air. Then she sat and cradled his head in her lap again. He looked at the sky, then took in as deep a breath as his failing lungs could manage.

"Ah," he said blissfully. "Thank you."

"It doesn't smell of green things, though," Harriet said.

"No. But it's clean, and fresh. That's enough." He lifted his arm, his fingers moving, and she took his hand in hers, squeezing it to keep him with her. "Harriet," he said, "you're flying free now. Keep flying. Don't let anyone, not even yourself, put you in a cage."

"I can't do it without you, Jem," she said.

"Yes, you can, it's natural for you." He swallowed, hard, and took another shuddering breath. "You can teach others to fly, as you taught me. If it's possible, I'll watch you do it."

"I don't want to fly without you. I don't want to teach anyone else. Jem, please, please stay with me!" She stopped then, feeling the hysteria rising, not wanting him to hear it in her voice. She wiped her hand fiercely across her eyes, then reached down and brushed his hair back from his face.

He looked at her then and smiled, his eyes, his face full of light, full of love.

And then, gently, as he had done everything in life, he was gone.

THE ECCENTRIC'S TALE: HARRIET

She looked at him, saw his hair was still moving, played with by the breeze, his hand was still clasping hers, was still warm, and told herself that he had not left her, could not leave her, not like this, not when they were almost home, when their lives stretched in front of them, full of promise. And then she looked in his eyes again, and knew.

The pain hit her, so overwhelming that for a moment it paralysed her, rendering her incapable of speech, incapable of anything. No one could suffer this and not die, she thought, and wished fervently that it was so, that she would die right now, and they would be together again, because she could not bear to be without him, not for a minute, let alone a lifetime.

But she did not die right now, and although she could not bear it, yet she did. The captain waited as long as he dared, the crew standing respectfully at a distance. All of them had seen death before, many times, were somewhat inured to it, but none of them had seen a couple so much in love as these two had clearly been. They had radiated happiness, and had infused the whole crew with their joy and love of life. No one could bear to separate them now, although God had already done so, in truth. They had seen women cry, scream, faint in grief before, were somewhat inured to that too. But they had never seen a woman in such silent, breathless agony. It was terrible, and those who could went to do chores, whilst others turned their heads, respecting her privacy.

In the end it was the captain who came to her, who knelt down next to her and spoke softly to her, telling her that they must take care of him, that they would normally bury at sea, but would, if she wished, allow her to take him home, although they must move him. He said this with such sorrow and distress for her that she could not object.

"Of course," she said, her voice raw with unshed tears. "Of course you must do it without delay. How many days yet until we land?"

"Four, maybe five, my lady."

"Yes. He loves the sea. We walked often along the shore. It will be fitting. Yes. Straight away."

"Oh no, my lady, we can wait," the captain said.

"No. He's already…" Her voice faltered, and she looked up at the sky, still blue, still cloudless. "I just need a moment to accept it," she said, "to say goodbye to him."

The captain moved away then, and went to make preparations, while Harriet said goodbye to the man she had loved since she was a tiny girl, to the man she would love until she died, although she knew that he had already left her, and was flying far freer than she ever would. Then she stood while they sewed a shroud around his body, while the ship's minister said words that were supposed to be comforting, but which she didn't even hear, and then while they slipped his body into the sea.

She stood on the deck and watched as he sank, and then the ship moved on. She stayed there for a long time, until the sun had set and the lanterns were lit. And then she went to the cabin they had shared and which still smelt of him, but in sickness, not health. She took her mattress and blanket on deck and slept there, in the spot they had placed Jem, breathing the pure fresh air that he had breathed in for the last time a few hours ago, that he would never breathe again.

* * *

Melanie, who had received Harriet's letter telling her they were on their way home, had prepared as much as she could to welcome them. She had sent the coach a few days ago, with Claire driving and two footmen behind for protection and to load the baggage, and had given them money to stay in inns while they waited for the ship to dock.

Then for the last few days she had stationed the fastest footman at the end of the road each morning, with strict instructions to run as fast as he could back to the house as soon as he saw the coach approaching.

So it was that when the Marchioness of Hereford arrived home, as many of the servants as could be gathered were in the courtyard waiting for her, Melanie standing on the steps, wringing her hands with anticipation. The coach drew to a halt, and she waited for the door to open and Harriet to jump down unaided as was her habit, but instead the footman climbed down from behind with the steps and opening the door, placed them in front of it then held out his arm.

Melanie's welcoming smile was replaced by a frown of puzzlement, but it wasn't until her sister appeared in the doorway of the coach that she knew something was terribly, terribly wrong.

The servants had started to cheer, but when they saw their mistress their voices faltered, and silence fell. She still wore her customary male outfit, but looked as though she hadn't changed her clothes for several days. Her hair was loose and tangled on her shoulders, and the combination of a suntan on top of extreme pallor made her skin yellow.

For the first time Melanie could see what her sister would look like when she was a very old woman. Harriet, who exuded life, who was always exuberant, even in hard times, was now utterly quenched. She took the footman's arm and stepped down from the coach, and then stood for a second staring at the house but clearly seeing nothing. She took a deep breath, then braced herself, as though preparing for a great battle.

Then she walked past the congregated servants without noticing them, and carried on up the steps to the house.

"He's dead," she said matter-of-factly as she reached Melanie.

Then she continued up the steps and through the front door.

Melanie stood for a second, wanting to go after her sister and find out what had happened, comfort her, but she could not just leave the servants standing there, clearly concerned. She had to deal with them first.

"It seems Lady Hereford is somewhat indisposed," she said. "If you go back to your duties for now, I will tell you when I find out what ails her."

"Would you like me to run for Doctor Smith, my lady?" one of the servants asked.

"Not just yet, but thank you," Melanie answered. The two footmen were unstrapping the baggage while Claire remained seated, waiting for them to finish so she could drive to the stables. Melanie walked to the front of the coach and stroked one of the horses' noses.

The young woman looked down now, removing her hat and dipping her head in respect. Like her mistress, she had adopted masculine attire, although only when she was driving the coach, saying it was more practical. It probably made life easier for her too to be mistaken for a man as she drove along, although what she had to deal with from other servants when stationery waiting for her passengers to return, she never said. She probably adopted the same impassive expression she wore now, which revealed nothing.

"Do you know what has happened?" Melanie asked quietly.

Claire nodded, then looked across the yard, and Melanie, turning, saw that the servants, rather than dispersing, were hovering around, no doubt hoping to find out what was wrong.

"See to the horses, then come to me in the library," she said. "You may go back to your chores," she continued loudly and firmly enough for the servants to start moving away. Then she went back to the house, discovered that Harriet had gone to her rooms and had locked the door, stating only that she wished to be left alone, and went to the library to wait for Claire.

She did not have to wait long. The girl arrived barely ten minutes later as Melanie was in the act of pouring herself a glass of brandy.

"I'm sorry for my state, your ladyship," she said. "I would have washed and changed, but I did think you'd rather see me quick. Matt is seeing to the horses and he's a good boy, loves them he does."

"You were quite right, Claire. Thank you." She took another glass and poured a generous measure into it, then passed it across to the dishevelled woman. "Here," she said, "you look as though you need it. Sit down."

Claire took the glass gratefully but looked at the pale lemon brocade chair uncertainly.

"I'm not too clean," she said doubtfully. "I doesn't want to dirty your—"

"Sit down," Melanie interrupted. "I don't care about the chair. I don't care about anything except Harriet. What's happened? She said he's dead. Jem should be with her, so I assume it's him?"

"She hasn't spoke to me, my lady. But yes, I believe so. When the ship arrived, the captain, he come down the gangplank with her, and she looked terrible, she did. And he said as I must be very gentle with her, as her husband had died of the bloody flux and she'd took it very badly. I didn't want to say that with everyone listening, my lady, because I knowed he meant Jem, and I didn't know if you'd want them all to know she'd married him."

She married him? Melanie couldn't believe it. Harriet would never marry again. She had said so, countless times. Not even Jem.

THE ECCENTRIC'S TALE: HARRIET

"You were right. Did the captain say it was Jem who was her husband?"

"No, he didn't. But who else would it be? They was so in love, when he was here. We all knowed that, all of us that was close to her ladyship. She wouldn't look like that for no one else. And you told me he would be coming back with her."

That was true. Melanie took a deep drink of the brandy.

"Where is Jem, then? His body?"

"That's what I asked the captain. He said that he was buried at sea, that he'd asked her ladyship if she wanted to bring him home, but she said no, he loved the sea too. And he said I must try to make her eat, because she hadn't et anything since he died, five days since."

"Did she eat at the inns you stopped at?"

"No. She didn't stay at them. We had to stop because of the horses, so's they could rest, but she told me and Tom and Jack to get rooms, that she couldn't see anyone, and she slept in the coach. Tom and Jack, they got rooms, but I couldn't leave her like that. I owes her everything, I does. So I ordered her some food and took it to her, but she wouldn't eat, said it'd choke her if she did. Then I climbed in the coach too and slept on the seat across from her. I didn't ask nor nothing, because if she'd said no I would have had to go, and I couldn't. And she didn't say nothing, just squeezed my arm in the morning before we set off again. So I slept with her last night too, which is why I looks like I does because I stayed with her all the time. And now we's home. But she hasn't et nothing, just drank some weak ale is all."

"You did right, Claire. God bless you. Thank you. I think you should go and eat something yourself now, and then rest. Take the rest of the day off and tell cook to feed you the same meal that she's cooking for me."

"Thank you, my lady. I won't say nothing to the servants, if they ask me. Nor will Tom and Jack. They're that upset too. They love her ladyship…most all of us do. If there's anything else I can do, if you wants me to get the doctor, I'll go now. She does need to eat, that's true. But I think she's just grieving, my lady, and there en't nothing a doctor can do for that, is there?"

"No there isn't. You're quite right. You go and rest." Harriet hated doctors anyway, in fact had never seen one, had never been ill enough to, in her life. Neither had Jem for that matter.

God, this was awful.

* * *

Harriet stayed in her rooms for five days, not speaking to anyone, not answering the door when Melanie knocked, not eating any of the food that was brought and left outside the door for her, although she did take the drinks. And then, just when Melanie was wondering how long someone could live without eating and whether she should get John to break the door down or send for a doctor, or both, Harriet suddenly appeared in the library after breakfast on the sixth day, and sitting down at the windowseat, looked out across the gardens.

Melanie, who was sitting at a table, and until her sister had entered had been reading, waited silently, allowing Harriet to make the first move.

"You've looked after the gardens well," she said after a few minutes, her voice somewhat gravelly through lack of use.

"I've done my best, although in truth your servants are so good that it's not been an onerous duty. I've missed you. The Earl of Highbury has asked after you too, was glad to hear you were coming home. He's not here today, because he's with Frances."

"How is she?" Harriet asked.

"Very unwell. William is home from university too."

"Ah, so she is near the end then," Harriet replied somewhat emotionlessly.

"Yes," Melanie replied, cursing herself for mentioning the Highburys. The last thing Harriet needed now was to talk about another death. "William will want to visit, as soon as he can."

"I can't see anyone yet," Harriet said. "Not yet."

Silence fell for a few more minutes. Melanie closed the book she'd been reading, and waited. Harriet continued to look out of the window.

"We took him on deck, because he wanted the last thing he saw to be the sky," she said softly. "He loved the sky. We used to lie outside together and look at the sky for hours. But the last thing he saw wasn't the sky, but me. He looked at me and smiled, and then he died." She bent her head, and looked at her hands twisting in her lap for a moment, then turned to look at Melanie, her grey eyes dark with pain.

"That's good. Because there's only one thing he loved more than the sky, and that was you. He died seeing the thing he loved most in the world. That must be a comfort to you," Melanie said.

"He said he would watch over me if he could. But he's gone. I can't feel him, not at all. How do I bear such loneliness, Mel? I don't know how to bear it," Harriet said. She shook her head, as if in anger. And then she started to cry, helplessly, brokenly. Melanie moved across to her then, and held her while she sobbed, not knowing what else she could do.

The sun moved past the window, a servant came into the library to make up the fire then left immediately when Melanie shook her head at her. And finally Harriet's sobs turned to gasps and then stilled, while her sister held her and stroked her hair, until finally she indicated that she had finished, had regained control. Then Melanie released her and sat back. Harriet blew her nose and wiped her eyes, and then opened her mouth.

"Don't say you're sorry," Melanie said. "There's no shame in grief."

Harriet smiled weakly, because that had been what she'd been about to say.

"How can I go on without him?" she said instead. "I don't want to. I don't know where to start, what to do."

Melanie thought for a moment, knowing she had to find the right words, honest words. No platitudes, not for Harriet, who hated such things.

"When you're feeling strong enough, you could look at the plants that you brought back with you. Patrick has planted them in the hothouse, assuming they should be there, but he doesn't know what to do or even what they are."

"They're bananas," Harriet said. "Yes, they need to be in the hothouse."

"Bananas. Well, I assume they're important, and that you and Jem chose them together. I think he would want you to look after them, wouldn't he?"

"Yes, he would," Harriet said. "He loved them. We both did. We ate them all the time in Gran Canaria. He grew one in the courtyard while he was waiting for me to come to him. And when the first fruit ripened, we peeled it and ate it together. He started at

one end, and me at the other, and we met in the middle, and—"
She was smiling as she said that, and for a moment Melanie saw a
glimpse of the Harriet she knew and her heart soared, but then
Harriet's face twisted in agony and she stopped mid-sentence.

"They are special, then, precious. You must tell Patrick what
to do to save them," Melanie suggested.

"He would want me to look after them. You're right," Harriet
said. She stood abruptly and then staggered, placing her hand
against the wall to steady herself. She hadn't eaten for twelve days.
For at least twelve days.

"You don't have to go now," Melanie said immediately. "You
need to eat something. Let me get some soup for you."

"No," Harriet replied. "I need to go now."

Melanie looked at her. Yes, she really did need to go now, right
now. If she didn't, she would never go, would never eat, would
die. She stood.

"We'll go together then," she said, taking her sister's arm. "I'll
support you if you feel dizzy, but when you come back, you must
eat something."

"Yes, when I come back," Harriet said, as though she was
going on a long journey.

They made their way out of the library and across the entrance
hall, slowly and falteringly. Mark opened the front door for them,
and they stood on the step outside and looked across the gardens
to the hothouse in the distance. Harriet's arm was trembling. Her
whole body was trembling, just from walking across two rooms.

"Mark," Melanie said. "Will you run and ask for the chaise to
be readied? We can sit outside in the sun and wait for it."

"No," Harriet said, her voice firm even if her body wasn't.
"I've never taken a chaise to the hothouse, and I won't now. I'll
walk there."

"Harriet, you're—"

"I need to do this, Mel. I need to do it right. I need to show
him I can fly."

Melanie had no idea what her sister was talking about. She was
delirious. Maybe later she would send for the doctor. She would
definitely do so if Harriet wouldn't eat. She sighed, and made a
gesture to Mark to follow them, then the sisters continued down
the steps and across the garden, the footman following discreetly,

THE ECCENTRIC'S TALE: HARRIET

but close enough to dart forward and catch his mistress should she faint.

The day had been still until now, but as they finally reached the end of the lawns and started along the short tree-lined avenue that led to the largest of the hothouses, where the bananas had been planted, a breeze suddenly got up, rustling the leaves of the trees and playing with the hair of the two women as they made their slow deliberate way to the door of the hothouse.

When they reached it Harriet stopped, and looked up. And then she smiled, a genuine smile that briefly brought life back to her face.

"Thank you, my love," she said to the clear, cloudless blue sky.

Then, lifting her hand from Melanie's arm, she opened the door and went through.

CHAPTER NINETEEN

June 1712

The couple lay on their backs near the river, enjoying the first truly glorious day of the summer. Between them on the grass was a pitcher of ale and a small pile of yellow peels. From the recumbent figure on the left a curl of smoke rose periodically into the air.

"They really are delicious. I don't think I've ever tasted anything quite as delicious before," the young man said. He was the epitome of relaxation; his lower legs were bare, his shirt sleeves rolled up and his expensive silk brocade coat flung carelessly to one side, next to which were his stockings and shoes.

"Most people haven't tasted them at all," the woman said. She was similarly attired, and equally relaxed. She opened her mouth and released a perfect smoke ring. They both watched silently as it ascended, became a wavering oval, then dissipated.

"Except for the queen," William said.

"And my servants, of course. And the Marlboroughs," Harriet added.

"Why the Marlboroughs?" William asked.

"I owe the duchess. She once did me a great service."

He waited, but she did not elaborate.

"The leaves are enormous. Are you sure it's not a tree? It looked like a tree to me."

"No, it isn't. The stem isn't wood – it's made of the leaves. They grow up through the middle of the plant from the bottom and make a stem in the end. Once it's fruited, it dies down, and new plants grow from little suckers at the base of it. We brought some of them back from Gran Canaria, and luckily I managed to

THE ECCENTRIC'S TALE: HARRIET

grow two of them. The others died though."

"Have you invited the queen to see them? I'm sure she'd be interested."

"I doubt it. I don't want to, anyway. I want no royals here, and none of her hangers-on either. I'm done with all of that."

It was certainly true that since she'd come home from her trip to Leiden for healing plants and to Gran Canaria for the banana plants, she'd lived very quietly, only going to Court when expressly invited to, and not always even then.

"And yet you're held in high esteem at the palace," William remarked.

"Am I?" Harriet replied indifferently. "No idea why. Maybe some of the plants from Leiden helped the queen then. I'm glad. If they all leave me alone, I'll be very glad."

A companionable silence fell between the couple.

"Sometimes, when we were in Gran Canaria, when it was raining, Jem and I would go outside and make a little shelter of banana leaves to sit under. It was really snug sitting there together with the rain pattering on the leaves, smelling that lovely scent you get when it rains for the first time in ages." She smiled sadly, and William, noticing, did not know how to reply to this. So he did the wise thing, as was his habit, and said nothing.

"I always think of him when I lie here," she added after a time.

"You lie here a lot," William remarked.

"I think of him a lot," she replied. "I always will. It doesn't hurt as much to remember when we were together now. It's bittersweet. One day maybe it'll just be sweet."

"I hope so. I miss him too. That surprised me at first, because I was jealous of him when I was a child," William admitted.

"Were you?" she said. "I didn't know that. You had no need to be."

"I know that now. But then, it seemed that he was taking you away from me. You were always so happy when you were with him. You seemed to light up from inside. I wanted to be able to make you light up from inside too."

"You did. You still do. But it's a different sort of light, that's all. You'll understand it when you fall in love, really in love, not just lust or infatuation."

"Yes. I suppose I will," he answered indifferently. "Papa says everyone at Court thinks 'Little Gem' a fine name for the fruit, because it really is a precious jewel."

"Ha! Do they?"

"Yes. Except your uncle, who said it should be named for the queen instead, as it's the queen of fruits."

"That'll be Percy, then. He can mind his own bloody business, the sycophantic shit. It won't happen, anyway."

"Why not?" William asked.

"Because as delicious as it is, the queen will not want her name to be given to something that looks like a man's prick. In any case, if they do change the name they'll never get another banana from me. I will have him remembered, even if the bastards don't know what they're remembering."

"You don't like the aristocracy much, do you?"

"I don't like them at all. Spiders in webs. With a very few exceptions." She looked at him and winked, and he smiled.

Silence fell again. Bees buzzed in the clover and dandelions, and a splash came from the lazily flowing river.

"So then, what is it that's on your mind? You didn't come here just to talk about bananas and memories. I thought it might be that you'd fallen in love with a young Mademoiselle or Fräulein while you were travelling around Europe, but it seems I'm wrong. You don't have to tell me what it is if you don't want to, though."

William sighed.

"I have to tell someone, and you're the only person I know who I can trust, will tell me honestly what you think, and who won't think I'm a fool."

"Hmm. Well, you can trust me. I'll tell you whether I think you're a fool or not when I've heard what you've got to say."

"Do you remember King James? James II?"

"Yes, I remember him, though I only saw him once. It was a memorable meeting. Tall. He could be kind, but he had no sense of humour. Took himself too seriously, and couldn't see any other viewpoint but his own. That was what lost him his kingdom in the end. He should have observed how his brother played the game. Why do you ask?"

"You think he lost the crown because he was too serious?" William asked. "I thought it was because he wanted to make Britain a Catholic state."

THE ECCENTRIC'S TALE: HARRIET

"Bullscutter," Harriet replied. "That's what the Whigs would have you think, because they need to justify why they replaced him. They can't just say, he was a terrible king so we got rid of him, because a lot of them are terrible lords, but don't want their tenants to get rid of them. That way lies anarchy."

William laughed out loud, and then sat up.

"Wasn't he trying to make Britain Catholic then? Even Papa says that."

"He certainly *hoped* Britain would become Catholic again, but I don't think even he was stupid enough to try to *make* us be, no. He certainly lifted all the restrictions on Catholics, and put a lot of them in high positions though. He thought all men should worship according to their consciences. His Toleration Act said as much."

"And do you think he really *believed* that?" William asked earnestly.

Harriet thought for a minute.

"Yes. Yes, I do. He truly believed that if people were allowed to hear about the Catholic faith, maybe to attend a Mass, that they couldn't help but see it was the only true Christian church and convert. Because that's what he'd done, and as I said, he was only capable of seeing things from his own point of view. He believed he wouldn't need to force them. Whether he would have tried to had he continued to reign we'll never know. He had no idea how terrified the British are of popery, and he was unyielding. That was why he lost the throne, and he deserved to, in my opinion. Charles learnt from their father's obstinacy, James repeated it. He was a fool."

"What about the son?" William said, so quietly that Harriet only just caught the words.

"The son? He's Catholic for certain. Whether he's as rigid as his father I don't know. Why?"

"Do you think he should be heir, rule when the queen dies?"

"Instead of Sophia of Hanover, you mean?"

"Yes."

"That depends on whether you believe in hereditary right being the only qualification, or if you think it more important that the monarch should be a Protestant."

"What do you think?"

"In truth, I don't care who sits on the throne as long as whoever rules leaves me alone, and doesn't plunge the country into another civil war, as James and William almost did. Why are you asking me all this?"

Another silence fell, and Harriet sat up, took a mouthful of ale, and waited.

"When I was in Europe, I met James," William said eventually.

"You met James, by accident, or you went to see him?"

"I went to see him. Or rather his Court, when I was staying in Paris. But he was there, and he graciously allowed me an audience."

"I'm sure he did," Harriet said. "It's in his interest to befriend as many British nobles as he can. Anne is in bad health and has no children living. He'll be seeking support in the hope of taking the throne when she dies. His claim is good, compared to Sophia's."

"Except that he is a Catholic," William said.

"Yes. Sophia's the first Protestant in line, which seems to be all that matters to the Whigs. Did James tell you he will turn Anglican? If he will, he has a good chance of being king after Anne."

"No. But I liked him. He seemed very honest, very passionate about the country and he told me he wished only to practise as he believes, and for others to have the same rights. All others. I think he should be given a chance to prove whether he would be a good king or not. It's ridiculous to pass over not only him, but fifty other people, and give the throne to an old woman who I'm sure doesn't care about us at all."

"Have you told anyone else how you think?" Harriet asked.

"No. No one."

"Don't. Because unless James is willing to convert, then he has no hope of being accepted by the majority of people in Britain, no matter how much he cares about the country. Although in honesty, I doubt he does. And openly professing what you've just told me could be very dangerous for you."

"I think he does care. He was very enthusiastic," William said.

"Of course he was. He wants power. He wants to be the king, to rule the country. It's what he's been brought up to believe he should do. And if he succeeds, do you think he'll care about you

THE ECCENTRIC'S TALE: HARRIET

or anyone else who helped him, unless it suits him to do so? No."

"You are very cynical," William observed.

"I'm very realistic. I have learned to be. You are seriously thinking to support James if he makes a bid for the crown? Answer me honestly."

"I am thinking about it. I must do what I believe is right. How can I hold my head up and feel proud, if I sit back and let wrong be done because I'm afraid of the possible consequences to me?"

Harriet looked at him, this passionate, dedicated child who was now a passionate, dedicated man.

"I see you're serious, and I admire your principles at least. So I will be honest with you, and tell you how I see it. When I was a child, I was a friend of King Charles. He wrote to me, and I to him, and I adored him. I would have given my life for him in an instant if he'd asked me to. I still think of him, and I will always hold a place in my heart for him. And I'm sure he genuinely cared for me too. But I will tell you this; if his crown or his power had been threatened, and throwing me to the wolves would have helped him keep them, he would have done it without hesitation. He did it to Montrose, after all. And so would James do to you."

"Have you met him?"

"No. I don't need to. Kings are all the same. All powerful men are ruthless, whether they seem so or not. If they were not, they would not be powerful. James is no different. Nor is Sophia, for that matter. Nor our current queen, the shy and hesitant Anne, who did not hesitate to abandon her father in his hour of need. You are a good man, William, and will be a wonderful earl one day. Don't throw it away because you've been mesmerised by royal glamour."

"I haven't been," he protested automatically. "Well, maybe a little," he admitted. "But don't you think that every man should worship God in the way he believes to be right?"

"I do, but it will never happen, neither under James, nor Anne, nor Sophia. Look at the ridiculous Occasional Conformity Act that was finally passed last year. This Act will not make dissenters become Anglicans. You will never bring a person to believe in your version of Christianity by forcing them to go to a particular church. It should be enough that they already believe in Christ; it's just in the details that all these groups differ, details that Christ never talked about as far as I can see. I think He'd be horrified if He saw what man was doing in His name. And that's why I don't go to church, like many others. I believe in my own way.

"This Act has been put forward time and time again by the Tories, not out of any religious concern, but merely to try to curb Whig power by depriving them of the electoral support of the non-conformists. It's they who are the hypocrites, not the poor souls going to a church they don't agree with once a year so they can keep their jobs."

"I don't think I've ever heard you speak about religion before," William said.

"No. For me it's a private thing between me and God, and if I'm wrong I'll answer to Him when the time comes. But I'll have no hypocrite tell me what God thinks I should do. I can read the Bible for myself, and I can't hold an official position anyway, as a woman, so I don't need to go to any church if I don't want to."

"That doesn't mean you're not powerful though."

"No, it doesn't. It just means I can't be openly powerful. But to get back to what you were saying. To me all churches are the same. Whichever one is in the ascendant will try to oppress the others and forcibly convert people. The Anglicans talk a lot about the Inquisition, and the tyranny of Rome, and they're right. But they are no different. Nor were the Presbyterians, when they had the ascendancy in Scotland. Don't put your life and the earldom that your father has nurtured for you at risk for an ideal that will never be realised. Churches are powerful, and power corrupts. It always has and it always will, in my view. So tolerance is a dream. James II found that out to his cost, and if his son thinks to repeat the mistake his father made, then he will fail too."

"You think if I support him I'm a fool, then?" William asked.

"No. I think you are a man of high principles, and I admire that greatly. But you are also young, and an idealist, and I care for you very much. I would not see you throw everything away for an impossible ideal."

"But you do believe that everyone should be able to worship according to their conscience."

"Yes, as I said. And if you believe that, then you would do a lot better to work quietly in the background to make it happen than to declare openly for James and lose everything. You will

THE ECCENTRIC'S TALE: HARRIET

likely be more successful if you do, too."

"It doesn't seem very honourable, though," William said.

"You can be honourable without the whole world knowing it. I cannot be a Member of Parliament, because I'm a woman. But I effectively control a number of MPs, and a number of church ministers, Justices of the Peace, and other influential men. If I want something, I don't go and demand it from them openly, because if I did I wouldn't succeed. They would resent me, and band together to curb me. Instead I make suggestions, very gently remind the men who have the power just how fragile that power is, how easily it could be eroded. I make them feel insecure, suspicious of those who could usurp them, so they do not band together, but remain isolated, vulnerable. I get what I want, and they keep their position that makes them feel so important. Consequently we're all happy. And I am telling you this because I trust you, as you are trusting me."

"I know that, and I value your view. So you think I should work in the background to restore James Stuart, if I really believe he should be king?"

"Well, in truth I think you should work in the background to grow your power as Earl of Highbury when you succeed to the title, and to hell with James Stuart. But you must act according to your conscience, as I act according to mine. And I might disapprove, but I will never condemn you for fighting for what you truly believe in. Just make sure it is what *you* believe in, and not what you have been beguiled into believing."

William bent his legs and wrapped his arms around them, resting his chin on his knees.

"I knew you would be completely honest with me," he said after a moment. "Thank you for that. And you didn't belittle me or say I was too young to know my own mind."

"How could I? When I was your age I knew my own mind very well, but I made life hard for myself by going about things the wrong way. And when I realised that, I became too cautious. I will never forgive myself for that. I swung from one extreme to the other, and didn't see the middle ground until it was too late. I would not have you do the same."

"You're talking about Jem," he said, and it was not a question.

"Yes. I was so intent on stopping others from taking away my

401

freedom, that I took it away from myself. I see that now. Just be careful. And think very long and hard before you make any decision. Follow your heart but think with your head, because if you don't your emotions will blind you to the right path, and you will regret it. You cannot undo what has been done. If you must do it, go about it the right way, a way that protects you and your family."

"Yes, I see that. I will think, long and hard, I promise you. Can I come to you again, if I need to?"

"You can always come to me. We are friends, and I don't use the word friend lightly, as many do. You know that."

"I do. I don't use the word friend lightly either."

She looked at him then, and smiled.

"No," she said. "You are loyal to your friends, always have been. There are not many like you. But even those you love and trust can turn on you if it suits them. And because of that I would say, choose your friends very carefully."

"As you have."

"As I have. Which is why I don't have many of them."

"I'm honoured to be among the number."

"I feel the same about you."

Silence fell again, and after a time they lay back down, each absorbed in their own thoughts. Bees buzzed in the clover and dandelions, and another splash came from the lazily flowing river. It truly was a beautiful day.

A light breeze rustled through the leaves and the grass, and feeling it play with her hair, Harriet smiled, and the sky, a clear cloudless summer blue, smiled back at her.

* * *

Harriet's story will continue in the next book in this series – The Ladies' Tale: Caroline and Philippa.

Follow me on:

Website:
www.juliabrannan.com

Facebook:
www.facebook.com/pages/Julia-Brannan/727743920650760

Twitter:
https://twitter.com/BrannanJulia

Newsletter:
http://eepurl.com/bSNLHD

HISTORICAL NOTE

It has now become a custom for me to write a historical note at the end of every book, which I confess I enjoy doing. In it I explore some of the historical incidents that I've written about, giving a bit more factual detail for those who are interested. If you are not one of those people, you can skip this part!

In the first few chapters I introduce King Charles II, with whom I am half in love. He was far more complex than the mere adulterous 'Merry Monarch' of various period dramas. In order to become better acquainted with him, I read a number of biographies and many of his letters, which give a good impression of the man behind the king, some of which I try to get across through his relationship with Harriet.

Upon his restoration in 1660 Charles recognised that the nation was sick of war and conflict, but was fearful of the return of a ruler who would use his power to wreak revenge on all those who had opposed monarchy. With this in mind, he addressed the issue in a series of letters that were edited into the Declaration of Breda, in which he promised religious toleration, property rights and to pay the soldiers their arrears of money. He also granted a 'free and general pardon…to all our subjects, of what degree or quality so ever'. The only exception to this was in the case of the men who had been responsible for the beheading of his father, King Charles I.

Family certainly was extremely important to him. He is renowned for being lazy and taking the easy way out of difficulties, and yet he refused flatly either to divorce his wife and remarry when she proved barren, or to agree to the exclusion of his brother James as heir to the throne, even though his life would have been made much easier if he had. James and Charles were unerringly loyal to each other, one of James' few redeeming qualities.

Similarly, although Charles did not enjoy writing letters, he kept up a constant correspondence with his sister Henrietta, who was married to the Duke of Orleans – I have stolen a line from one of his letters to her and had him send it to Harriet, in which he states: 'I beg of you, do not treat me with so much ceremony in addressing me with so many 'Majesties' for I do not wish that there should be anything between us two but friendship.'

He was also extremely fond of children, as is seen in the close relationship he enjoyed with his many illegitimate children, who he accepted as his without hesitation. He did indeed know about the duplicity and falseness of his courtiers, so it's eminently possible that he would have been endeared by a child such as Harriet who was profoundly honest and genuine.

Finally, the death of Charles, in February 1685. This took everyone by surprise at the time, as the king was profoundly healthy and always had been apart from a couple of bouts of fever. He ate moderately, drank moderately, and was well-known for taking exercise, particularly long, brisk walks. On the morning of 2nd February 1685 Charles cried out in pain, fell to the floor and had a number of fits. Over the next few days he alternated between rallying and failing, and finally died on 6th February. It's certain that the vast number of horrendous treatments given to the king by desperate physicians at the least made his last days a torment, and at the worst hastened his death dramatically. The amount of blood that was drawn alone would have weakened him catastrophically, to say nothing of the numerous bizarre remedies administered.

There are still numerous theories as to what was wrong with him, ranging from malaria to a stroke, viral encephalitis to mercury poisoning due to the chemistry experiments he engaged in. What was absolutely certain was that the death of Charles plunged Britain into another very uncertain time, which will be explored in depth in my next series, Road to Rebellion.

However, the basics are that Charles II died without legitimate issue, which meant that his brother James then succeeded him

THE ECCENTRIC'S TALE: HARRIET

as James II of England and VII of Scotland. The reason that many people were uneasy about this is because several years before James had become a Roman Catholic. It's difficult to imagine now just how terrified the country was of a Roman Catholic revival, but fear of 'Popery' was very real. There were multiple reasons for this fear, but part of it was due to the fact that the Tudor reformation with all its bloodshed and intolerance had taken place only a hundred and forty years previously, and part of it because King Louis of France was a devout Catholic bent on becoming the ruler of the whole of Europe and restoring it to the 'true' faith.

Nevertheless, kings were ordained by God, so in the main the country settled down to endure the reign of James rather than risk another civil war. This was not easy, as James was a firm believer in absolute monarchy, and resented any questioning of his decisions. But he was already in his fifties, both his daughters by his first wife were devout Protestants, and his second wife appeared to be barren. It was believed that when James died his eldest daughter Mary would become a more reasonable queen and the Protestant succession would be assured. But in 1688 the queen gave birth to a son, James, and it seemed that a line of Catholic absolutist kings would result.

At this point a group of politicians invited Mary and her husband, Prince William of Orange to intervene. William set sail for England at the end of 1688, and following a series of betrayals, King James panicked and fled to France, therefore allowing William and Mary to take the throne in his absence.

This is what started the Jacobite movement to restore the 'rightful' king to the throne, Jacob being the Latin for James.

In Chapter Four Harriet listens at the door as Stephen discusses finances with Amelia, and the special remainder that his great-grandfather took out to allow daughters to inherit the title.

Normally in a peerage the title would automatically pass only to the legitimate male heirs of the body, but in certain circumstances a 'special remainder' could be added, which would allow the title to pass to daughters or other relatives. This ensured the survival of the peerage if there were no sons to inherit.

Special remainders could also be taken out when a peer had

more than one title, which would allow a second son to inherit one of the titles.

Also in Chapter Four, Raphael discusses the Tulpenwoede with his bride-to-be. As far-fetched as it might sound, at one time a single tulip bulb could cost as much as a large house! Tulpenwoede means tulip madness, and in the 1630s it led to the first major financial bubble.

Tulips are native to central Asia, and it's said that an ambassador to Constantinople noticed the beautiful flower growing everywhere, and sent a bulb back to his friend in the Netherlands in the late 1500s. They were an instant hit, especially because there was a huge variety of colours available.

In 1602 the stock market opened in Amsterdam, and people started to trade in these new and beautiful flower bulbs. They also traded in other flowers, but tulips, being rare and new, attracted the highest prices. The most sought-after were the variegated flowers, which were a sensation at the time. It wasn't known then that these variegations in colour were caused by a virus which eventually killed the plant - the rarity made them even more desirable – and more expensive.

It became fashionable to trade in them if you were wealthy, and owning a rare tulip became a status symbol – a way of instantly showing how wealthy and powerful you were. Prices exploded, and by the 1600s, a number of tulip brokerages had opened and were trading briskly.

Things came to a head in 1637, when in just one month the price of some bulbs increased by over 1000%. And then the bubble burst.

There are numerous theories for why this happened, including panic about the insanely high prices, a bad deal in Haarlem, plague sweeping the country, and supply outstripping demand as people started to grow their own tulips. Almost overnight the whole market collapsed, bringing some to the point of ruin. Although the tulip bubble only affected a small number of wealthy people, it's remembered because it's a reminder of human greed and the wish to make money quickly overriding all common sense. There have been a number of financial bubbles since, and will no doubt be more in the future!

Finally, in Chapter Fourteen I have Harriet play a practical joke on her Uncle Percy by forcing him to stand under a 'water feature'

THE ECCENTRIC'S TALE: HARRIET

which looks like a willow tree, and then drenching him. I've loosely based Raphael's sumptuous home on the real-life Chatsworth House, which I visited a couple of years ago when I was researching for Harriet's book.

I was touring the gardens when I discovered the 'willow tree'. The current fountain dates from the early 19th Century, but it replaced a decayed 17th Century one. The original fountain was designed in 1695 by Grillet as a brass 'joke' tree, which drenched anyone who stopped to admire it closely. In 1696 Celia Fiennes wrote of it: all of a sudden by turning a sluice it raines from each leafe and from the branches like a shower, it being made of brass and pipes to each leafe but in apperance is exactly a willow".

It was just too good to be true, and I knew I had to use it in Harriet's book!

I will be writing blogs on my website www.juliabrannan.com over the next months about some of the other historical things featured in the book, including the bloody flux, and Catalina de Erauso and other women who lived lives as men. I already have a number of blogs on there about historical aspects of my Jacobite Chronicles, and if you want you can sign up for my monthly newsletter, which includes a historical feature. The sign-up link is http://eepurl.com/bSNLHD

Printed in Great Britain
by Amazon